UNSOLICITED

JULIE WALLIN KAEWERT

Unsolicited

ST. MARTIN'S PRESS — NEW YORK

A · THOMAS · DUNNE BOOK

Design by Judith A. Stagnitto

Library of Congress Cataloging-in-Publication Data

Kaewert, Julie Wallin.
    Unsolicited / Julie Wallin Kaewert.
       p.   cm.
    "A Thomas Dunne book."
    ISBN 0-312-11088-X
    1. Publishers and publishing—England—Fiction 2. Authors and publishers
—England—Fiction.   I. Title.
PS3561.A3617U57   1994
813'.54—dc20   94-1113
                                                              CIP

First Edition: July 1994
10 9 8 7 6 5 4 3 2 1

To William, who never doubted

Acknowledgments

Heartfelt thanks to Del, Mom, Jan, Herb, Nancy, Jenny, and Ned for making the dream come true—and to Josette, Peter, Simon, Sarah, and Timothy, who will know why. Thanks also to the Nantucket Historical Society, the reference librarians of Redwood City, the Menlo Park Fire Department, and the employees of the Radio Shack of Stanford Shopping Center for sharing their expertise.

Partial List of
Unsolicited Characters

Barnes Appleton. . . . . .reviewer for the *Sunday Tempus Book Review*

Simon Bow. . . . . .managing director and owner of Bow and Bow, Ltd., literary publishers

Ian Higginbotham. . . . . .managing director of Plumtree Press and friend of the Plumtree family

Nick Khasnouri. . . . . .Plumtree Press accountant

Romney Marsh. . . . . .Ministry of Defence official; one-time friend of the Plumtree family

Alex Plumtree. . . . . .owner of Plumtree Press; in love with Sarah Townsend

Max Plumtree. . . . . .brother of Alex and journalist with *The Watch*

Alison Soames. . . . . .respected publicist at Soames and Sons; daughter of Rupert Soames

Rupert Soames. . . . . .owner and managing director of Soames and Sons, Publishers, Ltd.

George Stoneham. . . . . .Alex Plumtree's best friend

Lisette Stoneham. . . . . .Alex Plumtree's secretary; wife of George Stoneham

Sarah Townsend. . . . . .investment banker; much admired by Alex Plumtree

1

When I received the telegram in Skópelos, I should have wired my regrets immediately: "Thanks, but no thanks. Having far too much fun leading sailing holidays. Must respectfully decline offer to take charge of family firm. Stop."

Instead, I said I'd be on the next plane, and it nearly cost me my life.

I'd had reservations about coming back to manage the small, sedate publishing house I'd inherited, but my worst fear was that I would die of boredom. No one told me that book publishing was a murderous business, and that within a single week in the not-so-distant future I would barely escape death in a dozen exotic forms.

The treachery of the business wasn't immediately apparent; far from it. For my first two years with the company it seemed that nothing could go wrong, and I was lulled into a false sense of well-being. It came as a nasty surprise when, on a drizzly October evening almost two years to the day after I'd returned to London, I got the first inkling that all was not as it should be.

I climbed out of Farringdon tube station jet-lagged and woozy, fresh off the plane from Boston. I'd spent two utterly unproductive days there trying to close a copublishing deal with an American company, and didn't much feel like going out that evening. But a promise was a promise. Two weeks earlier I had agreed to attend the publication party of a competing book publisher, Soames and Sons, to celebrate the release of *Fleet Street Beat*, the memoirs of one of London's more respected tabloid editors.

I turned down a cobblestoned alley under a sign that said CHURCHILL'S REAL ALES and sighed. Why Soames and Sons was having its party at this tourist trap of an old brewery, miles from the nearest tube station, I couldn't imagine. I'd been here once before, and the smell of rampant fermentation was still fresh in my mind.

I told myself to give Soames and Sons credit; at least they had a reason to throw a party. It was more than I could say for my little company.

No sooner had I straightened my tie and entered the brewery's yawning stone hall than Alison Soames wiggled up to me in a tight electric blue suit. She was the new blood in Soames and Sons, which I often thought should be renamed Soames and Daughter, as Rupert Soames had no sons.

"Alex! You came." She was flushed and slightly out of breath as she took my arm. Alison's décolleté fashions and breathy voice fooled some people into thinking she had more beauty than brains, but she didn't fool me.

I looked around and smiled, shaking my head. "You've done it again, Alison. I don't know how you expect us to compete."

It was clear to me now why Alison, a public-relations genius, had decided to have the party here. The brewery's size and general atmosphere of decay had allowed her to create a full-scale replica of Fleet Street, the infamous home of London's journalists. Pasteboard facades of the familiar buildings lined the walls, and costumed actors set type by hand at old-fashioned printing presses positioned throughout the room. I gazed in wonder at several giant rolls of newsprint hanging overhead, suspended from ceiling-mounted cranes.

I was impressed by Alison's authenticity. Not many people knew that when London papers had actually printed their news in Fleet Street, there had been no other way to get the big reels of newsprint into the cramped old buildings but through upper-storey windows. Cranes had hoisted the two-ton cylinders in from the back alley like tin cans on strings.

She gave me a look of mock reprimand, tilting her bleached blond head to one side. "Don't give me your hard-luck story, Plumtree. You're the one with the best-seller."

I smiled modestly. There was no point in telling her that, barring a miracle, within a week or so I would have to close the doors of Plumtree Press for good.

Alison beckoned to a passing waiter and lifted a pint off of his tray. She thrust it into my hand as if in condolence. "Drink it and weep, Plumtree."

Standing very close, she ran her hand down my back in a way that made me shiver. Then she winked and was gone. I stared after her for a moment, feeling slightly confused in her wake. Alison never failed to interest me, physically if not otherwise, and she would probably be a lot of fun if I were in the market. But I wasn't—not at the moment, anyway.

I took a sip from the dripping mug, trying not to spill it on my suit, and got my bearings.

Everyone was hard at it, the journalists drinking and the publishers talking as fast as they decently could. Most of the book reviewers from the major London papers and magazines were there, as well as the managing directors or senior editors of publishing houses like mine. They studiously avoided looking at their watches to determine which train they could take to their country retreats for the weekend; after all, it was well worth the investment of a Friday evening to establish a rapport with an influential reviewer. The return, in the form of a review in a Sunday paper, could be on their doorstep in the space of a few weeks.

With gratitude I spotted Barnes Appleton, the most influential reviewer of them all, and headed in his direction. A chat with him was a worthy excuse for not performing my real duty for the evening, which was a sort of Plan B in case the American copublishing deal didn't come through. Loathsome as the thought was, I would have to gauge the interest of several competitors, including Rupert Soames, in purchasing a chunk of my company.

It was unfortunate that the only people likely to be interested in a piece of Plumtree Press were my father's most bitter competitors, several of whom were downright obnoxious. But even more than the personalities involved, I hated the idea of selling out. Aside from the feeling that I was betraying my father and three generations of Plumtrees before him, I hated it because Plumtree Press had come so close to having more profit on its bottom line this year than any of its competitors had seen in decades.

3

Just not close enough.

Barnes Appleton saw me coming and raised his glass in greeting. He reminded me of a chubby leprechaun: short, fairly jolly, rosy cheeks. But this benign image masked a force to be reckoned with in the world of print. He wrote for the *Sunday Tempus,* and had won the prestigious Beecroft Award, the British equivalent of the American Pulitzer prize, the year before. His exposé on a third-world dictator had actually gotten the ruffian thrown out of office.

Barnes was also a recovering alcoholic, and of all his achievements I admired that one the most. I thought it must take a lot of courage on his part to come to these industry functions where alcohol flowed like the River Fleet.

"Alex," Barnes said, looking pleased. "I hoped I'd see you here tonight." He had to tip his head back to look up at me, and I was aware of our extreme difference in height. At six foot five inches, I was a full foot taller than he, and I wondered if he would get a sore neck talking to me.

"Well," I said, raising my eyebrows. "Same here." I was surprised at the warmth of his greeting and somewhat flattered. We were acquaintances, certainly, but no more. I wondered what was up. "How's the critiquing business?"

"That's exactly what I wanted to talk to you about." He glanced at someone over my shoulder, gave me a worried smile, and steered me off toward a nearby printing press. Assuming he was trying to avoid someone, I played along.

When we were safely behind the press, Barnes glanced surreptitiously around the room and frowned. Finally he spoke, barely moving his lips and speaking so softly that I had to lean over to hear him.

"I'm not sure I should be telling you this, Alex, but I think you've a right to know."

I looked at him with interest. I'd never seen him act so mysteriously.

"Know what?"

He reacted as if I'd shouted. He looked around nervously and held up a palm. "For God's sake, Alex, don't make a scene—act your inscrutable self."

"All right, all right," I said, chastised. His habit of looking around was contagious.

When he spoke again, it was in a stage whisper. "Something very big has happened with that sequel you gave me to preview." He swept the room again with his eyes. "And someone out there is doing his best to prevent me from telling the story. I wanted you to know before—"

"Barnes! Alex." It was Alison Soames getting her money's worth. The opportunity to talk to Barnes Appleton was one of the reasons she'd organized this party. With a mixture of fascination and dread, I wondered how close she would stand this time.

Barnes rolled his eyes.

"What are you doing over here all by yourselves?" She put a hand on each of our backs. Alison did a lot of touching, and people criticized her for using femininity to swell the bank balances of Soames and Sons. But I thought her very bright and genuinely kind, and accepted her flirtatiousness in good humor.

We turned and looked at her, and she rewarded us with a dazzling smile. I wondered briefly if it were possible for teeth to be that white naturally.

"Barnes." Her throaty voice was thick with innuendo, but the smile was all innocence. "I know you objective observers don't like to be told when a publisher likes your review, but your piece on our new Mountbatten biography was a work of art."

That was diplomatic, I thought. Barnes had, in fact, skewered the book, but had done it artfully, parodying the author's overblown prose throughout. I'd laughed out loud myself when I'd read it. But Alison knew that people would buy the book just to find out what Barnes had been writing about.

She touched his arm, and he looked down as if a mosquito had landed on it. He was happily married to a barrister—a very pretty one—and didn't like the thought of people seeing Alison touch him.

She removed her hand and withdrew slightly, unoffended. Without missing a beat she continued, "Tell me. Of all the reviewers at the *Tempus*, how were we so lucky as to get you?"

"What can I say?" Barnes smiled modestly, pink cheeks glowing, trying to make the best of the situation. "It'll do well, I think."

"Let's hope so," Alison said fervently, pressing her hands together and glancing at the ceiling. "We—"

She did a double take, her startled gaze returning to the ceiling. Her face froze, and I automatically looked up. I had the impression of something huge and white falling fast—onto us. I dived for the ground sideways, taking Alison and Barnes with me.

It was enough. A ton of newsprint—one of the cylinders suspended from the ceiling of the warehouse—slammed into the floor inches from where we had stood, creating an earthquakelike vibration and a deafening boom.

On the floor, the three of us looked into one another's stunned faces. In fact, Barnes's and Alison's faces were all I could see, as my glasses had come off in the dive.

Alison in particular was easy to see, as she was lying on top of me. It wasn't altogether unpleasant, and I waited for her to disengage herself in her own time before starting the hunt for my glasses. I didn't publicize it, but I was legally blind, and those glasses were all that stood between me and a seeing-eye dog. If they had been damaged, I was in trouble; they were a prototype pair made of a new German plastic. The wonder material, which was still not in full production, was able to incorporate the same correction in a quarter-inch-thick lens that required half an inch of ordinary glass. My previous lenses had been over half an inch thick, and the bulk and weight of them, not to mention their appearance, was unworkable. Contact lenses would have been the obvious solution if the shape of my eye hadn't precluded them.

Alison took advantage of the situation somewhat, generating a certain amount of friction as she slid off. I felt around as inconspicuously as I could for the frames. The rest of the room seemed to be suspended in time; no one spoke or moved.

I finally arrived at the conclusion that my glasses were nowhere within reach. They were a royal nuisance.

I turned to Alison and broke the reverberating silence. "Must you be so authentic in executing your party themes?"

She rewarded me with a shaky smile, and we slowly picked ourselves up. Voices began to buzz around us.

"Oh"—Alison's face abruptly disappeared and swam into view again—"these must be yours." Bless you, I thought as Alison pressed the glasses into my hand. I put them on, relieved that they had survived unscathed, and joined Alison and Barnes in contemplating the giant roll of paper that had nearly smashed us to a pulp.

"Look at that," said Barnes, wide-eyed and pointing. "It's broken right through the wood floor." The cylinder had evidently landed off-balance before toppling over onto its side, and there was a neat crescent-shaped imprint in the false, raised wooden floor.

I looked up and saw that the cable of the ceiling-mounted crane was intact, its hook swaying some thirty feet above us. Evidently the problem hadn't been a frayed cable. Perhaps the hook had been faulty—the metal fatigued—and it had snapped.

I was contemplating the hook when a movement near the ceiling caught my eye. Something dark had moved on one of the metal walkways that ran around the room at two-storey intervals, a sort of modern minstrel's gallery. I squinted, straining to catch it again, but it was gone.

"Back in a moment," I said to Barnes and Alison, making for a door on the wall to my right. The room began to buzz as I entered a narrow, dank hallway and banged through a set of double doors toward what I thought was the office section of the building. These old buildings resembled nothing so much as rabbit warrens; fortunately I had once had a self-guided tour of this place while searching for the well-hidden toilet.

On the other side of the doors I found myself back in the twentieth century, in a deserted room of desultory beige-burlapped cubicles. An exit sign glowed red on the opposite wall, and I ran toward it, hoping for a stairway. I was in luck. I listened for hurried steps descending, but heard nothing. Taking the steps two at a time, I bounded up to the first landing, the second, then the third, where I stopped short.

A maintenance man stood on the fourth landing, in gray trousers and a white shirt emblazoned "Acme Sanitation Services." He looked up at me in irritation, then resumed his listless mopping of the linoleum. For a fraction of a moment I entertained the notion that he might have been the one on the gallery, if indeed there had been anyone there at all. He was the only available candidate.

But his flaccid face and half-open eyes told me that he wasn't quick enough—or awake enough—to have rushed down the stairs, got into character, and mopped a whole flight of stairs without even being out of breath. The fourth flight of stairs behind him was freshly damp and bore no footprints.

On the off-chance, I said, "Have you seen anyone come down these steps in the last few minutes? Dark clothes, in a hurry?"

Had I been a glob of chewing gum on the floor, I might have

received a more enthusiastic response. He glanced at me again, but didn't answer.

"Please, it's urgent." I tried again, punctuating every word. "Anyone? Here?" Indicating the steps behind him, I made a little running motion with the fingers of my right hand and felt like an idiot.

He shrugged his shoulders and shook his head. Crazy Englishman.

Deciding he didn't speak English, I nodded my thanks and stepped around him, throwing open the door to the hallway. There were more offices here, and a door to the fourth-floor gallery.

I opened the door and stuck out my head. No one. Looking down, I saw that people were congregating around Alison and Barnes, who looked slightly bewildered. The controls for the ceiling crane were only a foot away from me on the wall, and the hook that had suspended the paper from a height of two stories swung in random air currents two levels below.

Easy enough to figure out the controls, open the hook, drop the paper, and duck through the door into the empty offices.

But why?

I made my way back down, past the Acme man. He still hadn't made it past the third landing, and I eyed him suspiciously. All my life people had teased me about my vivid imagination. Maybe I hadn't really seen anyone. It had only been the merest suggestion of movement, after all, and it was dark up there.

I had an uncomfortable feeling that it hadn't been an accident, but I decided to keep that cheerful thought to myself.

As it turned out, I wouldn't have had the chance to share it with anyone.

Glad to be back with the crowd, I made my way toward Alison and Barnes amid sympathetic murmurs and concerned inquiries. Rupert Soames hovered near Alison like a bear guarding his young, furiously berating the manager of the facility. The pasty-faced young manager quaked in his boots, and I couldn't blame him. Rupert looked fierce at the best of times, a hulking, twenty-stone giant of a man with wiry reddish gray eyebrows that formed an angry V at the bridge of his nose. Like a bear, he could be particularly intimidating when angry and seemed to arouse an almost primal fear in those unaccustomed to him. It occurred to me that anyone who got past Rupert to date Alison, who still lived at home, was a man of great courage.

Alison, obviously embarrassed, did her best to silence him.

"Really, Father, it's not his fault. And everybody's all right," she said urgently. "Can we just get on with the party now, please." It was an order, not a question. Alison could be all business when she wanted to. She saw me and grabbed my arm, relieved. "Alex. Help me out, would you? The band." She nodded sternly across the room to where they stood, unsure whether to pack up or continue. "Tell them I don't care if there's an earthquake, if they want to be paid, they'll—"

Neither of us saw it coming. Rupert, whom I studiously avoided because of his long and bitter rivalry with my father, landed a whopping punch in my rib cage, and I heard a whoosh of air escape from my lungs as I sank to the floor. Stunned, and instinctively curled up in a ball, I spotted a wing-tipped foot coming fast in the direction of my head and I threw up an arm. It was a healthy kick, and I was glad my head hadn't taken it.

"Soames, for God's sake!" It was Barnes Appleton's voice, disgusted and incredulous. "What the hell do you think you're doing?"

If it hadn't come from Barnes, whose approval Soames desired more than that of any other reviewer, I doubt that it would have stopped him. He must have hesitated in his attack, because when I next looked up, Barnes and half a dozen others, including the respected literary publisher Simon Bow, were bodily restraining him.

Alison, who had been staring at her father in disbelief, now closed her mouth and took charge of the situation with her usual aplomb. As she knelt to help me up, perfume emanating from her cleavage like smelling salts, she looked up at Simon Bow. "Simon, would you be good enough to take Father outside?" Her angry eyes flicked between her apoplectic father and Bow, who was still restraining him. "And you." She looked at the brewery manager. "Get that band playing. Now."

"Y-yes, Ms. Soames."

By this time, Rupert appeared as if he was coming to his senses and looked more embarrassed than enraged. He glanced at those restraining him, then at the buzzing crowd, and seemed to realize that once again his temper had cost him dearly. Finally, his eyes rested on Alison, who was kneeling at my side. It seemed to sink in then that he had put the last nails in the coffin of her carefully planned press party.

"Alison, I—"

"Get out," she said with impressive force, jerking her head toward the door. "Now."

Simon Bow, with characteristic diplomacy, said, "Come along, old boy. Let's get a breath of air. Over here, that's the way."

As Simon steered him off, Rupert shot me a look that was more venomous than his physical attack. I looked him in the eye as I sat catching my breath, telling him as clearly as I knew how that I wasn't afraid of him.

I did, however, make a mental note to watch out for him in dark alleys.

Perhaps he really was unbalanced, as my father had suggested on several occasions. The thought had first occurred to my father when Rupert stuck a banana in his tailpipe almost ten years ago, nearly asphyxiating him, and then again five years later when a brick sailed through his office window from the direction of Soames and Sons.

Through the years there were dozens of similar incidents, and it became something of a family joke. "Rupert's gone barmy again," my father would say, smiling and shaking his head at the dinner table. We would clamor for the story, and he would tell us of Rupert's latest exploits.

It may have been the sight of me in close proximity to Alison that had set him off, not to mention that she had just nearly been killed. In his mind, because of his competition with my father, a Plumtree represented a threat. He probably thought I had something to do with the newsprint mishap.

I shifted into a semblance of an upright position, assessing the damage on the way. My rib cage would be blue, green, and purple in a couple of days, but it was bearable. It wasn't until I straightened all the way, too quickly, that I felt a stab of white-hot pain. I gasped and the room spun wildly.

Alison took my arm in a way that was, for once, devoid of sexual overtones. "You're hurt," she said, worried. "I saw your face just then. I'll get a doctor."

"No—no. I'm all right." And I was, really. I'd had worse punishment at the hands of my older brother, who had loved to beat me up as a child. Rupert may have cracked a rib or two, but it was nothing compared to the damage Max used to do.

Alison was looking slightly the worse for wear herself, I noticed. Her shoulders sagged with disappointment and there was a smudge of mascara under her left eye.

"I'm sorry about your party," I said. "But look at the bright side. It might be more newsworthy this way."

"Mmm." The ghost of a smile twitched at her lips. She was a good sport, I thought. "And I'm sorry about my father. This obsession of his with your father—and now you—has only got worse since your father died." She looked down for a moment. We had never discussed the subject on the few occasions we'd met, but somehow I'd known she thought it as ridiculous as I did.

With an obvious effort, she changed gears and squared her shoulders, looking me in the eye. "You're sure you don't want a doctor?"

"Yes, thanks. But I don't think I'll stay for the dancing. Thanks for an interesting party." I felt her eyes on me as I started to walk away.

"Alex."

I turned and looked. "Yes?"

"I'm glad you—well, you know." She looked at the floor with uncharacteristic shyness, then up at me again. "Thanks."

I assumed she meant my unceremoniously shoving her to the floor. "Any time at all," I said, and walked through the musty hallway into the night. The deed I had dreaded could wait, I thought, for another day—if on another day I could bring myself to sell a part of Plumtree Press.

The mysterious conversation with Barnes Appleton came back to me as my shoes tapped along the cobblestones. I wondered what he had to tell me. He said it was important, and confidential, but

Alison—followed by half a ton of paper and her rabid father—had prevented further conversation. When I looked for him after my scuffle with Rupert Soames, Barnes had been surrounded by the usual admiring crowd. I intended to call him later that night and find out.

Checking my watch, I headed for Farringdon tube station. There was barely half an hour before Sir Harold Plumpton's show, "Personalities," at nine o'clock. I rarely watched television, preferring books, but that night was different.

I was one of Plumpton's guests.

It was rumored that even the Queen was a regular viewer of this popular talk show, which was hosted by an ex-Member of Parliament only slightly more garrulous than he was corpulent. I hoped I wouldn't come off looking like a twit. After all, this was probably the last time I would enjoy such notoriety, I thought grimly. Unless something happened soon, I would no longer be an object of fascination for the British public. I would be a laughing-stock.

Gingerly descending the steps to the train, I found that my ribs didn't hurt as much as I would have expected. I entertained the hope that they were merely bruised and lowered myself into a seat on the waiting train.

It was my pride, I thought, that had sustained the real injury. I thought back to the happy days of just a few months ago, when one day it struck me that I had done it. After just two years of mind-numbing work, I had begun to transform Plumtree Press, the staid publisher of scholarly anthologies, into a dynamic trade publishing house.

I had focussed on developing a line of fiction while my father's trusted colleague and friend of forty-five years, Ian Higginbotham, had kept the academic anthology side of the business ticking over. Ian's expertise had made my risky new idea possible, and we had been rewarded with the nation's most-talked-about best-seller. Following the example of a best-selling American author, we had chosen a title straight from the King James version of the Bible for its familiarity: *Deliver Us From Evil.*

Then came the sequel, *Those Who Trespass Against Us,* which was now complete with the exception of its last five chapters.

I had used its projected profits to sign several respected authors in order to expand the fiction list. It had been easy enough to obtain the funds, as a friend of mine was in an influential position at an investment bank. Through her personal recommendation, she had persuaded the board to lend me a significant amount of money. After all, the sequel to a best-seller was virtually guaranteed the same success as the original book.

Though no one knew it but me—not even the banks, yet—it had all fallen apart. The author, the only writer I had ever known to be ahead of time on our mutually agreed upon schedules, seemed to have disappeared suddenly several weeks ago, leaving me high and dry without the last five chapters of the sequel.

His absence meant that the future of Plumtree Press, which was of course inextricably tied to my own, hung in the balance. The bills were coming due, and the sequel should have been off to the printer weeks before. I shifted uncomfortably at the thought.

If only my would-be American copublisher, Charlie Goodspeed of Bookarama America, Inc., weren't so maddeningly conscientious. Actually, it wasn't fair to blame Charlie for the delay in closing the deal. Charlie Goodspeed himself was a caricature of willingness and enthusiasm, fairly jumping out of his suit to make Plumtree Press's list his own. It was his army of lawyers who had found some arcane point of international law to quibble over in the contracts. Regrettably, they had sent me home sans contract and— still more regrettably—the rather significant check due on signature of the contracts.

My eyes felt gravelly. I rubbed them impatiently as my mind continued its catalog of Plumtree Press's problems. It only made matters worse that I had already kicked off the publicity campaign, certain that my star author would deliver. I knew that an actual review of the book couldn't appear until the book was off the press, but as a preview I had sent the partial manuscript to Barnes Appleton at the *Tempus*, care of the book review editor, so he could get started on it. It was all so embarrassing. Now I would have to tell him that I'd wasted his valuable time; there was no more manuscript forthcoming. Judging from Barnes's comments at Alison's party, he'd already read what I'd sent him.

I sighed as the train picked up speed. What was it that my

grandfather always used to say? "Easy come, easy go." Not that I hadn't worked like a fiend these last two years, but it was really Ian's talent and experience that had brought us such dramatic success—along with a peculiar form of manna from heaven.

The manna had come in the form of an anonymous, unsolicited manuscript delivered by courier one day about two years ago. I had glanced at the manuscript and found that I couldn't put it down. It was a riveting novel about the children of London who had been evacuated from the city during the Blitz. In an evil plot hatched by a corrupt official, the children were sold to childless Americans while their natural parents were informed that they had died. The children, in turn, were told that their parents had died in the bombing, and that they were going to foster homes.

That evening, long after I had decided that I would publish the book as the first work of fiction on Plumtree's list, a fax came in from someone who called himself only "Arthur." He identified himself as the anonymous author of the book, and detailed the terms on which he would allow the book to be published, including strict anonymity. That wasn't too difficult, as he had never let me in on the secret of his real name.

All royalties from the book were to be donated to the War Orphans Fund. He said it was pointless to try to find out who he was, as the courier who brought the manuscript didn't know his name and had never seen him. The fax number, he said, was unlisted and untraceable.

I had of course tried in every way I could to find out who he was, starting with the courier and the fax number, and ending with the manuscript itself. Over the years of our association, I had come to accept the arrangement and stopped trying. It certainly hadn't hurt sales to have an anonymous author; first England and then America had been fascinated by the idea, and readers had been compelled to visit their local bookstores to discover him personally.

The sudden success had been a shock, albeit a pleasant one. We did three reprints in one month, first of 50,000, then 100,000, then 200,000. I hadn't sought success of this kind, and certainly not at the age of thirty. I chalked it up to divine benevolence and plowed the profits back into the new fiction list which, by now, I wished I'd never thought of.

As the train plummeted through the underground tunnel, I had an uncomfortable feeling—and not just in my rib cage—that something was very wrong. It was unlike Arthur to be late, and still less like him not to communicate. He and I had grown to be friends, in a way; he had a keen sense of humor and seemed to be exceptionally kind. I knew all this from our fax communications; he normally sent a fax every other day or so to discuss the sequel, to pass on a joke or one of his pithy sayings, or simply to say hello.

Sometimes I had the odd feeling that he knew a great deal about me, and early on I had racked my brain trying to think who, of all the people I knew, Arthur could be. I thought that he must be older, not merely because his novel was set against the backdrop of World War II, but because of the rather formal tone of his prose.

But no matter how many names I considered, I always drew a blank. Maybe he would remain a blank forever now, I thought. Perhaps he was injured, ill, or even dead. Perhaps I would never know.

Newly disturbed at the thought, I looked up as the train screeched to a halt at King's Cross station. Standing carefully, I made my way off the train and was grateful that the elbowing masses of the peak period had long since disappeared. After a short ride I changed trains again at Holborn, then got off at Tottenham Court Road. I walked the several blocks to Bedford Square in a biting wind and tested the limits of my ribs, gently stretching and twisting to see what response I got.

By the time I'd reached the square, I thought I might be all right for the boat race tomorrow with a roll or two of strapping tape. The last thing I wanted to do was miss the final regatta of the season at the rowing club. It would be my last good excuse to see Sarah Townsend, whom I adored but seemed destined to admire from afar.

It began to drizzle again, a cold, comfortless near-November rain whipped into stinging gusts by the wind. I picked up my pace, catching a whiff of the wet wool of my suit as I wrapped my raincoat more tightly about me. Soaked, sore, and chilled to the bone, I thought of Rupert Soames and wished I hadn't. There was something depressing about his raw hatred.

I walked up to number 52 and unlocked the massive brass

lock, pushing open the heavy door. I had bought this building, just three doors down from the Plumtree Press offices, after coming to work for the company. The bottom two floors were rented to an Italian art book company, and I occupied the third-floor garret. It was just right for me, not much to clean, lots of dormers and skylights, and extremely convenient. Sometimes I wondered why I bothered to have a home at all, since I spent most of my life at the office, which was equipped with well-worn leather sofas that were all too conducive to sleeping.

In a small concession to my ribs I took the lift up for once, leaning against the wall as we rose. My watch said nine o'clock, time for Plumpton's show. I let myself into the flat, started the recorder, and took the opportunity of an advertisement to strip off my sodden clothes and climb into a warm woolen robe.

By the time Harold had introduced me as the new sensation in British publishing, I had a fire crackling in the fireplace, a glass of cabernet in my hand (a gift from one of Sarah's business trips to San Francisco), and a frozen lasagna in the microwave.

It was a good thing I had turned on the recorder, because my mind wandered. I kept wondering what good it was to be a sensation if there was no one to share it with.

The phone rang, and I struggled out of the comfortable chair to answer it. "Hello?"

"Al! Hey, buddy, you're not going to believe this."

He was right. I couldn't believe it. I had left Charlie Goodspeed and his platoon of lawyers in their plush conference room not ten hours ago. Already he was burning up the wire to London. "Charlie?"

"Yeah, it's me! Listen, we've got that little snag in the contract all worked out. The guys just switched around a few lines and took one out, and—bingo!" I could see him smiling on the other end of the line, Coke can in hand, leaning back and resting his size-twelve wing-tipped feet on the mahogany conference room table. "We think it looks pretty good, but obviously we need to talk it over with you. Think you can make it over here again sometime this week?"

It was impossible to be angry with Charlie; he was like a child. Frustrating, but lovable. He would offer you the shirt off his back in a blizzard, his last sip of water in the desert. I could see why he depended so heavily on those damn lawyers; if not for them, he'd give away his books to make people happy.

It was starting to seem odd to me that they required my presence each time they had some new question about the contractual agreement; but then they were almost paranoid about industrial espionage, by my standards, anyway. I had no reason to believe that this iteration of the contracts was any better than the last three, but if it was, I wished they'd just mail me the money.

I fought down irritation and fatigue and tried a rational approach. "I'm glad the impasse has finally been breached, Charlie, but don't you think you could come over here this time? Better yet, if you've got everything figured out to your satisfaction, why not just send them by overnight mail for my signature?"

"Come on, Al." He chuckled. "You know how I hate to fly. You also know that my legal beagles here won't allow a single word of the contracts out of this office until they're signed—not by fax, photocopy, or fiche. Hey, that was pretty good, huh?" He chuckled at the accidental alliteration. "No, seriously, Al, we're in a very competitive market over here. We can't have documents flying all over the airwaves for our competition to see."

I had attempted to talk them out of their paranoia several times now and had gotten nowhere. I didn't bother to try again. "Charlie, I think you know I'd do just about anything to get the contracts signed and the books rolling out under our joint imprint. But for me to come again this week—even if you pay again—well, I just can't. Plumtree Press can't run itself, you know. And my managing director is away on holiday. I've got to be there."

"Hmm. Well, think it over, will you, Al? I'll give you a ring again tomorrow. Ciao!"

He was gone. I looked at the phone in my hand and shook my head. The man was a human tornado, but a lot more persistent.

I hung up the phone and went back to my chair, turning my attention to the television as I sank into the cushions.

". . . haven't been in publishing long, have you, Alex?" Sir Harold asked the question and looked at me expectantly on the television, a benign smile curving between his rosy cheeks.

"No, that's right. Just two years now. Though in a way, you could say I've been in publishing all my life—visiting the office with my father, hearing him talk about it. I can't say it felt particularly new when I finally began doing it myself."

"How did you get your start—the experience, the background—for the success you've had? If you'll forgive me saying it, you are rather young for your position."

I had to give him credit. He asked the question as if he honestly didn't know what I would say, though we'd discussed all of this in detail a couple of hours before. I supposed his former career in politics had provided ample opportunity to develop acting skills.

I saw myself nod, slightly embarrassed, on the screen. "First, let's separate me from the success." How right I was, I thought morosely. "It's the people who've been at Plumtree Press for a long time who are responsible for that. But as far as my background goes, well, I suppose it's not exactly the usual career path. After doing some graduate work in English literature, I needed a break from the books, so—"

"Where did you study?"

"I got my undergraduate degree from Dartmouth, in the States, then went to Magdalen at Cambridge for a Masters."

"Hmmm. Go on. Away from the books, you were saying."

The interrupting and prodding were irritating, but I supposed he had to do it to keep his viewers interested.

"Yes, well, to get away from the books I led flotilla sailing trips for five years in America, Greece, Turkey, and the Caribbean. Each flotilla was a group of about a dozen yachts, all skippered by vacationing sailors. They were fiercely independent, but didn't want the hassles of maintaining their own boats, dealing with foreign port masters, and so forth. Oddly enough, besides having sort of absorbed the family business by osmosis, leading flotillas turned out to be one of the best preparations I could have had."

"Why do you say that?"

"Well, I'm no management expert. But people don't like to be managed; they like to be in charge of their own destiny."

He nodded pensively, encouraging me to go on.

"Each of the yachtsmen on the flotilla trips was in charge of his own vessel—where and how he sailed. I was just there as a backup in case something came up that he thought he couldn't handle, or didn't want to. If his toilet backed up, for instance"—

there was scattered laughter in the audience—"or the motor gave out, or the tender needed to be patched. We operate on the same principle at Plumtree."

"You don't find that they object to your youth and—pardon me for saying it—inexperience?"

I saw myself give Sir Harold a slightly sheepish smile. "Er, actually, I suspect that's worked in my favor. People see me as too young and inexperienced to be threatening. Besides, this way they can tell me everything they know as experts. I've never yet met a person who doesn't enjoy teaching a beginner how to do something he himself loves."

Sir Harold nodded slowly. I shifted in my chair and made a mental note not to philosophize about management again. The trouble was, he was disarming, and at the time I hadn't realized how much I was talking.

He tilted his head to one side and looked serious. "Alex, your parents were killed in the Sporades Islands in Greece when the propane tank on their yacht exploded." He looked at me for a response. Perhaps he expected me to disgrace myself in a burst of tears.

I took a bite of lasagna and saw myself nod, looking directly at him.

"How did that affect you?"

What a ridiculous question, I thought.

"I miss them very much; they were wonderful people. But we thoroughly enjoyed life together. I think dealing with death is easier when you have no regrets."

"And you gave up sailing for the helm of Plumtree Press after that?"

I rolled my eyes at his metaphor. I hoped he didn't think he was the first person to think of it.

"Yes." I didn't mention the six months that my brother had run the company before deciding it was too much work. As the eldest, he was the rightful heir by family tradition, and he had stepped in after my father's death. But he threw up his hands after taking all the cash out of the company that he could, and left it to the company lawyer to send me the telegram in Skópelos.

"It must be a good feeling to know that you've done so well in carrying on the family's interests—the top-selling book worldwide this year, and your first foray into fiction." He delivered this with an avuncular smile as he shook his head in mild wonder. I remembered feeling as if I'd been patted on the head, even as I admired his graceful segue into Arthur territory.

"Now, Alex, we're all terribly interested in this secret author—er, Arthur." He smiled at the play on words. "What can you tell us about him?"

I noted with relief that my face revealed none of the concern I felt about Arthur's disappearance.

"I don't know a great deal more than you do about him, Sir Harold, except that he has a great sense of humor in his private communications and cares a great deal for others. As you may know, all his royalties go to the War Orphans Fund. In the friendship we've struck up over the fax line, he seems to be a very kind person." I shrugged, smiling.

"And you honestly have no idea who he might be?" His cynical tone implied something that I had been accused of before: that I did know but was using Arthur's anonymity as a publicity ploy.

I shook my head. "Believe me, I'm as eager to find out as anyone. He seems to know a good deal about me, and it's an odd feeling. But I've tried everything I can think of—from following his courier, who receives packets at the post office without return address, to tracing the fax line. I've even analyzed the paper and typeface, but there are no hints there. It's ordinary white bond, and a fairly common typeface—Zapf Calligraphic. Comes on all sorts of personal computers. Now you know as much as I do."

He looked intrigued. "Will he be writing any more books for you?"

I shrugged and smiled. "Your guess is as good as mine."

Once again, my face effectively hid the fact that the sequel was planned and virtually ready for release—except for the crucial last five chapters. Only the *Sunday Tempus,* happily sworn to secrecy in return for a promise of exclusivity, had its partial copy for review. Watching the TV, I let out a pent-up breath and prayed that I would find Arthur soon.

Thank God, I thought, that so far the only person who knew about the sequel, besides the *Sunday Tempus Book Review* editor, was Barnes Appleton.

I sat up quickly. Barnes. How could I have forgotten to call him?

Sir Harold and I droned on in the background as I went to the phone, dialed directory inquiries, and asked for the number. A disembodied voice informed me that the number was unlisted by request.

Of course. No professional critic in his right mind would have a listed phone number. I would have to wait until Monday to call him in his office.

As I put down the phone I noticed that the light on my answering machine was blinking. One blink, one call. I pressed it and heard Sarah's refreshing American accent over a long-distance din that I couldn't place. Probably a train station or airport somewhere.

"Alex, it's Sarah. Sorry about the late notice, but I've just heard that Mike Holloway has the measles." She paused for a moment to let a tinny public address system announcement run its course: *"Attention, attention s'il vous plaît . . ."*

So she was in Paris again, most likely. I often wondered how she kept track of where she was, she traveled so much.

"He was going to row with me in the pairs race tomorrow. I wondered if there was any way you could take his place."

My spirits lifted marginally. It was pitiful, really, to be so delighted at being second choice. But I would have done anything for her, anything at all, at a moment's notice. The only problem was that I couldn't show her, couldn't say or do anything that might jeopardize the one consolation I did have—a sort of brotherly friendship that allowed me to spend time with her innocently on occasion.

Her voice finished, "I'll be home late tonight; if you can, call and leave a message. Thanks, Alex—bye."

It was small consolation, a casual phone message when I had spent most of the evening wishing she were with me. I dialed the familiar number and, keeping my voice casual, said it would be no problem to row in Mike's place tomorrow, that I would see her at the club.

I went to the kitchen, grabbed a handful of the Oreo cookies Sarah had brought me from her visits Stateside, and sat eating them as I stared at the television. If it weren't for rowing, I wouldn't know her at all, I mused. I had met her while rowing at university, an opportunity I would never have had had I not, as some of my father's friends put it, "thrown away my future" by declining my father's alma mater and going to the Colonies instead.

They would never understand how wrong they had been. My choice in favor of Dartmouth, encouraged by my unconventional American mother, had raised many British eyebrows but opened doors into a wonderfully unstuffy world—of which Sarah Townsend was a part.

Sarah and I had been involved with other people while at college, she with my best friend, Peter.

I had, of course, observed that Sarah had remarkably long, lithe legs, almond eyes that turned up slightly at the ends, and a quiet intelligence that sparkled through them. But by the time I had lost interest in the comparatively ordinary girl I'd been seeing at the time, it was too late—Peter and Sarah were engaged. The year before last, just three years after I was best man at their wedding, he was diagnosed with a rapidly metastasizing form of cancer. It spread like wildfire. They could do very little for him, and within sixth months Sarah was a widow at the age of twenty-seven.

She'd transferred to London with her investment bank, thinking that the change would help. In some ways, it had worked; she began to function again and threw herself into her work. She had risen like a rocket in her firm since arriving.

But Peter was still very much with her and between us.

I had long ago come to the conclusion that Peter would be glad for me to care for Sarah, to look after her in his absence. I literally dreamed of doing so, and had dedicated myself to Sarah in a way that bordered on a strange sort of one-way marriage. But Sarah's every move indicated that she felt differently. She avoided looking into my eyes too directly or for too long, and kept a good six inches between us at all times. It had come up openly only once, when I'd put my arm around her after a long hike. We'd gone up Ben Lomond in Scotland with some friends, and were the first to reach the eerily rimed summit.

"No," she'd said, tears starting from her eyes as she pulled loose. "He should be here." She had started back down the mountain alone and I'd followed, cursing myself and vowing to keep my distance.

I didn't know if her feelings would ever change, but I was willing to wait. My brother had nearly ruined things for good with a tactless overture of his own mere weeks after her arrival in England, making her more distant than ever.

"How was I supposed to know she was hung up on this bloke Peter?" Max had whined when I confronted him with his actions. "If you ask me, there's something wrong with a woman like that."

I'd been incredulous, then angry. It had been all I could do to refrain from launching a fast left to his jaw. Instead I clenched my teeth and mustered my self-control. "Don't go near her again," I said with ominous calm. "If you do, there will be consequences. You won't like them."

"You're a real piece of work, Alex," he sneered. "You and your goody-two-shoes stuff make me sick. Just my bloody luck to have a brother like you," he mumbled. He left, slamming the door so hard that one of its small panes of glass flew out, exploding into sharp icicles on the floor.

That had been a fairly typical exchange.

I couldn't understand how my brother had become the unfeeling lout he had, but I suspected that the drugs his fellow journalists shared with him—and later sold to him—had something to do with it. I also suspected that drugs had something to do with his almost-explosive violence, and a raging jealousy that knew no bounds.

Max was still hung up on Sarah, despite the fact that he had been warned off, and despite the fact that she would never willingly see him again. He thought that because I saw her occasionally, I was trying to take her away from him. It never seemed to register that I had been friends with her for a very long time.

I shook my head in frustration and flicked off the TV, where Sir Harold and I had given way to the news. My body was tired but my mind raced, and I knew sleep would be a long time in coming. Still, there was the regatta tomorrow, and I couldn't let down Sarah. If I couldn't rest my mind, at least I could rest my body. I rewound and labeled the videotape, cleaned up my congealed lasagna remains, turned out the lights, and stretched out on the bed.

There I spent the next two hours contemplating Arthur's whereabouts before deciding to get up and reread his latest book— minus, unfortunately, the last five chapters.

2

It was sleeting the next morning as I covered the last few miles to Henley for the final regatta of the season. Winter was coming early this year; it was only the end of October. The heater in my Volkswagen Golf, despite its teutonic efficiency, wasn't making much of a dent in the cold. Rowing was a toss-up between pain and pleasure at the best of times and it wouldn't be much fun in this weather.

Being with Sarah, on the other hand, would more than make up for it. I thanked God that I had fought Rupert Soames and won on admitting women to Threepwood, the two-hundred-year-old rowing club founded by yet another Plumtree. It was well worth it, despite the fact that Soames was suing me over an obscure clause of the 1820 bylaws, which could be interpreted as prohibiting women from entering the club. Everyone but Rupert thought the regulation ridiculous, but we had never bothered to convene the board of governors to change it. I could always count on Rupert.

It suddenly occurred to me that the same silver Rover had been following me most of the way up from London. Now he had followed me onto the private gravel road that led to the club, so I knew his destination was the same as mine. Not many of us who belonged to Threepwood lived in London, and none of the other city-dwelling members that I knew drove a silver Rover. Strange, I thought, the way he always followed at the same distance, at least five car lengths behind me. Stranger still, I thought, as I glanced in my rearview mirror again at the entrance to the car park and saw that the car had disappeared.

Puzzled, I pulled into the car park and sat for a moment listening to little bullets of sleet hitting the windscreen. My thoughts drifted from the Rover back to Sarah. Sometimes it seemed more difficult to carry on being her friend than to just give her up altogether, but I knew from experience that long, hard slogs can win the race.

Besides, I couldn't help it. It was Sarah or no one at all.

I told myself to buck up, grabbed my kit bag, and sloshed through the sleet toward the pillared entrance.

A flash of color caught my eye, and I saw Sarah jogging toward me with a long red scarf around her neck, dark hair gleaming. There was nothing I could do to prevent my heart from skipping several beats.

She caught up to me, slightly out of breath, and fell in with my step. "Hi." She didn't have to look up as far as Barnes did; she was a leggy five foot ten.

"Hi yourself," I said, marveling that she would run out in this weather just to say hello. "Have a nice time with the Frogs?"

She rolled her eyes. "Oh, you know, they hate doing business with American banks. And they refuse to speak French to an American. So I spoke French the whole time, and they spoke English, and neither of us ever said a word about it." She shrugged. "What can I say? They need our money, and I was happy to give it to them."

"For an extortionate fee, of course."

"Of course," she agreed cheerfully. "They can afford it."

She ran lightly up the steps and pulled open the front door. As we stood dripping just inside the door, I had the feeling she wanted to tell me something.

"Alex, I really appreciate you standing in for Mike today."

"The pleasure's all mine," I said.

She hesitated, and I knew there was more. She was completely transparent to me, perhaps because I cared to notice everything about her. It often surprised her that I knew when she was pleased, upset, sad.

"Well, what is it?"

She looked at me, bemused. "I forgot. You read my mind."

"Come on, out with it."

"Well, it's a lot to ask, Alex, really."

"Nothing's as bad as the suspense. What is it?"

She steeled herself. "You've been so good, I hate to ask it. I mean, things like stepping in for Mike and fixing my plumbing at three in the morning. And rescuing me from your brother." She looked down at her sneakers and sighed. "If you weren't such a good friend, I wouldn't ask."

I cringed inside. Just a good friend. Still, it was better than nothing.

"Oh, Alex, I've got myself into a jam." Her arms flopped against her sides in a gesture of frustration and defeat. "It's Alan." Alan was her boss at the bank, a lecherous man twenty years her senior who, according to Sarah, had revolting personal habits. "I told him that I couldn't go out with him because I've got a date. I've fobbed him off before, but this time I made a mistake."

She frowned and picked at the fringe of her scarf. "He asked where I was going on my date, and my temper got the better of me. I said I was going to the Waterside Inn." The Waterside Inn was one of the most elegant—and expensive—French restaurants in England, on the Thames in the Berkshire countryside.

"Ah." I looked at her, but she was still preoccupied with the microscopic fibers of her scarf. "I think I understand. You don't really have a date to the Waterside Inn, but you want me to take you there anyway, because you know he'll go and take his mother if he has to, out of spite, just to see if you really have a date."

"How did you know that?" she said, looking at me incredulously.

I sidestepped that one, not wanting to tell her that I could sympathize with her boss. "Well, we can't have your career going up the spout, can we?"

"No," she said. "We can't."

We were late; people were rushing around us, getting ready for the first race. I was in it and hadn't even changed yet.

"Right," I said. "Waterside Inn. I'd be delighted."

She beamed an incandescent smile in my direction. "Alex, you're a peach. I'll pay, of course."

I waved the mention of money aside. If only she knew how much I wanted to take her there at any price. "On what night is this deception to take place?"

"Er—tonight, actually. I thought eight o'clock." She looked up at me to see if I minded.

I laughed and shook my head. "You don't expect much, do you? Lucky for you I'm not busy tonight." I looked at her sideways. "What would you have done if I'd been otherwise engaged?"

She shrugged but had the good grace to look embarrassed. "I didn't think you'd let me down."

It didn't occur to me to mind being taken for granted; I was grateful for any crumb she would toss in my direction. I smiled and nodded. "You were right."

She looked relieved that I hadn't taken offense. "Right. See you at the dock, then." She was off, jogging toward the women's locker room. I moved off in the opposite direction with an unrestrained grin. If ever there were a romantic setting, the Waterside Inn was it. At this rate, before long we would be moving on to candles and Tchaikovsky.

Perhaps I was inspired by the thought, or else I was in good form at the end of a long season. At any rate, to my great pleasure our eight won the heavyweight race. To my even greater pleasure, I escorted Sarah to victory as well, for which I earned an enthusiastic—if sisterly—peck on the cheek. She was a powerhouse in a boat. She wasn't big or visibly muscular, but she was highly skilled and had long legs as well as remarkable endurance.

I was settling down to a victory pint with her and most of my eight at the customary postrace party when I felt a tap on the shoulder.

"Plumtree, my boy." It was Simon Bow, the distinguished gray-haired eminence of Threepwood and the publishing industry in general. I stood and faced him.

"Hello, Simon."

Perfectly groomed as usual, he gave me his well-modulated smile, which I was certain he practiced in the mirror. "I didn't get to talk to you last night after the fracas at the party. You must be feeling all right, or you couldn't have won your races." The measured smile again.

"Yes, thanks. Rupert did let me escape in one piece, after all."

Simon chuckled. "How're things at the Press? Still nose to the wheel on the mass market stuff?"

Simon Bow was an expert at cloaking insults in innocuous verbiage, but I was equally expert at cracking the code. His barb was aimed at Arthur's novel, which was much more popular—read profitable—than the literary masterpieces Bow and Bow, Ltd. published. I liked to think he was just jealous.

I could read Simon Bow like a book because everyone in our tiny, incestuous London publishing circle knew everyone else's business. Family firms like Bow's and mine had carried on generations—sometimes centuries—of competition. It was because there were relatively few of us, I suppose, that we were so intensely competitive. Yet we all continued to keep our offices in Bedford Square in the West End, a vague sense of suspicion hanging over the square like a fog.

I smiled civilly. "Yes, *Deliver Us* is still keeping us busy; we can't seem to order the reprints fast enough. But then, all this hard work has the advantage of keeping me out of trouble."

It may have been less than kind to hint at Simon's recent troubles; he'd been caught red-handed by photographers with a girl half his wife's age on a Mediterranean holiday last month. Still, if I didn't show him I could give as good as I got, he'd walk all over me.

Simon laughed with genuine amusement and lifted his glass in a toast. "Touché, Alex. So much like your father." Looking at me, he probably saw a pretty good resemblance of my father, Maximilian Plumtree; the same dark hair and incongruous blue eyes behind thick horn-rimmed glasses, and—I'm told—the same inscrutable expression.

Simon and my father had fought it out on the playing fields of Eton and Cambridge, and later in a race for a seat in the House of Commons. Even after my father won, they had remained friends, not exactly close, but friends nevertheless. This was no mean achievement, considering that generations of viciously feuding Plumtrees and Bows had gone before them. Somehow, my father and Simon had managed to break the cycle.

"Cheers." Simon gave me a last appraising smile and floated off to grace another part of the room.

As I turned back to my eight I saw the general manager of the club threading his way through the room in my direction. "Call for you in the office," he shouted.

I nodded and followed him back to his lair. "Thanks, Sam. Any idea who it is?"

There was a hint of a smile on his rugged lips. "Someone calling on behalf of Rupert Soames."

I hadn't missed Rupert, but now I realized that I hadn't seen him. He was normally there on regatta days to uphold the newly forged Soames tradition, show off his beautifully made tweed jacket, and generally cast his long shadow over the proceedings. No wonder I'd been having such a good time.

Bracing myself for another verbal siege, I sat down on the manager's leather-topped desk and gazed out at the sleet.

"Alex Plumtree here."

"Good afternoon, sir. This is Graves; I am calling for Mr. Soames." It was Rupert's majordomo.

"Yes."

"Mr. Soames and Miss Alison would be most grateful if you would pay a brief visit to Auldwood this evening—say, between six and seven?"

I was shocked speechless. A Plumtree in the Soames residence? My father had tried on occasion to get Rupert into the Plumtree abode to mend fences, but never the other way round.

Graves cleared his throat. "I am aware that it is rather late notice, sir, but I've been asked to tell you that they would be most grateful if you would come."

"Er—yes. Yes, of course. Please tell them I'll be there at six."

"Thank you, sir."

I shook my head and returned to the party, glancing at my watch. It was only five o'clock now; there would be plenty of time to get to Sarah's by eight after this courtesy visit to Auldwood, which was just twenty minutes from the club. Rumor had it that Auldwood was decorated with enough valuable antiques, family crests, and gold-encrusted coats of arms to persuade the most snobbish visitor that the Soames family had been in these parts for centuries, and not just the last thirty years. Evidently Rupert was ashamed of having come from the wrong side of the tracks in

Liverpool and had surrounded himself with convincing props, now that he had the money to do so. He'd even gone to an elocution instructor to have his Liverpudlian accent exorcised. I would have respected him more if he had just been Rupert Soames, successful publisher, and hadn't felt that the rest of it was so important.

I looked in on the party. My eight was so convulsed in laughter—over some unrepeatable joke, no doubt—that for once they weren't making any noise. Sarah smiled broadly and retreated to a more civilized group, and I headed in her direction, waiting at her shoulder until the current version of the race was finished. Eventually she turned and saw me.

"About dinner tonight," I said.

"Mm."

"Anything else I need to know? Am I supposed to be anyone in particular, or just a mystery man?"

She looked flummoxed. "No . . . no one in particular." She put her beer mug down on the lid of a battered baby grand piano and wiped her hands on her jeans. We weren't big on formality at Threepwood. "But be presentable, will you, Alex?"

I took this to mean that at the very least I should change out of the old running shoes I had taken to wearing through the mud and rain on weekends, which was the only time I ever saw her. I wasn't sure if she had ever seen me in a suit; she probably thought I didn't own one.

"Presentable—right. I'll try. See you at eight."

I ran through the freezing wind to my car. It was already dark. If I dashed straight off to Soames's now, I could pick up my suit, get to my London flat, change, and still be at Sarah's in Hampstead by eight.

All this would be much easier if we lived in the same house, I thought wistfully, fishing for car keys in my pocket. I had inserted them in the lock when I heard something rustle behind me. I whipped round, startled, and heard as much as felt a whoosh of air, as if a cricket ball had just missed my head.

I pulled back from it, and in the lamplight caught a glimpse of a dark globe coming toward me again. I twisted to get out of its way, instinctively protecting my glasses, and it smashed into the passenger-side door with a heavy thud. The ball seemed to be on some kind of leash, like a tetherball. The third time I felt its breath I whipped around, lunging at my attacker's stomach. As I brought him down, I heard the ball rushing toward me. I threw my arms up to protect my head and sank down to cover my vulnerable ribs as best I could.

When it came, the pain bit deeply into my shoulder. The ball had iron teeth—like a mace—that scraped across the top of my arm and then sank into my flesh. They stuck there, and my attacker had to yank the ball away by its leash to get them out. I cried out, clutching my shoulder, momentarily paralyzed by pain. He scraped to his feet in the gravel, crunched away toward the holly bushes that lined the car park, and was gone.

For a moment it was silent. I heard only my breath coming in ragged gasps. As I stood, gripping my shoulder with the opposite hand, I heard someone coming toward me at a run.

"Alex!" It was George Stoneham. He was an old friend, a fellow oarsman, and the husband of my secretary. At the moment I was grateful that he also happened to be a doctor. I could hear his two boys, Michael and Edward, messing about behind him on the gravel.

"I heard something on my way out . . ." His eyes raked over me and my bashed-in car door, and he underwent a rapid transformation from rowdy crewmate to authoritative physician. "Boys, I want you to go to the car and wait for me there." They heard the change in his voice and scampered off obediently. George came near and gently pried my fingers off the wound to take a look.

"Good God, Alex. What kind of animal did this to you?"

I shook my head, teeth clenched. "Human animal, I'm afraid. One with—it's crazy, but—I could have sworn it was a mace."

"A mace . . ." His face registered confusion, then anger. He closed his mouth and gently put a hand on my back. "Let's get you inside, it's freezing out here."

I shook my head again. "No—not inside. I don't want Sarah to know. I'm seeing her tonight."

He looked at me carefully, as if trying to decide whether I had already gone into shock. Evidently he decided I had my wits about me, as he didn't argue. He was one of the few people who knew about my complicated friendship with Sarah.

"Sit down here, then," he said, opening my car door with a gloved hand. He tried to help me in and couldn't have known that in putting his hands firmly on either side of my chest he would set off fireworks in the area of Rupert's handiwork. He heard me breathe in sharply.

"In the chest, too?"

"No," I said, eyes closed. "That was Soames, yesterday. I think he cracked a rib or two."

"Right. Yesterday. And you rowed in two races today." He shook his head, emitting a little burst of air through his teeth. I could feel his eyes on me. "I'll just get my bag. Be right back." I heard his footsteps recede, his boot open and close, and his footsteps return.

"Okay?"

I nodded, teeth still clenched.

"It must hurt like hell. I'm sorry. I can give you something to take the edge off." He pulled a bubble-wrapped packet of two pills out of his bag and held them in his hand, thinking. "The only problem is, you'll have to let me drive you. You're not meant to drive while taking these."

"Out of the question then."

He raised his eyebrows. "I see." He thought for a second and rummaged in his bag, then brought out a syringe. "I'll give you a local anesthetic, then, but I'm afraid it'll wear off in three, four hours at the most."

I nodded, and he began cutting the hopelessly mangled mackintosh, sweater, shirt, and vest away from the wound. When he had a neat square, he began cleaning the skin around it. George was nothing if not meticulous.

"I hope you won't think me ungrateful, George, but I don't suppose you could hurry. I've got a lot to do before I fetch Sarah, and I don't want to be late."

He looked at me as if I were out of my mind and stuck the needle into my arm just above the wound without a great deal of gentleness. "You've gone round the bend, you know," he said definitely. "Absolutely stark raving. You're only just escaping stitches, someone's mangled your arm with a—a mace, of all things." He wrinkled his nose in disgust. "God knows what could make this kind of a mess. And you're telling me to hurry up and let you get on your way."

"Thanks, George."

He kept shaking his head as he cleaned the wound, which was, thankfully, already beginning to lose some feeling. "You didn't see who it was?"

"No—he was wearing some sort of hood."

"Maybe it was a violent punk, looking for someone to terrorize."

"Hmm." I didn't express my doubts that an anonymous hoodlum would lie in wait for me in the shadows around my car. I suddenly remembered the silver Rover but didn't mention it. I was afraid that he would insist upon calling the police if he thought I had been targeted personally.

"Don't you think you should call the police, Alex? Just to report it, if not to start an inquiry."

I sighed. "I would, but then it would go in the paper, and the gossip columnists would have a field day. They'd imply that I was involved in all kinds of dark business in car parks. Besides, I'd spend the evening at the constable's office, looking at mug shots."

"Mmm. See what you mean." He wound layers of gauze around the damaged flesh, and sighed. "I will never understand how you get yourself into these situations."

He had bandaged the wound, which was now totally, blessedly, devoid of feeling, and closed his bag. "Right, then. Let's have a look at the ribs."

We heard voices and looked toward the club entrance; people were beginning to leave the party and make their way to their cars. I glanced at my watch.

"Sorry, George, must dash. I'm due at Soames's in fifteen minutes. Thanks for the repair job; I'll call you next week."

"Soames's!" I heard him say as I started my car.

"Yes. As in Rupert and Alison."

I saw him in my rearview mirror, standing with his head cocked to one side, watching my tail lamps incredulously.

Driving the ten miles to Auldwood, I let a thin stream of cold air blast through the window onto my face. I needed to think. The mace brought back a distant memory of some kind . . . . I had seen it, or one like it, somewhere before. With a bit of rust on it, it seemed.

It was so unexpected, so bizarre. Why would someone want to crack open my head with a mace? Who would even have a mace? They hadn't been used since World War II, and then by only the Germans.

Then I thought of the roll of newsprint at Churchill's and wondered if that accident had been engineered to do me in. At the time, I hadn't considered that I was the one under siege.

There was still no answer to the question why, but it came to me that the only people who could have known for certain that I would be at the party last night and the rowing club today were the Soameses. It was their party and Rupert's rowing club.

Then again, I supposed it wouldn't have been hard for anyone to follow me to the party and then the next day to Threepwood. After all, it seemed that someone had managed it quite nicely in the Rover. The little scene of Alison putting her fingers together and looking up just before the newsprint fell haunted me. Had she positioned me directly under the roll, then signaled someone to let it go? Heaven knew that Rupert Soames would be only too delighted to eliminate one of the last Plumtrees from the face of the earth.

No, I told myself; Alison had been as frightened as I, and hadn't been prepared to move out of the way. If I hadn't shoved her aside, she would have been killed, too. Rupert wouldn't have risked her life, even to end mine.

Besides, why, then, would they invite me to their home? Perhaps I had better be on my guard. Perhaps they had lured me to their house for my demise.

"Get a grip, Alex," I told myself sternly. My wheels hit the gravel of Auldwood's circular drive, and I pulled up to the porticoed front entrance. As I opened the car door I felt an odd sensation in my arm—not pain, but more of a tickle. If not for the shot, I didn't like to think what it would feel like.

Just as well the rowing season was over for the year.

I went round to the trunk, opened it, and fished out an old green shooting coat of my father's that had mud on it from who knew when. I kept it in the car in case I had to change tires or dig myself out of the mud one day. Taking off my mackintosh with the neatly cut square hole in the shoulder, I substituted the wool coat and brushed off what dried mud I could on my way to the door.

I rang the bell, and a seventyish man in a uniform appeared to show me into the last place in the world I ever thought I'd see as an invited guest. Graves, I presumed. He eyed my coat with very slightly raised eyebrows. "May I take your coat, sir?"

"No, thanks," I said. "I'll keep it on."

He bent his head in acknowledgment and indicated that I should follow him. My running shoes squeaked on the marble as we walked through the rectangular two-storey entry hall, which had four hallways running off of it. Each hallway had a number of doors off of it, all closed. We entered the southwest hallway, and the butler opened a set of French doors to reveal Alison and Rupert in heated discussion in what appeared to be the library.

They stopped short and looked up, surprised, when they saw us. A fire burned brightly beyond them, and they sat opposite one another on matching chintz loveseats.

"Alex Plumtree, sir," Graves said, and closed the doors as he withdrew.

I noticed now that Alison, in a relatively tame suede skirt and mustard silk blouse, looked upset. Rupert looked at his watch and stood, but didn't come to the door.

"Why don't you come in," he said gruffly. I wondered briefly if I should make my escape, even then. Judging from my father's experience, not to mention my own, Rupert couldn't be trusted.

But I had always enjoyed risk; this was no different than sailing into a squall for the challenge it might present. "Thank you," I said, and left the relative safety of the doorway.

Rupert gestured that I should take the corduroy-covered armchair next to his sofa, and I sat down filled with equal proportions of curiosity and apprehension.

"Get you a drink?" Rupert stood next to a huge gilded globe, the top half of which folded back to expose a generous bar.

I saw two half-full glasses on the table in front of me and decided it would be rude to decline. I didn't want to sabotage the peace talks before they began—if indeed they were to begin.

"Yes, thanks, whatever you're having." Whatever they were

having wouldn't have arsenic in it, or something else used to dispose of unwanted people.

Rupert gave me a small nod of approval and hefted a bottle of Glenfiddich. Alison and I sat in uncomfortable silence, her eyes down. She was unusually subdued, and I wondered what they had been discussing before I arrived.

Rupert delivered the glass and redeposited his bulk on the small sofa. He looked incongruous here, much too large and unruly for this tasteful room of rosewood and chintz. He cleared his throat, glanced at Alison, and said, "I owe you an apology, Plumtree." He actually blushed at these words, the act of being civil to a Plumtree evidently difficult for him.

I blinked, trying hard to believe my ears. I heard myself say, "No need."

He waved me into silence. "Unforgivable. Absolutely unforgivable." He shook his head, ruddy jowls flapping, and looked down at his drink. I was on the lookout for sarcasm, but found none. "You know that your father and I"—at the mention of my father he ground his jaw around a bit in an act that must have been second nature—" . . . uh, well, we had our differences." He swallowed and looked up at me. "But nothing excuses one man striking another. I'm sorry."

Silence reigned. I nodded and said nothing, too stunned to come up with anything appropriate. After all the things Rupert Soames had done to my father—a partial list included attempted murder, blackmail, libel, slander, industrial espionage, and sabotage—it was a shock to learn that his idea of decency was to not strike a man.

Alison sat forward, clasping her hands and resting her elbows on her knees. The blouse fell away from her chest slightly to reveal the edge of a lacy black brassiere, and it was an effort to keep my eyes on her face. Tears glistened in her eyes. "Why don't you tell him, father? I know Alex. He won't tell anyone if you ask him not to."

Her voice seemed to work magic on him. He looked at her for a moment, then nodded. "You see, Alex, I have high blood pressure. Have had for many years. The medication I take makes most people touchy, irritable. The reaction is severe in my case, possibly because I'm forced to take considerable amounts of the stuff.

"I've fought against being belligerent for years, and though I've always had a temper"—that's an understatement, I thought—"I've never actually harmed anyone before. Physically, I mean." He looked at me, then away again. "But the day before yesterday my doctor increased the dose again, and it just got out of hand. I couldn't control it."

He walked over to Alison and put his hand on her shoulder, as if for strength. It had the effect of making her tears spill over. "I've only just told Alison about the medication. She lost her mother young, you know. I didn't want her to worry about losing me, too, all these years."

I was touched by this display of fatherly love and suddenly felt that I was intruding upon a private family moment. I stood up, gently setting my glass on the table.

"I understand, and I'm grateful to you for telling me. I won't breathe a word."

Rupert started to disengage himself.

"Please don't. I'll show myself out." I quietly closed the doors behind me and nearly backed into Graves, whose buttling sixth sense must have told him that I was leaving.

"This way, sir," he said neutrally, unable to resist another glance at my filthy coat as he led me to the door. "Good night, sir."

He closed the massive door behind me, and I stood for a moment, glad to be in the bracing air. It would take a while to get used to this idea of Rupert Soames being a decent man. He had always been my larger-than-life incarnation of evil. Even now I felt some part of myself wondering if this were merely a very convincing trick.

I descended the front steps to the drive and got in the car. For shame, I told myself. What I had just seen had been no act. It was sad, really, a man's life taken out of his control by medication administered to save it.

I started the car and headed for home, of sorts, revving up the heater on high. The village of Chess, named for the river flowing through it, was my childhood home. I still kept my parents' home there, with just enough heat on to keep the pipes from freezing, because I couldn't bear to sell it. Only the barest essentials had been moved to my tiny Bedford Square garret, and the particular suit with which I hoped to impress Sarah tonight was still in my closet at the house we called The Orchard.

If I had been entirely honest with myself I would have admitted that I was keeping the house in hopes of having a happy family of my own there some day. I envisioned Sarah reading the Sunday paper over endless cups of coffee, while I took the kids out for a walk with the dog. When people asked me about the house, though, I simply said I hadn't gotten around to doing anything about it yet.

I came to a gap in the hedgerow and a weathered wooden sign that said THE ORCHARD. I turned in and drove the quarter of a mile along a drive barely wide enough for my car—it had been built for horses and carriages—with boxwood and holly hedges brushing it gently if I swerved a bit to either side.

I still got the same old thrill when the house appeared through the trees; the brick and timber building was so well integrated with its surroundings that it looked a part of the natural landscape. Shrubbery hugged the front walls, and ivy climbed to the roof at varying intervals. It looked as if nature had been allowed to take its course, but that was a clever deception. The gardener maintained it just enough so that it continued to look that way. My parents had hated any kind of artifice, including overly manicured gardens.

Perhaps that was what had struck me about the Soameses' home: its total lack of naturalness. Things were too . . . perfect. The white pea gravel drive had been lined with perfectly trimmed and potted topiary trees, and the stilted, formal interior was out of keeping with Rupert's character. He was a rough-and-tumble man, yet his home looked like a museum. There were some beautiful pieces in it, certainly, as befit a museum, but it was not designed to comfortably accommodate several people sharing their lives. It was designed to impress.

Again, the house mirrored the man, I thought. Rupert didn't seem to work in publishing because he loved it; he did it because it lent him credibility as a gentleman and earned him the respect of people with whom he would otherwise never associate.

I had bypassed the little parking area for guests in front of The Orchard, studded with a fountain now closed for the winter, and turned into the side drive when something made me put the car into reverse. Backing around, I looked up at the front door. The heavy oak slab with its bull's-eye window was standing ajar, barely notice-able except to someone used to seeing it every day for most of his life.

No doubt Max had come for something and left it open, I thought with resignation. I had long ago given up hope that my brother would grow up and be responsible. Now I merely wondered how he could be a successful newspaper reporter and writer—for *The Watch*, one of London's leading papers—and still be so absent-minded and irresponsible.

I turned off the ignition, mounted the stone steps to the door, and pushed it open. It was dark inside, but with the ease of long familiarity I found my way to the hall table lamp and switched it on. Everything looked just as Amelia, the woman from the village who cleaned the place once a month, usually left it, but I had the odd feeling that someone had been there recently . . . or was still there. No lights had glowed from the outside, but it was possible that Max was in a back room somewhere with the door closed. I wouldn't have been surprised to learn that he'd been kicked out of another flat for tearing up the place with his wild parties and was crashing here at night. The last thing he'd do would be to tell me.

"Max?" I called, mounting the red carpeted stairs that rose out of the middle of the entry hall to the second-floor hallway. "Are you there?"

Silence. I shrugged and decided that my imagination was becoming entirely too active. I went to my room, got the suit that I hardly ever wore for lack of appropriate occasions, and went back down to the car, turning off the lights and locking the door securely behind me.

I strapped myself in, turned on the ignition and the heater, and suddenly realized that the front door had been open again when I came back downstairs. I was certain I'd shut it when I came in. Staring at the door, I decided that if Max were sneaking around the house for some reason, I'd been lucky to avoid him. The house was solidly locked now, anyway, and there was no point in worrying.

Turning my thoughts to Sarah and the Waterside Inn, I set off on the twenty-five-mile drive to London with an idiotic smile on my lips.

3

Back at the Bedford Square flat, I said a fervent prayer of thanks as I poured two brandies in the kitchen. I had brought the huge snifters from my parents' house months ago for just such a possibility. The evening had been a total success, candles and all. Sarah's boss had even been persuaded that she was on a real date, judging from the look he'd flashed me.

Sarah was in the sitting room making a phone call to her roommate, who was evidently nursing a nasty cold. I could see through the service hatch that the room, covered with books on three walls, looked warm and inviting in the light of the log fire I had started. Sarah looked even warmer and more inviting. She was wearing a touchable burgundy silk dress in a simple shift style, nipped in at the waist to show off her slender figure. Its simplicity only accentuated her other natural assets: perpetually rosy cheeks in a creamy complexion, sparkling green eyes, and dark hair that curled slightly below the shoulder. I had noticed that the dress was cut to fall an inch or two short of her knees, but when she sat down more of her legs showed. Her legs begged to be touched; the little curves where her muscles bulged ever so slightly, the intricate sculpture of her kneecap—they were works of art, proof that there was a God. I treated myself to a long, luxurious look, my eyes following the filmy black stockings up her leg until they disappeared beneath the dress.

"Do you always have this many messages after an evening out?" She sounded incredulous as she finished punching her roommate's number. "Your answering machine is blinking up a storm."

"Is it?" I didn't care about the messages, which were in all probability from Charlie Goodspeed. I only hoped that I didn't sound guilty; I'd been staring at those gorgeous legs and allowing my hopes to get way out of control after our evening together. But I knew better than to press my luck.

She got through to her roommate and I stood listening for a moment in the dark kitchen, not to her words, but her voice. I savored its warm, slightly-lower-than-you'd-expect timbre as it reverberated in my own sitting room. I allowed myself the luxury of pretending, just for a moment, that it was like this every night.

I suddenly realized that she might wonder why I was standing quietly in a darkened kitchen. I quickly picked up the two glasses and headed toward the sitting room. I heard her exclaim "Really?" into the phone with some excitement as she followed me with her eyes. I walked past her and deposited the brandies on an old chest that served as a coffee table.

"Hmm, he probably gets it the night before, too. Thanks, Liz—drink your hot tea and lemon and go to bed." I heard the laugh that made me feel warm all over. "All right, then—whiskey and lemon. Bye."

She gave me a mysterious smile as she hung up the phone and jumped up, heading for the hatchway to the kitchen. We had put a pile of papers there that had accumulated outside my front door during the day: the Saturday paper and the nonnews portion of the thick *Sunday Tempus*, which was often delivered on Saturday night.

"Just wait till you see this," she said, glowing as she carried the bundles back to the sofa. "Liz hasn't read it, but she says there's something about your book on the cover of the book review section."

My heart sank. How could Barnes possibly have run a review without the entire manuscript? He must have done some sort of preview piece. I hit the table with my fist in a gesture of frustration. Damn. My name would be mush, and the financial situation not much better. I thought guiltily of Sarah in her role as my banker, and regretted that I had never told her the depth of my business problems resulting from Arthur's disappearance. She knew that I had put off repaying the loan well beyond the agreed date, but she also knew all about cash flow in small businesses and had won extra time for me. Perhaps I would have to tell her now. If only I had found a way to tell Barnes at the party that Arthur and the rest of the book were missing . . .

Sarah looked up at me quizzically from the sofa, where she was digging through the paper for the section. "What is it?" she asked. "Aren't you pleased?"

I swallowed. "Well, yes; it's just that it's come a bit early. It's rather a long story." The phone rang, and I waved a hand at it, mumbling, "The machine will get it." The machine clicked on, and my message played silently, but the message-receiving tape must have been full. It clicked off again before anyone could leave a word. It was rather late for a call—nearly eleven—but Charlie Goodspeed was oblivious to such norms of human behavior. I was just as glad not to get the message.

I was tempted to tell Sarah about Arthur's disappearance and the incipient ruin of Plumtree Press, but it occurred to me that in sharing the burden I would put part of it on her shoulders. She turned back to the paper and pulled out the book review section, flopping it onto the table.

We stared in silence at a garish red cover that announced:

DELIVER US FROM EVIL: WERE BRITAIN'S WAR CHILDREN KIDNAPPED?

Barnes Appleton reveals that mystery author 'Arthur's' best-selling novel and its soon-to-be-published sequel are much more than fiction—and the sequel promises to reveal the identities of the kidnappers who stole Britain's children from their parents.

An overly creative art director had chosen to illustrate the title with an eight-headed monster locking a group of young children in a grotesque and sinister embrace.

Now I knew what Barnes had been trying to tell me at the party.

He had merged his literary and political interests and come up with a whopping story. Those damn missing chapters, I thought. They held the identities of the men who did this, and as a favor to me Barnes had written the review as if he'd had them. I remembered from having reread the manuscript the other night that the novel foreshadowed the exposure of the criminals, but that hadn't mattered when I thought it was all fiction.

"It's incredible," Sarah said, riffling the pages and eventually finding the beginning of the cover story. Dumbfounded, I sank onto the sofa beside her and began to read. The phone began to ring again, and I ignored it.

Barnes's article espoused the theory that Arthur's novel had actually taken place and was history, not fiction. Roughly a thousand children who had been evacuated to the countryside from London during World War II had evidently been sold by charity officials, who were to have evacuated them temporarily to the States. Americans eager to help were told that the children were orphans, and were asked to contribute a substantial fee to the charity in exchange for their passage. The real parents, in England, were informed that their children had died in freak accidents or bombing raids in the countryside.

To make matters more interesting, Barnes had learned that the records of the charity handling the evacuation of several boatloads of children had been destroyed in a fire, not long before the end of the war. The Ministry of Defence was conducting an inquiry, interviewing everyone involved to find out who had been in charge of the children's transport. At $250 per child for about a thousand children, it was estimated that the kidnapper had come out of the scheme with a cool $250,000, a small fortune in wartime.

"This couldn't actually have happened," I said, not wanting to believe. "It's horrible." It had made a nice plot for a novel, but that was because I had known it was fiction.

Sarah handed me my brandy and took a sip of her own.

"Why wouldn't Arthur have told me?" I asked, half to myself.

She turned back to the story as if she would find the answer there.

Unfortunately, I had to admit that it was probably true. First of all, Barnes was no sensationalist. Others could have written this story and I would have disregarded it as an effort to make a name for themselves.

But not Barnes. He'd already won his Beecroft Award for journalistic excellence and no longer had anything to prove. Besides, he had proof that couldn't be ignored. His article said that through ads he'd placed in American and British papers, he had found five sets of parents and children who had been separated in 1945 when the parents were notified that their children were dead, and vice versa.

He told the story of one child in detail, who had been older than two at the time. The child remembered that he had another set of parents before the war. The story of his reunion with his parents had brought tears to my eyes; the children were now in their late forties, their parents seventy.

All those lost years.

My mind flew off on a number of tangents and ended on the disturbing thought that Arthur's disappearance might in some way be linked to the release of this story in the paper. Perhaps he had written the story to expose the truth; perhaps the reason for the secrecy surrounding his identity was fear of retaliation by the kidnappers. It seemed to me that he must know who was responsible.

I had to find Arthur.

Perhaps Barnes knew something I didn't, after all his research. I lifted the phone off the side table into my lap and punched the number of directory inquiries. "The *Sunday Tempus*, please," I said.

Sarah raised her eyebrows, her way of asking what I was up to now.

"I'm calling Barnes's editor to get his number . . . Hello, could I have Nigel Wexford please? Yes, that's right." I waited for several moments before receiving a peremptory harrumph on the other end that might have been a hello.

"Alex Plumtree here. Is that you, Nigel?"

"Y-y-yes, it is. I w-w-wondered when you would c-c-call."

I thought, not for the first time, that perhaps he had gone into literary criticism because reading and writing didn't involve speaking, which for Nigel meant excruciating stuttering.

"Yes, well, it's quite a story, isn't it."

"Quite a . . . good God, you d-d-do know about Barnes, don't y-y-you, Alex?"

"Yes, I've read the story about *Deliver Us From Evil*, if that's what you mean."

"N-no." A pause. I had the feeling he was composing himself. "R-r-read t-today's paper, will you, Alex, and c-c-call me back if you st-still don't understand. We're a b-b-bit unglued around here, I'm afraid. S-s-sorry; I know you t-two were friends."

The phone went dead in my hand.

I rummaged for the Saturday paper in the pile Sarah had brought over from the hatchway. A wave of shock washed over me as I unfolded the paper to see Barnes's face under a headline that read, "Prize-winning journalist found dead in Notting Hill flat."

I sank to my knees and spread the paper on the coffee table, skimming the article. His wife had come home late Friday night from her office to find him on the floor by the fireplace, bleeding from the head. At first she thought he was merely unconscious and had fallen against the raised brick hearth. She went to help him but saw that it was hopeless. He was already dead. Services would be held on Sunday at one o'clock, St. Brides Church, Fleet Street.

If only I'd called him, got his number from the paper's offices last night. Maybe I could have stopped the intruder, scared him off. . . .

I became aware that Sarah was very quiet and still, looking over my shoulder at the paper. I turned and saw that her face was white, her eyes huge.

"Are you all right?" I put a hand on her shoulder, then took it away again as the alarm bell went off in my head.

She nodded resolutely. "Yes—all right." She looked down and her eyes came to rest on the empty ring finger of her left hand. "How awful for his wife."

"I know." Of course I didn't, not nearly as well as she did, but I was trying.

We were quiet for a moment; then she surprised me.

"Alex . . . are you thinking what I'm thinking?" Her eyes held more sadness than I could bear, but they also twinkled with intelligence.

45

I took the bait, relieved that I hadn't dragged her back into the depths of grief with my problems. "What would that be?"

"Well . . . doesn't it seem a coincidence that Barnes should be found dead just when people became aware that he was doing this story? I didn't know him, but I read his articles. He seems, seemed, too smart to trip and die in front of his own fireplace."

"Mmm." The thought had crossed my mind.

"Someone at the *Tempus*—or contacts there—could have known about this article days ago. His editor, of course, knew even sooner."

She frowned and looked at me. "You do realize this has implications for you, beyond the publicity your books and Plumtree Press are receiving as a result. Someone was behind this kidnapping plot and they can't be too pleased at being exposed. You don't think anyone's out to get you, do you?"

"You sound as if you read too many Nancy Drew mysteries as a child."

"I'm serious, Alex. If they want to silence this story badly enough, you could be in danger. You're the only one Arthur communicates with."

She looked at me with enough warmth and concern to melt me. I tried to keep my mind engaged and waved my hand dismissively to hide my certainty that she did have a point.

Unfortunately, she knew me too well.

"Look me in the eye, Alex." I did. "Has anyone threatened you?"

She saw me waver, and that was enough. "I knew it," she said. "Out with it."

I told her about the roll of paper at the press party, minus the half-seen man in the gallery, and decided to spare her the detail of the mace episode in the boat club parking lot.

She listened wide-eyed. "Why don't you tell me these things, Alex? You could have been killed!"

"And you could worry yourself to death if you're not careful. It could have been an accident, you know." I noticed her glass was empty and picked it up with mine to get more from the kitchen.

The harsh ring of the phone startled us both, and this time she picked it up. "Hello?"

I loved her casual American way of answering the phone. Growing up, I had always had to say, "Chess Four-six-three-one." Quite a mouthful.

"George, yes, how are you?" Sarah said. "You're what?" She was silent for a moment, watching me carefully through the hatch.

"I see," she said. "Alex, it's George calling to see how your arm is doing—the one he patched up today after you were attacked in the car park, that really should have had stitches. He wants to know if it's very painful, if he should come over and give you another shot."

I rolled my eyes in the dark kitchen. Just like him to call and check up on me. Now she knew the whole story anyway.

I popped my head through the hatch. "Tell him it's fine, thank you very much." With envy I saw that the phone cord was brushing innocently against her right breast. I would have given a lot to trade places with it for a moment.

"It's fine, thank you, George, he says." She listened for a moment. "I'll tell him. Thanks—yes, you too. Bye."

She looked at me with amusement as I covered the few steps back into the sitting room. "He says that if you want your ribs taped up properly, you should come by his house tomorrow. He says he knows the hack job you will have done."

"Mmm." There seemed to be no way to keep secrets from her—not that I genuinely wanted any.

" 'Mmm,' " she repeated, her eyes laughing. "The classic English response. That's all you're going to tell me—'Mmm'?"

"It was nothing, really. Rupert Soames lost his temper at the Soames and Sons press party and hit me. And then as I was leaving Threepwood this afternoon, some out-of-sorts young punk chose to take out his anger at the world on me. It was just unlucky that I was the first one out."

She looked at me as if she expected more.

"That's all."

"You're sure."

"Of course I'm sure." I took a sip of brandy.

"I should have known something was afoot when you suggested having brandy."

She really did know me well. I normally disliked postprandials, but had decided the brandy would be a good anesthetic, now that the shot had worn off. And I knew her well enough to know that she was probably thinking about the Dartmouth Outing Club hiking trip up Mount Washington when I sprained my ankle and refused to take the codeine in the first aid kit for the pain. I had always had a deep mistrust of pills and drugs in general.

"You know," she said, her head on one side, "I remember the time on Mount Washington when you—"

"Yes. I thought you might dredge that up," I said in exasperation. "Listen. Since you know so much about me anyway, I'm going to tell all. We might as well put your superior intelligence to work on this thing with Arthur. And Barnes."

I shook my head. Poor Barnes.

Then, feeling that I owed it to her anyway, I told her everything. About Arthur disappearing, about the way the business was bet on the sequel, about Barnes mentioning to me at the party that something had come up about the book.

She thought for a moment. When she spoke, I was impressed that her thoughts were of my problems, and not hers. She was the one who would have to explain to the investors at her bank if Plumtree Press failed.

"Maybe whoever was behind the kidnappings really is trying to get back at you for exposing the truth, for publishing the book in the first place. And then, of course, there's always Rupert."

Yes, there was always Rupert. She knew about some of the nasty tricks Rupert had played on me at the rowing club, spreading rumors, the bylaws suit, even loosening my rigging so that I was thrown from the boat during one race, thereby destroying my boat's chance of winning.

I would have thought Rupert a likely possibility, with his jealousy of me in my father's shoes and the company's success, and all the old pent-up feelings toward my father. But I couldn't consider it after what I'd seen at his home this evening.

Or was I supposed to think that?

"I can't explain it all, but I have reason to believe it's not Rupert."

"Hmm. Okay." That was one of many things I liked about Sarah; she was reasonable. She would never beg me to tell her something I couldn't. "Any other business rivals you can think of? I can't imagine that you have any personal enemies."

I shook my head. "No. But now that you mention business rivals . . . well, something rather interesting did happen with Simon Bow."

She sat up and looked at me with interest.

"About the time word got out that there was going to be a sequel to *Deliver Us From Evil,* he called and asked me to Bow and Bow for lunch." My taste buds reverberated at the memory of the Tournedos Rossini that Simon's caterers had served on the antique conference room table, preceded by smoked salmon and accompanied by new potatoes and crisp vegetables—a startling contrast with Plumtree Press's meager sandwiches and crisps.

"He offered an exorbitant price for the rights to the sequel, and the paperback rights to the first book as well. Needless to say, I wasn't interested, as I wanted them to build the reputation of our list, and to bankroll the new line of fiction."

I leaned back and rubbed my eyes, feeling tired. It seemed I had far too many enemies all of a sudden. My arm stung with new vigor, and it was beginning to sink in that perhaps someone did want me to disappear, like Arthur. And Barnes . . .

There was a rustle, and when I opened my eyes, Sarah was standing. I automatically started to get up, but she gently pushed me back onto the sofa. "You stay there," she said, pointing a finger at me authoritatively. "You're exhausted, and I'm leaving. But I want you to promise me something."

I nodded dumbly, looking up at her like a child. "Keep your door locked and call me tomorrow night. Let me know if you're still alive."

I nodded again, never one to turn down an invitation to call her. "I will," I said. "Thanks."

"Is there anything I can do for you before I go?"

I thought of quite a few things.

"No," I said a bit wistfully. "Thanks."

She turned, the burgundy silk gliding smoothly over what it covered, and left. That was it; she had been here, in this very flat, and now she was gone.

Another man might have wished that she had said "I had a

great time" or "Thanks for tonight." In our case, we were good enough friends to know that we'd both had a great time. What I wished for was some glimmer in her eye that said things were changing between us.

But I could wait; I would wait.

I turned out the lights, fell onto the bed in my clothes, and dreamed I was with Sarah in a long hall full of closed doors. She held a huge ring of keys up in front of me, and was unlocking a door when, to my great dismay, my alarm clock went off.

Eventually, groggily, I realized that it wasn't an alarm clock; it was the phone ringing in my ear. My shoulder throbbed viciously. I picked up the phone using the other arm and squinted at the clock. It was just six o'clock. "Hello?"

"Alex Plumtree?"

"Yes."

"Mike Dobbins here from the *Daily Herald*. Did you know that *Deliver Us From Evil* was factual when you published it?"

"Did I—look, would you mind if I called you back?" I refrained from shouting down the line that it was an uncivilized hour for a phone call, knowing that any anger I showed would come back to haunt me in the paper tomorrow.

He wasn't at all discouraged. "I just have a few questions. If you don't mind, I'd quite like to—"

"I do mind. If you want me to call you back, give me your number." You couldn't be subtle with journalists, as I knew all too well from dealing with Max.

"I left it on your answering machine last night. That's how I know you don't return messages."

I rolled my eyes. These people were unbelievable. "Well, give it to me again."

Sighing, he did. The moment I hung up, the phone was ringing again. Through a sleepy haze, I realized that I was under journalistic siege, and that the calling hours of this uncivilized breed begin at six in the morning even on weekends. They were at least as bad as Charlie; perhaps worse. I reached down and unplugged the phone, then rolled over for what I hoped would be another hour or two of blissful oblivion.

I had no sooner pulled the duvet over my head than the doorbell rang. Growling on the way to the closet for my bathrobe, I realized I would have to deal with these people somehow. Last night, in the glow of Sarah's presence, and then the haze of exhaustion, I hadn't thought about the press. But this story involved one of their own, and they were bound to be thorough.

I went to the door and looked out through the panes of glass toward the top, totally unprepared for what I saw. A camera flashed, and one of them said, "Heads up—here he is." I opened the door and was met with a full frontal assault: questions, lights, flashes. There must have been ten of them, and they weren't particularly friendly.

"Do you think the death of Barnes Appleton had anything to do with the story he wrote on the Arthur books?"

"Why did you pretend the books were fiction?"

"Are you cooperating with the government on this?"

I took it all in and knew what I had to do. "Thank you all for coming. I'm afraid I can't meet with you today, but you're all invited to Plumtree Press tomorrow morning at ten for a full briefing. By then I can provide you with copies of faxes from Arthur, and anything else you might be interested in. All right?"

They weren't satisfied. The questions flew, the cameras rolled on. But it was the best I could do. I had to think, not to mention go to Barnes's funeral and talk to his wife. "Thank you. See you tomorrow. Fifty-eight Bedford Square."

I closed the door on them and took the phone in the sitting room off its hook. I made a new answering machine message that explained the time and location of the press briefing.

Then I did something I'd never done before: I decided to call Ian on his sacred vacation, knowing that he wouldn't want to be kept in the dark any longer. For five weeks now I had refrained from calling, much as I could have used his advice. I dialed his home number, which I knew would be answered by an answering service. "Ian Higginbotham's residence," said an engaging voice.

"Yes, hello. This is Alex Plumtree; I work with Mr. Higginbotham. It's urgent that I reach him. Can you give me his number on holiday, please?"

"I'll put you through—we aren't allowed to give out the number. One moment please." I heard a click, and then the single long ring of a non-British telephone. Perhaps he was in America or Canada. I let it ring twelve times and then the engaging voice cut in. "Would you care to leave a message?"

"Yes, please; could you ask him to ring Alex?"

She took my number and we said good-bye.

I looked at my watch and saw that it was still only six-thirty. It was just as well that the esteemed members of the press had gotten me up early; I had a lot to do today. After a hot shower, a cup of coffee, and some toast, I felt nearly human.

I put on an extra sweater, as the heat would be off in the office on a Sunday, picked up my briefcase, and had my hand on the doorknob before I heard them. Assorted bumps and rustles and cries of, "Here he comes!" alerted me to the fact that the press was encamped on my doorstep. They had seen my head through the glass when I walked into the entry hall, scrambled to their feet, and turned on their lights again. I pretended to pick something off of the hall table and retreated. They couldn't see below my shoulders, and didn't know I was ready to go out.

They were a right nuisance. No wonder Max liked the business; he could make people miserable all day long.

A smile spread over my face as I had an idea. I had always wanted to try walking to the office via the roof; the houses on Bedford Square form one long, connected terrace. I had a skylight in my bedroom, and there was one in the storeroom on the top floor at the office. Both of them were also emergency exits and had metal rungs leading up to them. Provided I could somehow open the office skylight from the outside, I saw no reason why my plan shouldn't work.

I would also find out firsthand how good our security was at Plumtree Press.

It was a great deal of fun walking about on the roof tiles and breaking into my own office—a fresh perspective on Bedford Square—and I vowed that I would do it again soon. I felt a small thrill at having outsmarted both press camps, the one outside my flat and the one that I had spotted outside the office door. Considering the circumstances, I was fairly cheerful until I opened the door leading from the storeroom into my secretary's office area.

I was greeted by an unholy mess of files strewn about the floor, and the filing cabinets overturned for good measure. The screen of Lisette's personal computer had been smashed, and the bookcases holding all of our published books overturned.

My heart sank. I stepped into my office which was, if anything, worse. Peeking through the door of Ian's office, I could see that it had been gone over, too. My instinct was to check to see if the Arthur file was still there. Like most of the files, it was missing from the open file drawers, so I stooped and picked up the files and replaced them in alphabetical order. When I had picked up the last one, there was still no Arthur file among the A's.

I leaned against the file cabinet, contemplating for a moment what it was that someone wanted badly enough to break into this office. Information about Arthur? His *Those Who Trespass Against Us* manuscript?

Whoever it was would be very surprised to know that the only one of those commodities that I had was not even complete—the partial manuscript. But that might have been what they were after. Barnes had had one too, and they'd killed him, after all. I frowned. This simply didn't make sense. If the book were going to be published anyway, why would they have to steal it?

Then it struck me. Barnes had said it at the party, but I hadn't understood. Someone didn't want the sequel published. Now that the story was known to be true, the perpetrator would be revealed at the end of *Those Who Trespass Against Us* if the two protagonists finally found their man.

I didn't know what had happened to Barnes's copy of the manuscript, nor to Arthur's. The only other copy that existed, to my knowledge, was mine; I'd waited to send any of it to production until it was complete. Fortunately, by accident I had ensured that it was safe. I had a habit of reading manuscripts in bed at night. In the morning I put the rubber bands around the unbound sheets of paper and stowed the whole pile in the top of my dresser. Not in a drawer, but behind the four-inch dentil molding that ran around the top of it. I had never thought of it as a hiding place; it was just a convenient way to get the massive piles of paper out of sight and out of the way until I needed them again.

I went to the stairwell and took the steep steps three at a time until I reached the production department. The production manager contracted with typesetters and printers; if the manuscript hunters had thought to look through his file on *Those Who Trespass Against Us*, they might think there was a copy of the manuscript there. If they had made as great a mess of production as they had of the editorial offices, we might never get all the right pages in the right books again. As I bounded off the landing and into the large room populated with a dozen desks, each of them stacked high with paper, I breathed a sign of relief. The stacks were intact, as were all the computers and file cabinets. It looked as if the intruders hadn't been smart enough to think of the production department.

I climbed the stairs again and tidied up; it wouldn't do to entertain the press this way. I replaced the books on the shelves in all three offices, then brushed the glass from all three broken computer screens off of the desks into a dustbin, thinking as I did that breaking the screens had been rather unnecessary. Perhaps these people were not very smart; surely they should have known that breaking the monitor wouldn't affect the information on the computer disk. Had they messed with the disk, they would have found that we didn't have the book on the computer yet anyway. Arthur's manuscripts were some of the very few we still received on paper instead of magnetic media.

I sighed and revved up the ancient office vacuum cleaner, listening to the bits of computer screen fly around inside as they were sucked up. What a farce tomorrow would be, I thought; I had promised the press copies of Arthur's faxes, and now, without the file, we didn't have any. It's true that they wouldn't have proved that I didn't know who Arthur was, but I thought it might help if I looked them in the eye and told them that this pile of paper was everything we knew. It was the best I could have done and now I couldn't even do that.

Still, I told myself, there was a lot that I could do—not necessarily about the press, but about Arthur and the manuscript. This was no time to be discouraged.

With the place in reasonable order, I sat down and penned a factual history of how we had come to have Arthur's books. I included all the facts that I thought might interest them except for three: Arthur's disappearance, Barnes's comment at the party, and the fact that the last five chapters of the book were still missing.

Then I picked up the phone and called Lisette, George's wife and the best secretary in the world. She needed warning of the onslaught tomorrow. I got their answering machine and left a message.

I checked my watch and saw that it was just nine o'clock. Three hours until I would have to get ready for Barnes's funeral.

The phone rang, and I picked it up automatically. I had already said hello before realizing that perhaps I should have let it ring.

"Al! Thought you might be at work on Sunday."

I was incredulous. It was four in the morning Boston time. "You never sleep, do you, Charlie?"

"Nah—too much exciting stuff going on." He paused. "Hey, I saw that piece in the *Sunday Tempus Book Review* by Barnes Appleton. You keep getting that kind of publicity, and you won't need the academic side of your business." He chuckled, sincerely pleased at what he thought was a success for Plumtree Press. Of course he couldn't know that Barnes was dead.

I described the situation, omitting the detail of the incomplete manuscript to preserve my reputation, and for once Charlie was silent. When I finished there was a pause. Then he said, "Gee, I'm sorry, Al. That's terrible." He sounded crushed. "Is there anything I can do? Do his wife and kids need money or anything?"

No kids, I told him, and his wife would be all right in that respect. I thanked him for thinking of it.

"No problem," he said, sounding subdued. "I'm really sorry, Al. With the funeral and all, I don't suppose you'll have much chance to think about coming over. I'll give you a call tomorrow." Click.

At least I would have a twenty-four-hour reprieve from Charlie. I sighed and pushed myself up from the desk, thinking it was time I did some more investigating on Arthur. I went back into the storeroom and climbed the metal ladder to the skylight, then clambered onto the roof. In order to get down to the street undetected, I would have to walk across the roofs of several buildings, then down one of their fire escapes. Fortunate, I thought, that today was Sunday and the square was deserted.

Choosing the Soames and Sons building for the fun of it, I

found its fire escape stairway at the back of the building and trotted down into the alley. It felt good to be doing something, anything, to try to find Arthur. At Tottenham Court Road tube station I took a Central line train to Oxford Circus, switched to the Piccadilly Line, and got off at Brixton. Here I would visit the only other person I knew of who had some type of contact with Arthur: the motorcycle courier who had delivered various chunks of his manuscript.

I had been to this unsavory neighborhood only once before, when I'd first followed the courier to his home. I'd asked our receptionist to let me know when a courier came with anything from Arthur, and she dutifully obeyed. The taxi I hailed outside the office had been pushed to its limit to follow the man, who rode a motorcycle as if he had a death wish. In the end we made it to the courier company, Deadline Deliveries, not far behind him.

The taxi driver had said dryly, "More like Dead*man* Deliveries, if you ask me." We agreed it was incredible that the man had stayed alive to reach his forty-some years.

He'd hopped off his motorcycle and walked back to his flat in a dingy little alley. Since I wasn't sure he'd talk to me, I didn't confront him until after I saw him go through his door, so I'd know which room was his. On that first visit, he hadn't answered the door at all, though I'd seen the one-way peephole darken in his door when I announced my name and company.

This time, I happened to catch him in the hall, on his way out. He looked altogether more decent out of his black leather trappings and motorcycle helmet, smaller and almost delicate. He wore round, wire-rimmed glasses and had a thin, sandy-colored ponytail. I was halfway up the stairs before he turned from closing his door and saw me coming, and he ran back to his door and fumbled with the key at the lock. I stood calmly behind him, watching.

"You know who I am, don't you?" I spoke gently, not wanting to alarm him. He backed up against the door, the whites of his eyes huge. I could see that he had recently had a black eye, which was now a sickly greenish yellow.

"You stay away from me. I don't want any trouble. I've never asked for any; I just want to be left alone."

"I'm not going to hurt you. I only want to talk to you for a few minutes."

Some of my calm seemed to be wearing off on him, but he stayed pressed up against the door. "That's what they wanted, too," he whined. "They said they just wanted to talk."

"Who's they? Did they do that to your eye?"

Pale and sweating profusely, he nodded.

"Do you think we could go inside for a moment and talk? It's about Arthur. I'm afraid there's something wrong."

He looked me up and down, and after a final look at my eyes he relented. "Well, just for a minute, then." He had no difficulty with the lock this time, and let me into a minimal one-room flat with a single dirty window as its focal point. I smelled his breakfast of fried egg and was unaccountably depressed at the thought of it.

He didn't offer me a chair and remained standing himself, still prepared to dash out the door in case he'd misjudged me.

"It's about Arthur," I said. "You know who I mean, don't you?"

"Bloody right I do. Everybody wants to know about him all of a sudden."

"I'll be honest with you. I'm sure Arthur's been good to you—I know he deals with you directly because there's no Deadline dispatch number on his packages." He colored slightly, and I saw his defenses rising. "Don't worry—I'm not going to tell anyone. I wanted to talk to you because I think something may have happened to him. I thought you might be willing to help."

He nodded. "I didn't tell them; I've come to like Arthur. He's helping me get out of debt, and tell the truth, this cat-and-mouse business makes a nice change. I wondered what happened when I got a notice, like I always do, that there'd be a package for me to deliver—let's see—three weeks ago now. Then it never came. He's never missed a date before."

My hopes soared. "Have you actually met him? When you've received the packages, I mean?"

"Oh, no. He's careful, isn't he—doesn't want anyone to know who he is. He sends them to me by mail. There's no return address and everything's typewritten."

"The postmark?"

He shrugged. "London."

I was disappointed. I hadn't really learned anything.

"The funny thing is, I can't figure out why me. One day about a year ago there's a letter in the mail asking me if I'd do some delivery work for a bloke named Arthur. If I wanted the job, I just had to deliver what he sent to your address there in Bedford Square, and I'd be paid fifty pounds each time." He raised his eyebrows. "Out of the blue."

I had an idea. "How does he pay you?"

"Always the next day; it's like he knows I've done it."

That wasn't exactly what I'd meant, but I could see what was most important to him. I tried again. "Does he pay by check or cash?"

"Oh, always cash. Under the door in an envelope. I take it to the bank straightaway."

"Yes, of course." I tried to hide my disappointment. If only he'd paid by check, we might have been able to trace him through the bank. But of course Arthur would have thought of that.

I moved on to my next question. "Who were the people who gave you the black eye?"

He shuddered. "I don't know who they were. I'd know them again, though, I can tell you that much."

"Can you describe them?"

"One was sort of medium height, with dark hair—foreign looking. His eyes were what really got to me; cold as ice. He did the talking. The other one was big, really big. Not tall, but muscular, like. He did this." He pointed to his eye.

"What did they want to know?"

"They thought I knew where Arthur was and wouldn't take no for an answer. Thought I was lying. Maybe they finally believed me when I still couldn't tell them after they started the hitting, I don't know. But they haven't been back."

"Was that all they wanted to know?"

He shrugged. "Where he lived, that sort of thing. How I'd come to be involved with him. Of course I couldn't tell them, because I don't know."

I felt sorry for him. "Do you know that Arthur's a famous author?"

"Books, you mean?"

"Yes—I'm his publisher. If you'd be interested, I could send

58

you the one that's out so far." It may be the only one that's ever going to be published, I thought.

He looked pleased. "I'd like that."

"Um, I don't know your name."

"Oh—right. Derek Huggins. Here, let me write down the address for you."

While he scribbled on a scrap of paper with a pencil, I asked, "Would you let me know if you hear anything from Arthur, or if those men come back?" I took out a business card and wrote my home phone number on the back.

He nodded as we exchanged papers.

"Sure. And let me know if you hear anything."

He opened the door and we clomped down the filthy wooden stairs. We parted at the street entrance to his building. "Thanks," I said. Suddenly I stopped. "Wait a minute—one more thing. How did they know you were Arthur's courier?"

He shrugged again. "Beats me. How did you?"

I smiled. "Good point. I followed you. But out of all the couriers that come to our office, how did they know that you were the one who brought Arthur's manuscript?"

He knitted his brow and shook his head. "Don't know."

"Well, thanks, Derek. Take care on that motorcycle."

"Right." He smiled, obviously proud of his prowess on the bike.

On the way back to the tube station I mulled over my conversation with Derek. It hadn't been a total loss; at least he had confirmed that Arthur had suddenly gone missing, and that he had planned to send me the last five chapters or some portion thereof three weeks ago.

Now I was really worried.

I got on the train and hurtled home through the tunnels. There wasn't really time to squeeze anything more in before Barnes's funeral; I didn't want to be late. Back at Bedford Square, I peeked around the edge of the building on the corner to see if the press people were still there. I sighed. If anything, their number had grown.

Walking around to the back of the Soames building, I marveled at their tenacity. Not that I should have been surprised; I had heard Max rave enough on the subject of the "big story" he needed. Each of them was hoping for instant fame, something they could catch before someone else did. In some cases, like Max's, they needed it to save their jobs.

Back in the flat via my new private entrance, I left the skylight unlatched, knowing I would need it again. I rang Ian's answering service and got a different cheerful voice, but Ian still did not pick up his phone. After twelve rings I left another message for him to call me. I thought that perhaps he neither answered phones nor called in for messages while on holiday. He could be stubborn. He was due back in another week or so, but that was a long time to wait for the kind of news I had for him.

I dressed and climbed out of my skylight in a black mood.

Barnes's wife, Judy, looked at me with something like hope. "You do understand, then," she said. "It wasn't an accident."

My mouth hung open in astonishment.

We were standing in her Notting Hill flat, where the mourners had proceeded after the funeral for a reception. Judy, normally a sparkling personality, stood a little slumped, looking at me through dark-circled eyes. She was an elegant woman, with a slim figure that complemented her tailored black coatdress, and warm brown hair pulled back austerely with a bow.

Everyone else had left, but I'd wanted a few words with her in private. I was still reeling from the revelation that Barnes had been drunk at the time of his death; at the time of the autopsy they'd found three times the amount of alcohol in his blood that was legal for driving.

But the bombshell she'd dropped on me next was, if anything, more shocking—and heartbreaking. She was three months pregnant, she said, something she and Barnes had been hoping for for seven years.

"He never would have started drinking again now," she said. "He was so happy about the baby. Everything had fallen into place for us." She stared blankly at the cup and saucer she held in her hands, neither seeing nor caring that she had been holding the cold liquid for half an hour.

I was filled, then, with so much anger at Barnes's murderer that I would gladly have killed him at that moment. Such promising lives, all three of them—and whomever it was had tried to discredit Barnes besides. I was thankful that that little detail hadn't made it into the press. No doubt his friends in the profession had made sure of that.

I looked at the capable woman in front of me whose life would never be the same again. "I'm going to find out what happened," I said. "I know it wasn't an accident. I'm quite sure it had something to do with a book he reviewed—*Those Who Trespass Against Us*. It was one of ours at Plumtree."

I wanted to tell her that I'd give anything to never have heard of the sequel or thought of sending it to the *Tempus* for review. But it wouldn't do any good now. She was the one who needed comfort, not I.

She was looking at me intently, her eyes alive again. "You mean—these questions you've been asking me about Barnes and the last few days—you know something . . . ?"

"Let's sit down," I said, guiding her to her own sofa. "There are a few things you should know." I felt certain that she could handle the news that someone wanted to stop publication of *Those Who Trespass Against Us* before it was complete, and that this was a possible motivation for her husband's death. She wouldn't want to be shielded from the truth.

She hadn't heard about the press party and the newsprint accident, as by the time she got home on Friday night Barnes was already dead. She didn't flinch as I told her, and it occurred to me that she was thinking as a barrister again. I was giving her evidence for her newest case. "Go on," she said authoritatively, as if to a client.

I told her next about the attack on me, the ransacking of the office, and the frightened courier, filling in bits of information about Arthur and his secretive communications along the way. I left out the news about Arthur's disappearance, as I couldn't see that it would make any difference.

"So someone's afraid of being exposed in this book," she said thoughtfully. "They knew Barnes knew something about them—or thought he did."

I felt I owed it to her to tell her the full story, tragic though it was. "Judy, you need to know that Barnes didn't even have the last five chapters—the part of the book that would incriminate the kidnappers. I don't even have them." I sighed. "He did me a favor and wrote the review as if he had them; he knew from the synopsis that Arthur provided at the beginning of the book that it ended as it did. But he didn't know who the perpetrators were; they assumed that he did. For all I know, they might not even be exposed in the book."

"I see." She nodded and for the first time, remarkably, fought for composure. I understood; it was all so futile. She didn't ask why the chapters were missing, and I left it there.

We agreed that I would call her as soon as I knew anything, and I said good-bye feeling as if I had murdered Barnes myself.

"Don't," she said clearly at the door.

I turned back to look at her.

"Don't feel that you're responsible. He loved doing this sort of story. Don't think it's your fault."

I didn't know what to say, so I nodded. She closed the door behind me, and we were alone with our thoughts.

The last thing I needed was what I found back at my flat, which, for once, was mysteriously devoid of press vultures. I wasn't sure which was worse, finding Max there or finding that in my absence, judging from appearances, a hurricane had swept through the place.

Max didn't see me right away, stalking angrily about the sitting room as he was, crunching bits of glass into the rug with every step. I stood for a moment outside the open door. Every bookcase and surface had been swept clean of its contents; every lamp was smashed on the floor. The only way he could have been more destructive would have been to set it ablaze.

I stepped in and Max looked up. His eyes looked strange; the pupils too small, the whites too wild. I braced myself for one of his chemically induced tirades.

"Hello, Max. If I'd wanted redecorating, I'd have asked."

He looked at me through narrowed eyes and snorted bitterly. "You've got a hell of a nerve. I didn't do this." He dismissed it as insignificant with the wave of a limp hand and fixed me with an ominous glare. "No, Alex, little brother, you're the one who's made the mess."

"Oh?" I waited.

"You're the one who's ruined my career, my entire life. You had a story that could have made my name, and you gave it to a total stranger, that Barnes Appleton bastard. The fat ass already had a Beecroft Award." To my total surprise, his next utterance was an angry sob. "Don't you see, Alex? I needed that story. I needed it." He sank down on the sofa, face in hands.

I had never seen him like this. The unbridled hate was almost easier to deal with; I was accustomed to it. Warily, I walked over to him and put my hand on his back. He flinched slightly but didn't move away. "Max. I'm sorry this is so hard on you. But you must realize; I didn't know the books were based on truth. I learned about it in the paper, just like you."

The sobs stopped, and he sat composing himself for a moment. The next thing I knew, he had, in one remarkable leap, flown off of the sofa and gained a very respectable stranglehold around my neck. It was a shock, more than anything else; in his drugged state—and even in an unaltered state—he was no match for me physically. That was yet another thing that had made him insanely jealous through the years; once I had equaled his height and weight, he could no longer beat me at will. I grabbed his wrists and squeezed, pushing them away from my neck at the same time.

It wasn't particularly difficult. He grunted, and his hands released their death grip. I held his wrists away from me, in front of my chest. He struggled furiously to regain his hold, though, grunting and straining until in the end I got tired of it. I wrapped a leg around the back of his, confusing him no end, and hooked both of his feet with my right heel, pulling them suddenly toward me. We both went to the ground, with me on top, and I pinned him there, arms at his sides.

"You bastard," he hissed. He was calmer now, his eyes marginally clearer. The exercise had probably done him good, I thought. We stared at each other for a moment, unaccustomed to this close range after so many years. "Let me up. I won't hurt you," he sneered, "though God knows I'd love to kill you."

With that brotherly sentiment, obviously heartfelt, I let him go and stepped back a few paces just in case.

He got to his feet, still panting, and walked to the door. He turned and pointed a finger at me, stabbing the air for emphasis even before he began to speak. "You can't fool me, Alexander *Christian* Plumtree." He spoke my name with venomous sarcasm. "You're just like father—always pretending to be so noble and true. But you won't even help your own brother. Underneath it all you're a crook, just like he was."

He wasn't finished. "Have you ever wondered what it was that made our dear father so reticent about the war?" He gave a short, nasty laugh. "I think there are a few secrets about this whole *Deliver Us From Evil* sham that you'll wish had never come out." Now he looked smug. "I've been researching it in the family archives. Good luck to you, Alex. You'll need it."

He slammed the door and left me standing, bewildered, in my own private disaster area. I couldn't face cleaning up this one too, at the moment, and decided to give Ian another try.

There was no answer.

4

Monday mornings, and this one in particular, were made bearable only by the saving grace of Lisette's coffee. It was such an extreme shock to the nose, tongue, and stomach that everything else—including my problems at the moment—seemed positively anemic. She deposited a cup on my desk, then stood back, head cocked to one side, and looked at me.

"A hard weekend, *n'est-ce pas?*" Her French accent alone lifted the spirits.

"The best and the worst rolled into one," I said, lifting the life-giving liquid to my lips.

She raised her eyebrows and made her mouth into a little round o.

Lisette, full of figure and full of life, was one of the sexiest women I had ever seen. She was also very bright and had a great sense of humor. If not for Sarah, I might have had trouble working with my best friend's wife. I didn't like to think how much her clothes cost the Stoneham family budget, but I had to admit they did their job. They magically clung to all the right curves and minimized the rest—except her hips. Nothing could minimize Lisette's hips. They were the axis of her power. She moved in a cloud of scent that smelled expensive, with a slight swish that I speculated was the sound of nylon on nylon where her thighs brushed together. She wore improbably high heels to make up for the fact that she was just five feet tall, but they didn't slow her down for a moment.

Lisette was the best change I had made at Plumtree Press since my arrival. Ian agreed thoroughly, often muttering, "That woman's a godsend," as she left the room. "Absolute godsend. Don't know what we ever did without her."

She and George had started having children almost immediately after they were married, and Michael and Edward were both in school now. Lisette had been miserable during the long days at home without someone to take care of.

Laughing, I mentioned one night at their house that we could certainly use her at Plumtree, never dreaming she'd be interested. But to my astonishment she chose to apply her considerable talents to our office, and the place hadn't been the same since.

She winked at me now and said, "I won't even ask. About the best part, I mean." George had evidently told her about my date with Sarah. Before I could say anything, she went on. "And as for the worst, George said he had to patch you up. Again."

"Well, as you know, George works wonders. It's feeling much better, thanks." I took another sip of coffee and felt the jolt at the back of my tongue. The clock on my desk told me it was eight o'clock; two hours until the vultures came to roost. "I suppose we'd better prepare for the onslaught." I sighed and sat up straight. "We'd better get them some food, and—"

Lisette waved dismissively. "I got your message. It's all taken care of. Caterer, chairs, photocopies—don't worry about it. Now be serious, Alex, and listen to me—just for a moment." She sat down in one of the two chairs facing my desk and gave me her mother hen look, clutching a dog-eared legal pad to her chest. "We're worried about you, Alex. This book has, you know, brought a lot of weirdos out of the wainscoting."

She paused to let this sink in, and I suppressed a smile at another of her attempts at English slang. She had learned her English from American movies, an Irish nanny they'd had for the boys, and blue-blooded George. It made for an interesting dialect.

Lisette leaned forward across the desk, deadly serious. "Come stay with us for a while, Alex, eh? Just for a little while, until things cool off a bit."

I hesitated for just a moment, tempted by the thought of their company, not to mention her coq au vin and pear tart. "That's very

kind of you, Lisette, but for goodness' sake. No one's after me." I
eyed her across the desk. "I had no idea you were such a wor-
rywart."

"Alex, that person in the car park hurt you. He might have
killed you—George told me. And even before that, you almost
snuffed it—yes?—at that press party. Surely you have not forgotten
this so soon."

I looked up. How did she know about the press party?

She cocked an eyebrow at me.

"You think I am in the dark, yes? I have friends who tell me
what is going on." She frowned with real concern. "My friend, I
think perhaps you should worry a bit more."

When she put it like that, it did sound bad, and she didn't even
know what had happened to the flat. Still, they hadn't really hurt
me, not yet. Puzzling, that; if someone wanted to kill me, they'd had
ample opportunity. It was as if someone were trying to scare me,
though I couldn't imagine why.

In any case, I wasn't going to hide. Besides, how would I ever
figure out who was behind all this if I didn't continue to play the
worm on the end of the line?

"Thanks, Lisette. I certainly appreciate the offer. But try not
to worry. I don't need to hide, and I can't come stay with you and
George, though it would be fun. Maybe I could book in for a long
weekend over the holidays?" It was my smile, in the end, that
seemed to exasperate her.

"Oh, you . . . you swine." Lisette could swear a blue streak
when she felt like it; it was the one part of the language that she had
mastered absolutely. She worked hard at keeping it under control in
the office and around the kids, though. Her lips stuck out in an
angry pout. "I wish you cared half as much for your own hide as we
do." She stood up and walked out of my office, banging the door
behind her.

I had just looked back down at my papers when the door
opened again and Lisette's head peeked through. "Charlie Goodspeed has called six times already this morning. I am telling him you
are unavailable." Her head withdrew and the door closed again. I
sighed and slumped in my chair, wishing I could somehow postpone
the day.

As it happened, Lisette was right; I should have worried a bit more. But I didn't know that until later.

The day passed without any walls collapsing or bombs going off, but either of those possibilities might have been preferable to the press conference. The only bright spot was that Max didn't come.

The rest of them descended on us en masse at ten o'clock as planned and grilled me for two hours. There were sixty of them, all unbelievably hungry and thirsty. They were hostile from the beginning, evidently inspired by what they'd seen on morning television, and it only made them angrier that I couldn't show them any of our communications from Arthur as promised. They obviously thought I had staged the office break-in as well.

Had I always known that the book was a true story?

Why didn't I make it known?

Didn't I feel responsible for Barnes Appleton's death?

When was I going to tell the truth about Arthur's whereabouts?

Were we making any effort to contact the parents and children involved?

Who owned the movie rights?

The questions were endless.

Even when the briefing was over, that wasn't enough for them. Half a dozen wanted exclusive interviews to get me to say something everyone else hadn't already heard. Fortunately, Lisette maintained a schedule of military precision, allowing each of them just five minutes.

I had only just finished at two o'clock when I received a call from a Ministry of Defence official who happened to belong to our parish church in Chess. His name was Romney Marsh. I didn't know him well anymore, but he had been a friend of my parents. He lived alone, and from time to time he had come to our house, and we had gone to his.

Then something had happened, and we never saw him anymore. Even at church, my parents and he seemed to avoid each other. When I asked my father about it, his face had gone hard. Then he'd squatted down to my level and put his arm around my shoulders. "It's something you shouldn't worry about, Alex. Romney's done something very wrong, and we can't be friends anymore."

Back in the present, his upper-crust accent oozed into my ear. "Alex? Romney Marsh here. I wondered if I might pop over and have a word. Two-thirty all right?"

I was pleased to hear from him but secretly wished he would give me time for the lunch I hadn't had yet. Still, it didn't seem right to say anything but yes to someone from the MoD.

"Fine. I'm afraid you'll have to come round the back, though. We can't seem to make the press go away. . . . They're sitting on the front step like vultures."

He chuckled mellifluously. "The eternal problem—for us, too."

"I can imagine. There's an alley off Gower Street; our back door is the first on the right. Lisette will be watching for you."

As I hung up, Lisette came through the door and held up a brown paper bag.

"Tuna and pickle all right?"

"God bless you, Lisette. Nothing has ever sounded better."

"Would you believe it, I had to go out and get one. We had two hundred sandwiches in here, and—poof!—all gone. They are pigs, Alex—pigs." She shook her head.

"By the way, Romney Marsh from the MoD is on his way over. Would you keep an eye out for him in the alley and show him right in to the big conference room? I'll wait for him there."

"MoD—Arthur really has landed us in it, hasn't he?"

I pondered her words as I settled myself in one of the big, comfortable leather chairs in the conference room and bit into my sandwich. It had occurred to me, of course, that someone from the government might be contacting me, once I'd read Barnes's story in the paper. But I'd never thought it would be Romney Marsh. In fact, until now, I'd never been exactly sure of what he did for a living, except that he was a civil servant of some type. I wondered if he and his department weren't rather displeased to have this scandal break right now, just when things were going well for them in terms of public relations.

There was a knock on the door. I tossed my sandwich refuse

in the bin and stood up as the door opened and Lisette showed Romney in. I hadn't seen him in years, as I hadn't been to the Chess Parish Church since going off to university. He looked just the same except for the bulge around his middle, impeccably dressed as ever in a well-made suit and with a tan and a suave smile.

"Alex, so good to see you." He stretched out a brown hand and grasped mine firmly.

"It's been a long time, Romney. Good to see you, too."

I indicated a chair and he sat down, relaxed and confident. He glanced around the room, taking in the framed vellum pages of illuminated manuscript on the walls. They'd been there as long as I could remember.

"I see you're taking good care of your father's company. He would be proud if he could see you now." He frowned slightly and shook his head, looking down. "I'm so sorry about your parents— wonderful people."

"Yes." He hadn't been at the funeral, come to think of it.

He shifted gears rather quickly, unlike most of the people who had offered me sympathy over the last two years. Talk of death didn't seem to disconcert him in the least. "Well. I can see that you're busy, and I don't want to take much of your time. I'll get right to the point."

I wondered what he had done that was so horrible in my father's eyes.

"You can be a great help to us, Alex, in this whole *Those Who Trespass Against Us* affair." He looked down at his fingernails as if composing his thoughts. For the first time he struck me as being vaguely effeminate. "You can imagine that it's quite important to us."

I nodded. "Yes, I can see that."

He leaned forward and spoke softly. "I need to share a secret with you so you'll understand why I have to ask what I'm about to."

He seemed to be waiting for some acknowledgment, so I nodded again.

"Your mysterious author, 'Arthur,' has landed us in a bit of a mess. It was no problem while people thought it was fiction, but now that Barnes Appleton has portrayed it as fact, well . . ." He paused and let out a fairly dramatic sigh. "You see, he's told only one side of the story. The people whose children were kidnapped weren't just innocent parents. They were German spies."

His eyes bored into mine like laser beams. I became aware that my mouth was open and closed it. Good Lord. What had I done. And Arthur—what kind of person was Arthur?

I felt sick. "I—I don't know what to say."

"No. The damage is incalculable, to the country and to the MoD." He paused. "But there was no way you could have known. When we took the children, we saved their lives—you see, they weren't with legitimate guardians. They were being used as a cover by the agents, and were in danger. Besides that, they could have been killed by us when we went in for their parents." He looked vaguely disgusted.

"But what about the interviewees in Barnes's article—"

"We tracked those people down. Rather sad, actually. They got scared when they heard he'd been murdered, and admitted that he paid them off."

I didn't want to believe it. I couldn't believe it. Whatever had happened, I felt certain that Barnes wouldn't have done that. Besides, I didn't trust Romney entirely. I could see that I'd have to find some way to make him think I did, though, while I figured out what was going on. Otherwise I might wind up like poor Barnes.

I allowed myself to look disconcerted. My mouth hung open slightly, then closed and opened again like a goldfish. "But—I don't understand. Barnes didn't need to do something like this."

"No. One wouldn't have thought so." Romney shook his head. He could afford to show a bit of pity for Barnes, now that he saw I would cooperate. "But he drank, you know. Who knows, chemically inspired insecurity or something. They're susceptible to all sorts of things. In fact, they found that he'd been drinking just before he died."

I felt myself go cold and hoped that nothing showed on my face. Judy Appleton had said that information hadn't been made public, and I was certain that she wouldn't have told Romney. Here, I thought, was one of the ugly little beasts crawling out of the wainscoting. I made a conscious effort to relax my shoulders, but didn't trust my play-acting ability any further when it came to discussing Barnes.

I leaned forward and tried to shift the discussion away from Barnes. "But I still don't understand. What can I possibly do?"

Romney looked at me as if I were mentally deficient, a scowl between his icy blue eyes. Then he shrugged and gave a condescending little laugh. "Well. Obviously we can't allow the sequel to be published. I'm afraid we must insist that you give us any copies of the book, including computer files and so forth, in your possession. What's more, we must, of course, be given access to Arthur. You've had your little fun with the whole scheme—your million pound best-seller. Now it's time to come clean, for the sake of your country."

I was speechless. So Romney's people were behind the office break-in. But wasn't it a bit obvious to ask for the manuscript after he'd already looked so thoroughly? Surely he knew I'd made the connection. Either there was a lot more to this that I didn't know, some legitimate reason for what he was asking, or Romney was definitely a part of something that smelled foul—something that included Barnes's nonaccidental death.

"Romney." I concentrated on keeping my voice even. "Forgive me if I seem dense, but this makes no sense to me. What harm can the book do now? Even if what you say is true, how could you prosecute Arthur for writing a novel?"

He leaned back in the chair and brought the tips of his fingers together in a steeple. His voice was exaggeratedly calm. "Call it what you like, Alex, but some of us have to run this country. This is not a game." He leaned forward again, bringing his face close to mine. Something between a smile and a grimace crossed his face. "Are you going to cooperate or not?"

I could see that this was indeed a game; at least I would have to play it as such. I laughed a nervous laugh, which he would expect. "Well, of course, I'll cooperate. But I'm sure you already know that the office was broken into over the weekend, and all the copies we had of the manuscript have been stolen, along with Arthur's file. And I assure you, I have never had the slightest idea where Arthur is. He's been extremely careful to protect his identity at every turn."

The muscles in Romney's face tightened before he could stop them. He looked at me sideways, as if trying to determine if I was telling the truth.

"No, I didn't know that," he said. I believed him. He looked as if he were fighting for control. The muscles around his jaw bulged for a moment, then he reached into his pocket and brought out his wallet. He pulled out a white card, turned it over on the table, and wrote a phone number on it. "This is my home phone," he said. "If there's anything you can tell me about Arthur or the manuscript, anything at all, I want you to call me there. Since your father and I were friends, I'd like to deal with this privately—from home." He stood up, and I stood with him.

"Thanks for coming personally, Romney. I appreciate it. I'll give you a call if I learn anything." I stuck out a hand and he took it, with one more searching look into my eyes.

"Remember what I said, Alex. This is not a game."

On that ominous note he turned abruptly and left. I heard Lisette intercept him in the hallway and usher him into the lift. "*Au revoir*, Monsieur Marsh." She popped her head in the conference room, where I stood thinking uncomfortable thoughts about what Romney was up to, and why he wanted me to call him at home. "There is a call waiting for you, Alex—the gentleman would not tell me his name. Do you want to take it in your office?"

"Yes, thanks, Lisette." I followed her out of the room and down the hall, every floorboard creaking beneath me. Suddenly my whole life seemed fairly creaky, nothing certain, nothing as it seemed to be. I sank down into my father's leather chair and punched the blinking button on the phone. "Alex Plumtree here."

"Listen carefully, I'll only say this once." I froze, my ear glued to the receiver. The voice was subhuman, ultra-bass, distorted. I knew immediately it was a tape recording eerily slowed to half the speed of a man's voice, but that didn't reduce its chilling effect.

"I know you have the manuscript. Leave it on the bookstand in front of the fifteenth-century illuminations in the rare book room of the British Library by noon tomorrow, or accept the consequences." The voice paused. "Should you decide to play the hero, be advised that you are not the only one who will suffer." There was a click, and it was gone.

I took the phone away from my ear and slowly hung it up. My shoulders were painfully tense, and I shrugged them back and down. That unnatural voice had given rise to a primitive, instinctive fear that had me in knots. But it wasn't just the voice. Whoever had made that call had probably killed Barnes and taken his manuscript.

I leaned back in the chair and clenched my fists, cheeks hot with anger. Whoever it was knew how to get to me; they had to know about Sarah. I wouldn't put it past Max, but there was always the possibility that it was Romney. He would have made it his business to find out about Sarah. Someone could have made the call and played the tape for him as he walked out the door just to throw me off the track.

I slammed my fist against the desk, sending coffee flying out of my cup and onto a stack of royalty statements. Swearing under my breath, I took out my handkerchief and mopped it up. Even if I had the complete manuscript, I wouldn't put it in the hands of these people, whoever they were. The only thing to do was to somehow get them before they got me—or anyone else. But I would have to be terribly, terribly careful about Sarah.

The purple rage I felt at the thought of anyone harming her even scared me a bit. Pity the man who tries it, I thought.

Then I picked up the phone and did something stupid.

"Yeah." It was the way Max always answered the phone.

"Have a tape recorder handy, Max?"

"A tape—" He sounded completely flummoxed. Perhaps it hadn't been he, I thought. It wasn't long before he got his second wind. "Well, if it isn't little Alex Two-Shoes. I can't believe you would condescend to call me, even if it's to ask a favor."

I just listened, and he didn't know what to make of it. "Seriously, you want to borrow my tape recorder, is that it?" His voice was almost normal, the old Max. He even sounded slightly pleased that I would call and ask something of him. "I wouldn't mind, but it's packed up. I just had a long interview, and it seized toward the end. I had to borrow someone else's to finish it."

I knew him well enough to know that he was telling the truth.

My voice came out thick and uneven. "Thanks, Max—thanks anyway." I started to hang up, but he was saying something else.

"Oh, Alex. Make sure you read the paper tomorrow." He almost sounded cheery.

"Right." I hung up and swiveled the chair to look out of the picture window at Bedford Square. Another drizzly day was developing into a windy night; we often had a week of this sort of weather in late autumn that brought down trees and made a leafy mess. At four-thirty, it was nearly dark already. I watched a young woman across the square struggle to get her umbrella open in the wind, only to have the wind catch it and turn it inside out. She threw it in the gutter and ran toward Tottenham Court Road, holding her purse tightly against her.

I sighed and watched the wind strip the last leaves from the trees and shrubs in the park below. I had better prepare for the worst, I thought. By tomorrow at noon, when someone went to the bookstand in front of the British Library's fifteenth-century illuminations rack and found no twentieth-century manuscript on it, all hell would break loose.

I heard someone come into the room and swiveled my chair away from the window. It was Nick Khasnouri, our accountant. He gave me a worried smile. Nick was a young man my father had personally tutored in reading and math as part of his volunteer work with Publishers for Literacy. My father had his plate full with a million other things, but never got too busy to chair the board of the charity or to tutor Nick. And what a difference he had made in Nick's life. Nick's parents were poor Pakistani immigrants who couldn't speak English, but they found help for their son through Publishers for Literacy.

When it was time for him to go to university, my father helped him study for his admittance tests, and when Nick earned a place, my father agreed to pay his expenses. He had just graduated a year ago with honors in mathematics, and I'd snapped him up immediately to do our accounts. He seemed delighted with his first professional job, but worried incessantly about dotting every *i* and crossing every *t*. I took every opportunity to reassure and encourage him, but he still worried. Perhaps it was necessary to worry in order to be a good accountant, I thought. At any rate, we enjoyed a casual friendship, and I felt fortunate to have him working for me.

"Nick-o. Glad you dropped in. I wanted to talk to you about the bank's repayment schedule. Have you persuaded them to—" I broke off when I noticed that Nick was staring at the paper in his hand, totally preoccupied.

"What is it?"

He looked at me, a puzzled frown creasing his forehead.

"It's these first-quarter numbers from the charity's books," he said, plopping himself in a chair in front of my desk and looking back down at the paper. "I'm caught up on everything current here, so I thought I'd come to grips with them." Nick had asked if there was anything he could do for Publishers for Literacy, and at the next board meeting we'd voted him in as the deputy treasurer under Simon Bow.

He continued, obviously troubled. "I've put all the existing yearly accounts on my spreadsheet to analyze, all the way back to 1972, when they started again after the fire." Publishers for Literacy was pitifully short on historical records; one fire had destroyed them all toward the end of World War II, and another in 1972.

Nick looked me in the eye, frowning. "Alex, if I didn't know better, I'd swear someone's been dipping into the coffers."

"But how—"

Lisette popped her head in the door. Nick saw my eyes move and turned to see who was there. "If you don't need me for anything else tonight, I'm going to go cheer for Mike at his football game."

Oh, for such innocence, I thought. If only Mike knew how lucky he was.

"Sounds like a pleasant end to a rotten day."

"What a night for it, though," Nick said, throwing a glance at the window, which was hit intermittently by violent gusts of rain.

Lisette rolled her eyes. "They play raining or shining, floodlight or sunlight. Both of the boys are obsessed with the game. George encourages it."

"He would," I said, shaking my head. "Tell Mike good luck for me."

"Have fun," Nick said.

"I will." She smiled. She waved and was gone. I was glad she was going early; normally I couldn't persuade her to leave until at least six-thirty.

Nick and I got back to business. "Look at this," he said, holding out a wide computer printout of spreadsheet cells. "Every year at the same time, when we pay our fund-raising firm, an extra ten thousand pounds goes missing."

"Ten thousand!"

"Every year."

We looked at each other, no doubt thinking the same thoughts. The only people who had access to the charity's bank account and checks were the acting chairman, who was Ian; the vice-chairman, myself; and the treasurer and his deputy, Simon Bow and Nick.

"I'm sorry," Nick said. "I know you've got a lot on your mind already with this Arthur problem. But I thought you should know right away."

"Thanks, Nick—you did the right thing." I thought for a moment. "Let's wait until we can really make a case, and then take it to the authorities. You should probably let Simon Bow know right away, but don't tell anyone else, all right? This could do a world of harm to the charity."

Nick nodded and left quickly, sorry to be the bearer of bad news.

I rubbed my hands over my face and thought of Ian again. It was more important than ever that I reach him now. I dialed his service and got the same woman I'd spoken with before. The last few times I'd tried Ian, I'd been desperate enough to ask the answering service people if they'd heard from him before asking to be put through to his number.

"Mr. Plumtree," she said hesitantly. "You know that Mr. Higginbotham normally calls in at least every couple of days, because we take messages if people ask us to. Well, it's been a full week now since he's called us or answered his phone. I'm worried that something might have gone wrong."

I didn't like the sound of it. It had seemed strange to me, too, that he had never returned my calls, but I'd told myself he was off doing something interesting and hadn't worried too much about it.

"Can't we trace the number you have for him? We could start a search there."

"I'm afraid not," she said. "He didn't actually give us the number. We forward his calls to his home number, which he personally programmed to forward on to his holiday number. So no one knows what it is. Even British Telecom say they can't get it; I've checked."

Ian's passion for privacy reminded me of Arthur's. Privately,

I wondered why he was so careful about giving out his holiday number, but I told the answering service woman that he was probably having such a good time that he didn't want to answer his phone. She laughed nervously and said she certainly hoped so. He wasn't due back for another week, after all; everything could be just fine. Each of us promised to let the other know if we heard from him, and said good-bye.

I tried to put Ian and the charity out of my mind, and for the next three hours busied myself with trivial things that nevertheless had to be done. I wrote a couple of rejection letters to authors I didn't want to offend, mailed *Deliver Us* to Derek Huggins in Brixton as promised, and looked over the new author contract proposed by our lawyer.

I decided also to write a note to Judy Appleton, telling her that I thought Barnes's memorial service was a fitting tribute to him and just what he would have wanted. I searched in my drawer for ordinary stationery, as Plumtree Press letterhead didn't seem appropriate, but found none. Ian would have some, I thought; he was always lending me things that proper gentlemen wouldn't think of being without.

I got up and went to his office. There was a slight smell about the place that brought him to mind instantly, but I couldn't put my finger on it. Patchouli, perhaps, as at his flat. As I opened his drawers I found myself wishing I could speak to him. He was a kind, comforting man. In some ways I knew that I had adopted him as a father, and I thought that he had also adopted me.

I sat down in his desk chair and continued searching. Ian was also a pack rat, always tucking away little snippets of information he thought he might find useful. I pulled out a poem that he'd cut from some sort of magazine. It was entitled "Sorrow," by Johann Wolfgang Goethe:

> *Who never broke with tears, his bread,*
> *Who never watched through anguished hours*
> *With weeping eyes, upon his bed,*
> *He knows ye not, O heavenly Powers.*

I knew that Ian was deeply religious, a firm adherent to Christianity, and we'd discussed the finer points of the faith far into the night on several occasions. Otherwise he rarely spoke of his faith and was a quiet, studious, absentminded professor type, sharp of wit but never of tongue. He had been the rock upon which Plumtree Press was built, I knew.

He was a strong man, I thought as I sat staring at the poem. Solid to begin with and tempered by pain. My father had often referred to the fact that Ian had been through a lot, but never said exactly what. He had a heavily lined face, with a touch of sadness behind the smile. His skin was often weatherbeaten from some hiking or sailing exploit, and I noticed that he seemed to take comfort from loneliness in strenuous—even dangerous—sport.

I smiled as I opened a drawer filled with unused paper napkins and plastic forks and spoons, and thought of his lean form sporting its rumpled corduroy jacket. He was the sort about whom people said, "He needs a woman to look after him." I would have concurred, if only because of his dietary habits. He hated to cook and would often buy something unappealing like a chunk of raw tofu for dinner. Quite often he ate at the office, over his desk, though once a week we went out for a bite to eat together. The phone rang. Knowing that Lisette was gone, I absentmindedly picked it up, forgetting that we were under siege. "Hello?"

"Hey, Al."

Well, I told myself, be grateful it isn't the press.

"Hello, Charlie."

"Everything okay there?"

"Yes, we're doing all right." I couldn't let him think things were as bad as they were, or he'd never agree to do business with me. At least his lawyers wouldn't.

"How about tomorrow, Al? Can we get it done tomorrow?"

I thought of the British Library and the manuscript, and knew that the last thing I'd be doing was flying to see Charlie. "Charlie, this week just isn't good, okay? I promise I'll call you when I can come. You might as well stop running up your phone bill, be-cause—"

"Oh, hey, don't worry about that. I don't mind. I'll call you tomorrow, see how things are going for you. Take care, now."

So much for subtle tact.

Shaking my head, I roused myself from Ian's chair, closed the drawer full of things other people would have thrown away, and found the box of plain white stationery in the last drawer. Perhaps inspired by him, I said a brief prayer that he was all right and went back to my own office, where I focussed my energies on writing the note to Judy. Then I started the printer reprinting the royalty statements I had soaked in coffee, and turned my attention to laying my plans for tonight and the next few days. I worked best with lists, a trick Ian had taught me, and wrote in a column:

"family archives"?
store manuscript
watch
tape
phone
ans. machine
appt.
Ian's

Cryptic, yes; but no one else had to know what I was up to.

I was folding up the list to put it in my pocket when the bell rang downstairs. It was unusual for anyone to come by the office in the evening. I peeked out of my dormer window but couldn't see anyone standing on the front step; whoever it was was under the overhang, out of the rain. I trotted down the three flights of steps to the front door and opened it warily.

It was Sarah.

"Sarah—" I felt a little upwelling of joy in my throat. I was almost happy until I realized that tomorrow I could be risking her life by not delivering the manuscript. The threat had been quite clear; I would not be the only one paying the price, the caller had said.

"Whew!" she said breathlessly, stepping in and wiping her feet on the mat. Her cheeks were bright red, and stray wisps of hair were stuck to her face with rain. "It's wild out there. Another good pair of shoes ruined. English women must buy ninety percent of the footwear sold in the world." She put down a plastic bag she was carrying and closed her umbrella as she looked up at me, smiling. "I thought you might need a little cheering up tonight." The smile faded, and she looked at me closely. "Alex, are you all right?"

I wanted more than anything to hug her, dripping raincoat and all. A wonderful scent emanated from her, a mixture of things brought out by the rain—probably her shampoo, perfume, maybe even a little perspiration. It was almost irresistible, but with great restraint I reached out and took her umbrella instead. "Of course I'm all right. It hasn't been the best day of my life, but it's improving dramatically now."

She didn't look convinced as she pulled off her raincoat. I was momentarily distracted by the way her blouse stretched beneath her suit jacket as she struggled out of the coat, and almost missed the opportunity to help her with it. Such innocent opportunities to touch her were few and far between, and I had to make the most of them. Still slightly taken aback by my good fortune, I hung her coat on the hall coat-tree and turned back to her, smiling.

"This is a pleasant surprise, I must say."

She picked up the bag, which had Indian characters on it, and said, "We'd better eat it while it's hot. Do you keep any plates around here?"

Five minutes later we were up in my office with a fire going, eating vindaloo and onion *bhajis* as if we hadn't seen food in weeks. I had taken something of a risk in lighting the fire, as this fireplace hadn't been used in years; any sort of creature could have built nests in the flue by now.

But fortunately a cheery blaze burst into life from the logs stacked in the grate for window dressing, and I pulled two of the biggest, most comfortable leather chairs up close to the fire. The food gave off exotic scents from the coffee table between us, and brass sconces on the walls shed a soft light on the hunting prints and manuscript pages some Plumtree had hung in this room long ago. I had even managed to find a bottle of gewürztraminer, which I thought particularly good with Indian food, in our small store of party supplies in the office fridge.

The food, warmth, and companionship seemed a welcome relief to her as much as to me, and she spouted off about her day through mouthfuls of incendiary curry as if some sort of dam had burst. I watched her, storing up the memories, the sound of her voice, and the way she moved. What was it that her voice reminded me of? It was a musical instrument, low and throaty and rich. It didn't come to me, but I knew it would. I was careful not to do anything to disrupt her, to make the music stop.

She finished telling me the saga of an impossibly demanding elderly investor of hers who had caused her current deal—the backing of a small Midlands-based software company—to fall through. She sighed and stuffed a shred of nan bread into her mouth. A tantalizing crumb hung on the left corner of her mouth for a moment before she felt it and brushed it off, unembarrassed, with her napkin. I would gladly have licked it off for her, I thought.

"But enough of that," she said, still chewing. "What happened at your press conference?"

"They weren't pleased."

"Are they ever?"

I smiled. "Good point." I took a sip of wine. "The real problem was that someone broke into the office on Sunday and took the Arthur file, and I had promised them copies of his faxes. I had a crazy idea that they would believe me—that I don't know who he is any more than they do—if I showed them everything I had." I shook my head. "Now they think I teased them, that I staged the break-in. And the questions they asked—you can't imagine. It's almost as if they think I'm responsible for the kidnappings myself." I put down my plate. Several grains of rice were all that remained.

"It's no good, Sarah. I'm going to have to find out who's behind it all—Arthur's disappearance, the break-ins, people with maces in car parks—before it's the end of, well, this." I gestured to the room, and the fire crackled quietly in the silence. I didn't add, "And me."

"Let me help you," she said.

That hurt. She didn't know that tomorrow at noon, without her permission, I could well be risking her life when I didn't hand over the manuscript. "You already have," I said, indicating the remains on the coffee table.

"You know what I mean," she said, mildly exasperated. "I mean *help*. How are you going to find out who it is?"

Against my better judgment, I told her about the first item on my list. "Oddly enough, Max suggested that there was something about all this in what he called the family archives. I don't know what he's up to, but he seems to know something I don't. He must be referring to some family memorabilia at my parents' house. I thought I'd drive up and check it out."

"Let me go with you, then." She matter-of-factly stood and picked up both of our plates. "Where do you do the washing up here?"

I laughed, surprised. "You don't wait around, do you." I paused. "You mean that you actually want to go with me tonight?"

"Well of course." She looked at the clock on the mantelpiece. "It's only eight-thirty. We'd have a couple of hours up there at least."

This was a woman after my own heart. I had planned to go to The Orchard tonight, but when Sarah came I thought it could wait until tomorrow. The fact was, I desperately wanted to get up there before any more time went by and to find out what Max had been talking about.

"All right, then." I smiled. "But you need to know what you're in for. It's cold up there in the attic, which is where we're going, especially on a night like this. We'll have to stop off and get some warm clothes at my flat. And there will be spiders and things."

"Remember the snake?" she said.

I laughed. Once during college I had gone camping with Peter, Sarah, and a girl I'd long since forgotten in the White Mountains of New Hampshire. The girl had stuck her toes into her sleeping bag one night and felt something move. She'd screamed, startling all the wildlife, including us, in a three-mile area, and leapt straight into my arms.

"What is it?" I'd asked, trying hard to keep a straight face. "An—an *animal!* In my *sl-sleeping* bag!" She cried hysterically. Sarah had got up and opened the bag, exposing in the moonlight a healthy specimen of a black garter snake. She picked it up and stroked it calmly in front of the girl, saying, "Cute, isn't he? Nice snake." I could still see the look on the girl's face. She hadn't come with us again.

"All right," I said, grinning at the memory. "You've made your point." I pushed the fireplace screen tight against the fireplace and picked up the wineglasses. Then, like a young married couple, we went into the kitchen to do the washing up.

Thirty-five minutes later we pulled into the lane leading to The

Orchard. "You're really out in the country here, aren't you?" Sarah said. "I'd pictured suburbia."

"God willing, it'll be quite a while before either Watford or London pushes out this far." We drove up the drive in silence and crunched to a halt outside the front door. The moon hung above the house like a spotlight. It was, I had to admit, a beautiful sight, though with the wind making such a racket it was anything but peaceful at the moment.

"I hope we don't lose any of the trees in this wind," I mumbled. Leaves and small branches had come down all over the front courtyard and were hitting the car like rain.

"What a beautiful house," Sarah said, looking at it. "It looks as if it's been here forever." We left the peace of the car and struggled against the wind up to the door. I had the key ready and pushed the heavy door open, then stepped quickly to the hall table to switch on the light. After everything that had happened in the last few days, I didn't know what to expect. But the house appeared to have been left in peace. I walked back and shut and bolted the door against the wind, checking to make sure it was locked.

"How lovely," Sarah breathed.

I didn't even notice the entryway anymore, but it always captivated visitors. My mother had begun a renovation of most of the downstairs only a year before her death, and she had commissioned wallpaper to replace the original ivy and plum tree motif paper on the walls.

I had hung the new wallpaper myself and hired a professional to carry out her rather exotic plans for the entry hall. White material was gathered at the highest point of the two-story, circular passage and draped in a teepee shape above our heads. It was light and airy; the perfect bridge between leafy green countryside and English manor house.

Standing here inside the door we could see the reception area ahead, with a large circular table in the middle that always used to hold a vase of flowers from the garden. To the right a staircase led up to the second floor, turning left abruptly and left again to run the width of the room. The effect was a sort of second-floor gallery that led to the west wing of rooms.

I rubbed my hands together briskly. "It's cold in here; it'll be much worse in the attic. Would you like some coffee or something to take upstairs?"

"No, thanks. Go ahead, though, if you want to."

"No, we'll go straight on up, then. I'll just get the torch." I walked through the reception area, turned right down a little hall-way that led to the kitchen, flipped on the light, and pulled open the tool drawer. No torch. I always kept one here, so that I wasn't continually packing equipment back and forth from London.

"That's odd," I said, coming back through the swinging door. "It's gone. Max has no doubt been here and hasn't replaced it." I sighed. "We'll have to improvise. Do you want to come with me?"

Sarah nodded and followed as I led the way to the dining room where the candelabra and candles were kept. I knew that I should have them locked up somewhere, as they were real silver, but there was so little crime in this area that it seemed ridiculous. Still, with all the strange goings-on, I should probably do something about it.

I turned on the lights in the dining room, which consisted of a newly (as of the renovation) rigged set of concealed spots over the huge mahogany table. My mother had wanted them so that she could focus them on the flowers in the middle of the table, which she said normally got lost in the candlelight.

Our eyes were drawn away from the empty table toward the sideboard. There they were: two candelabra, forty-eight candles in all. Plenty of firepower to do what we had to do in the attic. They were fully stocked with white candles to complement the dark blue and white–striped decor, and I found matches in a drawer in the buffet. "All set," I said, using a Massachusetts expression picked up from Sarah.

She smiled and stepped up to the table to assume her load: one sterling silver candelabrum. "I think I'm going to enjoy this," she said cheerfully.

"Don't speak too soon." I followed her out of the room and extinguished the light.

We both heard it. There was a creak in one of the floorboards above us, one of the characteristics of the house my mother hadn't changed in the renovations. She had always made good use of it to figure out what my brother and I were doing.

Neither of us spoke. We stood still and listened. Minutes

85

passed, but no one moved, not even whoever was in the hall above us.

Finally I whispered, "Stay here, okay? This door locks; turn it behind me. I'll go see who it is."

"Are you crazy?" I could smell her perfume; I had done some research and knew it was called Ysatis. Sometimes in a department store I stopped and smelled it, just to be reminded of her. It was spicy, Oriental. I knew she must be perspiring, or the scent wouldn't be so definite.

The vehement whisper continued. "I'm not staying here. It could be one of—you know—*them*."

I knew better than to argue. I moved to the side of the hall, put my candelabrum down, and indicated for her to do the same. Then I switched off the light and turned around. "I'd rather move in the dark, so if you're coming, you'll have to hang on to me. Remember to stay to the sides where the boards won't creak."

"Right."

I went as noiselessly as possible to the foot of the stairs and stopped again to listen. Sarah was absolutely silent, and if it hadn't been for the gentle tug on the back of my shirt, I wouldn't have been sure she was there.

Nothing.

We started up the steps, and I knew to avoid the eighth one altogether, as it was extremely noisy. Again, Sarah picked up on it and followed suit. What a truly remarkable woman, I thought.

We reached the top of the stairs and made the left turn. We were getting fairly close now. I took still more caution crossing the gallery; I had learned from grim experience that every tiny noise made there echoed fiercely in the reception room below. I still hadn't heard anything move again in the hall, and I would have if they'd moved off the board. We rounded the corner and I reached for the light switch.

I couldn't think when I'd been more embarrassed.

It was a cat.

Not just any cat; it was Sheba, the pride and joy of the woman who came from the village to clean. Sheba must have weighed thirty pounds, if she'd ever allowed herself to be weighed. She was sitting in the middle of the hall as if she owned it, smack on top of the squeaky floorboard. The blasted animal had a pass-through door and came and went at will, as Emma, her master, had practically lived with us for twenty years.

"Sheba." I raised my hands in exasperation. "For God's sake."

Sarah laughed loud and long, pointing at the cat, then me, then the cat. Eventually she wound down. I didn't think it was very funny.

She looked at my face and gave a mock scowl, trying to match my seriousness.

"A dangerous criminal, to be sure." She went forward and knelt down, stroking the cat. "Are you here to restore our sense of humor, Sheba? Taking ourselves too seriously, were we?"

She burst into a new round of laughter, holding her stomach, and this time it was infectious. We laughed the slightly crazed laughter of people who had been too tightly wound, as Sheba stared at us with condescension. Tears spilled from my eyes, and, I noticed, Sarah's too.

She said, "I thought—I thought—" Our eyes met and we burst into another silent spasm of hilarity. When we were thoroughly spent I staggered to my feet, took off my glasses, and wiped my eyes.

We slowly pulled ourselves together, and I for one was sorry the moment had passed. I felt something had happened between us that we wouldn't forget, some sort of new companionship. She sniffed and wiped her eyes.

"Ready?" I said.

"Ready." We stumbled down the stairs and reclaimed our candelabra, sniffing and groaning, then started back up the stairs.

"My smile muscles hurt," I said, smiling nonetheless.

"Hmm." She nodded. "Perhaps if we exercised them a bit more . . ."

"Good idea."

I could hear the wind shifting the ancient timbers and wasn't sure I'd been here in a gale this strong before. But the house was built to last; I'd seen how it was constructed and didn't think that any modern structure could withstand wind and weather as well as it could—and had, for some 250 years.

We arrived at the narrow door that led to the attic. I opened it and looked up at the single, long, steep flight of stairs. No cobwebs hit me in the face, no dead mice on the stairs. Either Emma had exercised her featherduster up here fairly recently, or someone else had been snooping about.

"We'd better light these now." I took the matches out of my trouser pocket and handed my candelabrum to Sarah. They were heavy, but she took it in stride. I struck a match, lit one candle on each, then put the matches away. I took my set of candles back and we lit the remaining wicks quietly, as if it were some sort of religious ceremony. Sarah looked very serious.

I started up the stairs. "If I ever come to live here, I'm going to personally run electricity upstairs. I can't imagine why they never did it."

"Perhaps they didn't think it would be necessary." Her voice was thoughtful. "Come to think of it, I don't think we had lights in our attic in Boston, either. It wasn't really a finished part of the house."

I reached the top of the stairs and stopped. I had entered another century—or more precisely, three centuries at once. Wind whistled at the windows at either end of the long, narrow room. I stepped aside, and Sarah stepped up to share the view. There were faded red velvet bodices with long dresses on them, a huge World War II vintage radio, and a Victrola. Portraits, a leather children's horse, and box after box of something that had probably seemed worth saving at the time.

"Wow," she said.

"I know what you mean. I used to beg Dad to come up here when I was a kid. Sometimes, on a rainy Sunday, he'd indulge me, and that's how I know exactly where we're going tonight."

I made my way to the far end of the room, where my first bicycle leaned against the wall and an ancient croquet set moldered. The triangular wall was covered with bits of family memorabilia: my grandfather's Scripture Prize from grammar school, my great-grandparents' wedding picture, a pictorial history of the kings and queens of England ending with George III.

I walked over to a drab green trunk and set down my candelabrum on a box next to it. "Whatever Max might have been thinking of that related to my father in the war is probably in here. This is where my father kept . . ." My voice trailed off as a distant memory returned. "The mace," I said.

"What?"

"The mace, the thing someone hit me with in the car park on Saturday night. It used to be here, by the trunk."

"I'm still lost," Sarah said. "Why would there be a mace in your attic? I thought they were used by the ancient Romans."

"Yes, they were, but barbarians in more modern times used them. My father spent some time behind the front lines before he was wounded and transferred to the American liaison office. Some Germans surrendered to his group outside a small town in France, and he found this on the field. He kept it as a macabre reminder of what the Germans were like as enemies."

I wasn't going to say it, but it seemed pretty clear to me now that it had to have been Max in the car park that night. Who else could have known that the mace was here? The whole episode was puzzling, though; Max might be violent, and even irrational, but he wasn't the sort to run about car parks with bizarre and ancient weapons of torture. Besides, the mace was heavy. Max had never been strong, and whoever planted those spikes in my shoulder had packed a respectable wallop. The only explanation I could think of was the power of adrenaline.

Had he really wanted to kill me? I wondered.

"I'm sorry," Sarah said quietly, watching me.

I looked up and saw that she had caught my train of thought. It was horrible to suspect one's own brother, but I didn't see any other answer. I cleared my throat and set about opening the trunk. The wind was, if anything, growing stronger, rattling the windows at either end of the room and demanding entrance. The beams creaked and shifted as if the whole top of the house might blow off. Sarah looked up at the sound of one particularly great crack, and I began to wonder if we really were safe up here. I resolved to do my business quickly and get out.

A leather strap held the trunk tightly closed; my father had told me he didn't want mice getting into the trunk and eating up his treasures. As I unfastened the strap I noticed that the dust on the trunk underneath it had been disturbed recently. So Max had done some snooping up here, and this was indeed the family archive he had meant. I wondered if he had left anything for me to find.

I was struck by an odd feeling of having been led to this place to do what I was doing now. If Max had been here and found something of interest, he wouldn't have replaced it for me to find. He wouldn't even have closed the trunk . . . unless it suited his purpose. Feeling rather like a rat in a maze, I lifted the lid and gazed down at my father's well-worn field uniform. An image of him as a young man flitted through my mind, lithe, fun-loving, full head of thick dark hair. I lifted it gently out of the trunk and placed it on a box.

Sarah looked into the trunk with interest. The next layer turned out to be four packets of letters addressed to "Miss Alexandria Packard," my mother's maiden name, in my father's abominable handwriting. They were tied with a red ribbon. I was tempted to tug on the end of ribbon immediately and begin reading, but it would be much wiser to gather the materials I wanted and look at them at home.

"Would you hang onto these?" I passed the letters to Sarah. "We'll take them with us. It would have been like him to confide in my mother about what he was doing."

I pushed aside several packets of old meal rations, sealed in labeled foil packets and probably hardened into something like rock by now, and a compass. They were the stuff of childhood rainy-day memories, my father having told me the stories behind them at least once a year when I coaxed him up here.

Among similar familiar clutter I saw the top of his old beat-up lap desk and pulled it out. It was a box about a foot wide, eight inches deep, and eight inches tall, with a brass crest inlaid in the top. It was the typical British design of a lap desk, with a lid cut at a slant which opened out to make a smoothly sloping surface for writing. He told me he'd had this with him in America, on his Anglo-American liaison duty in Washington. It had never occurred to me to wonder why he'd locked this piece away instead of using it; perhaps there was something inside.

When I got it out and balanced it on the edge of the trunk, I could see why he hadn't used it. The hinges were loose and the lid slid about precariously, threatening to detach itself with the least provocation. Still, my father was the quintessential frugal conservative, and I was surprised he hadn't rehabilitated it. I sat down on the floor and opened it carefully on my lap. A loop of green ribbon protruded from the base of the red felt writing pad, and I pulled on it. It was typical for these desks to have a cavity below the writing surface, where stationery could be kept. With high hopes I looked into the little space and found nothing more than a sheet of paper. Office of Anglo-American Liaison, Washington, D.C.

"This was the office my father was appointed to even before Britain got into the war," I said, holding the sheet out for Sarah to see. "I think it was a sort of pseudo-diplomatic corps. He served there in 1940, ever so quietly trying to persuade the Americans to join the effort, then went back to the European theater until 1943. He'd been slightly wounded, and things were heating up between Britain and the States again thanks to Monty and Patton, so they sent him back to Washington. He finished out the war there. We never could get him to say much about his time there."

She nodded, taking the sheet to look at herself.

We heard a huge swell of wind noise, complete with creaking and moaning courtesy of the house. We both looked up in apprehension as something slid off the roof above our heads. "It's a piece of slate," I said. "We're going to have some damage from this one. I'll hurry. There could be trees down; it could take us some time to get back."

Sarah was looking at the lap desk with fascination. "Is it true that these often had secret compartments in them? I was shopping once in Portobello Road and a vendor there told me about them."

I shrugged. "It makes a good story, and probably helps them sell their antiques. I did see one once, though, at a friend's house. It had a pressure panel right here, and a little drawer popped out when you pushed on it. His sister kept love letters in there and thought we didn't know about them."

"You're naughty," she said with a sly smile, sliding her hand down the side of the desk. "Wouldn't it be fun if we found—" She stopped and got to her knees, bending closer. "Wait a minute, Alex," she said slowly, squinting to see better in the candlelight. "There's a ridge here."

A thin drawer, almost the entire width of the bottom of the

desk, slid out as easily as if it had just been oiled. Two thin, black leatherbound books rested on the red felt inside. Sarah and I looked at each other, openmouthed. I picked up one and looked at the first page. "October 21, 1940. Nantucket, Massachusetts. My father's handwriting." I took hold of the drawer, pulled it out farther, and found a white envelope.

"Photographs," I said, pulling open the flap of the envelope. I pulled out two black-and-white pictures and held them at an angle so Sarah could see. One was of my father and Ian lounging about on the lawn of what might have been an American military base, judging from the barbed wire fence. Ian had been a handsome young man, even then looking rather fierce with those piercing light blue eyes. They were both smiling and wearing civilian clothes.

"My father met Ian—that's Ian Higginbotham, who's worked at the Press ever since the war—when they were both sent to the States on the Anglo-American Liaison team."

I flipped to the second picture. It was my father and Ian, looking very somber indeed, standing in front of an old, dilapidated building surrounded by beach grass. A sign on the front of the building said WAUWINET HOME.

Sarah said, frowning, "Hey, I know that place. They've fixed it up now—it's an old people's home on Nantucket."

A mental shock wave hit me hard. In Arthur's first novel the children had been kept at a place called Surfside House, on Windborne Island off the coast of Massachusetts, until their American foster parents came to pick them up and make their "transport donation." It was obviously meant to be Nantucket.

Now my father and Ian stared me in the face, smack in front of "Surfside House." They could reasonably have been there for two reasons: they were the kidnappers or they were trying to help the children. I couldn't believe that they had innocently happened to visit Nantucket on leave and wound up at the children's home by chance.

The whistling wind suddenly sounded eerie, unnatural, as another remarkable thought came to me, piece by piece.

Ian.

Ian and his passion for secrecy, Ian and his extraordinarily long holidays, Ian and his sudden lack of communication with his answering service, Ian and his sad, mysterious past that my father referred to but would never discuss . . .

Why hadn't I seen it before? Ian was Arthur.

It all fit: Ian's love for computers and gadgets, his experience in the war, his editing and writing ability, his solitary life.

My mind raced. If this were true, how much of the Arthur books were Ian's actual experience? In *Those Who Trespass Against Us,* the protagonist, a British military officer, is told that both his wife and daughter have died at roughly the same time, shortly after his daughter is evacuated to the United States. He refuses to believe it and searches for them on the brief personal leave he is allowed.

He learns from friends in London that his wife did indeed die in a car accident, and has her recently buried body exhumed so that he can be certain it is she. He is unable to go to the States to search for his daughter until after the war, but when he does, he can find no evidence of her death, and all the records of the charity that had brought her had been lost in a fire.

Just as the records of HELP (Humanitarian Efforts by the League of Publishers), which became Publishers for Literacy after the war, had been lost in a fire in 1945.

Arthur's protagonist continues his search for the lost daughter for twenty years after the war, writing tirelessly to everyone from county sheriffs to missing-persons bureaus in the States who might know where she is. In the early 1970s he recruits a friend to help him find both his daughter and the people who kidnapped her. They attempt to find a paper trail to the kidnappers and become certain that they're onto something. And, as luck would have it, it's at that critical point that the story comes to an abrupt halt, awaiting Arthur's next five chapters.

I was quite sure that if the protagonist was indeed Ian, his friend was my father. Did Ian have a daughter somewhere? If she'd been born in 1939, she'd be fifty-four now, probably with children of her own. Ian's grandchildren.

I told myself to keep my imagination in check, that it was a wild idea, but I couldn't help being more worried than ever about Ian. What if Romney had figured out that he was Arthur and taken care of the problem with another kidnapping? What if he had taken care of Ian in a more permanent way? . . .

I realized I was still staring at the photo and looked up at Sarah, who was staring at me. She had read Arthur's first book and knew what the photo meant. I replaced the photos in the envelope, and tucked it and the books into the pocket of my jacket.

"Let's go," I said, putting the desk back into the trunk. "It's getting late, and we've found what we were looking for."

And a whole lot more, I thought.

I closed the trunk and fastened the leather strap around it, and we got stiffly to our feet. Despite the drafty cold, the atmosphere suddenly seemed oppressive, as if the weight of all that history was too much for any one room to bear. I gestured for Sarah to go ahead, as I didn't think she'd like to come after me with all that darkness behind her. At the top of the stairs she paused, and I looked around her shoulder.

"I thought you left the lights on in the hall."

"I did," I said, apprehensive. "Don't tell me the power's gone out." I thought for a moment. Then, more quietly, I said, "I don't suppose I could persuade you to stay here while I take a look around."

"You suppose right," she whispered.

I blew out my candles and put them down, and Sarah followed suit. Then I switched places with her and led the way down the stairs. I wondered if I were worrying too much about someone else being in the house. It was not unusual for the power to go out in storms like this; all it took was one big tree to fell a wire.

Halfway down I paused and whispered, "It's probably Sheba; she's been trained to turn off light switches." This won me a playful poke in the back.

At the bottom of the stairs I flicked the light switch off, then on again. Nothing. The power was out. By now I was suspicious enough to wonder if someone had turned off the power at the main switch in the kitchen. No matter, I thought; the best thing I could do would be to leave quickly with our information and get Sarah home safely. The candelaba would be safe enough in the attic until I came again.

I led the way to the front door, walking quickly in case my

worst fears were justified, and opened it, reaching for Sarah behind me. We stepped out, and the wind sucked the door closed, slamming it noisily behind us. Sarah looked back, startled, and I gave her what I hoped was an encouraging smile. I was glad to see she was hugging the packets of letters under her coat so they wouldn't blow away.

We bent against the cold wind and started for the car, then stopped in confusion. A massive grinding sound, like stone on stone, seemed to be all around us, loud enough to make itself heard above the storm.

"What on earth—" Sarah shouted her question and the wind swallowed it.

"Let's go!" I shouted, and urged her toward the car with a firm shove. We had just run down the steps onto the gravel drive when we heard a crash and felt the ground shake. Whirling around, I saw the finialed pediment from above the front door roll over onto its side on the front porch.

It had missed us by one second and three feet, not enough if you asked me.

I looked at Sarah and there was no mistaking the terror in her eyes. She ran to the car and got in. I followed, slamming the door shut on the wind. She sat staring straight ahead in the freezing car, not appearing to see anything in particular.

"Sarah," I said softly. "I'm sorry. It was a close call. Are you all right?"

She nodded, her face stony, and I kicked myself for involving her in this.

The only thing I could think to do was to start the car and head for London, and hope that the car's heating mechanism would warm up relatively soon. More words would only make things worse.

We drove in silence for twenty-eight minutes, and with every second I became more convinced that we had reached some sort of point of no return. She would have to be crazy to willingly involve herself in such violent goings-on. She probably never wanted to see me again, ever. Other men probably took her on dates to movies, the theater, concerts.

And where did I take the woman I loved? I took her to a cold, dark attic in a house where things went bump in the night, the power failed, and large stone ornaments nearly crushed her to death. The doubt was there in both our minds, I knew; had someone pushed the stone, or had it chosen this moment, after two hundred stolid years, to succumb to wind and weather? I doubted it very much indeed.

I pulled up to the narrow gate in front of Sarah's house and stopped the car.

"Sarah," I said. "You're a loyal friend. But you've done enough. Even the bank can't expect you to risk your life trying to get its money back."

I paused, as she looked as if she were going to say something. I waited, but she remained silent.

"Good night, Sarah."

She looked at me again, as if she were going to speak, but in the end she just put the letters on the seat, got out, and closed the door.

I drove home in a blue funk. Things would never be the same. Her eyes had been different—not colder exactly, but more distant— when she got out of the car.

I would have to learn to live with it.

5

At six o'clock the next morning I found myself still staring into the gray, cold fireplace, the diaries and letters strewn in front of me on the coffee table. The traffic noise was getting louder, and I realized that all over London, and the world, happy people were getting up, kissing their spouses and their children, and trotting off to work.

I, on the other hand, had driven away the only woman I had ever loved. In addition, according to the diaries, my father and Ian had quite possibly committed one of the most hateful crimes imaginable, my brother was trying to kill me, and my company was going out of business.

I sighed and leaned forward, rubbing my eyes. I couldn't just roll over and give in. Perhaps if I kept the usual routine, tried to pretend it was a normal day.

I got up, shoveled some coffee grounds into a filter, glugged bottled water into the top of the machine, and punched the On button.

The phone rang as I trudged downstairs to pick up my morning papers, but I made no attempt to intercept it. I reflected that I had had nightmares before, but last night's was by far the worst— and I had been awake. I kept asking myself why, if Ian was Arthur and the story was about his daughter, and he'd known about this crime all these years, he hadn't done something about it. Evidently my father had been in on the secret, too. He hadn't done anything about it, either.

I'd arrived at the disturbing conclusion at about two in the morning that it had to be because they were hiding something; that perhaps they had been involved in some way.

I shook my head. It still didn't make sense. I would have put my father and Ian at the top of the list of the people who would never participate in such an unforgivable scheme.

The diaries hadn't helped, either; far from it. They had proved to be completely ambiguous. It was almost as if they had been written deliberately to give no impression of innocence or guilt. My father had recorded events, yes, but in such a way that I couldn't tell whether he was kidnapper or savior, which seemed very odd.

A typical passage follows:

Ian and I arrived on Nantucket late last night, and this morning went to the Wauwinet Home on the northeastern edge of the island. It is a temporary billet where the evacuated children will stay until their foster parents receive word of their arrival and can pick them up. The operation seems to have been extremely successful; all of the children appear to be in good condition and have taken the news of their parents' death remarkably well. The foster parents will come over the next few weeks to pay their fee and fetch the children, and the Wauwinet Home will be ready to accept the next HELP boatload. Ian and I promised to stop in again tomorrow, and will do so for the entire week of our leave.

The letters had been equally unhelpful. They were almost entirely of a personal nature, which I had to admit was fascinating, but all of them had been written in the period during which my father had been stationed in Europe. Not a single word about the Wauwinet Home or evacuated children.

How naive I had been when my father told me he was going sailing with Ian that year; I'd invited them both to join me in the British Virgin Islands, where I was leading a flotilla. Now I realized, of course, that they hadn't been sailing at all. They'd either been tracking the kidnappers to find Ian's daughter, which was the version I preferred, or they were trying to cover their tracks.

I opened the heavy front door and stopped to pick up the papers. A photo caught my eye and I froze.

With horror I stared at my father's strong, proud face as it peered up at me from the front page of the *Tempus*. A bold headline ran above: "Maximilian Plumtree Implicated in 'Arthur' Kidnappings." I grabbed both papers and retreated inside, hearing the blood pound in my head.

I put one foot in front of the other and climbed the stairs like an automaton. Who could have done this? No one knew that my father was guilty of the crime. I didn't even know for sure, and I had his diaries. I looked at the name on the byline of the *Tempus* story, but it was unfamiliar to me.

With a feeling of dread I looked at *The Watch*. My stomach turned inside out as I read the name Max Plumtree in bold, small type at the top of the story.

I walked to the kitchen, sat at the table, and read both stories, then picked up the phone. With violence I punched the seven numbers that would put me through to Max's flat. No one answered. I let it ring, knowing he was there, probably passed out from celebrating the night before. For five minutes I sat on the phone, listening to the ring, hoping it was irritating him.

It was just as I had thought.

Max picked up the phone with a string of swear words so vitriolic that anyone else would have hung up.

"You've gone too far," I said calmly.

"Ha," he said. "I thought you'd call." A pause. "You liked it, then. I owe it all to you, you know—you and your best-selling novels." Sarcasm dripped down the line.

"I said, you've gone too far." As I spoke, the strength of my convictions returned and I was furious with Romney and Max for suggesting something that simply couldn't be. Something foul was going on with the two of them, with these diaries, with Arthur's— Ian's?—disappearance.

"Romney Marsh fed you this story for his own ends, Max. It may be his version of things, but when the truth comes out, you're going to look extremely foolish. No one wants a journalist who gets his story wrong."

Finally, silence on the other end of the line.

"I also wanted to thank you for sparing us last night, though I can't imagine why you did it." I paused. "I suppose I'll be seeing you at noon."

When he answered, I knew I really had his wheels turning. His voice, when it came, was defensive. "Wait a minute. What do you mean, I got the story wrong? And what makes you think Romney Marsh told me?"

"You have got to stop underestimating me, Max."

Silence. "Underestimating . . ." He sounded confused, then defensive again. "I—I don't know what you're talking about. I didn't get the story wrong, and I didn't see you last night. And if I can possibly avoid it, I am not going to be seeing you at noon."

I could hear it; he was telling the truth. He had done the story all right. And he had gotten it from Romney. But he hadn't pushed the pediment on us.

"I have to find out one more thing." I paused. "What's happened to father's mace?"

"How the hell should I know?" he whined. "You were the one always digging around up there with him." It was quiet for a moment, and I could almost hear the cogs whirring. "Was it valuable?"

"Thanks, Max." I felt no regret at hanging up on him, and ignored the phone when it rang a moment later. I pulled a London Book Fair mug out of the cupboard and sloshed coffee into it with irritation. Someone was playing a game with me, and I wouldn't be played with. Max was a part of it, but there was someone else, someone behind him, using him. And whoever it was, he was far more sinister than my pitifully insecure brother. They would never persuade me that my father had been a kidnapper, nor Ian.

Then it hit me. I sat up and stared with absorption at the empty wall opposite. The feeling I'd had in the attic of having been led there; the lack of cobwebs; the disturbed dust under the leather strap; the unusual tidiness of it all, considering that Max had been there.

Of course someone had wanted me to find those diaries. They were not the originals, not my father's. And the letters, the ones with mention of the kidnapping scheme, had probably been removed from the packets. I was certain he would have written to my mother about his investigation of the kidnappers; even then, especially then, he would have had no secrets from her.

It had to be Romney. He was the one who had asked me for the manuscript, having failed to find it either here or at the office the previous day. It wouldn't do any good to wallow in self-pity or remorse; I would simply have to right those who had been wronged. That included my father, Arthur, and the families who had been torn apart. I had to prove that Romney was up to no good.

It was even more urgent that I find Ian, just in case my wild theory was justified. But I couldn't think of any way to find him without first proving that Romney was the kidnapper. Somehow I didn't think it would work if I barged into Romney's house and demanded that he come clean and tell me where Ian was.

I carried my coffee into the bathroom and showered, depression and despair falling away like so much dead skin. My mind flew ahead to the challenge of exposing Romney, and I felt almost elated. It would have to be done carefully, so he wouldn't know I suspected him. I wasn't much of an actor, but I did have the gift of inscrutability.

It wasn't long before my plan took shape. Romney would never even know I was onto him.

I toweled dry and switched on the television to see if Max's story had made breakfast TV. Rupert Soames's florid face and cloud of reddish, wiry hair practically filled the screen. "And as much as one would like to be charitable, I must say that I had my doubts. Mind you, Plumtree was careful to maintain a good front—family, charity, public service—but some of us knew better." He looked meaningfully at the interviewer, who was off screen, and added, "And none better than I." He shook his head regretfully.

Saint Rupert.

I wasn't going to let him get me down, but I resolved to become less trusting. To think that I had been ready to believe his cock-and-bull blood pressure story . . .

"You've been acting as the chairman of the League of Publishers since Maximilian Plumtree's death," the interviewer cooed in a low voice. The camera shifted to her, and Britain's viewers got a shot of miniskirted leg and fluffy hair. "Have you found any indications of impropriety in the way he represented the publishing industry?"

I pulled my tie through the knot with a certain amount of violence, noting that Rupert could barely conceal his delight at the opportunity to voice his favorite complaint. "I always said it wasn't fair for a Member of Parliament to hold this position—conflict of interest, you know—but it was as if he had everyone under his thumb. No one would listen. I still say it was all wrong."

Rupert the Crusader for Justice.

Poor Rupert. I had never seen a man so consumed by jealousy. My father had been dead for almost two years now, and even that hadn't set his mind at ease.

Lisette met me at the door with a silent hug, then went off immediately to get me a cup of coffee. It was as healing to the spirit as chicken soup.

With gratitude I accepted calls throughout the morning from concerned friends.

"Alex, it's just terrible. I don't know what to say, except that we're thinking of you, and that no one believes this nonsense for a moment." My mother's best friend.

"Everybody knows that Soames is off his rocker." George Stoneham.

"Dammit, Al, I didn't know your Dad. But I'd sure as hell like to throttle those jerks in the press!" Charlie Goodspeed (at three A.M., his time).

"The truth will out in the end, Alex, I assure you." Neville Greenslade, the family lawyer.

The most memorable call was from the prime minister, a university friend of my father's, who expressed his support. "These publicity hounds really are the limit," he said irritably. "And that Soames fellow. What the hell does he think he's playing at?"

But the most helpful call came from Simon Bow. "Alex, if there's anything I can do, just let me know. You know I have the greatest respect for your father, and nothing will ever change that." I thanked him, and he said, "Listen, I was going to call you this morning anyway. I've a little business proposition for you. Are you free for lunch?"

With regret, I told him I had an appointment. Bow's catered lunches were the envy of Bedford Square. I didn't tell him that I would be standing in the British Library, stomach rumbling, watching a bookshelf at noon. But, I said, I'd be glad for an excuse to walk across the square if he had a few minutes right now.

I put on my coat and stepped out into the weak autumn sunshine. It was unusually pleasant for the last days of October; the storm had blown all the clouds away. With every step I crunched a thick layer of downed branches and leaves into the pavement.

I wondered what Simon had in mind. Whatever it was, this would be an excellent opportunity for me to propose cooperation on the academic list for him and entry to the American market for me. Over the last few days I had developed deep reservations about working with Charlie Goodspeed and his eccentric organization. I had doubts that the agreement would ever come to pass, no matter how many times I crossed the Atlantic. I felt guilty at the thought of disappointing Charlie, but the thought of doing business with predictable, familiar, normal Simon Bow was almost irresistible. And his success in the American market had been considerable on the literary side; I was certain our academic books would benefit from his established distribution channels and reputation in the United States.

I decided to do it, but to pursue the Bookarama deal with Charlie at the same time. Surely one of the options would work out to my satisfaction.

The idea of copublishing with Simon was so new to me that I hadn't thought about what terms to offer. Perhaps I'd let him make a suggestion, then counter if necessary. I knew that I needed at least £250,000 in short order to save Plumtree Press.

My mind played with Simon's motivation for this sudden interest in doing business with me. There had always been such a healthy rivalry between Bow and Bow and Plumtree Press, despite Simon's rough-hewn friendship with my father, that I was a little surprised at his invitation. But it was no secret that Simon was in line for a knighthood and was only lacking some depth in his charitable work. Recently he had been written up for the adult literacy program he'd started operating out of the Bow and Bow offices in the evenings, which would certainly help him achieve his goal.

But I speculated that he wanted to add a bit more credibility to his background as educator, and a strong academic list in his company's catalog would help. How better to achieve that quickly than by buying it from us, the leader in scholarly anthologies? We were a perfect complement to a trade literary publisher like Bow's. If we'd been in the record business, Simon would be selling singles and we'd be selling albums—of classics.

I walked into Bow and Bow reception and stood for a moment in front of an elegant, mature woman with silver-white hair who was evidently the secretary. Someone Simon's wife had vetted, no doubt, given his reputation. She smiled and signaled for me to wait while she finished with her phone call.

"We'll be expecting you then, Mr. Vasquez," she said silkily. I started. Emilio Vasquez was only the hottest name in literary fiction this year. If Simon had persuaded him to join his stable of authors, it was a major victory.

"I'm sorry to have kept you waiting," she said. "What can I do for you?"

"I'm Alex Plumtree, here to see Simon."

The woman's eyebrows raised a fraction, and she let out a nervous laugh. "Yes, of course." I could see that she'd read the morning paper. "Why don't you sit down. I'll let him know you're here." She picked up the phone and punched a button as other lines began to ring.

"Thank you."

A shelf of Bow and Bow books lined the wall to my right, and while I waited I caught up on what they had been publishing. There were very few mass market books; he published mainly sophisticated works of art that would have a dedicated following, and made them relatively expensive to buy. Most of them were hardcovers with specially designed endpapers; thick, soft paper; and pages with deckled edges. Collectors' editions, really.

I heard heels clicking in the marble hallway, and Simon stepped into the room, an elegant, silver-haired man in a soft camel suit. He was the senior statesman of book publishing in the kingdom, now that my father was gone.

"Do we pass muster?"

"Indeed you do. I can see that the fine craft of book making is alive and well," I said. "They're beautiful. Not many people can afford to produce this sort of book today."

"No," he said, looking a bit sad. "No, you're right. Well, let's go on up." I followed him up a flight of stairs, which were elegantly clad in an Oriental runner. He had evidently chosen to put his offices on the second floor, which had by far the best view of the square. I knew this because all of the buildings around Bedford Square were the same; it was an example of Georgian tract housing. When these buildings were private homes, the second floor had been the room where visitors were entertained and balls were held. The front wall of the second floor, where Simon was headed now, was almost completely covered with floor-to-ceiling windows. At Plumtree Press, our production department occupied this area, as they needed the most space.

He opened the door to his inner sanctum and ushered me in, indicating a pale peach wingback chair that looked directly out at Plumtree Press. His office was very formal and proper, fitted out in the style of a fine London house: antiques, brocade upholstery, wooden floors with Aubusson carpet. I wondered if he had ever been inside our offices, and if so what he thought of our well-worn forest-green-and-burgundy gentleman's club atmosphere.

He walked around his desk and stood next to a massive coffee-and-cream-colored leather chair. "Tea? Coffee? Anything?" He waved at a fully stocked bar.

"No, nothing, thank you."

He sat down and looked straight into my eyes. "Alex, I know you've got a lot on your mind. I won't waste your time." He leaned across the desk, pressing the tips of his fingers together. "It strikes me that you have something I need, and I have something you might want." He paused, looking pensive. "I had always hoped that I might be able to do business with your father, but—well, it wasn't meant to be. We still have the opportunity, though, and it's not too late." He stood up and began to pace, hands in his pockets.

"It occurs to me that the academic anthology market would be a good one for me to have a finger in, as a literary publisher. Sort of fits with our line, you know."

I couldn't believe my ears. Had he read my mind?

He continued to pace. "And when I was thinking about it, it

occurred to me that perhaps we could work with Plumtree. We could copublish with you on your Modern Classics line; our literary publishing reputation in exchange for your name in academic anthologies." He wheeled to face me. "Split the profits. Naturally I would expect to compensate you for the fifty percent of sales you would be missing on those volumes, and I have a couple of ideas on that."

He appeared to be gauging my level of interest and was evidently satisfied. He began pacing again.

"I don't know if this would interest you, but you may know that we have a considerable presence in the U.S. market: distribution channels, book clubs, public relations contacts. Have you ever considered introducing your anthologies to the American market?"

I wrestled with a momentary feeling that this was too easy, too good to be true. What was the catch? But he was waiting for an answer. I nodded. "I've wanted to get into the U.S. market ever since I joined the company. In fact, I think my father was interested in going in that direction for some time. No one got around to doing anything about it—it's tricky stepping into a new market, especially that one."

"No question about it," he said emphatically. "That's why I think this is a mutually beneficial situation. If we copublish, you have access to all of our American resources and facilities for all your books—not just the ones on which we cooperate." He stopped and looked pleased with himself, as if we'd reached our conclusion. I wondered if that was all.

Cash, I thought with disappointment; my company needs cash.

"Now, I've been thinking about the terms," he continued. Perhaps he'd read my mind again. "I'll just throw out a couple of ideas, and you tell me if you think they sound reasonable. One option is for us to pay you a one-time fee of a million pounds, and be done with it. This is important enough to us to make it worth your while. Naturally, we'd still split the profits from the books fifty-fifty.

"The other possibility is to work out a schedule whereby you receive a larger percentage of the profits on the copublished volumes for a time, and gradually even out to fifty-fifty over the years. Like an author's escalating royalties clause, but declining instead of escalating." He sat down on the desk. "What do you think?"

I thanked God for the gift of inscrutability. If not for that, I might have made a total idiot of myself. This was a far, far better deal than Bookarama had been able to offer.

I nodded slowly, as if considering. "Copublishing is an interesting idea, Simon. Naturally I'd like to discuss it with our lawyers and accountants first." I couldn't believe it; I was beginning to sound like Charlie.

"Of course," Simon said. "I took the liberty of having these drawn up to simplify things." He handed me two separate documents. I could see at a glance that they were copublishing contracts specifying the terms he had just outlined. The lure of knighthood really had him scrambling.

"I'll send them to my lawyer today," I said, standing. My watch said ten forty-five, and I had a couple of things to do before planting myself behind a shelf in the British Library in an hour. Some sort of gesture of tentative agreement seemed in order, and I reached out my hand, looking him in the eye. He seemed taken aback, but took my hand and shook it firmly. "You might not believe this, Simon, but I had something similar in mind myself. I'm glad you put it into words first."

He shrugged with self-deprecation and smiled. "You know what they say about great minds. Speaking of which, now that the situation has—er—changed considerably, I wonder if you're ready to sell me the Arthur rights yet."

I smiled and narrowed my eyes. Every time I saw Simon, practically, he asked me the same question. "I thought you didn't deal in such commonplace literature. What was it you called *Those Who Trespass Against Us*—'that mass market stuff'?"

He waved a hand dismissively. "You mustn't take me so seriously, Alex."

"Don't worry," I said lightly. "I don't. And no, I'm still not interested in parting with Arthur's works."

"Ah, well." He sighed with exaggerated drama. "I'll try again another day."

He saw me down the stairs and out and paused after opening the door. "I want to reassure you, Alex, that no one believes these things in the paper or on the television. People know what kind of man your father was."

I nodded. "Thanks, Simon. You've been very kind." I waved the envelope of contracts at him and stepped out. "I'll be in touch soon."

"Right. Bye, then."

I thought I felt his eyes on my back as I walked toward the park and had the uncomfortable feeling that he was looking after me with pity. That was the one thing I couldn't bear. I squared my shoulders and walked with all the dignity I could muster. It was possible, after all, that this whole offer had been made out of pity. I gritted my teeth. Poor young Plumtree can't quite cut it, needs a bit of help, you know.

Still, I thought, it was too good to refuse. And no more Charlie, besides. If it became definite before Bookarama did, I would take it no matter what it cost my pride.

Something was niggling at the back of my mind. This was the easiest solution I had ever come across to a truly thorny problem— almost too easy. It might have been the remnants of Nehemiah Plumtree's (born 1721, died 1777) puritanical blood in my veins, or my suspicious nature. But I felt uncomfortable when things came so easily.

Look where the sudden arrival of Arthur's best-seller, free of charge and entirely without effort on my part, had gotten me.

I ran back up into my office, fetched my briefcase, and told Lisette I was going to a meeting that might take all afternoon. She knew my schedule as well as I did and knew that there was no meeting on my calendar.

"Of course," she said. She looked around to see if anyone was within hearing distance, and shook a finger at me. "But you had jolly well better be careful," she whispered meaningfully. She knew me too well.

I went back to my flat to fetch the manuscript, waving to my gregarious Milanese publisher tenant as I started up the stairs. If I stopped for a moment, he'd take all afternoon. But he was insistent, waving at me and calling my name as he came toward the French glass doors that separated his office from the entry hall.

"*Signore Alex! Signore! Momento.*" The doors swung open. With resignation I turned to greet him. He was so friendly, I thought, and he might be lonely in London. I really should make more time for him.

"Hello, Riccardo."

His blinding smile was accentuated by his tan face. "You *just* missed him. He left only a moment ago."

"Who?"

He looked puzzled. "Why, your cousin, of course. I saw him go upstairs and asked if I could be of help, but he said it was all right, you were expecting him." His smile lit up the stairway again. "Is so nice he could come from Scotland to be with you."

Alarm bells went off in my head. "I don't have a cousin, Riccardo." I bounded up the stairs, and he followed, concerned.

I knew there was a problem when I saw the smoke pouring out from under my door. "Call nine-nine-nine. Quickly!" I heard him take the steps down two at a time, a heroic effort for someone with such short legs.

Above all, I had to save the manuscript.

I took off my coat and wrapped it around my arm as a sort of shield, then turned my key in the lock. As I pushed open the door, flames leapt out, drawn by the new draft. I jumped back and held the padded arm in front of my face, hearing the soft roar of the fire. When I looked again, the flames weren't leaping out the door; they were coming from the runner in the center of the entry hall. I could barely see for the smoke, but the flames seemed to be confined to the rugs and furniture so far. The floor itself wasn't burning, nor the walls. That, at least, was something to be grateful for.

I took a deep breath, held it, and stepped inside.

My books, I thought. I felt more than a pang of regret for them. If they weren't already burning, they would be soon. I used to think that in case of a fire, if I were here alone, I'd save them first.

But that was then. Now there was far more at stake.

It says on the back of hotel room doors that you should stay close to the floor in case of a fire. I'd never had the opportunity to use that piece of information before, but now I got down on my hands and knees. I crawled through the entry hall toward the bedroom, close to the wall, avoiding the smoldering runner down the center and praying that my glasses could withstand this kind of heat. This would make a nice test for the plastics company.

"Damn!" I felt a sudden, searing pain above my ankle. I

looked back and saw that my cuff was on fire. I was coughing, having gulped in a mouthful of sooty smoke. I reached back with the padded arm and beat at my leg, then hastily pulled trousers and sock away from the spot. There was no time to waste; I had to either turn back and give up, or hurry up and do it.

I turned the corner, still on hands and knees, and saw that the bed was engulfed in flames. It was burning as if it had been soaked in gasoline, as well it may have been, I thought. A racking cough shook me as I looked at the roaring bed, then at the dresser, and decided to do it. There was no other way.

It was hard to breathe; when I inhaled, no air came, just choking clouds of soot. The bed generated incredible heat as I ran alongside it to reach the dresser, and I had the feeling that my clothes were blistering off of me. I reached up, groping for the manuscript, found it, got my fingers around it, and pulled it over the molding and down. It was so hot, too hot. I was gulping for air now, working to pull oxygen into my lungs. The smoke they got instead was unacceptable, and they expelled it in coughs as quickly as they could.

I wasted a valuable instant looking up at the skylight, thinking I might be able to use it for its intended purpose of fire escape. I quickly realized that even if I could climb the hot metal ladder, the moment I opened the skylight it could very well create a chimney that would instantly incinerate me—and the manuscript.

I turned to escape the way I had come, trying hard not to breathe, to keep the bad air out until I was outside. But a strange thing happened; everything went dark, and I couldn't see anymore. Then I was on the floor, making crawling movements, but my face was on the floor and my legs wouldn't work properly. I remember thinking, You're losing it, Alex; don't, don't, don't . . . the manuscript. I couldn't control the coughing; even though I wasn't inhaling any more smoke, the expulsion mechanism was working.

My last memory was the gargantuan battle of getting the thick manuscript between me and the floor, then between me and my waistcoat. The next thing I knew there was something over my face, but it wasn't a shroud. I was breathing hard and fast, as if I'd been running and was out of breath. The air was good; breath felt good, a relief beyond words.

"He'll be all right now." The voice came from right above me, but I still couldn't see anything, and I certainly didn't feel all right. There was pain and also the ache of my lungs. The floor was vibrating and there was a loud noise. In the next moment I realized it was an ambulance siren.

With sudden panic I realized that they were taking me away, away from the British Museum and the only chance I would have to see who would try to pick up the manuscript. I tried to sit up to tell them I was all right, could they please just let me out here, I had an important appointment. But nothing happened; I couldn't even open my eyes, let alone move.

"Thank God," said a voice with a thick French accent. I felt a squeeze on my hand. It was Lisette.

Then I was tired, much too tired, and everything drifted away.

When I next awakened, it was in a hospital room. I knew this mainly because I could smell the antiseptic before I opened my eyes and I was in a bed, not my own, that had very white sheets. I could see that much even without my glasses, and I noted their absence with dread. If they were broken or melted, I was in a real fix. I turned my head and saw a brownish, indefinite blob next to the bed. I leaned forward and reached out my hand to see if perhaps it was a bedside table with glasses on it.

It was a mistake. A spasm of painful coughing consumed me and made me forget I'd ever worn glasses. I closed my eyes and let it have its way.

A hand gently squeezed my shoulder, and as the coughing subsided I sank back on the bed feeling as if my lungs were punishing me for the abuse I'd dished out.

"Just relax." The voice was Sarah's. It was soothing, quiet. Her hand stayed where it was. I felt ridiculously weak and just laid there, trying to catch my breath, my eyes closed. There wasn't much point in opening them if my glasses were gone. After a moment she squeezed my shoulder and said, "I'd better tell the nurse you're awake. I'll be right back."

I tried to say, "Please stay," but a weak croak came out that she might not have heard, let alone understood. Things in general weren't working properly. There were bandages on my arms and legs, for instance, which considering the situation were probably covering burns. But burns are painful, and I didn't feel a thing. Perhaps they'd spiked the IV with painkillers.

She said again from the door, "I'll be right back."

As I waited for her to come back with unwelcome company, it came back to me in a rush. The manuscript. Romney. The library.

It was useless for me to grope about; I would have to wait and ask someone where it was. After an eternity, I heard a rush of air as the door opened and knew that they were back. One pair of squeaky nurse's shoes, one pair of city pumps. I would do all right as a blind person, I thought, if that day ever came; I had already developed my other senses to compensate.

"Well, I see we're awake at last." Judging from her voice, my nurse was the mercilessly cheerful type. That was all right, I thought, as long as she didn't take it too far. She came over and picked up my wrist. Taking my pulse, I presumed. "It's late, but we'll see what we can do about getting you some tea."

"Is—" It came out a croak again. I could see that I was going to have to find another way to communicate.

"Shhhhh. Can't you see I'm trying to count here?" She was close enough that I got the impression of a big, friendly smile. When she had finished pulse taking, she picked up the blood-pressure cuff, fastened it on, and started pumping. "Your friend told me you wanted to tell us something. I brought a pad of paper and a pencil with me. I think that'll be best for right now, don't you?"

I felt as if I were back in second form, but at least she was considerate. I waited while she listened to whatever it was she listened to, and she handed me the pad and pencil. "In case you're interested, Alexander, you're doing very well. You've got the constitution of an ox. Fit, too, by the looks of it. Must be a regular athlete," she said lightheartedly.

"He is," Sarah said seriously as I scribbled. "He was on the American Olympic rowing team." She didn't add, bless her, that President Carter had decided to punish the Olympians that year for the Soviet human rights record. After all our backbreaking work, we hadn't got to go. It wasn't something one forgot overnight.

"Aha," she said, with a look of appraisal. "That explains it, then."

I passed her my pad. It should have read as follows, though I couldn't actually read it myself:

1. Glasses.
2. Ask Sarah: manuscript. Was it on me when I came in?

"Oh. Sorry. Your glasses are right here." She pulled open the top drawer and drew them out. "Mmm. I can see why you need them; thick ones, aren't they?" Little did she know.

She helped me put them on, and I felt human again. It was an enormous relief to be able to see clearly; it made me feel altogether better. She was still beaming at me, a large, capable woman with big teeth and a black plastic nametag that said FIONA. I smiled back.

"That's what we like to see," she said, patting my arm. "I saw you looking at the flowers. They're from someone named Charlie." That figured, I thought. I marveled at his ability to know precisely what was happening in London at all hours of the day and night. I glanced at Sarah, but as the nurse stood and took the note to her, her ample figure obstructed my view.

When the nurse finally moved out of the way, I was stunned at Sarah's appearance. She looked terrible. She was leaning precariously against the wall, and her peaches and cream face was gray. Deep lines extended downward from the corners of her mouth.

The nurse evidently had the same thought. "You'd better sit down before you fall down, love."

Sarah looked up distractedly. "Who, me? Oh, no." She waved a limp hand. "I'm all right."

What had happened to her? While she looked at my first note, I scribbled furiously on the pad.

I tore it off and got it ready to pass back to the nurse. I felt as if I were in a game of charades.

Unaware of my scrutiny, Sarah rubbed her temple. She had perked up a bit after reading my question about the manuscript. "Fiona, where would a patient's personal things be kept, something Alex might have had with him when he was brought in."

"Normally in that locker by the door—I've got a key—or in this bedside stand. We find they go missing less often that way. I wasn't on duty this noon, or I'd know where his things are."

She sounded disappointed that she couldn't tell us right away. One by one, she rattled through the drawers in the rickety bedside stand. Nothing. Next I heard keys tinkle as she moved to a small closet behind the door and turned her key in a lock.

"One smoky pair of trousers. Cor, what a pong," she said, waving her hand in front of her nose. Then I heard her rummaging in a paper bag. "Would this be it?" I could tell from the way she hefted the bag that it must be the manuscript, all 450 pages of it. Arthur was not particularly concise, and he still had five chapters to go . . . I hoped.

Sarah nodded behind her, and Fiona brought the bag over and plopped it on the bed. "Tomorrow, sir, you can tell me how you managed to get this wad of kindling out of a fire unscathed, when you fared worse yourself. But right now, I'm going to see what I can scavenge around here in the way of food." She turned to Sarah and spoke gently. "After he's eaten, I'm afraid you'll have to go. He needs sleep."

Sarah nodded and came to sit on the bed as the nurse left. I handed her my note: *Are you all right?*

She looked at it and bit her lower lip hard.

Then, to my total surprise, she put her hands over her face and sobbed uncontrollably. In all the time I'd known her, I had seen her cry only once—that time at the top of Ben Nevis. The entire bed shook, and she was silent aside from an occasional choking sound. I put a hand at the base of her back—considering that this was a special circumstance, I assumed it would be all right—and gently rubbed it up and down. There must have been some disaster at work, some family problem.

I longed to pull her close and tell her it would be all right, but I could do neither.

She shook her head and snatched three tissues out of the box on the bedside table. "I'm sorry." She swiped at a runaway tear. "It's just that I couldn't sleep last night, and then when Lisette called from the hospital . . ."

She succumbed to another round, holding the tissues to her face. She sat that way for a long time after the sobs stopped, sniffing and composing herself. I kept my hand on her back as she'd kept hers on my shoulder.

Finally she blew her nose with determination, tossed the sodden tissues into the dustbin, and turned to look at me. "I thought I'd lost you, Alex. You're my best friend."

It took some time for it to register: She'd been crying because of me. She cared that much about me.

"You didn't exactly look like a rose when I got here, with the IV and the breathing apparatus around you, making that horrible sound." Her upper lip flinched involuntarily.

Of course. I should have realized sooner. She had lived at the hospital those last few weeks with Peter. Hospitals and all that goes with them must be torture for her.

She did her best to put on a cheery face. It only made her look more tired. "Still, all that was more than twelve hours ago now, and you're almost good as new."

Twelve hours ago . . . that meant it was nearly one in the morning. No wonder she was tired, and I was hungry.

"They said you should be able to leave tomorrow morning, providing you don't do calisthenics during the night."

I smiled. That was great news. I had things to do, people to see, namely Romney Marsh.

I picked up the pencil again.

1. Thanks for being here.
2. Would you do me a favor and take the ms to the City with you and put it in a bank vault tomorrow morning?
3. Go home and go to sleep; you're making me feel tired.

She laughed, and it made both of us feel better. "I can take a hint. You just don't want to share your dinner." She stood up and gave me a brisk peck on the cheek, but some of her hair brushed against my face, softening the kiss considerably. I noted with interest that the effects of the fire didn't interfere with the attraction I felt to her.

She was looking at me, smiling. "I'm glad you're feeling better. I'll talk to you tomorrow. And don't worry about this. It'll be in our vaults at the bank first thing." She hoisted the bag off the bed and her pumps tapped softly out of my room.

As the door swung shut, I leaned my head back against the pillow and sighed.

When I opened my eyes, there was light flooding through the window, which I could now see looked out on Gower Street. So I was at Great Portland Street Hospital; it made sense, as it's only minutes from Bedford Square, but I hadn't bothered to ask last night.

Fiona was fiddling with some plate covers and a tray, and when she heard me shift she turned and stood with her hands on her hips.

"Well, well. And I suppose now you want breakfast. You've got a lot of cheek, you know. I found a nice turkey sandwich for you last night, not to mention fruit and a sweet, and when I came back in you were out cold." She dropped the act and smiled as she rolled a massive amount of food in front of me on the over-the-bed tray. "How are we feeling this morning?"

I rubbed my eyes and took stock. "I feel all right," I said, surprised. The bandaged areas on my legs and arms smarted, especially the one where my sock and trousers had been on fire, but my head was clear and that was what mattered. I even had a croaky version of my voice back.

She laughed. "Let's see." She came over and did the usual routine, and pronounced me fit as a fiddle. "As far as I'm concerned, you're wasting a bed here." She winked. "Your doctor will be in later. Oh, and the police want a word, too."

She bustled out and I tucked into sausage, eggs, toast, juice, and coffee with a gargantuan appetite. I couldn't remember ever having been so hungry. It wasn't until after I'd finished that I began to think about the fire, Romney, and the rest of it.

Somehow I'd arrived at the conclusion that Romney had been responsible for the fire, though I couldn't exactly say why. It had something to do with the noon meeting and the fact that he wanted that manuscript. I tried to concentrate. It must have been close to eleven-thirty by the time I saw the smoke coming out of the flat. If it had been Romney behind the British Library threat, he'd have known that there was very little chance of me being at the flat then. But why burn the place down?

I watched the traffic go by and thought about it, and came up with only one idea. If he thought I wasn't going to take the bait and hand over the manuscript, he might have wanted to destroy it. Eleven-thirty should have been a good time to do that undetected, but he didn't count on Riccardo being there. And he certainly didn't count on me.

Riccardo. He had seen the man who started the fire. As I pulled back the bedcovers to go in search of a telephone, the door opened and a police constable entered. "Alexander Plumtree?"

I nodded.

"I'm Inspector Hawkins. I wonder if I could have a few moments."

"Of course." I sat back down on the bed and covered my bare legs with the bedclothes again. The hospital provided the most minimal nightclothes I had ever seen, hardly the sort of thing in which one wanted to be seen walking about. I wondered what was on his mind.

"Thank you, sir." Inspector Hawkins sat down in the standard National Health Service chair and took out a small notebook. He seemed slightly embarrassed, but for what reason I couldn't imagine. He was some ten years older than me, but was already gray at the temples and thick around the middle. A comfortable life of pints and pork pies, I guessed.

"Well, sir, the first thing I'll need is your account of what happened yesterday. We understand that arson is suspected, judging from, er"—he looked down at the notebook to be sure of the name—"Riccardo SanGiacomo's conversations with his colleagues. Plus, we can't find any evidence of an accident. No problems with the heating system, gas stove—nothing like that." He blushed and cleared his throat. "Aside from the newspaper coverage about your father, sir, can you think of any reason why anyone should have wanted to start a fire in your flat?"

Now I understood. He was embarrassed for me; he thought that I was the target of hate crimes as a member of a scandalized family. I thought quickly; did I want the police in on this situation? I could hardly turn the police onto my own brother and I wasn't sure who else was responsible yet. And he was ready to believe that it was someone furious with Maximilian Plumtree for the loss of hundreds of London's children.

"No," I said. "I can't. But Riccardo saw the man; surely you've got a description from him."

The inspector raised his eyebrows, then shuffled his feet as he concentrated on the speckles in the linoleum floor. He cleared his throat and mumbled, "I guess they didn't tell you, then." He looked straight into my eyes and said, "As best we can reconstruct it from evidence, sir, Riccardo ran into the flat after you once he'd called nine-nine-nine. When they found him, it was too late."

I felt a sinking sensation, as if I had suddenly been accused of murder myself. This was the second decent, innocent man who had died this week because of me. Was there no way out of this? How many more people would be dragged into it before it was over?

"I'm sorry, sir. Perhaps you'd like me to come back . . ." He sounded almost hopeful.

"No, that's all right, Inspector. Let's get it over with."

I told him what had happened that morning when I came into the building, about my conversation with Riccardo, and seeing the smoke. I replayed the scene inside the flat for him, and he wrote furiously all the while. When I stopped, he put his head to one side and frowned at me, not unpleasantly.

"If I may say so, sir, you just don't seem the type. I mean, lots of people will run into a fire to save jewelry, valuable objets d'art, etcetera. What was so important in your bedroom that you risked your life to save it?"

I hadn't been overly impressed with Inspector Hawkins, but now I could see that he found it convenient to allow people to underestimate him—rather like Alison Soames. "A manuscript," I said. "I'm not sure there's another copy of it." I wasn't about to say which manuscript.

"One that you are planning to publish?"

"Yes."

"I see. Well, I'd call that extraordinary dedication to your work, sir."

He watched me for a reaction, but I didn't provide him with one. I said calmly, "No one cares about Plumtree Press more than I do, Inspector."

We both turned as the door swung open and Lisette and a man in a long white lab coat walked in. "Alex—" Lisette started toward me, then caught sight of Inspector Hawkins. "Are we interrupting? Should we come back?"

The inspector stood. "No, I've taken enough of his time this morning." He turned toward me and looked far too deeply into my eyes. I had the feeling he saw something there, something I wasn't telling him. "Thank you, sir, and I hope you'll be feeling better soon." He gave me a formal little nod of the head and left.

Lisette came over next to the bed and held my hand. "You

look almost human," she said. "*Mon Dieu*, you are a different man from last night, no?" She looked pleased enough to pop a button or two.

The doctor looked at my records, then at me, and pronounced me fit to leave if I didn't run any marathons in the next day or two. Lisette thoughtfully provided me with one of George's sweatsuits which, though several inches short, easily covered all the vital areas, and drove me home to her cozy guest house in Couch End.

She seemed to understand that I didn't want to go back to the flat just then for a look at my waterstained books, if there were any left. She casually mentioned along the way that there were several boxes of my belongings at their house. As we rolled up the drive, I saw that my car was already parked outside their garage.

As we walked to the guest house, Lisette insisted that I stay away from work for the rest of the day.

"Why, are the mice playing?" I asked, teasing.

She looked at me in exasperation. "You can be so difficult, Alex. You should listen to me more often, you know. Remember, I warned you before all of this happened. I have a sense about these things." She stuck her lips out in a pout and turned her head at an angle. "Everything is in perfect order at work; I am seeing to that."

I smiled in spite of myself. "I'm sure you are." I thought of everyone running scared at the sight of Lisette in charge.

"Good. Then you stay here and rest, and I will come see you when I get home tonight. We are having your favorite for dinner, you know, coq au vin." She pointed across the room. "There is food in that refrigerator, and drinks, and there is the phone on the desk. Call me if you need anything and remember that Nicole, the maid, is at the house. You can just press that button on the phone, and she will answer. Okay?" She was overflowing with energy and cheerfulness, completely fulfilled in her role of meeting other people's needs. She loved nothing more.

"Okay." I chuckled. "You're incredible, Lisette. Thanks."

"Don't speak of it." She breezed out of the sunny, pickled pine room, and I reached for the phone. I had some calls to make. Although I hadn't told her, I had no intention of returning to work until I had this problem sorted out. Besides, it seemed that wherever I went, other people got hurt.

Or killed.

I had watched the side mirror all the way en route to Couch End to make sure we weren't followed. All the same, it was surprising that they, whomever they were, hadn't sent someone to the hospital to try to recover the manuscript.

I puzzled over that with vague disquiet as I waited for directory assistance to answer. "Ministry of Defence, please." I copied down the London number and dialed it.

"Yes. Romney Marsh, please."

A pause. "One moment." There was the click of a transfer, then a new voice—this time a man.

"May I help you?" He was hesitant, questioning, as if he wasn't quite sure what to expect.

"Yes. I need to speak with Romney Marsh."

Silence. "I'm afraid we don't have anyone here by that name, sir."

I hung up.

Romney Marsh didn't work for the Ministry of Defence.

6

I drove up the A40 to Watford at over ninety miles an hour, the burn on my ankle stinging smartly as I pressed on the accelerator. Fast driving was my vice, my equivalent of Max's drugs. I drove fast when I was angry, and I was beyond anger now.

Romney Marsh was at the root of it all.

I was convinced that he was the kidnapper as well as Barnes's murderer, and that he had used Max to remove suspicion from himself and place it on my father.

But there was a way to prove to the world who he was and what he had done.

I noticed that the sky was clouding up as it regularly did in the afternoons, but this time the clouds were not the usual blanket of lead. They were brilliant white puffballs with blackened bottoms that fairly raced across the sky. It was a New England sky, I thought, intensely blue, black, and white, and so fast-moving it was almost violent. I flinched at the reminder that Barnes and Riccardo would never see another day like this and pushed down harder on the accelerator.

I had made several more calls from Lisette's guest cottage before leaving. I'd asked British Telecom if I could have calls to my home phone number automatically routed to a mobile car phone. They said yes, for a fee, but I'd have to stop in to authorize it; it couldn't be done over the phone. For an even more exorbitant fee it could be done on the same day, and I decided I would be extravagant for once.

My other calls were to Nantucket Island, Massachusetts, where I had sought and tentatively obtained further proof that Romney was the culprit. I had dialed Nantucket directory assistance and asked for the Wauwinet Home, and had subsequently gotten through. But after forty-five years, no one there knew anything about the time when it was a children's home. They'd referred me to the Historical Society, where I'd struck gold. The head of the society had referred me to an elderly woman who worked at the children's home; she remembered a boatload of British war orphans kept at Wauwinet temporarily, until they were sent to Boston to be met by their foster parents.

I'd held my breath while she told me that a "nice British officer" had brought them. Did she remember his name, what he looked like? "Oh, my dear boy, I'm afraid after all this time I don't remember his name." She giggled like a schoolgirl. "But I'll never forget him: He was rather tall, with dark hair, and the most wonderful eyes . . ."

I was disappointed, thinking that could be just about anyone, when she continued.

". . . in fact, I've still got a photo of him." I nearly leapt through the phone wire. "I know it's here somewhere; I saw it when I moved last year and went through my things. Give me a few days to find it, and I'll mail it to you."

The most wonderful eyes, she'd said. I sighed impatiently. Almost any young man could have wonderful eyes in a young woman's opinion. I hadn't been able to get any more details out of her, such as the color of those eyes, but felt incredibly fortunate to be on the receiving end of the photograph. She'd agreed to send it by overnight mail once she'd found it, and I'd already dropped a note and check into the post to her.

At last I pulled into a public car park in Watford, the northwest London suburban shopping mecca, and made for a branch of the country's largest electronics equipment store. Normally I would have gone to Tottenham Court Road next to Bedford Square for such things, but the last thing I needed was to be spotted by someone I didn't want to see.

A young sales clerk walked up to me and offered his assistance. "Yes, I'd like to buy a car phone with an answering machine and something that will allow me to tape both sides of a telephone conversation."

He looked interested. "Someone else's telephone conversation?"

"Exactly."

He gave me a conspiratorial smile. "Follow me, sir."

It was surprisingly easy, I found, to listen in on others' conversations. I had my choice of a ballpoint pen, a paperweight, and a number of other forms of electronic bugs. I bought the most basic variety for just £25, a pair of magnetized semicircles, each the size of a thumbtack, that came with a miniature voice-activated tape recorder. The bugs, one of which went into the earpiece and one into the mouthpiece, were actually tiny radio transmitters. There was a receiver in the tape recorder unit, he said. He showed me how to use them and informed me that the only trick was obtaining the opportunity to plant the devices. The bug had to go in Romney's telephone, but the tape recorder could be located anywhere on the premises.

"Used it myself on the girlfriend," he said with a wink. "I found out what I needed to know. But I should warn you," he added, "lots of people find out things they'd rather not know. I've had people tell me they wish they'd never had the idea."

I'd much rather not know about any of this, I thought; I wished that none of it had ever happened. But I had little choice at this point.

I purchased the surveillance equipment and the car-phone-cum-answering machine, then thanked him and headed for the door, carrying my boxes.

"Good luck," he said.

I appreciated his good wishes but had no idea that the most difficult part of my day would be getting British Telecom to do its job. Although technically possible, it seemed that what I wanted them to do hadn't been done by this particular office before. I speculated that even feigning cooperation with Romney would be less difficult than persuading them to activate my car phone with my existing number, but in the end I won.

I then continued on to a department store where I purchased

several outfits of clothing, including a warm, brown leather flight jacket. I also extracted my electronic gear from its packaging and hid it, ready for use, in the inside pocket of the coat.

Eventually I was en route to Romney's cottage in Chalfont St. Giles, a storybook village that was a peaceful country retreat heavily settled by stockbrokers and BBC executives. The town had achieved fame once upon a time when John Milton sought refuge here from a plague that ravaged London, and each summer tourists came by the busload to pay homage to the great poet.

The thought of anyone as blatantly nefarious as Romney living in a rose-covered cottage here was absurd, but then perhaps he thought it presented a good image to the rest of the world.

I had called him from just outside the electronics shop to ask if I could pay him a visit to chat about Arthur. He'd been surprised and pleased. I didn't have the first idea what to say to him on the subject; all I needed was a minute or two alone with his telephone.

I hadn't been to his house for roughly twenty years, but when I pulled up, it was just as I had remembered it. It was a listed building, like Plumtree Press's at Bedford Square, which meant that it had historical significance. White stucco, diamond-paned windows, thatched roof—it was the quintessential English cottage. The last time I'd been here it had been for Sunday lunch immediately following church. For some reason Romney had attended the parish church in our neighboring village of Chess instead of the one in his own town, and my parents had often entertained him with other friends from the parish. Once or twice he'd returned the favor. My brother and I had been shy, I remember, not sure what to do, as it had been made quite clear to us that we mustn't fight in someone else's home.

But then Romney had shown us his train set, which was the most amazing I've seen to this day. If I were ever to be blessed with fatherhood, I would want to provide my children with a train set like Romney's. It occupied an entire room and was a miniature version of the region, complete with recognizable local churches, train stations, and houses.

The train set was the main reason I had been so upset when my father had fallen out with Romney. It was out of character for him to write off anyone the way he did Romney; my father was a firm believer in forgiveness and reconciliation. I was bitterly disappointed when I learned that we would not be visiting Romney again. Perhaps I hadn't exactly said "How could a man with such a wonderful train set do anything wrong?", but I thought it.

I shook myself from the past and got out of the car, putting on the leather jacket. I put my hand inside the pocket and fingered the bugs and miniature tape player. Would I be a good enough actor to pull this off? I reminded myself once again that there wasn't much choice.

Before I could ring Romney's bell the door opened and Romney's well-shaped head popped out.

"Come in, come in," he said, searching my face for a hint as to the information I had for him. "I was pleased to hear from you, Alex." He was warm on the surface but reserved underneath; in fact, I had the feeling that he was going along with my act. It made me uncomfortable.

I smiled anyway. "I appreciate it that you would see me on such short notice."

"Well, this is by far the most important thing I've got going," he said seriously, looking into my eyes.

Yes, I'm sure it is, I thought, considering that you have no job at the Ministry of Defence.

"Sit down, Alex; make yourself comfortable. Can I offer you tea? Something stronger?"

"Tea would be great, thanks," I said, sinking into one of his overstuffed green corduroy chairs. It felt good to sit down; the world was still a bit wobbly, and I was unreasonably tired for two-thirty in the afternoon.

"Right. I'll be back straightaway."

This was my chance, probably the only one I would get. I stood up again with an effort and went to a telephone on a small round table against the far wall. It was near the dining room table, which I thought might be his working surface, though it was now free of papers and clutter. From slight familiarity with the house I remembered that there weren't many rooms to the ancient building. I remembered only two upstairs, one tiny bedroom with a bath for Romney and one room for the train paraphernalia. I didn't think he had a study per se.

I could hear him clattering about in the kitchen with mugs, the milk bottle, and the kettle as I got out my goodies. All I had to do was unscrew the mouthpiece, then . . .

"You do take cream, Alex?" My heart pounded and I turned to face Romney, who had popped his head out of the kitchen. Fortunately, I hadn't yet picked up the phone.

"Yes, thanks." My voice came out clear and steady, much to my relief.

"Ah, looking at my train memorabilia, I see. I finally framed those this summer, a shame to have them all in boxes."

"Wonderful idea." I nodded and returned my gaze to the wall opposite my face. Fortunately for me, the wall was filled with old train-route maps, photos of steam trains, and even old, yellowed schedules.

"Won't be a moment." He was gone again.

I worked fast now, unscrewing the plastic mouthpiece cover and inserting my bug as instructed. I then replaced the cover, quickly unscrewed the earpiece and planted my bug there, then walked back to my chair at a leisurely pace. After I left, I would reconnoiter and install the recorder in what I hoped would be a far more accessible place. The bugs were actually tiny radio transmitters, and the salesman had assured me that as long as I placed the recorder in or near the same building as the bugs, the setup would work beautifully.

Romney was quick about the tea: Before I'd sat down again, he was back in the room, bearing a tray that held a plate of shortbread and two steaming mugs.

"I'll show you something, if you're interested," he said, placing the tray on the footrest and indicating the memorabilia wall with his head. He walked back toward it, looking at the simple frames housing his carefully matted treasures. "Some of this is quite rare. As I recall, you were interested in trains."

"You have an excellent memory, Romney."

"Are you all right?" He had turned to look at me as I got up, and there was concern in his face.

"Why, of course," I laughed. "Why do you ask?" What was he playing at now? I wondered.

"It looked like you had a bit of trouble getting up just then.

You don't really look very well, now that I think of it. Are you ill, or is it just a rowing injury?" He appeared to be serious.

I looked at him. It was a bit much for him to pretend he didn't know about the fire. There was no doubt in my mind who had set it.

Two could play at this game, I thought.

"How did you know?" I tried to assume a mildly chagrined expression.

"Ah, I was right." He smiled, relieved. "Another Plumtree doing battle with the oars. I hope it wasn't too serious."

I smiled in embarrassment. "If you must know, Romney, I tripped as we were carrying the shell up the path to the boathouse. Terribly clumsy of me. Fortunately, no one else was hurt. And the boat was all right."

"Well, as long as the boat's all right." He chortled at his little joke and cast one more appraising glance over me, looking at my eyes particularly, and began his tour through steam train memorabilia. I felt as if we were both on a stage, acting out a farce. Eventually he turned and ushered me back to the chairs.

"Have some tea. It'll help what ails you. Help yourself to biscuits, too. I'm very eager to hear what you've got to say about Arthur." He picked up a shortbread finger and bit into it with relish. "To tell you the truth," he said through a mouthful of crumbs, "after our last talk I didn't think you were going to cooperate with me."

He was a clever one, all right. Some day, perhaps after he was in prison, I would have to ask him if he'd studied drama in university.

"I won't deny that I was shocked at what you had to say about Arthur, and Barnes, for that matter," I said. "But I've been thinking about it—Arthur in particular—and decided I should share with you all the information I've got, no matter how trivial it seems."

Romney's eyes glimmered with the hope of forthcoming information, but he just nodded and kept chewing. Behind the charade I could tell that he was virtually holding his breath. Evidently, whatever meager information I possessed was still more than he had. I would give him insignificant but truthful details, none of which would help him track down Ian any more than they had helped me.

I took a sip of tea to keep him in suspense for a moment longer. It was ordinary PG Tips, and it soothed my smoke-burned throat.

"The first thing I thought of is that Arthur appears to be an older man. The tone of his prose, his obviously first-hand description of the war, and the conditions of the various towns at the time . . . I think all of those things indicate that he is of an age to have fought in the war, say, sixty-seven or so."

Romney's face registered disappointment before he could mask it.

"Very interesting," he said. "Go on."

He put down his tea and leaned on one elbow, chin in hand.

"I'm not sure what this next item is worth, but he always communicated with us by facsimile. That indicates to me that he is up to date, a bright, interested person who keeps in touch with new developments. He does all his writing on a personal computer, which further supports this thought. He must be a man of some means, because when his manuscripts come through the mail, they are laser printed. That's quite a bit more expensive than using a dot matrix printer."

He nodded and continued to look at me, though by now I thought he looked fairly disgusted. He hadn't expected this sort of meaningless trivia.

"And there's one more thing." I paused. "When we do get things through the post, they come with a London postmark."

He continued to look at me for a moment after I'd finished, then sat forward. Now he wore no expression whatsoever. I hoped my face was as empty of information.

"Alex," he said casually, leaning forward for another biscuit. His eyes rested on the Portmeirion botanical plate for a moment as he selected a bourbon cream, then returned to my face. "Are you mocking me?"

I'm not sure what I expected, but it wasn't outright confrontation. I thought we had a tacit agreement to play the game.

"What do you mean?" I answered a touch defensively.

He chewed and looked at me without wavering, his head tilted slightly to one side. "I mean that I think you came here knowing that this information would be of little use to me. And I don't think you came just to see the train set after all these years."

He let this sit there like a small black cloud. He was neither angry nor hurt, but bemused.

"I'm sure I don't know what you're talking about. Didn't you ask me to call you if I thought of anything?" I did my best to look wrongly accused.

After a moment he leaned back in his chair and took a long sip of tea, then put his mug down with finality. "Yes. Well. As long as you're here, is there anything else you'd like to tell me, Alex?"

I shrugged. "I've told you everything I can think of," I said.

How could it be that I liked the man, despite everything he had done to make my life miserable? Perhaps I had jumped to conclusions. Maybe he wasn't the murderous fiend I thought he was. But then Rupert had convinced me of the same thing, and the next time I saw him he'd denounced my father on national television. I continued my charade for lack of a better idea.

"I'm sorry that it's of no use to you," I said.

I got to my feet and went to the door. He rose and followed me, then reached around me to open the door. I stepped through the doorway into the cloud-dappled sunshine.

"Alex." I turned to face him. "Thanks for keeping in touch. Come again, whether you have news or not. And be careful on those boat paths." He nodded cordially, the beginnings of a smile on his lips, and closed the door behind me.

Things were becoming more complicated by the minute. I trusted this man, even liked him. Was it his acting? Perhaps my ability to judge character was slipping; I'd always considered myself rather good at it. But remember what he said about Barnes, I told myself.

I plodded down the path to the car and told my mind to give it a rest. In time, my mind would sort out all of this on its own. It couldn't be rushed, and certainly not with millions of microscopic particles of burned rugs, paint, and furniture clogging it.

I got into the car with a slight straining of bandages, wishing that just one company in the world made cars for tall people, and looked out at Romney's house. I just couldn't see prowling around in broad daylight in a neighborhood like this. I was sure to be spotted by a little old lady having her tea by the window. I would have to come back when it was dark.

I shifted into first and set off for my next destination. It was three o'clock already. I'd let go for far too long the errand of doing some research on the relocated children of London in World War II. Even when I thought Arthur's book was fiction, I'd wanted to go to the British Library and enlist the help of a really good reference librarian to help me read up on the subject. I had never done it, and now it had been several days since I'd learned that the events of the novel had indeed taken place. Now it was more important than ever to me to find out what had actually happened.

As I drove back to London I thought that I would have to park in an out-of-the-way place on the far side of the library from Bedford Square. The library was only a couple of blocks away from the square, and it was possible that someone might recognize my car there. I should have bought something inconspicuous, like a gray Rover. My dark green Golf was just uncommon enough to render it a nuisance in these circumstances.

I involuntarily glanced in the rearview mirror, thinking of the car that had followed me to Threepwood. That car wasn't in sight, but I took stock of the others behind me and made a mental note to see if they followed me off the A40.

None did, and I parked successfully on a quiet side street off Russell Square near the library, wondering if I was becoming paranoid. My stomach was growling, and in order not to disturb the rest of the library, I ducked into an unremarkable pub called The Book and Binder and had the inevitable roast beef sandwich and orange juice. My body evidently expected to be compensated for the twelve hours I had deprived it of food the day before. I ate with a ravenous hunger and didn't even care that everything still smelled and tasted like smoke.

Body and mind seemed remarkably cheered by the lunch, and I walked out of the dark-paneled pub feeling almost good. My world might be falling apart around me, but they hadn't stopped me yet, and that was something.

The librarians had me fixed up in no time. Feeling like a university student again, I sat at a long table accommodating eight other readers and bent my head to the books they'd found. Two books in particular were dedicated to the experience of children in the war, including evacuation. I read them eagerly, skimming until I came to relevant sections.

I learned that the first wave of children was evacuated in September 1939, when the government decided that the threat of German bombs falling on London would soon become a reality. More than 750,000 children left London for the English, Welsh, and Scottish countryside. The children's teachers managed the exodus, and neither children nor teachers knew their destination when they marched together from their schools to the train station. Children were identified by large nametags that hung from their necks.

By the end of their evacuation day, many of the children were standing in a strange school in a faraway corner of Britain, hoping that they wouldn't be the last to be selected by a foster parent. Others were billeted in large country homes or public schools until accommodation could be arranged.

In all the books I found repeated references to the differences between these streetsmart Londoners and their foster families; many of the evacuees were quite poor, as the wealthier people had been able to make their own arrangements for living in the country. In general, the evacuees were considered undesirable by the families who were asked to take them in, and in some cases this attitude was reflected in the children's treatment. I had never thought of that aspect of the evacuation before.

The more I read, the more the thought of keeping track of all those children boggled my mind. But according to these volumes, at least, there were remarkably few difficulties in the whole process. Occasionally a child ran away and got lost, but within several weeks the Red Cross was able to tell the child's parents where he or she was.

Almost a year later there was a second evacuation. France had fallen, and a German invasion of England seemed imminent. A number of the children originally evacuated had returned home in the intervening year, and others had never left in the first place. The government strongly encouraged parents to send away their children, this time not just to the countryside, but out of the country. England was flooded with offers of help from private citizens and charities in Canada, New Zealand, and the United States.

To manage the evacuation process, the government formed the Children's Overseas Reception Board (CORB). The children eligible for government-sponsored evacuation overseas were those between the ages of five and sixteen attending grant-aided schools, who had good teeth and had been cured of impetigo and lice. Two hundred and ten thousand children applied by July 4, 1940, and 94 percent came from working-class families, as the sailings were free.

Fascinated, I read that the CORB sailings stopped almost as soon as they'd begun due to several unfortunate difficulties. One was a rumor that wealthy children were taking places on the ships that should have been given to working-class children. This criticism of the program spread to the House of Commons, where MPs claimed that CORB favored the rich, and the government was pressured to put an end to it. I shook my head, incredulous that there had been so much class struggle, even in wartime.

Sadly, there was also the problem of the children's safety. A number of the evacuation vessels were lost, among them the *City of Benares* on September 13, 1940. There were four hundred crew members and passengers on the ship, among them ninety children and nine escorts. Only seven children and two escorts from the CORB program were among the one hundred survivors.

I held my breath when I read on the next page that *six hundred* more children barely escaped disaster when their sailing was canceled just as they were about to board on September 30, the day the government discontinued the CORB program to satisfy its critics. Six hours later, the ship sank.

There was one bittersweet story about a woman who, at the last moment, couldn't bear to let her children go on the ship that would take them to the United States. Saying she had a premonition that something terrible would happen if they went, she led them home again from the docks. Two days later, they learned that the entire ship had been lost.

I turned the page. It seemed that even if the political and safety issues hadn't been in the way, the lack of ships—both liners for passengers and warships for escorts—would have stopped the sailings. The Admiralty needed all of the vessels it could muster for fighting off the invasion and couldn't allocate them to escorting children.

But private sailings continued for a short time, partially funded by charities and citizens. This was what had allowed the disaster chronicled in *Deliver Us From Evil* to take place. I shook my head and thought of all the kind people who had made the evacuation such a remarkable success. Now their record had been blemished, and it wasn't fair.

The people involved in administering the evacuation and caring for the children once they got to the United States had gone to great pains to ensure that the children were properly cared for. The *Deliver Us* disaster certainly hadn't happened through any lack of diligence on their part. In fact, people cared so much that they fought to change the law to allow the children in. Evidently some obscure child labor law prevented "unknown" children, that is, children whose parents didn't have friends in the United States, from entering the country. But in that same year of 1940 the U.S. Attorney General ruled that a charity or nonprofit corporation could guarantee the support of numbers of unspecified children, and within forty-eight hours receive blank visas for them. So that was how they'd done it.

I sat up and rubbed my hands over my face. There was a lot of detail here, but all of it was important if I were to understand the kidnapper. I sighed and thought that it would be much easier if I could just get my hands on the last five chapters of the sequel.

Plodding on, I repeatedly saw mention of the U.S. Committee for the Care of European Children, which was based in London. It had come into existence because people worried about the children being brought into the U.S. haphazardly, without a central authority to coordinate their care. How right they had been to worry, I thought. The Committee set up 170 local committees across the U.S. to interview prospective foster parents and worked out detailed standards even for the temporary shelters in which the children were placed. In October of 1940, after a good number of children were already in the United States, the Committee, through immigration reports, did its best to compile a central registry of all foreign children who entered the country unaccompanied after September 1, 1938.

Even this massive effort to keep track of the children hadn't foiled the kidnapper. He'd been clever, all right; he'd burned the records, and somehow he'd managed to get a boatload of younger children, many of them below the five-year-old minimum. His dirty work had been done before they ever reached the United States, so everything looked to be in order once they were there.

If only the Committee had known to worry about the charity officials, I thought. The kidnapper had to be someone like that, with authority and yet access to the children. Perhaps an escort, even, who made the trip overseas with them. But who would have thought that anyone involved with a charitable effort would kidnap children?

I read on, skimming some photocopies of magazine clippings the librarian cheerfully added to my pile. In some cases the people who sent their children abroad were well-connected upper-class families who knew similar families in the United States. The children of a certain lord and lady, for instance, went to live with a prominent American family in their mansion on Long Island. It was children such as these who received a good deal of the press coverage, and I looked at a news clipping from *Time* magazine that showed the lord and lady's children frolicking in the green fields surrounding their foster family's manse.

But there were only so many children of lords and ladies in Britain. Far more children, the ones whose families couldn't afford to evacuate the children themselves, went to families whom their parents didn't know. Though they were of course well cared for in those unknown families, those children were far more vulnerable to the *Deliver Us From Evil* plot than their well-heeled compatriots. It would have made the papers had the lord and lady been notified that their children died in an accident before making the trip to the United States, and that there were no identifiable remains. It also would have made the papers had the lord and lady's children been notified that their parents had died in the bombing and that the children would henceforth live in the Long Island manse.

But it would have been entirely believable to temporary American guardians that the parents of their charges had died in bombings in London—they read the news; they knew that it happened every day. Tragically, the children's real parents, back in London, had no reason to disbelieve a telegram informing them that their children died before arriving safely overseas. And since they didn't know the child's destination when the boat left, they couldn't even contact the foster family.

One newspaper story in my pile of clippings showed parents kneeling and sobbing at the site where their child supposedly died in a freak accident in Southampton before boarding the ship to sail to America.

I rested my head in my hands for a moment, trying to comprehend the cruelty of the person who sent those telegrams, the desire to cause so much unnecessary suffering in an already-suffering people. Who was capable of such a well-planned, grotesque operation? I couldn't believe that my father and Ian were.

What had Romney been doing during the war? Rupert? How could I find out?

I turned back to an article that discussed all of the relief efforts on the part of American charities. Dozens of them had sponsored sailings, some in cooperation with British charities. I reread the section that explained that Humanitarian Efforts by the League of Publishers (HELP), the children's charity that had become Publishers for Literacy after the war, had cosponsored a couple of sailings. I focused again on the paragraph that said the Anglo-American Liaison team in Washington had assisted in coordinating the evacuation activities at first, but had to back out and dedicate its limited staff to other urgent matters. Someone could easily make a case that Ian and my father had been in on the plot. Not only were they part of the Anglo-American Liaison staff but they had both been involved in Publishers for Literacy, or HELP at the time.

I sighed and looked at my watch. Six o'clock already. I would check one last thing and go.

Remembering that Barnes's review had mentioned something about money being the motivation for the kidnappings, about £250,000 worth, I checked the index of the most detailed book for mention of fees, finances, and donations. There it was in dollars. At the time, one dollar was worth .25 pounds, or four dollars to the pound. For each child sponsored, the charity had to pay $50 to be deposited by the committee in the government-required trust fund. They also paid $8 as a "head tax," and $2.50 as a visa charge. There were also transport fees, which amounted to around $75 per child.

I sat back and thought about it. Parents who badly wanted to help a child certainly wouldn't balk at paying even more than $135.50. The kidnapper probably asked for a great deal more, claiming that they had had to pay extra for the use of the ship because of the great demand for them, and just pocketed the difference himself. I decided I'd got enough of a feel for the situation for the moment and thanked the librarians.

The next item on my itinerary was Ian's house on Gower

Street. With the stories of the children still very much in my mind, I left the car where it was and approached Gower Street from the back, behind the University College buildings. To travel on Gower itself meant walking past the office. It was dark, of course, but all I needed was to have our errand boy spot me on his way home and spread the word that I was wandering aimlessly about the area. In fact, I'd read a mystery once in which the office gopher was the accomplice of villains, and reported to the villains on his boss's every movement.

You sound paranoid, Plumtree; stop it.

I walked as quickly as I could around the corner to Gower Street, then up the three houses to Ian's. Grateful that I'd had my keys with me at the time of the fire, I separated his from my bunch of a dozen, unlocked his front door, and slipped inside, pushing the big door shut behind me.

I flipped on the entry hall light, as it had long since grown dark. All was peaceful and quiet. The steady ticking of his grandfather clock was soothing after the noise of the street, and my smoky nostrils thought they detected a touch of patchouli in the air.

I walked into the living room and turned on a table lamp. Ian hadn't so much decorated his flat as allowed it to express itself. He'd painted the walls an off-white, then filled it with colorful Indian rugs and an eclectic mixture of old maps, original artwork, and books. I liked it very much, and my visits here had inspired me to do much the same with my own garret at Bedford Square.

I'd never given much thought to where Ian went on his vacations and assumed that he enjoyed the freedom of going wherever he pleased on the spur of the moment. Over a pint at the pub or dinner on a lonely weekend evening we had talked much of sailing, and I knew he had traveled widely by yacht, to many more far-flung destinations than I had in my flotilla sailing days. But I never attempted to question him about where he had been on the last holiday or where he was going on the next.

I flopped into a deeply padded white wool armchair. How to go about finding Ian from his personal belongings? I looked around the walls, my eyes taking in a map of the Gulf of Thailand, with what looked like ideal sailing waters. Next to it was a map of Cape Cod in Massachusetts, with Martha's Vineyard and Nantucket included.

Sailing charts, I thought. Ian must have an entire library of sailing charts that would tell me where he had been, where he liked to go.

I got up and walked into his study, flipping on the wall switch. His desk was cluttered with paper as usual, and the file cabinets hung open with random bits of paper sticking out of various folders. There was another, larger cabinet against one wall, about four feet wide by four feet deep, and I opened its door. It was very much like a display case for art prints at a museum; a rack perpendicular to the wall slid out and revealed a number of plastic pockets suspended from the spine at the wall end, each of which held a sailing chart. I flipped through and found charts for Yugoslavia, Turkey, Greece, the Virgin Islands, Denmark, San Francisco Bay, Monterey, Mexico, France, and, once again, Nantucket Island.

If Ian were Arthur, he would have known Nantucket well. As the book portrayed the story, he had not only spent time there on his leaves during and immediately after the war but had returned there later in life with his friend—evidently my father—to continue his search for the kidnapper.

Perhaps Ian was sailing off Nantucket now or had run into trouble there.

But the chart was here. Wouldn't he have taken it if he'd gone sailing there? I let my mind chip away at the problem as I stared at the chart. Why go to Nantucket now, with the mystery solved?

It flashed through my mind that all of a sudden there was a great deal going on in Massachusetts that was related to me. Was it coincidence? I had been in Boston three times in the last month to visit Charlie's Bookarama, and Simon Bow's American subsidiary was also located there. Nantucket had been prominent in my father's diaries, as had "Windborne Island" in Arthur's novels. And it just so happened that Sarah's parents, long time suburban Bostonians, had now retired there as well.

I closed the cabinet again and sat down at his desk, suddenly feeling very tired. He could be anywhere. I had no idea where he was, and my mind hadn't yet come up with any bright ideas as to how to track him from what was here in his house. I sat for a moment, enjoying the calm of the place and the closeness to Ian.

It was inexplicable, but I had the feeling he was alive. It might be unlike Arthur to drop out of sight with only a hundred pages to go, but this was not the home of someone who no longer existed. If Romney's people—or others—were holding him somewhere, or if he was in danger or distress at sea, he had survived.

So far.

The thought got me up and moving again, out of the flat. I wasn't getting anywhere here.

Seven o'clock. I had planned to meet Sarah after work, ostensibly to remind her to be careful and not walk into dark alleys alone until this ordeal was over. Once I had spoken to her I'd leave, or at least she would think so, but I planned to follow her home to ensure that she arrived safely. I didn't worry about her at work with her colleagues, or at home with her roommate, but I did worry about the times in between. On a jammed Underground platform people might not notice a man quietly threatening a woman and forcing her to go with him.

I had enough time to get there, since she never left work until seven-thirty or eight, and decided to take the tube. I walked to Russell Square instead of Tottenham Court Road in order to avoid passing the office, and made my way to the Bank station. On the way to her building, I approached a pub that had people pouring out of its door onto the street, laughing and teasing one another. An office party of some sort, I thought.

I remembered times that we'd had like that at Plumtree, celebrations over Arthur's success, and more raucous occasions with the sailing company staff. I liked to think that there would be times like that again when all of this was over, though I couldn't be sure that it ever would end. What if I never found Arthur—Ian—and never proved Max's article and Rupert Soames's statements about my father wrong? What if they got to me before I got to them?

Stop it.

Then I heard them, young voices from the pavement I'd just passed in front of the pub.

"Oy, wasn't that the young Plumtree?" He didn't make much of an attempt to lower his voice. "You know, the publisher. The esteemed MP's son." He guffawed.

"Yeah," another said slowly. "You're right. Some high and mighty family that turned out to be. Father's a war criminal, namesake's a crackhead, and this one's hiding that Arthur bloke."

"Gawd, I couldn't believe that story in the paper," said a high, sarcastic voice. "By his own son, too."

"Shhhh," one of them said. "He might hear you."

I kept walking. In time they'd know they'd been wrong.

After I'd milled about with others on the pavement outside Sarah's office block for forty-five minutes, I saw her. She came out of the door with a startlingly good-looking blond man. She threw back her head and laughed at something he said as they turned together and walked down the street, her dark, shiny hair bouncing.

Well, well, I thought bitterly. At least I know she'll be safe. He won't let her out of his sight for a moment.

I paused for a moment as they were absorbed in the stream of people hurrying away from work and flowed farther and farther away, almost out of sight. Was it decent to follow them?

I couldn't help myself. I hurried after them and when I got to within about thirty feet, I kept my distance. After five minutes of more laughing and high-spirited talk, they turned into La Grenouille, one of the city's best French restaurants.

What did you expect? I asked myself angrily. She had never said she wanted to go out with me, and I had brought her little but trouble recently. I had even less to offer her now than I had a week ago. Even if my company went belly up, I could have offered her a proud family heritage. Now that was gone, too, unless I could do something about it. Exactly what that would be, I didn't know.

I turned and plodded in the dark back to the tube station, then got off at Russell Square and reclaimed my car. The phone was ringing when I got to it, and I quickly unlocked the door, got in, and picked it up.

"At last," Sarah said with exasperation. She must have called from the restaurant. "I've been trying to call you all day at Lisette's. She told me you were there. As a last resort I tried your number at the flat, but . . . where are you? I hear noises in the background."

"I'm in my car—I had the number switched to a car phone." It was hard to keep the disappointment out of my voice. I should have realized long ago that she was seeing someone else; she'd certainly made it clear that she wasn't interested in me.

"Oh." She sounded a little puzzled.

"Where are you going?"

"Back to Lisette's." It wasn't exactly a lie; I was headed there for some much-needed fellowship with friends after I placed Romney's tape recorder.

"Well, are you all right? Feeling okay? You sound a little quiet." I heard muffled restaurant noises and classical music in the background.

"I'm fine. Listen, Sarah, I wanted to mention to you—"

But she was already talking again, evidently unable to hear me because of the noise.

"Okay. Well, take care, then. I can't talk now, but call me tomorrow—let me know if there's anything I can do." She didn't sound enthusiastic, just busy. "Bye for now."

She was gone. I turned off the phone and sat for a moment with it in my hand, too discouraged to make the effort required to place it in its holder. I could see them sharing a bottle of Veuve Cliquot by candlelight, laughing as they had at the office door. I had never felt more discouraged in my life. I rested my forehead against the top of the leather steering wheel and allowed my shoulders to slump forward.

The phone started to ring again immediately, and I let it go. I didn't know what I would say to anyone who called, especially if it was the eerie voice that made the threat when I was at the office.

Sarah. If only I had her beside me, I could do anything . . .

I sat up suddenly, eyes wide, as a horrible thought occurred to me. I might not want to answer the phone, afraid of another threat. But if I didn't, I might not be where I had to be to save Sarah's life. I had tried to tell her on the phone to be careful, to stay around other people, that she might be in danger, but she hadn't heard.

Perhaps the golden-haired boy would stay very close to her indeed, and I needn't worry.

I took a deep breath and picked up the phone. "Hello."

"Alex! *Mon Dieu!* We have been so worried!" I heard her cover the mouthpiece and say to George, "It's Alex. I've got him. It's okay." Then to me, "Are you all right? Where have you been? I didn't even know how to tell Charlie to reach you." Good. She wasn't really angry.

"Thank God for that. I'm sorry I worried you, Lisette. I'm perfectly all right. I had a few things to check into today, and now I'm back in my car on a car phone."

"Mmm." She didn't like the sound of that. "I found your note. We thought you were probably all right, but you should be resting. You looked so tired, and—"

"Lisette, you're obsessing again. It's very kind of you to be so concerned, but—"

"You don't sound right to me."

I closed my eyes and smiled in spite of myself. "Why don't you let me tell you all about it at dinner? I have just one more errand to do, but if you and George will still have me, I'll be there in an hour or so."

She cheered up considerably at this. "Good. We will be waiting for you. Your coq au vin will be *fini.*"

We said good-bye and I started the car, grateful for the comfort of their friendship. Where I would be without them, I didn't know. Sleeping in the car, I supposed, and eating at McDonald's. It would have been hopelessly depressing without the thought of their well-lit home and friendly faces urging me on.

I drove back to Chalfont St. Giles and parked up the road from Romney's. The miniature tape recorder was still in the pocket of my new leather jacket. I touched it and hoped that I could find an appropriate place for it, and also hoped that none of Romney's neighbors would happen to look out of their windows.

According to the man in the electronics store, all I had to do was put the recorder in an inconspicuous place and set the switch to "on."

I got out of the car and hiked back to Romney's neighbor's yard, then jogged back to the treeline, where I hovered for a moment. No lights snapped on; no voices shouted. As far as I could tell, I hadn't been spotted.

I stepped over a line of shrubs delineating the property boundaries and walked over to the woods in back of Romney's house, where I waited again for a moment before advancing up the garden toward the cottage. When I was twenty feet or so from the house, I stopped to take a closer look.

There was an appendage to the main house, a rustic-looking shed that might have been there for three centuries like the rest of the place. It was hard to tell. It had been meticulously whitewashed, like everything else, but was small. I wondered if he had knocked the wall through to make it a pantry, or if it were some sort of garden shed. Either way, it might make the perfect place for an inconspicuous little tape-recorder-cum-receiver.

I decided to check it out and tiptoed up the garden path. The house was completely dark from the back, and I speculated wishfully that perhaps Romney was out for the evening. Drawing even with the shed, I noticed that it had a side door. I tried the latch, a simple old-fashioned black bar that lifted out of its bracket, and stepped inside.

It was so easy, I could have sworn it was a trap. I quickly closed the door behind me and waited for my eyes to adjust to the darkness. I heard absolutely nothing in the meantime, and it made me envy Romney's life in the country. After ten seconds or so of blinking and looking around, it became clear that this was Romney's garden shed. His spade, hoe, shovels, and pots lined the walls. Could it be that the Romney I knew also grew carrots? Or daffodils?

I shook my head at the irony of it all and looked for a suitable place for my particular variety of plant. I found it against the wall shared with the house, under an upside-down terra-cotta flowerpot. Not wanting to waste time, I took the tape recorder out of my pocket, used my fingernail to flip the tiny switch on the side to "on," and set it on the ground. The man at the electronics shop had already inserted a tape in the machine and given me several spares, which remained in my pocket for future use. I put the flowerpot back in place and prayed that it would work.

Then I ran back to the car and drove like a madman to George and Lisette's in Couch End.

In front of a fire after dinner I told them some of what I had done that day, excluding Romney Marsh and the surveillance gear as well as Sarah. The boys had gone to bed an hour before.

"You don't hang about, do you?" said George incredulously. "And I envisioned you languishing in the guest bed with a book. Not without envy, I must say." He shook his head. "Should have known."

"I told him—"

The doorbell interrupted Lisette, and she looked at her watch. "A bit late for someone to call, isn't it?"

George stood, frowning, and went to the door.

"George Stoneham?"

"Yes." George took in the two blue uniforms of the local constable's behind the short, dark man in an oversized raincoat who was speaking. "Is there a problem?"

"I'm Inspector McLeish. We're looking for Alex Plumtree to assist us with our inquiries. We've been told that he might be staying here."

"Well, yes—come in, please."

McLeish was the caricature of a Scotsman, with big bushy eyebrows that angled off in all directions, and a bold, forthright manner. I liked him immediately, though, as it turned out, not what he had to say.

He walked into the room and caught sight of Lisette and me on the sofa. "Mr. Plumtree." He recognized me right away. "Would you like to talk in private, sir?"

I looked at Lisette and George, who looked concerned. As far as I was concerned, anything he had to say they could hear. "No, this is fine."

"Please, Inspector. Sit down." George indicated that the Inspector should take his place on the opposite side of the L-shaped sofa from me, and started to get chairs for the constables. Lisette watched, speechless, from her perch on the edge of the sofa.

"Thanks very much, sir, but these boys will wait outside, keep an eye on things." They left, closing the door behind them. He sat down, opened his mackintosh, and extracted a small spiral-bound notebook from an inner jacket pocket.

"Coffee, Inspector?"

"No, thank you."

"Something else?"

"No. Thanks."

"Would you like me to take your coat?"

"I'll keep it, thanks."

"George!" Lisette exploded in one of her incendiary outbursts. "Would you stop asking questions and give the man a chance to tell us why he is here?!" We all looked at her, wondering where this had come from. She must really be concerned, I thought.

In total exasperation she turned to poor Inspector McLeish. "Well?"

She didn't faze him in the least. "I am here because evidence has been found which suggests that you, sir," he looked at me meaningfully, "murdered Barnes Appleton."

The three of us probably gave a reasonable impression of a small school of goldfish. Lisette was the first to speak.

"You can't be serious. I mean, you can't just say something like that! You—you have to have proof!" She got up and stood directly in front of the inspector, forefinger raised. To his credit, he held her eye and did not flinch.

"Lisette, darling, the man is just doing his job," George said soothingly. "Let him explain. Besides, he said he *did* have proof."

I looked at George and raised my eyebrows.

"Sorry, Alex—I didn't mean it the way it sounds. Of course you didn't murder Barnes." George laughed nervously. "I'm merely repeating what the man said."

All eyes returned to McLeish. After a moment, Lisette sat down, glaring at him suspiciously.

"Thank you. I'll be happy to tell you the rest of it. The reason I didn't just haul you down to the station and lock you up is that the whole thing looks a bit odd to me, and to tell the truth, I don't really think you did it."

He paused and my heart started beating again.

"But I do need to ask you some questions, and I'd appreciate it if you wouldn't take any sudden trips to faraway destinations just now."

"I understand." I swallowed. Romney, or Max, or someone, was certainly making sure that I knew he was displeased over my failure to turn over the manuscript. "What exactly is it you've found, Inspector?"

He nodded and relaxed a bit back into the sofa, crossing his arms. I had the feeling that he relished this. "As you may know, sir, Mr. Appleton's wife repeatedly asked us to consider his death something other than an accident. We went back and looked at the body again from that point of view and saw that the bruises he had could have been consistent with a struggle. Sloppy work not to have found it the first time round, actually, but then we weren't looking for it."

He cleared his throat, making a sweep of our faces with his eyes. "At any rate. We did another autopsy and found that the

144

wound on his head was more likely caused by a blow with an instrument than a fall on the hearth bricks. The autopsy showed us something else, too; he had so much alcohol in his stomach at once that it suggested he may have been force-fed, so to speak." He looked down as if disgusted at the thought, his first real display of emotion.

Poor Barnes.

"Then we went back through the flat, and though many things had been disturbed since the night of his death, his wife said she hadn't gone near the hearth—couldn't bear to go near those bricks, she said." He looked at us and said confidentially, "Hard to get the stains out, you know."

"Oh my God," Lisette said, sounding choked.

"Yes, well, we checked the fireplace tools for fingerprints—there had been a fire in the fireplace the night of his death, by the way, rainy, cold night—and that's where you come in, sir."

"Sorry?"

He looked at me as if I were a bit thick. He spoke distinctly, as if to one hard of hearing. "That's where we first found your fingerprints."

"You found my fingerprints on Barnes's fireplace tools?"

"Well, not exactly. Not on all of them. Only the poker."

Lisette and George looked at me, uncomprehending. George raised his chin in defiance. "It can't be," he said.

"You have made a most horrible mistake," Lisette said threateningly.

Inspector McLeish put his palms up. "Wait a minute. I already told you I think there's something strange about all of this. The fingerprints were extremely clear, complete. There was absolutely no mistaking whose they were."

He looked at us proudly, and when we returned blank stares, his shoulders fell. He sighed as if disappointed in us. "Well? Don't you see? It was too clear. Fingerprints are never that clear, not in the best of cases. They get smudged, rubbed off, and if the murderer has a grain of intelligence, they disappear completely."

"Now just a minute," George began, as if that had been the last straw. "Are you saying Alex is stupid? Because if you are . . ."

145

"Thanks very much George, but he said if the *murderer* has a grain of intelligence he wipes the weapon clean."

George looked at me in horror. "Of course, of course, yes. I didn't mean that. It's just—"

"You know," Lisette said thoughtfully, "I think I see what the inspecteur is getting to."

"At," George said irritably.

Lisette looked puzzled. "What?"

"What he's getting *at*, not *to*."

Lisette made an almost-animal sound of frustration and threw up her hands. "This is not the time for English lessons!" she shouted. Making a visible effort to compose herself, she said, "I am trying to tell you that the inspecteur is trying to tell us that Alex is too smart to have left his fingerprints on the fireplace poker!" The sentence began in exaggerated calm and ended in an angry fortissimo.

George cringed, and the inspector looked bemused.

I said, "How can you be so sure that I'm not the murderer?"

Lisette and George looked at me aghast, but I was happy to see that Inspector McLeish looked pleasantly surprised.

"Ah. I'm glad you asked. We actually have some quite good evidence to show that you are, in all probability, not the murderer."

He looked as if he'd just swallowed a canary. Obviously he was more concerned with the intellectual challenge of his job than with slamming me in a jail cell and saying the case was closed.

"First, we have Mrs. Appleton's personal reaction to our findings. She expressed total disbelief and anger—at us, mind you, not you—when we told her. She said it wasn't possible, that we had mixed up our files. She had quite a lot to say about you—said her husband had told her all about you." He eyed me with an air of amusement, and I wondered exactly what Barnes had said.

"Second, our records show that two phone calls were made from your home at what we estimate to be the time of death—nine-forty-five P.M." He ventured a smile. "So you see? You couldn't very well have been making phone calls at Bedford Square at nine-forty-five, got all the way to Notting Hill, and murdered Barnes Appleton by nine-fifty."

I breathed an inward sigh of relief. The first phone call had been to directory enquiries to get Barnes's phone number, the

second to Sarah to answer the message she'd left about the regatta.
Lisette and George simultaneously lifted their mugs and took
a gulp of coffee. George coughed.

"It means you were framed, as they say," said Inspector McLeish.

The word sounded sinister, as if it had a life of its own. It made
me think of the people behind the act who wished me ill. No, Alex,
they don't wish you ill; they wish you dead. I felt a tickling sensation
on my arms as the hairs were raised by gooseflesh.

"And now I have some questions for you," said the inspector
matter-of-factly, uncrossing his arms and finally putting pencil to
paper. "I understand that you were at a party with Barnes on the
night of his death. Tell me about it."

Our eyes met for a moment, and I realized that this was the end
of my privacy, what was left of it. True, my family's life had already
been ripped open and poured out for public consumption, and what
the public had was not even the truth—we had been lied about,
maligned.

But once I told the police everything, it would be worse. The
financial condition of the company, the fact that my brother was
somehow involved and might have tried to kill Barnes or me that
night—these were not things that I wanted splashed on the front
page of the tabloids.

A strange look had come over the inspector's face, something
akin to suspicion, and I realized I had been thinking too long. I
quickly decided I would tell him everything about the party with the
exception of my real motive for being there.

I began by explaining that I had spotted Barnes across the
room and walked over to say hello. At first, Inspector McLeish
watched me intently as I spoke. But as the story continued he
apparently became satisfied that I was telling the truth and spent
more and more time looking down at his little book as he scribbled
furiously. He listened without interrupting and scribbled faster
when I described Barnes's cryptic comments about "something very
big" having happened with Arthur's book that "someone" didn't
want made public. I ended the story with my attempt to reach
Barnes, the subsequent call to Sarah, and reading the manuscript
before bed.

147

When I stopped, he put his head on one side. "You're not stupid," he said.

"Thank you," I said as cheerfully as I could.

He smiled at my attempt at levity. "You have noticed by now that it looks as if someone is rather eager to—er—incapacitate you. The newsprint, the fire—" I looked up. "Oh, yes, I know about the fire. It's all over the paper today."

Of course. It would be all over the paper. Probably under Max's byline, now that the Plumtree saga was his story.

Lisette, bless her, didn't say a word. Neither did George. They both knew about the car park mugging and the break-ins. They looked at me with wide eyes.

"Yes," I said. "I know."

"Any idea why?"

The question hung there for a moment. I finally decided upon a simple answer.

"No."

"Hmmm. Must be very puzzling to you."

"Yes, it is, indeed." His eyes bored into mine. They were brown, flecked with gold.

"Well," he said, standing. "I've taken enough of your time tonight. As I said, don't go on any long trips in the next week or so. We might have some questions for you, Mr. Plumtree. You will be staying here?"

"Yes," I said, "if they'll have me."

Lisette waved her hand dismissively and George rolled his eyes. "Do shut up," he said. "Of course you're staying here."

We all walked the inspector to the door.

"Thank you," I said. He looked up at me doubtfully. "For not manacling me and dragging me off to the constable's, or wherever it is you drag people off to."

He nodded and buttoned his coat, then drew himself up to his full height and faced me directly. "Anything else I should know, Alex?" I knew the sudden use of my Christian name was meant to prompt me to pour out my soul.

"No," I said.

"Right, then. Here's my card in case you should think of anything you'd like to tell me. Good night."

He collected his bobbies and they got into the car. George closed the door. "God, what a night," he said, leaning against the back of the door. "Alex, isn't there something we can do? Can't we help you find these people? Shouldn't you have told him about the rest of it?"

They didn't even know all of the rest of it, I thought. The pediment, the threat, the missed rendezvous at the British Library, the "cousin" behind the fire.

"No," I said, shaking my head. "You've been a great deal of help. But I don't want you involved any more than you already are."

They looked hurt.

I didn't want to scare them, but I wanted them to understand my reluctance to draw them in further. "The boys need you," I said gently.

Lisette put her hands to her face. They were shaking. "Oh my God," she said weakly. George put an arm around her.

Suddenly I realized what I should have seen long ago: I had already endangered them. Not just my friends, but their innocent children. I had to get out of there. I was poison to everyone I touched.

"I must go," I said. "Now."

They followed me out to the guest house in silence. I tried to look positive as they helped me pack my few new clothes, partly to reassure them but even more to reassure myself.

"Keep things going for me at the office," I said as we walked out to the car. Then into George's ear, "I'm going to hire a security firm for both the office and here, round the clock." He nodded and tried not to look worried.

"Oh, Alex," Lisette blurted, hugging me as she cried. There was nothing to be said; they wished me the best, but we all knew that their sleeping children were more important.

I gave her a quick kiss on the cheek. "I'm not going to call," I said, "until it's over. Better that way."

George nodded and grabbed my hand, then my forearm with his other hand. "Be careful."

"Where are you going to stay?" Lisette sniffed, then blew her nose.

"I don't know yet, and I wouldn't tell you if I did."

She nodded, then burst into a new round of tears.

I got in the car and drove off. They both waved at me, and I watched them in the rearview mirror until I turned out of the drive. Unsure of where to go, I drove to the only place I really wanted to be: Sarah's.

The phone rang on the way, and I picked it up, wondering what would go wrong next.

"Al! Glad I finally caught you. You okay? Hey—sounds like you're on a car phone." A brief pause. "It's almost midnight there, buddy. You oughta be in bed."

I didn't point out that if I had been in bed, his call would have awakened me. "Don't worry, Charlie. Thanks for the flowers—that was very thoughtful."

"Well, Jeez—I just can't believe all this stuff that's been happening to you. I really wish I could do something to help."

"You could send the contracts over for me to sign, along with the check, if you really want to help." It was worth a try.

His laughter was so raucous I had to hold the phone away from my ear. "No can do, Al, you know that." An entire millisecond of silence followed, and it made me wonder if perhaps he sincerely regretted that he couldn't do it my way. "But listen. I've got an idea. Why don't you come out here for the weekend? Sign the contracts, spend a quiet couple of days with my wife and me looking at the foliage. Kick back and relax. We'll have a check for the initial payment ready for you to take back on Monday." I realized too late that he was taking my stunned silence at his outrageous suggestion for an acceptance. "Excellent! I'll call and arrange for a ticket to be left at the British Airways counter for you for the Friday night flight from Heathrow."

"Wait, Charlie, you don't understand. I can't—" Click. The man was a hopeless case. Kind as they come, but he lived in a dream world where everything turned out the way he wanted it to. I wondered what his wife was like and felt a little sorry for her.

I didn't have the energy to call him back right away, but as I hung up I told myself I'd do it tomorrow. He could always cancel the ticket and get his money back.

I found a good spot on Sarah's street where I could see the entrance to her house clearly. I got the blankets I kept in the trunk for emergencies and wrapped them around me, reclining my seat all the way back. I called the security firm my father had used to watch The Orchard when we were on holiday, and asked them to immediately, yes, even at this hour, even if it cost a bomb, put a couple of men on George and Lisette's house around the clock. I asked them to be as unobtrusive as possible, but told them that there were two young children in the house who might be the targets of accomplished kidnappers.

I also asked to have one man outside and one man inside Plumtree Press from eight o'clock weekday mornings until the last person went home at night. Marginally comforted, I settled in for a long night as Sarah's own personal security service, prepared to respond to whatever disaster might arise.

Half an hour later, it came. I heard voices on the pavement behind me, and my eyes snapped open. I must have fallen asleep. I unwrapped my left hand from the blanket and yawned. Midnight. There was laughter, two sets of shoes tapping as they came from the direction of the train station. I would know that voice anywhere. Sarah and Prince Charming were home at last.

I adjusted the rearview mirror to see them better, but they were already close enough to be in my blind spot. Their conversation was audible, coming into focus as they came closer. The words of the man at the electronics shop came back to me and I grimaced. I might hear things I would wish I hadn't.

". . . really funny thing is that he'll never even know how it happened." She sounded tired but happy.

Who would never know? I wondered. How what happened?

"Even considering everything we know, you have to feel sorry for the guy." So he was American. Perhaps that was it; she felt more comfortable with someone of her own nationality.

No, I told myself; stop making excuses. She just isn't attracted to you.

They were right next to the car now. It was ridiculous to think that she would actually look at the cars parked along her street, but they were so close . . . if she looked over and saw my familiar car with its Bedford Square resident's parking sticker on the windscreen or glanced inside and saw me swaddled in blankets like an invalid while the American film star looked on . . .

Walk on. Please, please, walk on.

They stopped by my left front fender. I held my breath and tried, without actually moving, to shrink back into the darkness as he put his arm around her. He gave her a strong, familiar squeeze, as if they'd known one another all their lives. He was obviously very certain of her feelings for him. Someone from her past, I thought; a longtime family friend, now grown to be more. Sarah was facing me. She looked serene, her shoulders relaxed, not at all uncomfortable with his closeness or his touch as she was with mine.

"I know," she said, shaking her head. "Especially with all that business in the paper. I'm surprised he can hold his head up."

My God, I thought. They were talking about me.

"Yeah," he said. "Shame about that. Well, here's my car—I'll say good night. See you tomorrow." My heart stopped for a moment, wondering if she would look at his car and notice mine behind it. But she wasn't thinking of such things. She was looking up at his face, as relaxed and happy as I'd ever seen her.

She gave him a peck on the cheek. "Thank you, Rob. It was a lovely night."

She looked back once and waved from her door as he drove off, and I thought she might spot me. But, as usual, I needn't have worried; she was oblivious to me.

I watched her disappear into the house, feeling displaced. Even the boxwood around her house looked foreign all of a sudden, like something I'd never seen for what it was. I might as well have been on another planet. My home was gone, Arthur gone, Ian gone, my company all but gone, and I had been able to accept those facts by clinging to the hope that Sarah might some day come to care about me. It was a worse blow than all of the others to find that she wasn't as perfect as I thought she was.

It was impossible for me to be angry with her, but I was filled with bleak disappointment. And I had to stay in touch with her; she had the manuscript. What was it she had said to Prince Charming? Something like, "The strange thing is, he'll never even know how it happened."

I looked up at her window and suddenly felt very cold indeed.

7

I awoke when the birds made such a racket that I realized I could endure the cold and stiffness no longer. I hadn't intended to sleep, but I kept waking up and realizing that I had. Still, having awakened at least twenty times since midnight, I wasn't much more refreshed than when the long night began. I had at any rate made it to morning, and I was learning to be grateful for small favors.

More important, I was awake in time to make sure that Sarah wasn't intercepted by one of my unknown enemies on her way to work.

Sarah. Even in the uncertainty of dawn, seen dimly through a windscreen made foggy by body heat and breath, I felt a remnant of certainty that she was the Sarah I thought she was, the woman for whom I would lay down my life and never question the decision. I didn't know how to explain away her remarks of the previous evening, but again, I was willing to wait.

I made myself undo the blankets and wake up; there was no substitute for cold if one wanted to do it properly. With curiosity I peeked under the bandages on my ankle and side; they were both much the same as the day before. As far as I could tell, there was nothing badly wrong.

My watch said six-thirty. I passed the next fifteen minutes wondering just how early she got up. On the infamous hiking trip that she, Peter, my girlfriend, and I had taken, she had been awake before any of us. At seven-fifteen, I thought she must be up soon.

She was. I had barely finished remembering how she'd looked that summer morning—she was just Peter's girlfriend at the tender age of nineteen—when a light came on in Sarah's corner of the house. It was somewhere in the back—probably her bathroom. I'd seen her bedroom and bath a few times and mainly remembered baskets. There were baskets filled with towels, baskets filled with soaps, and baskets filled with flowers—real ones, of course. She loathed anything artificial.

An hour later I saw her come through the door, looking radiant even in an ordinary fawn-colored trenchcoat. She was carrying a black umbrella and walking toward the train station, which meant walking directly past my car again. She did, without so much as a glance, and I let her get almost to the corner before I commanded my legs to change position and go after her. Stiffly, they obeyed. I felt as if I'd been on a coach flight to Australia, and considering the length of my legs, that was no small ordeal. I wasn't sure if I felt more pain or pleasure as I stretched out the kinks on the hill down to the station.

I felt stronger and sharper this morning, possibly because of the disturbing possibility I'd faced last night that Sarah was some-how involved in the manuscript hunt. When faced with the idea that I couldn't trust Sarah, my primary hope and comfort, I had felt like an animal concerned solely with survival—tough, ruthless, every sense alert for possible threats. My intuition said that she was com-pletely trustworthy, but the animal said not to be so naive.

Sarah arrived at work without incident. It occurred to me that it was remarkably easy to follow someone; people did not instinc-tively turn and look behind them, as the movies would have us believe. I had been following Sarah for quite some time and, as familiar as I was to her and as intelligent as she was, she hadn't spotted me. After watching her go through the door I ducked into a coffee bar and turned my mind to deciding which branches of the maze I would explore that day.

A young waitress in jeans and a sweatshirt brought hot coffee and took my order for an omelette and toast. I asked her if I could borrow a pen, and she pulled a black Biro out of her back pocket. "I need it back," she said doubtfully.

I reflected that I probably looked untrustworthy in my rumpled clothes and beard, and reached up self-consciously to feel my whiskers. "Yes, of course. Thanks." I pulled some napkins out of the dispenser on the Formica-topped table and began to write.

When I feel out of control, I often write things down. Problems seem far more manageable in print. By the time my omelette came, the small napkin was filled with questions and, unfortunately, no answers. I stared at it, running over the items time and again as I ate.

Who is kidnapper/wants manuscript?
Why is Romney Marsh involved if not MoD?
Is Ian Arthur?
Where is Ian?
Rupert involved?
Sarah?
Diaries—why ambiguous?

The tape would tell me a lot, I hoped, once I had it. I wondered if Rupert had had time to incriminate himself yet, since I'd installed it yesterday afternoon.

There were a few things for me to check into today in addition to the tape, and I made a mental checklist. I would have to call Simon, as the contracts he'd given me to look over had disappeared in the fire with my briefcase, and I had to get that process started with my lawyers if I wanted to accept his route out of bankruptcy instead of Charlie's.

Then there was the Bedford Square house. It was a mistake not to have gone there before now, I knew, in case any valuables remained to be salvaged. But the most valuable things there were my father's diaries, and they had certainly been destroyed in the fire. Still, I would ask Lisette to leave the key somewhere for me.

Then there was Ian's house. I refused to believe that there was no clue as to his whereabouts there. I couldn't think of anywhere else to look. Besides, I hadn't been at my best yesterday and may well have missed something. But first I would get the car from Sarah's street and drive to The Orchard to freshen up. At least there would be no one there for me to endanger.

I paid the check, leaving the girl's pen conspicuously on top of my money, and made my way back to the train station near Sarah's office building. It was drizzling lightly, and I walked with my head down, thinking. While at The Orchard I could exchange my Golf for the old family wreck—one 1976 vintage black Mini. It was well weathered, having been driven by both Max and me when we were younger and more reckless. Despite its many dings and creases, it worked beautifully and would keep me from being recognized instantly by my car.

Like the rest of my tidy little schedule for the day, that was an erroneous assumption, but I wasn't to know that until later.

As I took the tube back to the station near Sarah's house, I thought again of the strangeness of these last few days. Whoever my enemies were, they seemed content with attempts to frighten me. Ominous as my encounters with them had been, they hadn't actually tried to kill me yet—assuming the newsprint at Churchill's Real Ales had been intended for Barnes. The fire had only been a close call because I'd happened to come home in the middle of the day; they had evidently meant it to destroy the manuscript, not me.

What, exactly, was it that they wanted? Perhaps they had nothing more in mind than harassment. I would be almost certain that it was merely Max in his misery and jealousy, trying to make my life difficult, if not for our phone conversation the other day. Unless he had suddenly become a better actor than I suspected, I didn't think he was behind it. I took some comfort in the fact that whoever wanted the manuscript had to be smart enough to know that he couldn't kill me, or he'd never find it. He merely had to scare me enough to make me tell my secret.

I didn't spend time imagining what he would think of next.

I walked up out of the station into the drizzle and jogged up the hill to my car. My hands were red and stiff from the wet cold, and I fumbled with the keys. For the thousandth time I wondered who would have had the motivation to kidnap the refugee children. There was money in it, yes; but to commit a crime like that for the sake of money . . .

I got in the car and automatically headed for The Orchard. I had the feeling that the answer was buried somewhere in the recesses of my mind, that I could unlock the secret if I could just get all the pieces to fall into line. My father's diaries said that a fee of $250 was charged to each set of adoptive parents when they came to Wauwinet Home for their foster child. There were approximately one thousand children in all who passed through the home in the last three years of the war, which meant that the kidnapper had pocketed a quarter of a million dollars. That was a lot of money then, particularly just after the war. Enough to get a good start in a business or investments. Enough to make someone quite wealthy now.

But could there be something else, something more sinister than simple greed? I wondered. A chill made me jerk involuntarily, and it wasn't just the cold of the car seats seeping through my clothes. Some of the most horrific crimes I could think of had involved children. They were worse than other crimes because their victims were people who had never done anything to deserve them—innocent, beautiful children. There were the Humbert Humbert types who were satisfied with admiring and caressing and there were the sicker varieties who enjoyed inflicting punishment on children. God only knows what happened to those poor children on Nantucket.

Disgusted, I turned off the A40 in the direction of Chess, speculating that if someone were unbalanced enough to kidnap children, and sociopathic enough to deliberately separate them from their parents for life, he could easily be a pedophile or worse. Surely he couldn't have children of his own and still have gone through with it.

My mind flew again to Romney. Childless and childlike, with his train obsession, he certainly fit the profile. And my father may well have learned that Romney had a weakness for children; that would have justified his keeping us away from him as well as the contempt and revulsion he seemed to feel toward him.

So why had I begun to like him yesterday? Perhaps it was a longing for a time long past, for endless Sunday afternoons with his train set, comforting voices of my parents and the other adults droning on in the lounge beneath us.

I shook my head and told myself that I wasn't feeling up to par yesterday, that I shouldn't take too seriously any wild new insights that came to me then. Perhaps I was imagining the whole incident with Sarah, too; perhaps she hadn't been talking about me and I only thought she had. In my exhaustion I could have judged it wrong.

I turned into The Orchard's drive. There were no masked men hiding in the garage or in the house when I walked to the kitchen to turn up the heat. By the time I had put the clothes I was wearing in the wash and gathered up some old ones, then showered and shaved, I was almost persuaded that I would be left that day to straighten out my life in peace.

I continued in that happy illusion until I was driving down the Chess High Street in the old Mini, at which point I noticed the silver Rover behind me. To have found me in this car, they must have been waiting for me somewhere around the house. Again, they hadn't tackled me or killed me while I was in the shower, as they could easily have done. They were just harassing me.

I was angry enough to make an irrational decision as to how to find out what they wanted once and for all. Driving as if I hadn't seen them, I headed for an isolated corner of the town Common, a rolling ten acres of Chiltern Hills filled with trekkers and impromptu football games on weekends. On weekdays it was empty, except for the home of an old friend of mine and its two occupants. I would use an old childhood trick on the two people I could see in the car. It was a trick that had given me a fleeting moment of triumph over Max once when he had deliberately bent the handlebars on my new bicycle.

I checked to make sure my seat belt was fastened and cranked the Mini up to top speed. I had to be ahead of them by at least fifty yards to make it work. It was early-closing day, Wednesday, and the town appeared to be deserted—all the better for speeding. Within five minutes I was there, at the corner of the Common where huge elms hung over the road and the road made a sharp jog to the left into the shadows.

I cranked the wheel hard to the left, and lifted the hand brake so that the nose of the car spun around to face the grass of the Common. I jumped out of the car, ran a couple of steps, and dived for the trees. I made it not a moment too soon. When the crash came, aided by the inevitable rain, leaves, and mud on the road, it was fairly impressive. Noisy, to be sure, and from the looks of it, not without its effect on the car's occupants.

I peered out from behind a giant old oak and was interested to see the Acme Sanitation Services man from the Soames press party angrily unfastening his seat belt. "Don't just sit there, you idiot— he's got to be nearby," he hissed. "Get out and start looking for him." The muscle-shirted young redhead sitting next to him looked startled and hurried to get out of the car. So Acme was the brains, and Red was the brawn. I had a way to deal with both of them.

What I did next was riskier than the car accident, because I had no way of knowing if they were carrying guns. I thrashed about in the bushes loudly enough to be sure at least Acme would hear, then started to run.

"This way!" shouted Acme, and when I turned to look after a few seconds, they were both hot on my trail. All was going according to plan. I took them over a little hillock, through a thick stand of beech trees, and after about five minutes I had them where I wanted them. I jumped a weathered wooden fence and kept running, but more slowly now. I didn't have to act; I still wasn't firing on all cylinders after the fire, and tired more easily than usual.

They had no sooner followed me over the fence than I heard the savage barking of my old friends Hans and Fritzy. The two Alsatians were growing old but were no less protective of their master's territory. They bounded toward us with all the energy and enthusiasm of their youth, and I continued to run toward them across the broad expanse of lawn. I had been here at Reggie Kingsford's place the day the new pups had come to live here, as Reggie was my best friend at school. I had been seventeen. Reggie's dad had bought a book on training Alsatians, and we'd taken it from there. It had occupied our spare time for months. After we had them trained, we would proudly parade them around town and tell them to "Stay!" outside the sweetshop when we went in for magazines and chocolate bars.

I hoped they remembered me, as it had been a couple of years since I'd visited them. Reggie had his own home now in the nearby town of Gerrards Cross, and his somewhat elderly parents spent a lot of time in Spain these days.

"Hans! Fritzy! Good dogs!" They had come even with me and

given little yelps of glee, but didn't stop to be petted. They had a job to do.

I stopped running and watched, enjoying the growing consternation on Acme and Red's faces as the dogs approached them. The men hesitated for a moment, looking between me and the dogs, then turned and ran in the opposite direction. Despite their adrenaline-induced speed, the dogs were faster. I let them get within six feet of the men and then called them off. I gave the short, sharp whistle we had used in training them from the beginning, and called, "Sit!"

It was magic. The snarling dogs skidded to a stop and sat, docile as lambs.

"If you don't stop, I'll put them onto you again." I said it casually, enjoying the moment. Red stopped immediately, giving a good imitation of a statue, but Acme was more reluctant. I could see he wasn't used to being beaten. In the end, though, he stopped, and stood perfectly still, facing away from me.

"Turn around and hold your hands where I can see them," I said, walking toward them. They turned around slowly, hands out from their bodies. I covered the twenty yards and felt them for guns. I didn't fancy being killed, though it didn't seem that that was what they wanted. I found a nasty little switchblade in Red's sock, and something even more sinister, in a way, in Acme's trouser pocket: a cattle prod for humans.

I stepped back and eyed them, slipping their knickknacks into my coat pocket. Acme looked at me with barely suppressed rage, his half-open dark eyes glittering. He was a piece of work. A two-day growth of stubble made him look even more disreputable than he would otherwise have been. His wavy dark hair was greasy, and a lock of it hung untidily on his forehead, stuck on by drizzle and sweat. He was of average height and build, but I had seen him run. He was lithe and fast. Even graceful, I would say, despite his baggy gray sweatpants and sweatshirt.

Red just looked scared, and about ten years younger than Acme and I. He barely took his eyes off the dogs, except to hurriedly glance at Acme occasionally as if to ask what was going to happen next. He had obviously spent a fair amount of time lifting weights to achieve the sculpted look of a bodybuilder, and even on this cold wet day he wore nothing more than jeans and a tank top to expose his muscular arms to full advantage.

After letting them stew for a moment or two, I said, "One move toward me and they'll be all over you. Understood?" Red again looked at Acme, imploringly this time. Acme graced me with a barely perceptible nod, insolence oozing out of every pore.

"We've met before," I said, looking Acme in the eye. He didn't respond. "The night you tried to kill Barnes Appleton—or was it me?" His face might have been carved out of marble. Not a muscle moved. "I need to know who you're working for. If you tell me willingly, now, it'll be much easier for you." Red cast a worried glance at his partner. I didn't have any plans to hurt them, but I had to motivate them somehow.

Acme only sneered.

I shrugged. "All right, have it your way." I turned to the dogs and gave the whistle. "Ready . . ." They got to their feet immediately, eyes riveted on the strangers, every muscle tense. "Attack!" The dogs leapt at them, snarling. I was somewhat worried. I wasn't sure if they would actually harm the intruders or not, but I certainly knew it was in their power.

Acme put his arms up, obviously terrified despite his defiance. Red frantically blurted, "Please! No! Okay!"

I gave the command for the dogs to sit, then looked from one man to the other and waited as a heavy mist fell. Red said, "We don't know their names—honest, we don't." He was American, I noted with interest. And shaking. Whether from cold or fear, I didn't know.

His simple statement had told me something else: that there was more than one person involved. "What do they look like?" Acme gave him a sharp look of warning, but Red was bent on ingratiating himself.

"The one has dark hair, dark eyes. Tall. He looks an awful lot like you, but skinnier. Paler, sort of." He shrugged.

It had to be Max. We did look a lot alike, but Max's drug habit had taken off at least thirty pounds. He didn't exactly look emaciated, but he didn't look well. I could practically see the drugs killing him—everyone could, except Max himself.

"And the other?"

They looked at each other. I whistled again, and the dogs got ready. Acme sighed and spoke for the first time. "All right. But you're going to be disappointed." I let the dogs stand at attention while he spoke. He had an earthy London accent and a bored voice that indicated he had seen it all. "We don't know who he is, never seen him. Goes to a lot of trouble to keep himself a secret. Sometimes he calls us, sometimes he gives us orders through the other bloke."

"Then you know his voice."

He sneered at me again. "I told you you'd be disappointed. He uses this weird slowed-down tape recording to tell us what he wants. Sounds like an effing crackpot to me, but he pays well. Satisfied? Or is this going to be an all-day event out here with you and the dogs?"

The threat I'd received over the phone had come from a slowed-down tape recording.

Acme and his big mouth were beginning to irritate me. I put my face close to his and the dogs shifted, snarling menacingly.

"No, I'm not satisfied. I'm very dissatisfied. People have followed me, burnt down my home, attacked me with exotic weapons, murdered my friends, ruined my business, and in general destroyed my life. I'm not going to be satisfied until I find out who is responsible and see them locked away for a very long time."

I must have been somewhat convincing, because Acme backed away slightly. "So far I can't prove that you've got anything to do with anything that's happened to me, so I'm going to go easy on you this time. But if I find you anywhere near me again, or near anyone else I know, you're going to wish Hans and Fritzy had got to you first." With that I turned and stalked off, leaving them to realize that they were going to have to devise their own way to get off the property with the dogs watching.

The thought pleased me, and I laughed a little as I walked back across the Common and down the little hill to my car. The local constables hadn't arrived at the wreck yet, I was glad to see; nor had anyone else. I folded myself into the Mini, luckily without any serious damage, and drove off. I didn't think the trunk would open, but it didn't matter in a Mini; I could reach whatever I needed from the backseat.

I picked up the phone and dialed Simon Bow's number. The silky voiced secretary answered and told me that Simon was out. I asked her to please let him know that I had misplaced the contracts and ask him to forward a new set to my lawyer, Neville Greenslade.

I gave her the name and address, then on a whim dialed Neville's office.

Neville was both our family and company lawyer, and his firm had handled my grandfather's affairs and his father's before him. It certainly made things easy; they knew our affairs intimately, which relieved me from worrying about them. I was put right through to Neville, who at sixty-five was the head of the firm.

"Alex, I'm glad you called." Confident, authoritative, and kind, Neville was a pleasure to deal with. I could practically see him leaning back in his big leather chair, with his broad, almost-smug smile and tortoise-rimmed glasses. "I read about the fire; Mary and I were worried about you. We left messages with Lisette but didn't know how else to get in touch with you."

"Thanks, Neville." For a moment I was tempted to spill the beans to him, recruit his help in getting out of my mess. But reason got the better of me and I told him about the Bow and Bow contracts instead. He showed no surprise at a second set of contracts; he had gone over the Bookarama ones as well. "I'd be grateful if you could look them over right away and let me know what you think. The sooner I get those settled, the better. You'll have to call me on my home number; I'm not going to be in the office for a few days."

"Yes, yes of course." He sounded hesitant. I waited. Perhaps he thought the idea of copublishing was a bad one. I valued his opinion and wanted to hear it.

"What is it, Neville?"

He made an uncomfortable sound, somewhere between clearing his throat and coughing. "I—er—I've been thinking." Long pause. "I would never want you to think that the promises I make to you, or indeed your entire family, would ever be broken willingly."

"No, of course not." Uh-oh. Had someone gotten to Neville?

"But sometimes my judgment, as a father, a lawyer, a human being, makes me question whether in the best interests of my clients I should break an occasional promise when I see fit."

"Go on."

He let out a long, pent-up breath. "Alex, your father left certain documents with me which I have been instructed to release to you at some point in the future. Exactly why he chose the date he did, I don't know, but I think you should have those documents now instead." I listened. "They might have some bearing on the— er—situation in which you are currently embroiled."

I relaxed. It was good news, not bad—or so it seemed. "I'm intrigued. Just now I'd jump at anything that might offer proof of my father's innocence." I stopped to think for a moment. "Could you tell me what these documents are?"

"I don't suppose it could do any harm. There are two small books filled with your father's handwriting. They're well worn and quite old. I haven't read them, naturally, but I'd say they might be journals."

My mind leapt to the implications of what he was saying. More journals . . . why wouldn't my father have put them all in safekeeping? Perhaps there was something in these that he didn't want lying around in the attic.

"All right if I pop 'round for them now?"

He gave a throaty chuckle. "No moss on you. Just like your father. Don't suppose I could persuade you to stay for a coffee as long as you're here."

I laughed. "Thanks, I'd like that. See you in a few minutes then."

I had time to think as I flew down the A40 toward Neville's office near Gray's Inn Road, always watching for any car that lurked for too long behind me. I was quite sure it would not be the silver Rover, given the damage it had incurred that morning.

It was odd. I knew that I was in a race, a race to save Ian's life, probably my own, and possibly even Sarah's. But I didn't know my opponent, and this was no ordinary race. I had no idea how to win.

I had allowed myself to feel that I was at a dead end today, that something had to happen in order for me to move forward. Now it had happened. The diaries piqued my curiosity. Perhaps they would tell me what I needed to know. My father had been a very thorough man; I wouldn't be surprised to find names and dates and a very complete account of how he spent his days.

I parked in one of Neville's firm's reserved spaces in a nearby car park, glancing around me for any suspicious characters, and walked around the corner to the impressive entryway of Escutcheon, Monaghan, Greenslade and Mathew. It felt familiar in the same way Romney's house had; I had been there several times with my father, and it hadn't changed in the slightest, as far as I could tell. A secretary showed me into Neville's inner sanctum. It was still dark and slightly musty smelling, like a library, which wasn't surprising. One high-ceilinged wall, from waist-height up, was covered with huge legal volumes that looked like antiques. Neville greeted me warmly, put his hand on my back, and ushered me over to a comfortable settee. After pouring me some coffee from a silver pot, he settled back in his chair with his cup. He looked concerned.

"I've been worried about you, Alex. Especially after reading about the fire. Mary and I wanted to know if you were all right, have you to dinner, but Lisette said you were out of the office. Couldn't be reached, she said. We couldn't think where you'd gone. Certainly not to stay with Max, I dare say." He scowled and took a sip of coffee. He seemed to be almost as disgusted with Max for souring the family name as I was.

"Are you all right?" he asked kindly. "Really all right? This is a lot to handle all at once."

I nodded. "Thanks, Neville. I've never appreciated my true friends more than I do right now." He looked pleased. "And I must say, your call came at an opportune time. The sooner I can disprove all this rubbish about my father being a child thief, the better."

His head bobbed up and down emphatically, then he snorted. "It's hard to believe that this story has got so far, gained so much credibility." He looked like he wanted to say more on the subject but stopped himself short. "I suppose you'd like to see those books now. And if I might make a suggestion . . . I suspect that they are much sought after by the person who really did commit this crime. So if you'd like to leave them here in our vaults, well, they've been safe here for quite some years now."

He had a point. "Yes, that's a good idea. Perhaps I could look at them now in your reading room, then leave them with you." That way they would never be endangered at all.

"Fine." He showed me into the small room with a leather-topped library table, then left, presumably to fetch the books. I became aware of an irritating noise, then realized that it was my fingers drumming on the table. If the diaries had nothing at all to do with the children, I would be very disappointed. But then why would he lock them up here with Neville?

The door opened again and Neville put a plain brown envelope on the table, labeled in the upper-right-hand corner with "Plumtree, Maximilian: for delivery to son Alex." A jumble of numbers and letters followed the words, and Neville hastened to explain. "The first number is the date on which we were originally to have delivered this to you—see, it's the first of next year. Then, this long number is your client reference number, and these letters indicate the type of item it is. In this case it's P for personal, followed by N/V to indicate that it has no intrinsic value beyond what it might mean to you."

I nodded and Neville left, locking the door behind him. It was for my security, I presumed. I broke the heavy wax seal and opened the envelope with fumbling fingers, wondering why my father had specified January first of next year for me to see these. He had been a habitual planner; few things he did were done without forethought.

I reached in and pulled out the two little books. They were almost identical to those I'd found in the attic, bound in thin black leather, with narrow-lined paper and a tattered red ribbon anchored to the binding for a marker. If anything, these books looked slightly more tattered than the others. I opened one of them and looked at the date at the top of the page. Oddly, it began on exactly the same date as one of the attic diaries, October 21, 1940.

My eye raced off down the page and with growing excitement I read what I had expected to find in the first set of diaries. There was no ambiguity here, only disgust at what had been done to the children and rage for the elusive person who had done it to them.

The first entry had a puzzled, tentative tone, as my father and Ian began to perceive that something was wrong.

Ian and I are here on beautiful but desolate Nantucket Island for our one-week leave from the Anglo-American Liaison office in Washington. The woman who runs our boarding house told us about a home filled with British children in Wauwinet, a remote corner of the island. We came to visit them to cheer them up several days ago for the first time, and I'm afraid we've stumbled onto something very disturbing. We know now beyond the shadow of a doubt that there is something odd about the circumstances of the children at Wauwinet Home, and wonder if perhaps they have been taken against the will of their parents. Today Ian and I spoke to several of the older ones, against the strict instructions of their caregivers, while they were playing on the beach. They did have parents in England, and had heard from them shortly before sailing to America. All of the children we spoke to had been evacuated to the countryside from London to be safe from the bombing there, and were in foster homes. Shortly before departing on the ship, all of them had been visited in their foster homes by a HELP official, who said that with the approval of their real parents they were being sent to America, where people were opening their homes to war refugee children. They would be very safe there, the official said, until the war was over. Then, once the children got here, they were informed that their parents had been killed in the two weeks it took to make the journey, and that they would be staying in America permanently with adoptive parents. Ian and I can't imagine that this could be true of all the children—there are fifty here at the moment—and wonder what the hell is going on. An interesting detail: one of the older children was watching as foster parents picked up his friend the other day. He claims that the foster parents handed over "a whopping wad of money" before taking his friend away.

Several days later, my father wrote the following:

I have put calls through to everyone I can think of at Help the Children and the Anglo-American Liaison who might be able to shed some light on the children's situation, but am dissatisfied with their answers. I was impressed that Old Knock-knees himself is in charge of the evacuation operation, as his old man arranged to have him sent back to the UK several months ago for personal reasons. He personally assured me that only children whose parents had died and who had no living relatives in England had been assigned to American foster parents, and all of this had been done under the auspices of the Anglo-American Liaison's Charitable Activities Committee. I then called Nigel Wexford, the chair of the committee, and he confirmed what Knock-knees had said. Why do I feel there is something rotten here?

Nigel Wexford. I was interested to see the book review editor's name surface here. I hadn't realized Barnes's coworker had been with the Anglo-American Liaison, too.

The next day, my father's handwriting was spiky and even worse than usual. I strained to read it, and caught my breath.

Dear God, I'd give anything to find out it's all been a ghastly mistake. Ian is in shock, and hasn't spoken since he got the phone call. Both Lily and Angela are dead. Even as I write this he is stumbling about on the beach, unaware of where he is or what he is doing. Naturally, he refuses to be comforted, and who could blame him. I've followed him for most of the day to make sure nothing happens to him. I'm going to write this as a prayer, God, because I need to talk to You. Why Lily? Why Angela? Lily was such a beautiful wife and mother, intelligent, kind, faithful. And Angela—barely two. Ian and Lily had her when they were so young, and then the war came. Ian has barely seen her.

There was a knock on the door. A key turned in the lock, and the secretary entered bearing a tray of sandwiches, fruit, and a soft drink. "All right?" she asked cheerfully.

Startled, I made the transition from the forties to the nineties. "Thanks," I said, mustering a smile, and gratefully picked up a roast beef sandwich. "Very kind of you." She smiled and left as quickly as she'd come. I sat back for a moment, chewing. So this was the tragedy behind Ian's lonely life. I understood him much better now.

I stood and walked around the room as I wolfed down the sandwich. The only way I could make sense of these diaries was to assume that the previous set was false. They were elaborate forgeries, planted there in the attic for me to find.

Suddenly it was all clear. Max knew me well, knew that with a few well-planned words he could get me to go to the attic looking for something like diaries. He could easily have copied my father's handwriting from other documents, and he would have enjoyed writing the prose. He must have seen the real diaries once, before my father put them into safekeeping. And he had hidden them so well; the desk idea was really rather clever. He had made it just difficult enough so I would be sure I was the first to find them.

I shook my head and popped open the Coke. Some big brother Max was. I took a long drink and enjoyed the bite of the bubbles in my mouth. No matter how ingeniously Max had led me to suspect our father, I knew that he was not the mastermind of this operation. Romney, in all probability, was using him to sidetrack me as he had used him to write the newspaper article. I was impatient to listen to the latest round of Romney's phone conversations, and sat down again to finish the second journal.

When I was finished, I closed the books, replaced them in the envelope, resealed the clasp, and allowed myself a moment in that quiet, safe room to bask in the joy of knowing that my father was who I thought he was. No, he was more: he, along with Ian, was the hero who had discovered the plot using the children and found the man responsible. The diaries paralleled Ian's novels almost exactly. It was all here, with just one disappointment: The kidnapper was not named. I knew a lot about him now, certainly; he was known to my father as Old Knock-knees, and he'd worked with both the Anglo-American Liaison and HELP. But I couldn't be sure exactly who he was. That would take some research.

I thanked Neville and left the diaries in his capable hands, feeling better than I had since the night of the Soameses' press party. Even the grim, drizzly day seemed to have improved slightly. I looked around as I left the firm's door, half expecting to see some unwelcome person waiting for me. But no one seemed to notice as I walked to my car and got in.

The car phone answering machine was blinking when I got there. I punched the button and played the message. "Alex, this is Alison Soames." She hesitated. Her voice was quiet, urgent. "I need to talk to you—today. It's important. Meet me at Nico's Taverna in Charlotte Street at five-thirty. I hope you've heard this message by then." Another pause. "Whatever you do, don't call my office. If I don't see you there, I'll call you later." Click. She'd signed off in a hurry.

There was information pouring in from all quarters, it seemed, all of a sudden. If Romney's telephone would provide me with something really interesting, I'd be even more pleased. I looked at my watch as I started the car and pulled away from the curb. Just after two. I would have plenty of time to go back for another snoop round Ian's house and then listen to the latest gossip from Chalfont St. Giles before meeting Alison.

She had chosen a small, inelegant place where the owner, chef, and waiter—all the same person—served up some of the best Greek food to be found off the Greek Isles. By five-thirty it would be half-filled with the after-work crowd enjoying bottles of retsina and bowls of *taramosalata* with pita bread. It was a noisy, inconspicuous place to talk—just right for the likes of me these days.

Filled with curiosity about what Alison could have to say that was so important, I drove to Ian's and parked, again, on the street behind the row of houses. I prayed that Alison would be able to shed some light on where Ian was and who was behind it all. But I had a feeling it wasn't going to be that easy.

The sky was growing darker as I tried to melt into the pavement and the brick walls of the houses on my way to Ian's front door. I climbed the steps and reached for the lock, key in hand, but I needn't have bothered with the key. The door pushed open with the barest touch of my hand.

I stepped over the threshold quietly, with a sense of trepidation, and listened. I couldn't hear anyone moving about now, but from the look of it, whoever had been there was rather violent with Ian's belongings. Someone had the same idea of looking for Ian, or his belongings, here, which I probably should have expected. But this someone had an obvious disregard for the property of others. I cringed to see Ian's fine book collection strewn about on the lounge rug, old leather bindings cracked with the shock.

I couldn't help but wonder what they were doing to Ian.

Without really thinking, I picked up a few of the older, more valuable volumes, placing them carefully on an empty bookshelf. The open spine of Ian's favorite book caught my eye, and I pulled it out from under the others. It was *The Razor's Edge* by Somerset Maugham, unlike the other books in his personal collection in that it wasn't a special edition or particularly beautiful in its construction. For the first time I realized that perhaps Ian liked it so well because it was set in Paris, where he'd first met Lily, the woman who would become his wife. He had lost so much, so young.

I opened the cover, and bold, angular handwriting leapt out at me. "To my darling Ian. All my love always, Lily."

I stood looking at it for a moment and thought for the hundredth time that it wasn't fair for any one generation of people to have suffered so much. My father and mother had come out of it all right, but people like Ian had lost everything. A little daughter, a wife. And he hadn't had the worst of the war by a long shot; he was alive to tell. At least I hoped he was.

Out of habit I riffled the pages to get a look at the typeface and design as well as a whiff of old-paper-and-ink smell. A stiff insert stopped the pages fluttering, and I pulled it out.

It was a photograph of Ian, a decade or so ago, judging from his still-graying hair. He was standing with an attractive couple, perhaps twenty years his junior, in the stern of a very respectable-looking sixty-foot yacht. I squinted at the name painted on the stern in rather delicate block letters: CARPE DIEM, NANTUCKET.

My heart beat faster. *Carpe diem*, "seize the day" in Latin, was one of Ian's favorite sayings. He often came out with odd phrases in foreign languages, but that was far and away his most frequent. And there was something about the shape of those letters . . .

I stepped over to Ian's desk, being careful not to tread on the books on the floor, and picked up the magnifying glass on top of a pile of papers. Looking closely, I could make out that the letters were in Ian's treasured Botticelli font, a sixteenth-century typeface he had studied in great depth. The serifs were thin but exaggerated, with a tiny curve at the end of many of them. We had used it several times at the press, though it was difficult to get printers to use it. Most of them had standardized to use more common fonts.

I put the magnifying glass down and concentrated on the unknown people in the photo. Like the typeface, there was something familiar about the woman. I knew I had never seen the other man before, but the woman . . . I stared at her. Perhaps it was her eyes. They were almond shaped and tilted slightly upward at the outside. Sarah's eyes were a bit like that. Maybe that was all; I was quite certain I had never actually met the woman.

I allowed myself to speculate about what this photograph could mean. A part of me wanted to dash to Nantucket immediately and look for Ian there. If he had painted the name on the yacht, perhaps he had some stake in it, or even owned it. He had never mentioned that he owned a yacht, but then he was a private, even secretive man. And modest. He wouldn't be one to boast about an expensive toy like a yacht.

If he did own a yacht registered in Nantucket, perhaps he had roots there—a favorite inn where he liked to stay, or even a vacation home of his own. And, evidently, friends. It was certainly the best lead I had yet. If I didn't turn up anything else soon, I would go to Nantucket.

I put the photo in the inside pocket of my jacket and took a quick walk through the rest of the house to make sure that there were no open windows, smoldering cigarettes, or other calling cards. The rest of the house was messy, but not seriously damaged. Judging from what they did to my house and the office as well as Ian's, when these people didn't find what they wanted, they went on a destructive rampage out of spite. I could almost perceive a certain style to the chaos.

The worst mess was in Ian's study, where they had ripped the charts from their racks and raked all of the carefully stacked papers off of Ian's massive desk and onto the floor. The drawers were open, their files on the floor. I took a quick look through them, feeling guilty about snooping, yet not wanting to miss anything important. But Ian's life on paper was nothing if not mundane. His records consisted of the usual bills and receipts people keep as well as some statements from his stockbroker and bank. I wondered if perhaps he had carefully weeded out any papers that would have provided significant information about him as a precaution against this very event. If indeed Ian was Arthur, that would have been the prudent thing to do.

It was time to retrieve the tape from Romney's shed. Long shadows fell across the street now at three o'clock, a grim reminder that another day was slipping away without any progress on finding Ian. Time was running out for him, and perhaps for me too.

I closed his door tightly and pulled my coat around me as I hurried to the car, wondering if perhaps I should stop trying to be clever. Perhaps I should simply confront Romney, Max, and Rupert with my worst suspicions and watch their reactions. One of the three of them knew where Ian was, I was sure of it.

In retrospect, I can't believe how blind I was. But, after all, I do have remarkably bad eyesight.

8

I left the car in a remote corner of a pub parking lot in Chalfont St. Giles. There had been no visible tail on the way here, and I'd become quite good at spotting them.

Nonetheless I took a roundabout way to Romney's house, using a series of streets and footpaths and staying close to trees and shrubs. It was positively gloomy as the light began to fade. A nearly full moon was due later, but thick clouds would totally obscure it unless the temperature got brutally cold. I avoided the gravel on a narrow path that cut through a block of homes, not wanting to crunch through it and call attention to myself. It was impossible to be too careful, especially now that I knew they weren't playing games anymore. If something happened to me, Ian was as good as dead. No one else knew to look for him.

In ten minutes I was in the bank of trees at the rear of Romney's back garden. He was there; I could see his deep-blue Ford Cavalier in the drive.

I made my way silently through his herb garden and down a long line of yews on a brick path. Just to be on the safe side, I ducked off the path halfway down and hid behind a yew for ten seconds, then peeked out again. All was quiet.

Looking around me, I ran the last ten yards to the little white-washed shed tacked onto the rear of Romney's house and ducked inside, closing the door silently behind me. All was just as it had been the last time I'd been here. As far as I could tell, he hadn't discovered my little machine under the flowerpot.

I picked up the pot and looked at the machine while reaching for a new tape in my pocket. The tape machine's cheery green light was on, its wheels spinning; Romney was, at this very moment, talking on his telephone. I would have to wait; this call might be important.

I didn't have to wait long. Not ten seconds passed before the light went off and the tape stopped turning. I quickly took out the tape, fingers fumbling slightly in the cold, and inserted a fresh one from my pocket. I peeked out the door of the shed and, seeing no one, skulked back into the bank of trees with the used tape burning a hole in my pocket.

It required tremendous restraint not to run back to the car. It was completely dark now, but I thought someone, anyone, running down the streets of Chalfont St. Giles might be enough to bring out the local constable's. There was not, as a rule, a great deal of excitement here.

I made it back to the Mini, got in, and took my answering machine tape out of the machine. I replaced it with the tape of Romney's conversations and pressed the rewind button. Surprisingly little of the tape had been used; I prayed there was something on it that would tell me what Romney was up to. When the machine clicked off, I pressed play and listened to a succession of exceedingly mundane conversations.

His cleaning help had called to say she was ill but would come next week at the usual time.

The secretary of the Chalfont Historical Society called to ask if Romney was interested in helping to set up some sort of exhibit about life in the seventeenth century.

Romney called his dentist to see when he could get his teeth cleaned.

After the fifth such call, I feared the worst. Perhaps I wouldn't learn anything about Romney's activities from my phone surveillance. After the eighth, unwilling to believe that I was still empty-handed, I began to wonder if perhaps they were messages in code. His cleaning woman might have been saying that their criminal plot, whatever it was, would be executed next week instead of this. The historical society call might have been to indicate that something would take place at 1700 hours. Romney's call to the dentist might have been to schedule a meeting with someone sinister.

My imagination knew no bounds when it came to Romney's calls.

But the tenth call was different from the start. The conversation began abruptly, and I held my breath as it began to unfold.

"The word is that they don't think they're going to get the manuscript. They've made the decision to terminate the problem within the next forty-eight hours."

This was it. This was it!

"Damn," Romney expostulated. "If it weren't for his stubbornness, this wouldn't have had to happen. My contact with Plumtree has proved to be worse than useless."

Silence on the other end for a moment. "Can you get here right away? Take care of him yourself?"

"Yes, I'll be there." He sighed disgustedly. "Where exactly is he now?"

I wasn't sure if they were talking about me or Ian.

"Coatue," said the other man. "You know the place."

"Yes. I'll be there by midnight your time."

"Right."

The caller rang off, and I heard a distinctive series of clicks with a squeak, the sound of an overseas call if I'd ever heard one.

I stared at the machine in horror. They were going to kill him. And I didn't know where this Coatue was, though I could have sworn I'd seen the word somewhere before. The moment I'd heard it, I could see it, spelled in my mind. It sounded French, but of course that didn't mean it was in France. He'd said it was in a different time zone. Please God, I prayed, let there not be more than one Coatue in the world.

There was no time to lose.

I drove like a bat out of hell, which was acceptable even in Chalfont St. Giles, out of the parking lot and onto the road to Chess and The Orchard. I made it in under ten minutes and pulled into the garage. The car smelled hot. I banged into the house and ran through to the library, where I hoped to find Coatue listed in the world atlas. The huge volume, three and a half inches thick and roughly two feet square, was on the bottom shelf of one of the bookshelves along with the *Oxford English Dictionary, Roget's Thesaurus,* and the *Official Scrabble Dictionary.*

I lifted the atlas onto a nearby desk and switched on the table lamp, grateful that Emma had evidently arranged to have the power reinstated after the storm. I flipped to Britain first, then Ireland, Scotland, Jersey, Guernsey, France, Belgium, Switzerland, and the United States. No luck. The moments slipped away. It was, as usual, colder inside the house than out, and I rubbed my hands together as I tried to think of other likely locations for a place called Coatue.

In the end, I banged my fist on the smug volume in frustration, cursing it for not being more helpful. I didn't have any more time to spend looking for a needle in a haystack. I looked at my watch and remembered that I'd promised to meet Alison Soames at five-thirty.

"Damn," I said, and picked up the phone. Then I remembered she'd said in no uncertain terms not to call her at the office.

I hung up again with a bang. I'd have to go meet Alison; I couldn't let her sit there alone. It was four o'clock; I had an hour and a half to go.

As I slid the book back into place it occurred to me that perhaps Coatue was a mere village or a tiny island. The atlas didn't list every named place in the world, after all, and I told myself that just because it wasn't in there, that didn't mean it wasn't in one of the countries I had tried.

I went out through the library's double doors into the garden, a shorter route to the garage than going through the house. I jogged along the curving path through the rose garden, now barren except for an outstanding crop of thorns, and turned left toward the garage at a hedge by the roses.

I caught a glimpse of the total darkness that was wild pasture beyond the hedge and hesitated for a moment. I breathed the pungent, cold air and thought that I would be wildly happy to live here again some day—if I could save the company and in so doing save the house and myself. It looked less and less likely that I would be settling in any time soon with Sarah and several twinkles in my eye, but I wasn't going to give up just yet.

I had barely made it onto the A40 and got my speed up to a satisfying seventy-five when the car phone rang.

"Alex? Romney here. Good God. What a noise. Do you have one of those car phones?"

"Indeed I do." You know I do, I thought.

"I wondered if it would be convenient for us to get together for a brief chat this evening. Something's come up that I think you should know about. I'll be happy to come to you—are you headed for The Orchard?"

Suspicion flared. I didn't think I'd do any more meeting in person at the moment, except with Alison, whom I trusted more than I did Romney.

"Couldn't you just tell me now, over the phone?"

"I'm afraid I can't trust the phone for this, especially not one of those mobile jobs. No, I'd much rather see you in person, if you don't mind."

Now I was really suspicious. I'd lead him on a wild goose chase—good, harmless fun.

"All right. In fact, I was just headed for the office. I'll be there for several hours; come when it's convenient."

"Thanks, Alex. I'm on my way."

The security firm just inside the front door would, I knew, stop him before he got any farther. I had given them strict orders not to let anyone in without checking with Lisette to see if they had an appointment. Even those who had appointments were escorted during their entire visit. I wasn't taking any chances.

I had hardly put down the phone when it rang again. I seemed to be very popular all of a sudden. "Alex? Simon Bow here. Thought I'd check in and see how you're coming with those contracts."

"That's what I like; someone really eager to do business." Privately I added, and you're really eager for a knighthood.

He laughed. "For that matter, I've been eager to do business with you ever since you announced Arthur's first book. Gold mines, that's what they are. Changed your mind yet on those?"

"You never stop, do you, Simon?"

"I wouldn't be in this business if I weren't persistent."

He had a point. Publishing was not for the get-rich-quick artist, nor for the faint of heart. It was not a wildly profitable business at the best of times, and every year it seemed to become less so for all of us. Thus the everlasting pursuit of the block-buster—of the Arthurs of this world.

"No, I suppose not. Sorry, Simon, I haven't changed my mind. But the contracts are with my lawyer, and I'm sure I'll be able to get back to you next week." If I'm still alive, I thought. I couldn't imagine what the next week would hold, but I did want him to know I was interested.

"Good, good. I take it all that racket in the background is your car. Where on earth are you?" His voice was very cool, casual.

This was the second person in five minutes who had asked me where I was. Was I being overly suspicious again? I had an odd feeling that the phone call I'd just heard on the tape had something to do with these rapid-fire queries about my whereabouts.

With the hair standing up on my arms, I said lightheartedly, "I'm just on my way back to the office. Don't know what I'd do without this car phone. And—er—where are you?"

"Oh, I'm in the Boston office this week. They're having the annual book fair, and I decided to pop over for the occasion. It's a jolly little event—nothing like the London Book Fair, of course. Come to think of it, you and I should go together next time, have a joint display. Have some fun, too."

"Mmm. Good idea."

"It's settled, then. And I'll look forward to hearing from you next week on the contracts."

As he hung up, I heard the squeaky clink I'd heard at the end of Romney's phone call about Coatue.

Of course. The sound of an overseas call.

My mind ran in circles on the way to Charlotte Street to meet Alison. As I sped along I pulled up the sleeve of my jacket and tried to catch a glimpse of my watch. At the speed I'd been going, I thought I'd reach Charlotte Street in another ten minutes, which would put me well ahead of schedule for Alison.

I decided to take time for a little experiment. I drove past Bedford Square and parked on Charlotte Street. Then I walked the three minutes back to the square, pulling out my keys as I approached. The light had faded almost completely now. By Bedford Square standards, it was the peak time for leaving work. Quarter past five. I waited for a break in the traffic, crossed the street to the small oval of park at the center of the square, and followed the curve of the fence toward the gate, which directly faced the entrance to Plumtree Press.

It was a private park, requiring a key for entrance. If it hadn't been almost dark, standing at the gate long enough to unlock it would have attracted too much suspicion. Barring sunny summer lunch hours, it was unusual to see anyone at all in the park. Even in the dusk, I would attract attention unless I moved quickly. I walked rapidly to the gate, turned my key in the lock, and went in, shutting it quietly behind me.

I looked around; it was strange to be here at this hour and this season. A squirrel looked up at me from the sparse grass. I supposed he normally had the whole place to himself. I whispered, "Sorry," and sought the security of a small but strategically positioned holly bush. From it I could look out directly on the door to the office, which was lit by the glow of an old-fashioned Bedford Square street-lamp. If anyone looked in my direction, I was quite sure all they would see was a small holly bush.

Several minutes passed, and I saw one of our assistant editors come out of the door. It was early for her to be leaving, but then I couldn't expect that the maelstrom around Plumtree Press wasn't affecting the employees in some way. The morning before I'd gone to meet with Simon, the morning of the fire, I had casually walked around to visit the employees and discussed current events with them. I'd asked for their loyalty and assured them that I had complete faith in Arthur, that he hadn't been involved in the kidnappings, and it would only be a matter of time before my father's reputation was set right. Still, they didn't know either man as well as I did, and might be embarrassed to be working for a firm that was receiving such negative publicity. Besides, they were bound to be worried by my continued absence and the presence of the security firm, though I had asked Lisette to mention to a few employees that the guards were there to keep the press from interfering with their work.

After ten minutes had passed and I had seen half a dozen more employees trickle out, I began to realize that it was unlikely my suspicions had been warranted.

I was standing up to leave when I noticed two men moving rapidly toward the door, and I ducked behind the bush again to watch. They didn't look like businessmen; they weren't carrying anything and their clothes were wrong. One was in a black leather jacket, and the other in a sort of peacoat. I hadn't seen them before.

The door closed behind them, then opened again almost immediately. The men emerged, protesting, under the escort of the security guards. The older of the two guards appeared to be saying something not altogether friendly. He was not only built like a tank, but he was tall, and I wouldn't have blamed the visitors for being intimidated. I watched them walk away, muttering under their breath, apparently surprised by the presence of determined security guards. I felt justified not only in the expense of the guard but in my suspicions. These men looked considerably tougher than Acme and Red; the dog story probably hadn't gone over too well with their employer, and some new blood had been called in for this job.

I stood up to go. Five more minutes until I had to meet Alison. I rubbed my thighs and wondered what, exactly, Romney had had in mind for these two men. I found it difficult to believe that they would have tried to assault me in my own offices, and besides, the time for simple scare tactics was past. I knew that Romney and his people had given up on obtaining the manuscript and were planning to eliminate the threat by eliminating Ian. And aside from Ian, I was the only person still alive whom they thought had read the manuscript.

In the back of my mind I had acknowledged long ago that if they had a grain of common sense, they would try to eliminate me, too. It was true that they wanted the manuscript, but if they couldn't get that, they'd better get the two remaining people who had read it. Barnes was already gone. These men had probably come to have a little chat and entice me to a later rendezvous, where they hoped to accomplish their real business.

I had my hand on the park's wrought-iron gate and was lifting the latch when I saw two more men mount the steps to the office. They were dressed in business attire, probably with suits under their Burberry-style raincoats. I felt a wild urge to laugh; the men looked almost comical. They were nearly the same height and moved in the same serious, stiff way. Incredulous, I stayed where I was—it was totally dark now—and waited to see what would happen.

Though they were treated with somewhat more respect than their predecessors, they were rebuffed with equal indifference by the guards. These two were equally surprised, and protested for a moment like the others. But in the end they eyed the opposition, squared their shoulders, and marched off, affronted. The security guards looked at one another and watched them go, shaking their heads.

When the most recent visitors were out of sight, I walked with all speed to Charlotte Street. I would be a few minutes late, but I hoped Alison wouldn't mind. An unwelcome thought had introduced itself, and it bothered me. Both Romney and Simon had asked me where I was, and two sets of men had come to find me not long after. It could have been coincidence, but more and more I believed that coincidences didn't happen. Of course, both sets of men could have come from Romney; when the first was rebuffed, better-dressed reinforcements moved in to take their place.

By the time I arrived at Charlotte Street by a roundabout route, I found that I was looking forward to being in a happy, familiar place again, seeing someone I knew. It was dangerous, probably, but I would join the human race again for a few blissful moments in the restaurant with Alison. All of this solitude was beginning to have its effect on me.

No one had managed to pick up my trail again today, which was almost more nerve-wracking than if I'd known I was being followed. As I walked down the street toward Nico's Taverna I looked around carefully anyway for someone who could have been watching me. I didn't trust anyone anymore, not even Alison. She could be bait.

As I walked and watched, a red Porsche purred into a parking spot and closed its eyelids. Alison's car. I decided to watch from a doorway in the shadows to see if anyone followed her in or seemed to be watching her. Alison popped out of the car in an orange miniskirt with a hip-length orange leather jacket and matching high heels. She pressed a button on her key ring and a *beeowip* announced that the car's alarm was on. Then she flounced into the restaurant as if irritated. I watched for a few moments, but no one followed her in or seemed to be particularly interested.

I crossed the street and walked into the warm restaurant. The seductive aromas of garlic and rosemary assaulted my nostrils. I would have a quick chat with Alison, explain I had another commitment, and be on my way. Wherever Coatue was, I had to find it, and fast. I couldn't let the fact that it looked hopeless stop me from trying.

Nico himself, balding and shaped like the proverbial Grecian urn, greeted me inside the door. I had been a semiregular customer since moving back to London. "Alex, Alex. So glad to see you here." He gave me a bear hug that nearly knocked me off my feet while administering several hefty pats on the back—his way of saying that he didn't believe everything he read in the newspapers. A few customers looked over, but no one I knew.

"Thanks, Nico."

He shook his head, holding me at arm's length by the shoulders. "Bad things happen to good people. Your father, too—he was good person." Still shaking his head, he released his grip and picked up a menu. "Your usual table?"

"No, I'm meeting someone tonight. She's already here." I nodded toward Alison, who gave a little wave from an inside corner table.

"Ahhh." Nico raised his wiry black eyebrows and looked considerably cheered by this news. He opened his mouth and closed it again, evidently deciding that circumstances were inappropriate for his speech about the benefits of marriage. He ushered me to the table, deposited the menus, beamed an incandescent smile at both of us, and left.

"Too bad you don't have any friends," she said.

"With the enemies I have at the moment, I need every friend I can get."

Her smile faded and she looked down at the starched red-and-white checked tablecloth. When she looked up again, her eyes were sad. "That's why I called you today, Alex. I'm sorry to have to tell you this, but—well, you have a few more enemies than you think."

Marvelous, I thought. Just what I needed.

"My father would fly to the moon and back if he knew I were

here, telling you this." She looked around warily, as if she expected Rupert to appear at any moment, then leaned over the small table toward me and lowered her voice. "We had World War III at Auldwood last night. My fa—"

"Here we are," Nico bellowed, noisily depositing a bottle of red wine and two glasses. Alison jumped several inches, and I leaned back into my chair. "You want to taste?"

"I'm sure it's fine, Nico. Thanks."

He nodded, poured two half-glasses, and left discreetly.

"Whew." Alison waved a hand like a fan in front of her face, which was beet red. Perhaps she was risking more than I knew to be here.

"Go on," I said, pushing her wine toward her.

She took a sip automatically. "Right. As I was saying, we had an unholy row at the house last night. I was going out and stopped at the library to say good-bye to my father. I could hear him shouting in there with someone and decided not to interrupt. But when I heard what they were saying—I still can't believe it." She gave a derisive snort and swirled the wine in her glass, shaking her head. "*You're* not going to believe it, either."

"I certainly won't until you tell me," I said, trying to check my impatience. "Start at the beginning. Who was there and what did they say?"

She sighed. "It's evil, Alex—positively *evil*. Your own brother." So far, no surprises. "My father was saying that he wanted out, he hadn't counted on people being killed, fires being set, and so forth. And Max said it was almost all over, they had almost done it."

"Done what?"

She looked at me with something like pity, but her eyes were hard with bitterness. "Got you out of the way. Got Plumtree Press out of the way."

I looked at her, uncomprehending. "What do you mean, out of the way?"

Now she looked angry. "Put you out of business, removed you from the competition. And they're not the only ones, Alex. When I confronted my father, he refused to tell me who else was involved. He said he wouldn't put me in that sort of danger. But I know there are others. Max said that 'the others' wouldn't stop, and if my father wanted to see Christmas he shouldn't make too big a fuss about wanting out." She took a gulp of wine, and I saw that her hand was shaking. Rupert was no saint, but he was her father.

Nico set some pita bread and *tzatziki* on the table and went away again. I looked at Alison, a million miles away on the other side of the table, feeling as if I were back on the faraway planet of the other morning. The world was bleak and cold, and I was totally alone.

I'd thought I had it worked out, the puzzle solved—at least to some degree. But this latest revelation sent what I had carefully pieced together tumbling topsy-turvy. The person, or persons, wreaking the havoc in Ian's and my life hadn't been the villain of the Arthur books, afraid he would be found out. It was just some people who wanted me out of business, a publishing vendetta.

My mind reeled as I considered the implications. Plumtree was small fry, as publishing firms went; why should anyone care?

My voice, when it came, was surprisingly calm and reasonable. "What you're saying is that a group of people including your father and Max formed some sort of consortium to abolish Plumtree Press. I suppose I should be flattered that we're considered such a threat."

Alison looked at me with incredulity. "How can you laugh about this, Alex? Don't you see? They're not going to stop until the job's done. Max said so."

I looked at her, my head on one side. "What do you make of it? You know we're a small family publishing firm."

She nodded. "I know. I've had all night to think about it. I don't think it's just your business. I think it's you—you and your father."

"Thanks very much," I said, a smile involuntarily twitching at my lips.

She was serious. "You know what I mean. Your position with Publishers for Literacy, and your father's leadership of the League of Publishers, not to mention his political standing. You, and your father's political and social legacy to you, must be some kind of threat to someone. Several someones."

I supposed what she said could be true, and that was horrible enough. But my mind flew off on another tangent, one that was even more horrible to contemplate.

When I'd received word of my parents' death, I'd accepted the word of the local authorities when they pronounced it accidental death at sea. My parents didn't have a crew, they sailed the yacht themselves, and they were often in remote areas.

I surprised myself by mentally slamming the door on that particular subject. Self-preservation. Perhaps I would reopen it later.

Alison was looking at me. "What are we going to do, Alex?" Her voice was sympathetic and strong as she leaned across the table toward me, and her use of "we" didn't escape my attention.

I asked her to recount exactly what she had heard outside the library door last night, hoping to learn something helpful. She willingly did so, but she had already extracted the valuable nuggets of information from the garbage Max had spewed forth. I wanted to ask her if she had ever heard of Coatue, but decided to play it safe. I had learned a thing or two about trusting people. In case she was being honest, though, I thought we had better not stay here in public together for too long, for her sake if not mine.

I thanked her, warned her to be careful, and assured her that I would tell no one of our conversation. Then I left by the back entrance and came out of the alley farther down the block near my car. Alison was roaring away when I hopped into my Mini, quite sure she hadn't seen me in the dark, and followed her.

Despite my vow to trust no one, I was surprised when she turned onto Max's street, and even more surprised when she parked her car outside his building and went in. I exhaled in a rush and saw the little cloud of breath in the frigid air. "Nastier and nastier," I muttered. I began to wonder if there was anyone I could trust.

Don't, I told myself. Don't start feeling sorry for yourself.

As I pulled away from the curb, the phone rang in the car. I reached for it and answered, "Yes."

"Hi."

"Oh, hello, Sarah." Here was someone I trusted—almost. I still wasn't sure what to make of her conversation the other night.

She hesitated. "Lisette tells me you're living out of your car these days. Good thing you haven't got a Mini."

"Yes, isn't it." I didn't want to tell her she was spot on.

A sigh came down the wire. "Look, Alex, I want you to know that I'm not proud of myself for—well, you know—not being of more help to you the last few days. I was only thinking of myself, and after all you've done for me . . ."

"Sarah, I don't expect you to return any favors. I'd hoped it was clear that there were no strings attached."

"Yes, I know, but—"

"But nothing. You owe me nothing."

Silence. When she spoke there was a slight tremor in her voice. "I wanted to call before I left to make sure you were all right. I'm leaving for the States in the morning—taking a few days off to see my parents before a meeting in Boston on Wednesday. But . . ." She paused again and let out an explosive sigh. "But I also had to call because I can't hold my boss off any longer. I'm so sorry, Alex—I've done all I can. But he's demanding that I get something from you by the end of next week—something along the lines of twenty-five thousand pounds—or he'll start legal proceedings."

My face grew hot with the embarrassment of having put her in this position; I knew it would go on her record that she had made a bad investment. I should never have involved her with my business, but at the time Plumtree Press was going from strength to strength.

I got my mouth working with an effort. "I can't blame him. Thanks for all you've done, Sarah. I'll have it for you next week."

Mercifully, she tried to overcome the awkwardness by changing the subject.

"Need anything from across the pond?"

"Mmm, can't think of anything. But I'm glad to hear you're taking a vacation—I thought you'd forgotten the meaning of the word." I really did worry about her; she worked far too hard. In fact, to my knowledge she hadn't had a holiday since coming to London a year and a half ago. "Have a wonderful time. You deserve it."

"Thanks," she said. "Don't go running into any more burning buildings. I'll call you when I get back on Thursday."

"Right," I said absentmindedly, weaving through traffic toward her building as I pushed the Cancel button on the phone. She had no way of knowing that I was on my way to her office now to see that she got safely out and home, boyfriend or no boyfriend.

As I drove I thought about the £25,000, cursing Charlie and his lawyers for their indecision and paranoia. I hit the steering wheel so hard in frustration that my hand hurt. I had no choice but to go to Boston and get his money, given Simon Bow's trickery on the contract. Damn them! If I called and objected to going in person, but insisted upon having the money next week, they would know that I was desperate and would withdraw their offer. No one wanted to do business with a company in serious financial trouble. I was going to have to do it their way, absurd as it was.

Facing reality with clenched teeth, I looked at my watch. Of course. The last flight of the evening had gone at six o'clock, five minutes ago.

I swore blackly at the traffic and dialed directory enquiries for the British Airways number, got it and changed my reservation to the next flight, which left at seven-thirty in the morning. Next I steeled myself and dialed Charlie's number. He sounded taken aback to receive a call from me, for a change.

"Calling from the plane? We'll have someone at Logan to meet you, bring you out to the Cape . . ."

"Charlie, listen to me." I made a heroic effort to eliminate the impatience from my voice. "I couldn't make it tonight, but I'll be on the plane tomorrow morning. It arrives at about nine-thirty."

He seemed sobered by the seriousness of my voice. "Okay, Al—we'll be there."

"You will have the contracts ready? Everything's ready to go?"

"Well, of course." He sounded injured, as if my last three trips had never taken place. "In fact, they're on the desk in front of me now."

"Good." I sighed. "See you tomorrow, then, Charlie."

I hung up the phone without waiting for a response and relieved some of my frustration by driving with extreme aggressiveness to a parking garage near Sarah's building. It made me feel slightly better, though I received a number of annoyed honks from more sedate motorists. I never drove unsafely, just assertively—and yes, aggressively sometimes—but it seemed people couldn't tell the difference.

As I walked from the garage to Sarah's building, I suddenly knew how I would spend the evening. I would do some discreet snooping around Romney's rose-covered cottage, and with a little luck might find something to tell me where he had gone tonight, where Coatue was. I had already committed the criminal offense of wiretapping; a little breaking and entering couldn't hurt.

"Lord," I said, remembering that I would have to call Inspector McLeish before going to the States. His last words to me had been, "Don't go on any long trips in the next week or so." Surely, I thought, they would let me out of the country.

Wouldn't they?

I decided not to give them the choice; I would go and do what I had to do, which was to somehow find Ian at Coatue. They could arrest me later if they wanted to. Judging from Romney's phone conversation, Ian didn't have long to live. If Romney had gone tonight, by the time I found the elusive Coatue and got there after signing the damned contracts, I might be too late. I was horribly aware that I was saving my company, and, yes, Sarah's reputation at the bank, at Ian's expense. Without knowing where Coatue was, I didn't even have a choice.

I shuddered, only partly because of the cold, and picked up the pace until I was in my usual observation spot opposite Sarah's building. My purposeful pacing routine had just begun when I saw two familiar figures move with threatening casualness up the stairs to the bank's front door.

Running into the road, I willed the traffic to stop for me and made my way through the peak-hour crush amid screeching tires and enthusiastic expletives. I weaved through the last lane as Acme and Red disappeared through the glass doors, and as I ran in they were stepping into an elevator with a green Up arrow above it. I swam upstream against a powerful tide of workers eager to get home, and had to push my way through the throng. Just ten feet and twenty people away from the elevator doors, I saw them begin to slide closed.

I pushed a couple of middle-aged men out of the way and lunged for the rapidly vanishing opening. When the doors closed they hit my forearm and opened again. Evidently Acme and Red hadn't seen me coming; for a precious instant, they seemed stunned. That was all I needed.

Before they could react, in one sweeping motion I stepped inside, grabbed the fire extinguisher off the wall, pulled its ring, aimed, and sprayed it at them as the doors slammed shut again. For the thousandth time I was grateful for the experience of leading the sailing flotilla. I'd put out dozens of cooking fires on yachts for tipsy occupants, always amazed at what people will allow to happen to other people's property. The white foam would make them want to scratch their eyes out of their sockets but would not permanently damage them. I knew from experience.

They jumped back from me, yelping with pain and clawing at their eyes as I pressed the red Stop button on the control panel. Acme let loose with a string of virulent curses and threats as the elevator jerked to a rough stop somewhere between the fourth and fifth floors. Red suffered more graciously, uttering mainly groans and grunts. I knew how badly their eyes hurt and was sorry to have to go to such lengths to stop them. The next part was worse, especially because they couldn't see me, but I had to keep them from coming after me once their tears had washed the irritant from their eyes.

I pulled back my fist and hit Acme as hard as I could in the jaw, resurrecting a skill I hadn't used since Max left home for university, and then only in self-defense. He flew back against the side wall and slumped to the floor. Red put up a halfhearted protest, his arms flailing in front of him blindly in an attempt to stop me, but in the end he got the same treatment.

When he too had slumped to the floor, I stepped out of my shoes and hurriedly pulled off my socks, balancing on one foot at a time, then stepped back into the shoes and tied the socks together. I wound them tightly around Acme's hands, then stripped off my jacket, sweater, and shirt. I hated to lose the shirt but couldn't think of anything else that would keep Red from punching elevator buttons or dialing for help before Sarah got out of the building. With all the threatening hands tied, I pulled both men to the corner farthest from the buttons, looped an arm of the sweater through Acme's and then Red's knots, and tied the whole mess together around the piece of metal that anchored the elevator's waist-high stainless-steel railing to the wall.

I put on my coat again and pushed one of the ceiling panels upward and to the side. A couple of inches higher on the metal ceiling of the car was a metal handle that evidently opened the emergency exit. Being tall came in handy occasionally; I reached up, gripped the handle, and turned it, pushing the trapdoor out into the darkness of the shaft. Grabbing hold of the steel bars that supported the ceiling panels, I got my feet onto the waist-high metal rail and pushed my head and shoulders up through the top of the car. It wasn't too difficult then to hoist the rest of my body through the opening. I crouched on top of the car, squinting, trying to get my bearings in the dim light.

A whirring sound emanated from above and to the right, where I knew the other elevator must be. I waited, willing it to stop at this floor. It appeared to be slowing, but when it came even with me, it whirred past and came to a halt at the floor below, roughly twelve feet down.

It wasn't ideal, but I doubted I'd get a better chance. I stood up, hanging onto the cable, and, before I had a chance to think about it too much, jumped over a couple of feet of black abyss toward the cable and roof of the neighboring car.

For a leap of faith in the dark, it didn't turn out too badly, with the unfortunate exception of my glasses. As I landed on the roof of the car, the cable raced up to meet me and swept them off the bridge of my nose. I heard them clatter once against the wall of the shaft as they fell, and before they could travel down the remaining two floors to the bottom, the lift started to move again.

There was no time to think about this new disaster, about how totally incapacitated I was without my artificial lenses. The elevator was still going down, swaying a bit as it went, collecting people to deposit in the lobby. I had to get off the car before it started to go up again, as I didn't fancy being squished like a bug on the ceiling when it got to the top floor. Besides, I had to get to the bottom of the shaft to see if I could salvage the glasses. It would have been much easier to find them with the help of the building maintenance people, but they would want to know why I was crawling about in the bowels of their building.

I couldn't hear what was going on inside the car below me; the mechanism made too much noise in the shaft. But the passengers must have heard me and probably weren't too pleased about loud noises on the roof and the uncertainty of swaying to and fro when they weren't on terra firma. When the car reached the ground floor, which by my calculation was three floors away, I would make my move.

The car came to a shuddering stop and the doors opened in the wall, faintly illuminating the shaft as light crept through gaps around the edges of the car. It rose fractionally as people stepped out. I focused my attention on the network of beams between me and the other elevator car. I knew I had to move quickly, vision or no vision; it wouldn't be long before the elevator was on its way up again. There was no choice but to lunge for the blurry image of a beam roughly four feet away, just far enough so that I couldn't grasp it securely before relinquishing my footing on the roof. I reached out and then leaned toward the beam, which extended downward from its cross-support at a forty-five degree angle below me. Half-jumping, half-falling, I got hold of it and scrambled until I was astride it.

From there it was not terribly difficult to lower myself slowly to the bottom of the shaft in the near darkness, feeling my way down along the beams. The working elevator was making another trip up, leaving me alone at the bottom without the help of any light from around the doors. When I reached the floor, I put one foot down, then the other, and heard something scuttle away across the floor, squeaking as it went. Paper and other litter rustled and scraped under my feet, the accumulation of forty years of maintenance detritus. There had to have been a good three inches of dust on top of it all—good thing I couldn't see what I was getting into.

I got down on my hands and knees and rummaged through the debris, feeling hopeful that my glasses might have fallen gently onto a discarded bag of hamburger wrappers and remained intact. They were plastic, after all; perhaps they had survived.

I have no way of knowing how long I looked before I found the first small pieces of what felt like quarter-inch-thick hard plastic, but I heard the elevator make at least a dozen trips up and down while I searched.

After at least as many more trips I had crawled in a spiral from the edges of the room to the center, and had found what I believed to be the remains of the glasses. Unfortunately, they didn't much resemble glasses anymore and would be of little use. The imitation tortoiseshell frames had broken into only three pieces, but the plastics company had been right. The lens material was still too brittle and needed work, at least if it were to survive a fall of several stories. Roughly a third of one lens was intact, from what I could feel, but all that remained otherwise were pieces.

I picked up what I could, put it all in my coat pocket, and turned my mind to getting out of my dungeon. There had to be a door somewhere to allow maintenance workers access to the shaft. I walked around the walls, feeling for a doorknob and the outline of a door, which I found on the far side of the beams, under Acme and Red. I turned the knob, pulled the door open, and was rewarded with the bright light of civilization. The gray linoleum-floored corridor was deserted, and I walked toward a blue neon glow near the ceiling that I hoped was an exit sign. Hands in front of me, I reached out for a dark stripe bisecting a large rectangle, apparently a door, and pushed. I was out in the chilly night air.

Unfortunately, I wasn't going to make much of a protector for Sarah without eyesight. The only thing I could do was return to The Orchard for my long-disused pair of heavy glasses. I set off for Bank tube station grateful that I had them, at least, and told myself that it would be some time before Acme and Red's boss knew the outcome of their excursion to Sarah's building. I was in two minds about leaving her there in the building with them, if she was still there, even though they were incapacitated. When someone investigated the broken lift and found them, they would almost certainly be freed. I was banking on the fact that their eyes would be too painful for them to continue with their plan, whatever that had been, but I didn't like leaving it to chance for the hour and a half it would take to get to The Orchard and back.

Still, aside from calling her and alarming her, there was nothing to be done but to go get the damnable glasses and make sure she was all right afterward.

It was a memorable experience finding my way down the stairs, through the ticket booth, and onto the right train, and no one offered help when they saw me feeling my way along. I hated to come face to face with what might be a rather grim future, if my eyes grew measurably worse.

In the end I made it onto the train and changed twice successfully before I was on my way to Chess. Once there I got a ride to The Orchard with the taxi service outside the station and finally found the glasses in my old bedroom bureau drawer. They felt like lead weights on my nose, and the correction was not as strong as the newer pair. Still, they would keep me functioning.

Max should have thought of this, I thought; if he really wanted to do me in, all he had to do was destroy both pairs of glasses. Foolish of him to go to such lengths. But then I had the feeling that all of this had not been his idea; he had been an instrument of someone far more cunning and devious than Max's temper would ever allow him to be.

I decided to leave the Mini in the City garage and drive the Golf back into London. The Volkswagen was a luxury after the Mini, particularly its functioning heat. Forty minutes later I parked in the same garage near Sarah's building. I went inside to the security desk, a long black counter along one wall, and asked the officer to ring Sarah Townsend. I didn't intend to speak to her if she answered; I would ask him to relay some phony message I had yet to invent. As he picked up the phone and consulted his list of names and extensions, I peered into the lobby where a cleaning crew appeared to be cleaning out the mess inside the elevator. Acme and Red were nowhere to be seen, which could be good or bad; I didn't know yet.

"No one's answering," the guard said, putting down the phone. "Sorry." I looked at my watch: eight-thirty.

"It's important that I find her; would you know if she's gone for the night?"

The guard turned to his colleague down the counter. "Bill? Any idea if Sarah Townsend has left yet?"

Bill raised his eyebrows and gave me an interested, appraising look. "Yeah. Left with a gentleman friend, about half an hour ago."

The blond American, probably, but I had to make sure. I would have hated for it to have been Red.

"Ah," I smiled sheepishly. "The competition got here first."

They smirked and looked at one another.

"Was he tall, blond, wearing a well-tailored suit? American?" I asked.

Bill nodded decisively. "That's the one. He met her in the lobby. They stopped to ask about a couple of nutcases we'd just packed off in an ambulance." He narrowed his eyes and shook his head incredulously, obviously enjoying the chance to tell me about it. "Got themselves tied up in the lift, all blinded, like, by fire extinguisher froth. Don't ask me why people do what they do. You'd have thought we were sending 'em to prison, the way they fought us about getting into the ambulance, but it's company rules—anyone injured on the premises has to go in an ambulance. Legal business, you know."

I shook my head. "Bet you're glad they're off your hands. Okay, then," I said, sighing as I straightened up. "Thanks. At least I know what I'm up against."

As I turned to go, Bill said, "If she was mine, I wouldn't let her out of my sight. You don't see too many that are pretty *and* smart." He winked and busied himself with some papers on the counter.

I nodded in total agreement and walked out. Even if she had gone off for another long evening with Mr. America, I had the pleasure of knowing that I had protected her from Acme and Red, and perhaps even saved her life.

The only thing left to do before catching the blasted plane in the morning was to try to find some sort of hint of Romney's whereabouts. I knew I might not find anything, but I couldn't just waste the time between now and the morning, and I certainly couldn't sleep.

I made my way back to the car and set off again for the great Northwest, specifically Chalfont St. Giles. The one benefit of all this driving was that it allowed me time to think. Time to think about what I would do when I got back from the earliest possible return flight from Boston. Time to think what I would do if I couldn't find Coatue or Ian after that, and what I would do if I could. Time also to wonder whether my life would ever become normal again, and whether I would ever win out over Mr. America.

My fingers had a deathgrip on the steering wheel, and I made an effort to relax them. I relaxed my right foot a bit, too, as I glanced at the needle on the speedometer creeping over 100. It wouldn't do to have two blots against my name with the police, that is, speeding in addition to suspicion of murder—not to mention potential convictions for wiretapping and breaking and entering. I shook my head in disbelief and wondered about the precise velocity at which speeding became a serious crime.

When the town of Chalfont St. Giles came into view, I took a back route over single-track roads to Romney's. I parked a couple of streets down and made the same stealthy approach as I had the night I'd planted the recorder, except this time I aimed for the back door of the house instead of the garden shed. Romney had ancient locks on his doors, possibly the original ones, and with little more than a good jiggle the back door yielded itself up to me. Surprisingly easy, I thought; if I were involved in something as crooked as Romney, I'd make sure I could keep people out of my house.

I spent the better part of two hours going through every scrap of paper I could find in Romney's desk, file drawers, and table surfaces. I was rewarded with nothing. Nothing, that is, but bills, bank statements, personal correspondence, and clippings. None of it pertained to Arthur's books, Ian, or my father in any way. He'd been very careful indeed.

Disgusted, I walked back to my car in the cold, fired it up, and decided to fortify myself with a pint and a pub dinner at the Cock and Bull around the corner. As I started to pull away from the side of the road, a car sailed past me at high speed with its lights off. I slammed on the brakes and hit the horn, hoping to warn him. His lights snapped on, and as the instant replay ran through my mind, I realized that the car had been a gold Mercedes-Benz. I happened to know someone who lived in Chalfont St. Giles who drove a late-model gold Mercedes-Benz: Bartholomew Graves-Smith. Since I had nothing to do, I followed him a bit guiltily, wondering where he was going in such a hurry that he forgot to turn his lights on.

Graves-Smith, an absentminded, gray-haired pussycat of a man, had sold out to a large American publisher called Megabooks at the same time I had left the Greek Isles for Plumtree Press. Rumor had it that he was struggling to meet their aggressive goals for him—which included making people redundant and raising profits at the same time. It was unfortunate that he had chosen to cast his lot with a company like Megabooks, which was so incompatible with his own.

He was also, unfortunately, incompatibly yoked with a grasping, vain, overly made-up woman who, I was certain, was responsible for the gaudy car he drove. He was perfectly loyal to her, though one couldn't say the same for her. In fact, she and her incessant nagging to earn more money had probably driven him to distraction, including driving without headlights. She didn't bother to keep their squabbling private, and could often be heard complaining in public that she didn't have a certain piece of jewelry or clothing that another woman was wearing.

I followed Graves-Smith from a distance of several car lengths. It would be rather embarrassing if he were to learn that I was amusing myself by following him about. I myself couldn't believe that I was following him about, but there was something about his car hurtling past me in the dark that made me curious. I wouldn't have thought him capable of speeding, and tried hard to imagine something that . . . of course. A woman. It had to be.

Ashamed of myself, I planned to turn off at the Royal Standard, a famous and ancient pub around the next bend in Beaconsfield, and end the game of cat and mouse. Then I saw Graves-Smith's turn signal go on shortly after he'd passed the Royal Standard, and realized that there was only one place that he could be going. Auldwood, the Soames family home, was at the end of that country road.

More and more curious. I stayed behind him. I couldn't imagine Rupert and Bartholomew Graves-Smith having a conversation, much less at Rupert's home. About a year ago, Rupert had publicly denounced Graves-Smith for selling out to an American firm, and the press had picked it up. As much of a milquetoast as Graves-Smith was, he did have a certain amount of pride. I couldn't imagine him paying a social visit to Rupert.

Graves-Smith had nearly reached Auldwood's drive. I turned off my lights and pulled off to the side of the road in case he should look back. As he crunched up into the gravel drive, I found myself drawn irresistibly to find out what was going on. I would have to take a closer look, but I certainly couldn't pull into the driveway for a snoop around. I turned the car around, turned my lights back on, and drove back the way I had come until I found a narrow lane that shot off to the right. I followed it as it snaked through the fields, edging closer and closer to the Soames property. It was very convenient to know the area so well.

I finally parked the car a quarter of a mile away from the house at the edge of a farmer's field, between fence and road, and hoped the owner wouldn't mind. Then it was a matter of ten minutes to trudge through mud and dead weeds to the edge of Rupert's estate. There was little light, and I wasn't aware of puddles until I was in the middle of them. My feet squelched in my inadequate leather loafers and thin socks, rendering them all but useless in warding off the cold.

I thought of Ian and felt a knot in my stomach. There was nothing I could do for him now, except pray that Ian would not be "eliminated," in the cold words of the man who had spoken with Romney, before I could find him. I felt hopelessly guilty and inadequate, following people around in the dark while his life was at risk. If only I could have gotten on that evening's flight, and not wasted so much precious time.

I almost ran into Rupert's fancy wrought-iron fence. It rose without warning from the stubble of the field and, like most of Rupert's belongings, existed more for form than function. I doubted that he had a surveillance system, living this far out in the country; it wouldn't have fit with his carefully cultivated country squire image.

Still, I was cautious. I didn't fancy being caught red-handed by Rupert, crawling about his property at night. I had decided to approach from the back of the house and see if I could find a way to observe Bartholomew Graves-Smith and Rupert. Chalk up one more offense for the prosecution, I thought: trespassing. It hardly mattered anymore.

I moved closer to the house, keeping some sort of greenery between me and it when I could. Though Rupert had been here for fifteen years or so, his garden looked new. He had the gardener keep the shrubs formally squared off, in my opinion a totally unnatural appearance for any living thing. In the rear area of the garden there were shrubs planted in curving patterns and shorn low to the ground. There was evidence of roses and other flowers among the curves, and a fountain in the middle.

I kept to the back of the bushes and followed them around to the brick path that led through the middle of the semicircular lawn, then I peered around the perfectly manicured shrubs toward the house. There was a large window directly ahead of me, with French doors in its center. I could tell that the lights were on in the room behind a dark opaque curtain, judging from the light that crept around the edges. The rest of the house appeared totally dark from this vantage point.

I decided to nose around the front of the house. Maybe they were having a showdown at the front door. I crept back along the way I had come toward the fence, then traveled along it toward the front of the house. By the time I had come even with the house, I could see that Rupert was playing host to a number of people this evening. Four non-Soames vehicles were lined up in the pea-gravel drive—including Max's black BMW and Graves-Smith's Mercedes.

Though I can't say I was surprised, it was another nasty jolt to see Max's car here. It wasn't just that he was here at the home of my sworn enemy. It was also that Max and Rupert in one place, according to Alison, implied a gathering of the publishers out to destroy Plumtree Press, and I didn't like what that said about Bartholomew Graves-Smith.

I started back toward the rear of the house thinking about the other two cars I'd seen in the drive. I moved as noiselessly as I could, trying to avoid the dead leaves littering the lawn. Though damp, they whispered when I stepped on them. One of the cars had been an aging forest green Jaguar, and a rather ordinary—compared to its present company, anyway—beige Ford Escort. I knew I'd seen the Jaguar somewhere before . . .

In a rush it came to me. It was Nigel Wexford's, the *Sunday Tempus Book Review* editor whom my father had mentioned in his diaries. Good God. If he was on Rupert's sabotage team, how had we got as much positive coverage as we had in the last year or two?

I shivered and rubbed my arms, as a chilling thought came to me. Was Wexford the means by which someone had known, days before Barnes's review of *Those Who Trespass Against Us* was published, that Barnes and his knowledge on the subject had to be blotted out?

That would mean that for some reason the anti-Plumtree publishers were also interested in preserving the anonymity of the kidnapper. Why would a group of trade publishers care whether the identity of the kidnapper was revealed? Unless one of them had been involved in the kidnappings . . .

No, I told myself, too farfetched. I knew all of these industry people, had for years. It was laughable to think of any one of them as actually criminal, even if they might not be my favorite people. Take poor old Bartholomew Graves-Smith. He didn't have it in him to do something really wicked. Besides, he was too busy trying to please his greedy wife.

Please his wife . . . I had an unpleasant flash of insight. Perhaps somehow the consortium meant money for those involved. If anyone was desperate for money, besides me, it was Graves-Smith. Between his wife and Megabooks, he was being squeezed from both sides.

The beige Escort. Who drove a beige Escort? I had no idea, but with a bit of luck I would find out soon. Emboldened by the almost-total darkness, I edged forward, crouching slightly, until I was near one edge of the large curtained window. A triangle of light was just ahead of me, and I couldn't believe my luck as I squatted to peer through it. A straight chair had prevented the curtain from closing completely at a height of about two and a half feet above the ground. What I saw in Rupert Soames's extremely formal white brocade living room was a rough circle of men sitting in chairs formed by Rupert, Nigel, Bartholomew, Max, and someone I would never have expected to be there in a hundred years.

Nick Khasnouri.

He sat looking uncomfortable and intimidated, his hands empty while the others held some sort of drink. Unfortunately I could hear little of their conversation, but I could glean a surprising amount of information from mere observation. Nick clearly didn't want to be there and sat on his chair rigidly, touching as little of it as possible. He looked angry and incredulous, as if he'd just been insulted. Rupert was speaking, and from his gestures and the others' glances toward Nick, it was obvious that Nick was the topic of conversation.

Rupert didn't look any too pleased himself, and his mood deteriorated as I watched. Before I knew it he was shaking a threatening finger at Nick, speaking in ominously low tones. Whatever he said made the others stare at Nick curiously, except for Max. His sneer remained consistent. He wore the detached look he had when he was in an altered state, and as I watched he stood and walked to a portable bar in the corner. He poured his cut-crystal tumbler almost full of whiskey and earned a disgusted look from Rupert as he sat down again.

The others squirmed a bit as Rupert made his accusations of Nick. Bartholomew seemed to break in mildly with what might have been, "Here, now, Rupert, there's no need to be rude," and was totally ignored. He shrugged and settled back into his overstuffed chair.

Fortunately for me, and unfortunately for Nick, Rupert stood and began to bellow. Rupert's outrageous volume allowed me to hear his words through the window, but I felt sorry for young Nick.

"How dare you! You're about as ignorant of the alterations in the charity's records as I am! You can't pretend you're lily white, now you've come this far."

Evidently this was Nick's boiling point. He stood and faced Rupert head on, and shouted back, "Look, I don't know what you're playing at, but I've had nothing to do with falsifying the accounts. I might not belong to your posh clubs, and I might not have gone to the right schools, but at least I'm honest. It's more than I can say for you lot." It was his turn to eye the assembled group with disgust. "I'm not staying for more of this," he said, and headed for the door.

Rupert sat down with unnatural calm and said something which I strained my ears to hear. I caught snatches. ". . . afraid . . . find that difficult . . . unless you cooperate."

For the first time it occurred to me that some harm might come to Nick. Perhaps Rupert had a gun; I didn't have a clear view of him. The others, with the exception of Max, showed signs of nervousness at Rupert's statement, but didn't budge. Before I realized what was happening Nick had walked angrily to the French doors, parted the curtains, and kicked hard at the center of one of the doors. The wood splintered easily, and glass tinkled onto the brick patio not four feet from me. He was out in a flash, running past me toward the back garden.

I tore after him and heard others behind me. But Nick and I were by far the youngest and fittest, and we kept running long after we had hopped the fence. He thought that I was one of the others chasing him, no doubt, and I let him think that until we had crossed an entire hay field next to the Soames estate.

"Nick," I shouted, gasping, "it's me. Alex."

He slowed slightly, still running, then turned for a hesitant look. When he saw me, or at least a vague outline that resembled me, his expression was one of amazement, relief, and guilt at once. He slowed and stopped, turning toward me.

"What the—" He bent over to catch his breath and looked up

at me, squinting and panting. "What the hell are you doing here?"

"I might ask the same of you," I said, breathing hard. "But I heard enough back at the house to know that Rupert and his lads are framing you for the inconsistencies in the charity's books."

He looked at me with relief. "Thank God you understand. I thought you might think that—"

"No." I waved a hand dismissively and leaned over, resting my hands on my knees while I caught my breath. It would be a cold day in hell before Nick would become dishonest enough to tell a white lie, let alone abscond with charitable funds. I stood up. "Come on, I've got my car out here somewhere. Let's drive and you can tell me all about it."

We glanced nervously at the surrounding fields as we walked to my car, but it seemed that Rupert and his gang had given up the chase for that night. It gave me pleasure to think that a street-smart kid who'd grown up on the wrong side of the tracks could outwit Rupert Soames with all his money and bluster.

We lifted our muddy feet into the car and closed the doors with gratitude, glad to be out of the wind. I had seen Nick glance into the backseat as he got in. He waited until I'd started the motor, then said quietly, "You're living in here, aren't you?"

"Yes."

There was a moment of silence.

"It's odd, seeing you again. It's almost as if . . . well, as if you'd come back from the dead. You disappeared so suddenly. We were all worried sick about you, but Lisette kept telling us you were all right. You could have come to us for help, you know." This last was pronounced in an injured tone.

"I appreciate it, Nick, but I couldn't do that to anyone. They would go to anyone who knew where I was—anyone."

"Who are 'they'?"

"Excellent question. I only know part of the answer. Rupert and our friends back at Auldwood are part of it all right, along with a small army of men to do the dirty work. But there's someone else . . ."

I asked Nick how he came to be at Auldwood, and he explained that Rupert had invited him, ostensibly for a party, but then it had become the odd tribunal I'd witnessed from the garden. He shook his head. "They were crazy—Nigel, Max, Bartholomew of all people, and Soames, of course. They said they could make it look like I'd stolen the money from Publishers for Literacy if I didn't shut up about the cooked books and help them make it all look proper. I felt I'd walked into some other world, hearing them say that. I just can't believe they're all in on it. They're actually criminals! I've got to tell the authorities, I suppose."

I nodded. "There's more, though, Nick. And I need you to wait before going to the police until I check something out. I need everything to stay as it is, just for another day or two, until I know. Then we'll tell the authorities everything we know. Okay?"

He looked at me and nodded, but he was concerned. He didn't like deception of any sort.

I decided to clue Nick in to what I knew, about the consortium, about Romney, about Barnes. He was shocked, then outraged, then discouraged as the story unfolded. He asked questions and I talked, and the questions gradually grew fewer and farther apart until at last when I looked over, his chin was on his chest. Poor boy, I guess I'd overwhelmed him. I smiled and wondered if I'd looked that young at twenty-one.

I didn't feel tired in the least, though it was approaching midnight. Seven hours and forty minutes until my plane took off for Boston. I decided I might as well try to get some sleep, and drove to an all-night motorway complex near the airport where I parked among the dozing truckers. Nick didn't wake up when we stopped, so I reclined my seat and reached into the back for my blanket and threw it over him. I piled what clothes remained on myself, set my watch alarm for four-thirty, and closed my eyes. This could be my last night in the car, I thought.

I was right. But any other predictions I might have made that night would have been wildly inaccurate, so totally had I miscalculated my situation.

9

I awoke panic-stricken. It was too late; I had overslept and missed the plane. I sat bolt upright, my heart jumping into my throat, but found myself held back by some sort of restraint. . . .

Instinctively I fought against it, only to realize the next moment that it was my seat belt. With some embarrassment I realized that the flight attendant was leaning over me, saying with a bemused smile that it was time to put my seat back upright for landing in Boston. I obeyed, disoriented and somewhat shaken, and changed my watch to local time. Two-fifteen in the afternoon London time, nine-fifteen in the morning here. We would arrive five minutes early, the pilot announced. It was forty-nine degrees and mostly sunny in Boston, with a wind of ten miles an hour.

My mouth felt full of cotton. There was a plastic airline container of orange juice on the tray of the empty seat next to me, and I finished it in one long, thirsty gulp.

We were still high above the water, and even in a jet-lagged stupor I felt my impatience mounting. The absurdity of making this trip when Ian's life was at risk was overwhelming, and I had the feeling of unreality I had experienced outside Sarah's house several nights earlier. I rubbed my hands over my face vigorously and let a pressurized breath escape slowly through my lips.

Glancing around my airborne prison, I noticed the in-flight magazine in the seat back in front of me and yanked it out of the webbing. The cover story was a feature on autumn in New England. I turned to it impatiently. Something, anything, to pass these last eternal ten minutes. The Head of the Charles, cider-making in Vermont, hiking in New Hampshire, the annual Cranberry Festival on Nantucket . . .

I turned to the spread on Nantucket and skimmed the cranberry story, how the berries are harvested from the bogs and where they go from there, then looked at the hand-sketched map of places of interest on the island. A single word caught my eye, and all of a sudden the paper went white and my hands clammy.

I had found it; I had found Ian. A small strip of land on the north side of Nantucket Island bore the legend "COATUE." My heart threatened to jump through my chest, and I took a few deep breaths. I had to get there. Now.

If I could have parachuted from the jet, I would have. I looked out the window and saw that we were almost down. With every muscle taut, I listened to the engines whine as we descended. The 747 was still over water, coming closer to the whitecaps all the time, and it looked as if we would skid down on them instead of the runway. But at the last moment the runway miraculously appeared, as it always did, and we taxied to an excruciatingly gradual stop.

Before the plane had made its final violent jerk at the gate, I had my bag in hand and was ready to race out the door and down the jetway to customs. Every second mattered; I had a horrible feeling that I was already too late. The five minutes or so I had to wait before getting off the plane seemed an eternity, but I was one of the first in line at customs, and it was a cursory inspection. At last I was free to run down the concourse to the commuter airlines to catch the earliest flight to Nantucket. Thank God I didn't have to deal with Charlie, I thought; he was either late or waiting outside. I would get to him later.

The woman at the ticket counter was clearly baffled as to why anyone should be in such a hurry to get to Nantucket Island in November. "The next flight leaves in fifteen minutes," she said, bemused. A grand total of two commuter airlines served the island. "It's on time—weather's good for a change." She glanced at me and smiled as she stuck a seat number on my boarding pass. "Cheer up, honey. You'll be there in half an hour."

She was right. Our little Cessna had landed at Nantucket

Airport before it ever reached cruising altitude. Forty miles wasn't much for even a tiny plane to negotiate. I had watched with fascination as we approached first Martha's Vineyard and then the smaller island of Nantucket, shaped like a lopsided crescent moon. It was easy to distinguish Coatue, which appeared to be nothing more than a sandbar that was scalloped along one side. Coatue formed the inside curve of the crescent, its scallops facing inward toward a long, narrow harbor that ran almost half the length of the island. A sailor's heaven, I thought, all that protected water for mooring yachts. I shuddered at the next logical thought; all that protected water would be perfect for various forms of skullduggery, including the disposal of unwanted authors.

Then we were down. As I walked across the tarmac from the plane into the airport, I caught a whiff of salty sea. Nantucket appeared to be mostly flat and undeveloped, from what I could see, and the gray beach grass rustling in the wind where the pavement ended was curiously beautiful. There were few trees, and with so much sky visible, and the smell of the sea, I had the feeling that some sort of weight had been removed from my shoulders.

I ran through the airport and managed to catch the first taxi in line. The driver looked just about old enough to have a license, and obviously lived on the beach in the summer, judging from the long white-blond hair that peeked out from beneath a faded baseball cap.

He greeted me with a ready smile, and I asked him to take me to a reputable marina where I could hire a yacht. I knew it was an unusual request for this late in the autumn, but it was the only way I could think of to track Arthur at this point. If there was nothing on Coatue but sand, then they had to be holding him on a boat. I would have preferred to use a powerboat for its speed, but if the need for stealth arose, I would be less conspicuous on a yacht. Less likely to raise suspicions, too.

The boy raised his eyebrows good-naturedly and adjusted his cap down on his forehead. "Things are pretty much closed up around here this time of year. But we can always go see Frank—if you don't mind a little drive. He'll be at home today, not at the harbor."

"Whatever it takes; I'm eager to get on the water."

"Gotcha." He put the car into gear and we were off.

I settled back to pore over a map of the island I had picked up at the Gull Air counter in Boston. It wasn't intended for sailing use, of course, but at least I could orient myself. Maybe Frank could sell me some charts or lend me some. I expected to have to do some night sailing and knew I would have to study the charts to avoid shoals and other hazards after dark.

It occurred to me that I might be able to glean some information from the young man in the driver's seat. Surely most people who lived on this island year-round knew a bit about sailing conditions here.

I leaned forward and said, "My name's Alex, by the way."

He looked at me briefly in the rearview mirror. "I'm Mike," he said cordially.

"Do you ever sail around here?"

He shrugged his shoulders and moved his head from side to side in ambivalence. "Sure. Some, in the summer. But I'm not one of these diehards. Give me a few beers and a sunny day, and yeah, I'll go out on a yacht. I even crew for regattas now and then, if they provide the lunch. But I'd rather be surfing."

I nodded. Only those with the opportunity to do it every day could be so offhand about sailing. "I know what you mean. It's not much fun when it gets really cold."

He snorted and turned onto a small road posted with a remarkably long name. I turned my head to catch it before it disappeared: Sesachacha Pond Road. It appeared that the Native Americans had been first on Nantucket, too.

"Ever sailed on the ocean side of Coatue?"

He looked at me in the rearview mirror, his eyes earnest. "Sure; nice sailing there, not too rough. But don't make the classic mistake of trying to sail around the perimeter of the island. It gets pretty hairy out by Maddaket—the far western tip of the island, out by Tuckernuck." I had noticed the tiny scrap of land called Tuckernuck Island on the map, barely a mile from the Nantucket coast.

"The shoals are marked on the charts, but more people rip the hulls out of their boats out there than you'd believe." He paused and looked in the mirror again, frowning. "By the way, can you think of a reason why anyone'd be following you? This same car's been behind us since we left the airport."

I looked in his rearview mirror, not wanting to turn around

and acknowledge their presence, and saw a white Volvo following us at a respectable distance. I stared, feeling suddenly cold. Even at this distance, with my marginal eyesight, I could make out their striking outlines.

Mr. America and Sarah.

Why?

Their conversation came back to me from the night I had appointed myself guardian outside her house. "The really funny thing is that he'll never even know how it happened," she had said.

"No, I can't think why anyone would be following me," I lied, not wanting to confront the truth. The only answer could be that she was one of them, one of Rupert's lot.

I could see that we were no longer on the main road. It couldn't be a coincidence that they were behind us now. We had turned several times in quick succession off the Maddaket road and were now following a sandy little bit of a path I didn't think many cars had negotiated.

"I've been making turns for a few minutes now just to see if they'd stay on our tail." He gave me a quick look in the mirror. "Don't worry, I wasn't going to charge you."

I was impressed, not only with his honesty but his initiative. "Thanks," I said, and was wondering how I could get away from them and onto a boat when Mike spoke again.

"Hang on," he said, gripping the wheel. "Let's have some fun with 'em."

Before I could respond he had somehow managed to spin the car 180 degrees to face the oncoming Volvo. He stopped it there on the narrow road, let out a whoop, and jumped out of the car as the Volvo screeched to a halt inches from the taxi's grille. I climbed out of the other side of the car, amazed, as Mr. America leapt out and sputtered furiously at Mike.

"Do you realize you could have killed us all? I've never seen such a crazy stunt in my—"

"Don't, Robbie, please." Sarah ran and stood between him and Mike, who seemed to think the whole thing was pretty entertaining. "Listen," she said, looking sheepishly at me. "I can explain all of this. I'm sorry, Alex; I saw you at the airport and had to know where you were going. You looked so worried, and I knew you wouldn't tell me if I asked."

She was asking me to believe in her again. I was glad she didn't know how much I wanted to.

"Who's he?" I asked, indicating Robbie with my head.

Sarah looked at me in surprise. "You've never met my younger brother, Rob?"

It was my turn to feel a fool. Rob still didn't look any too pleased, and I don't suppose I did either. We glared at each other for a moment and then I stuck out my hand. He took it, his reservations apparently fading, and we stood on the sandy road in the November sunshine and shook hands with what seemed to me ridiculous formality.

"I've heard Sarah mention you," he said carefully, glancing in her direction. "I suppose it's not your fault if your taxi driver tries to kill his passengers." He scowled again at Mike, then looked at me. "Is there anything we can do to help?" Something resembling concern crept into his face, along with several question marks. I liked him, now that I knew who he was—or wasn't.

If I hadn't been in such a hurry, I would have attempted an explanation. Instead I shook my head and moved back toward the car, still looking at him. "Thanks, no."

Rob accepted this with a nod, but Sarah looked exasperated. "Sorry," I said and climbed into the taxi. "I'll call you tomorrow, all right?"

I tried to put all thoughts of Sarah out of my mind as we completed the trip to Frank's modest beachfront home, where Mike put me in the weatherbeaten and obviously capable hands of his friend. As I stood at the window of the car counting out the money I owed him, I had an idea.

"Mike, would you consider selling me your cap? A sort of Nantucket souvenir?"

He looked at me incredulously, then took off the cap and inspected it. "It's filthy," he said. "Besides—not quite your style, is it?" He may have been referring to the "Life's a Beach" slogan embroidered onto the front in faded pink script. "Don't you want something with whales on it?"

I shrugged. I only wanted it for its disguise value, to obscure enough of my face that Romney and his friends wouldn't know me immediately if they saw me at a distance. "I like your cap the way it is. But I understand if you'd rather not."

"Take it." He handed it to me through the window in exchange for the money I passed him, at which point he smiled and drove off in a cloud of sandy dust, tires screeching.

Frank came out to meet me. He proved to be a quiet, nononsense man with rough-hewn features who hadn't shaved for several days. Frank took me to the harbor in his pickup truck and matter-of-factly asked me how much sailing I'd done.

"About four year's worth, full time, and ten summers before that." I didn't tell him that I couldn't see clearly past about twenty feet with these glasses; what he didn't know wouldn't worry him.

He nodded and took his eyes off the road to eye me briefly. "That's a load off my mind. You wouldn't believe what some people do to my boats." I could imagine how painful it would be for him, as the owner, to see his expensive yachts damaged; I had flinched a good deal at some of my charges on the sailing holidays, and those yachts hadn't even been mine.

"Ever sailed around here before?"

"The Cape and Maine, yes, but not Nantucket."

"Okay. You'll need to know about the shoals," he said decisively. "I'll show you on the charts in the office." We rode in silence for a moment past the quaint clapboard houses and beach grass. Then he said, "You haven't said why you want the yacht, and I'm not going to ask, but something tells me it's not exactly pleasure. I just need some sort of assurance from you that you're going to be the skipper yourself and that what you're doing is aboveboard."

He stared straight ahead and kept driving as if he'd just commented on the weather.

"Yes, of course. What I'm doing is entirely aboveboard. I don't mind telling you; I'm looking for a friend who has the odd habit of taking vacations out here at this time of year. I need to reach him about an important business matter." Not a bad blend of truth and omissions, I thought, and hoped he wouldn't ask why I didn't just use a motorboat. I could hardly tell him that I had to approach by stealth—inconspicuously, at the very least—in order to take him home.

"Hmmph," he said, apparently satisfied, and parked in a reserved space near the harbor. He led the way to a shack at the head of one of the harbor docks, unlocked the door, and showed me into his office. I had to give him credit as a businessman; his first act was to take an imprint of my credit card (just in case, he said). Then he lifted some plastic-coated charts out of a rusty rack on the wall and pointed out the worst hazards.

"I'll give you some time with those while I get her ready." I heard and smelled him filling up a fuel can with diesel, and after a few moments heard him crank up the boat's motor to be sure it worked. I gathered up the charts and went out to the boat, a thirty-two-foot yacht named *Rosie.* She was a familiar design, and I was able to assure Frank that I had sailed others like her.

"Guess you're all set, then," he said, and handed over the key. He wasn't even watching as I motored away from the marina. I supposed he had learned to be so calm from regularly watching strangers take his hundred-thousand-dollar babies out to sea.

It seemed to me that it had taken forever to get onto the water, but when I looked at my watch it was still just eleven, barely an hour since I'd left the airport. My stomach was jittery, as before a race, and the wind cut sharply through my sweater and jacket. I headed for the open sea and the other side of Coatue, pulling hat and gloves on from my bag as I held the tiller steady with my knees. The motor purred satisfyingly, and I was relieved to be on my way at last.

But I was not alone. I heard something behind me, and I turned around to see Frank's motorboat in hot pursuit. He had a passenger; it was Sarah.

I cut the motor back to idle and waited. The thought crossed my mind that if her goal was to keep me from finding Ian, she was doing a very good job.

"She wouldn't take no for an answer," Frank shouted. "I hope I did right, bringing her out. Says you forgot something."

"Of course you did the right thing," she said to Frank. "Thanks."

He looked at me for an answer before coming alongside, and I nodded. I would have a little talk with her and deposit her back at the marina as soon as possible.

Frank shrugged, held the boats together as Sarah climbed into *Rosie,* and buzzed away. Sarah started to rummage in a locker under one of the cockpit seats for a life vest.

"Sarah, I'm sorry, but you can't come with me. It's not going to work."

Because it was her safety involved, I didn't have any trouble sounding convincing. Naturally, I did want her to come, in my heart of hearts. Not only could I use someone who could see properly but she knew the area intimately. And today was no different from all the other days that I would have given anything to be in her company, even if I did have vague questions about whose side she was on.

She smiled up at me from the vinyl-cushioned seat, where she now sat calmly fastening herself into an orange life vest she had unearthed. Another laid at her feet, apparently a broad hint for me to don one myself.

"Listen, Alex. For once I'm in a position to help you." I tried to concentrate on what she was saying, but it was difficult because I was also watching her mouth move. It curved and flexed tantalizingly, and for a moment I could almost imagine engaging those lips in a lingering kiss. I bit my tongue and forced myself to look up and into her eyes, though the lips were still moving. "You can't see very well, if you don't mind my saying so, and you don't know the area. And if it gets any rougher, who's going to help you reef and man the jib? There isn't a sailor in the world so good that he isn't better with a partner. You should know that."

She was right.

"And another thing," she continued, buckling the last orange strap on her vest with a flourish. "You forget that this has a lot to do with me personally. I know that this has something to do with your troubles at Plumtree Press, whether it's about Arthur, Ian, or you personally, and I'm the banker who lent you the money, remember? It's my responsibility to get it back." She stood, hands on her hips. "If you won't take my help as a friend, consider it business."

I stared at her. "How do you know this has anything to do with Arthur?"

She gave me an incredulous look, as if to ask just how stupid I thought she was. "Nantucket? Arthur? The diaries? *Those Who Trespass Against Us?* Come on, Alex—why else would you be here?"

So she knew. I decided that under the circumstances, the direct approach would be best.

"You could be killed, Sarah."

"I know." She looked at me with determination and something else I couldn't put my finger on. I wanted more than anything to kiss her.

Instead I limited myself to studying her as we rode the swells in the boat. The waves were much taller now that we were closer to the Atlantic, at least five feet. A relentless wind with a violent edge to it lent a foreboding note to the whole enterprise, and a small voice inside warned me that Sarah was not what she appeared to be. Still, I couldn't help myself. It was a risk I was willing to take.

"Oh, all right, then."

She smiled brightly in her victory and came toward me as I stood at the tiller. "Okay. I'm glad you see reason. Now what's the plan?"

I was grateful that she didn't choose this moment to pepper me with questions. Not only would it have been the wrong time, but for her sake I thought the less she knew the better, until it was all over.

"You might not believe this," I shouted as I went below to crank up the motor again, "but all I know is that we're looking for a yacht with Arthur on it, somewhere on or near Coatue."

She nodded as if this were the most natural thing in the world, then shouted back, "Do you know anything else about the yacht? Name, description, anything?" She had a pretty good set of lungs to make herself heard above the wind and motor noise.

I came back up to the cockpit and started to take the cover off of the sail, which was stored tightly folded atop the boom. Sarah quickly joined me in untying the bits of cloth that held the cover on. "I found a photograph of Ian aboard a yacht named *Carpe Diem*, registered in Nantucket. But that doesn't necessarily mean—"

"Did you say *Carpe Diem?*" She looked at me quizzically.

"Yes. It means 'Seize the day' in—"

"I know, I know." She waved a hand dismissively, then went back to untying. "But it doesn't make sense." Her eyebrows bent in a puzzled frown.

"Why not? It's a great name for a boat. Enjoy the day, relish the moment—"

"No, no." She was impatient, excited. Her cheeks were cherry red in the wind, her hair blowing around her head like a dark cloud.

If only I could have told her how I loved her. "I like the name too. But Alex, I'm afraid you don't understand. That's our yacht."

"What do you mean, 'our' yacht?" I was filled with a sense of dread.

"You know, Mom's, Dad's, Rob's. Mine. Ours." She pulled off the sail cover with a little flourish and looked at me uncertainly.

The little voice that told me Sarah was not what she appeared to be was screaming now. I averted my eyes and began to feed the small plastic wheels on the edge of the sail into the mast so we could raise it. She immediately helped by hoisting up the sail so there was less tension for me to work against. I hadn't sailed with her before, but from the looks of things it was going to be a pleasure. She knew her way around a boat.

But what could it mean that her family's yacht, and therefore probably her family, was involved in this whole mess? If she was involved in the Rupert or Romney affair, she was a very good actress. But to me she seemed genuinely baffled as to why *Carpe Diem* might be involved.

My mind wouldn't stop as we got *Rosie* ready to sail. Why would Ian have been photographed aboard the Townsends' yacht? It was possible that he knew someone who knew the Townsends socially and had been at a party onboard when the photograph was taken, but it seemed unlikely. He had never said anything of the sort when I'd introduced him to Sarah or when he'd seen her several times since.

We were caught up in our own thoughts as I steered the boat out of the neck of Nantucket harbor and into the Atlantic. It was fairly wild out here, with big whitecaps, and I was surprised that there were so many people out boating. We had seen at least a dozen yachts moving about in the harbor, and I could see at least a dozen more out ahead of us in the ocean, fighting the wind. It was a force-four breeze, by my best estimate, which would take some skill to handle. But then, Nantucket would be full of people used to the sea, the skill of sailing in all weather handed down from generation to generation, probably starting in childhood. Particularly at this time of year, there would be no fair-weather sailors.

I wondered if the barometer was rising or falling. I gave the tiller to Sarah and went below, tuning the radio to the weather station. The barometer was indeed falling; high winds, rough seas, and a low of thirty-eight degrees was forecast for the night. It was far from ideal, but not quite impossible.

We could conceivably come upon them any time now, and I told myself it was my last chance to change my mind about Sarah. Either I took her back to the harbor right now or I told her my plan for rescuing Ian. Yet again I decided to believe the best of her, regardless of the outcome. It wasn't a rational decision, but one of desperate hope.

I went back up and took the tiller. "We'd better go over what we're going to do when we find them." She nodded and listened as I related my plans. By my own admission, they were wildly optimistic, though the odds had definitely improved since she'd joined the enterprise. To her credit, her expression didn't change and she only blinked twice.

"Still want to go on?"

She nodded energetically, and I was aware of that look again. It was almost like—no, it couldn't be. I put it out of my mind with an effort.

"There's something else we have to think about. There's a chance they'll see us before we see them. We can't rely on them being aboard *Carpe Diem*, even repainted, so we have to suspect that they're aboard any one of these." I waved my arm at the yachts in view.

"In fact, they might not be at sea at all, but on land when we search there, so we'll have to be prepared for anything. The only one of them we know for sure is Romney, and he might not be in plain view. So we might not know they've spotted us until they're upon us."

Sarah nodded again, all business.

"I'm glad to see there's beach grass on Coatue; it's not just sand." There were even a couple of tumbledown beach shacks, I noticed. "If we come upon them on land, we can yell, 'Fire!' and run like mad. Fire always brings a crowd of would-be heroes, if there are people about." I could see a few hardy hikers out on the spit of sand; perhaps someone would hear. "Whether there are people or not, run like hell if you can see there's no hope." The thought pained me, for her sake. I would never forgive myself if something happened to her.

"Okay."

"And if things should go wrong while we're on the water, the backup plan is the same. If you can get back to *Rosie*, do it, and either motor away or lock yourself below and use the radio. If you can't get back to the boat, swim away if you can, or float until help comes."

She nodded again and didn't seem particularly bothered. I, on the other hand, was having all sorts of doubts, foremost among them whether I should have brought a gun. I loathed the things, but many Americans carried them—especially the kind of people we were looking for today.

I pulled Mike's cap down onto my forehead to help disguise my face and got some air into the sails again. I didn't have to tell Sarah what to do; she just did it, going forward over the rolling deck to take care of the jib.

By five-thirty it was growing dark. We had sailed the length of Coatue, always coming close enough to the other yachts to catch a glimpse of their crews with Frank's borrowed binoculars. None of the yachts remotely resembled *Carpe Diem*, nor were any of the people we were looking for—namely Romney, Acme, and Red— among the crews. During the course of the afternoon we had also anchored off Coatue in a secluded place and hiked to the far end and back, but again had found nothing.

At first I had been full of hope and determination, certain that we would beat the odds and find something to lead us to Ian. After half an hour I had begun to realize what a ridiculous enterprise this was. Romney could have met his collaborators at Coatue, and they could be anywhere on the Eastern seaboard by now. Even if they were still around here, Romney wouldn't be prancing about on the deck for me to identify him, nor would they be sailing *Carpe Diem* for everyone to identify. It was true that no one expected me to be here looking for Ian, but that was small comfort considering that the odds were so great.

At last we had returned to the yacht. I didn't know where we'd try next, but I went about pulling up the anchor purposefully, as if I could convince myself that this hadn't been a wild goose chase. As if I could convince myself that Ian wasn't really going to die. As if I hadn't humiliated myself in front of Sarah besides.

"You shouldn't be discouraged, you know," she said calmly,

unfurling the jib. "We still have all the waters out from Coatue to explore. And darkness could present new opportunities. Your friends might take a few more risks at night."

I didn't answer, but took my place at the tiller and steered us out into the ocean. I could see several yachts with their navigation lights on in the dusk, and for the first time in my life decided to leave mine off. It was irresponsible to say the least, but on the other hand, if there were any chance that Romney and his cronies were out there, I couldn't see announcing our presence.

She continued in the same calm, confident voice. "I don't know how to use the navigation system, but I'm sure you do. You could take us to the places that they think no one would ever go."

I snorted. "Well, that would be fine. And how do you propose we find out where those places are?" I heard the sarcasm in my voice and immediately regretted it. She was only trying to help, after all. "I'm sorry, Sarah. I really am."

"No, don't apologize." She paused, her mind evidently on something else. Thank God, I thought, she wasn't the sensitive type, bent on taking offense at every turn.

"You know, Alex, I've been thinking. It's a longshot, but . . . a friend of mine was a marine scientist, and she took me out to see the rare marine life in some deep pools near the boundaries of the shoals, over by Tuckernuck Island." I remembered seeing Tuckernuck Island on the map, about a mile from the westernmost spit of land on Nantucket.

"No one ever goes there," Sarah continued. "People avoid the shoals like the plague. But there are little inlets in a few places that let you get into the pools. If I were trying to hide from other boats, including the Coast Guard, at night, I think that's where I'd go." She paused. "I can show you where they are on the map, but it takes some pretty precise navigation to get in there."

We were both watching the sunset, a bleak, perfunctory stripe of pale orange in the sky that hardly deserved the word. I thought resignedly that, having come this far, I'd better try everything. "Okay," I said, sighing. "Let's try it."

"All right." She went down into the cabin and brought out Frank's charts. "They're not all marked, but there are narrow inlets leading to those pockets I mentioned." She studied the charts for a moment. "Here. There's one here, by this little bulge on the depth chart. We went into three or four of them, but I didn't ask how many there were . . . yes, here's another, just opposite Eel Point near Maddaket." She stared at the charts for a long moment, then shook her head. "Sorry. I don't recall any others."

"Mmm." I bent over her looking at the bulge she had identified. "These underwater inlets are large enough for a thirty-two-foot yacht?"

"Sure, even a sixty-footer like *Carpe Diem*. They don't draw more than ten feet of water. But there isn't a lot of room to play with."

Maybe Frank should have been more worried about *Rosie*, I thought; she was likely to come back with a few scrapes, though I would do my best.

We set out for the first inlet Sarah remembered, not exactly with high hopes, but with the comfort that comes from doing something—anything—to move toward a goal. The orange was gone from the sky, and any moon there might have been was obscured by the thick clouds that had moved in over the course of the afternoon. It was suddenly quite dark, and the nearest lights we could see were those of a yacht scuttling around the corner of Coatue into the harbor.

I really had the mood of this place now, even having been here for part of just one day, and it matched my own precisely. Desolate. Windswept. Full of raw energy that was powerless to make any difference at all, so it spent itself flailing against the water and the land.

Sort of like me.

I snapped to attention as a gust of wind caught the sail and slammed us nearly flat against the water. For some time now the wind had been gathering speed and was blowing with a violence that suggested we reef, or fold the bottom few feet of sail down to give the wind less surface to blow against. Reefing is never pleasant, as it's always blowing wildly when it becomes necessary, but this was as good a time as any to take care of it. I turned into the wind and caught Sarah's attention. She came to hold the boom while I brought down the sail, so it wouldn't knock me overboard in a strong gust. *Rosie* rocked wildly, the stability of motion gone. When I'd lowered it about three feet, I used the bits of cloth sewn onto the sail to tie the new bottom onto the rest of it, now folded up close to the boom. When I finished and hauled it up again, the sail didn't look much smaller, but I knew we would feel the difference. That done, we resumed our course for the inlet. The reefing helped, but it seemed I was continually winching the main sheet, as the wind was not only strong but shifty. Every other moment I had to let the sail out or pull it in. Sarah, meanwhile, had rolled up the jib and fetched the safety harnesses from below. They were made for nights like this, when a rolling sea and high winds threatened to blow sailors overboard. They consisted of a simple web of material that slipped on like a life vest. Several feet of sturdy nylon cable hung from the vest, with a metal hook at the end of the cable for fastening onto the boat.

Sarah passed me mine without a word, as the wind and the crashing waves made it difficult to talk. She took the tiller while I put it on, looking at the bluish glow of the digital numbers on the navigation system display on the cabin wall. It was the only light emanating from *Rosie*. We were fortunate to have a sophisticated navigation system; not all yachts did. The numbers on the display told me the coordinates of our position and our destination, as well as the course we needed to steer to get there. I had programmed the system with the map coordinates for the spot where the inlet opens into the ocean, just off Eel Point, and by comparing those with our current position I could see roughly how much farther we had to go. According to the coordinates, we were within one hundred yards of Eel Point.

We were beating against the wind, which meant that the wind was pretty well beating us. I like to think that that's why we didn't see the boat until it was upon us.

One moment I was back to cranking on the winch, and the next moment a jolt threw me to the other side of the cockpit. Someone yelled a ripe expletive from off the port side, and with horror I saw Sarah fly against the starboard guardrail and over it. I left the sail to turn into the wind on its own, vaguely aware that we had been hit by a yacht not unlike our own, and clambered over to where Sarah had disappeared. Her safety harness had held, and she was suspended there over the edge of the boat, valiantly trying to reach the deck to haul herself up again.

I wedged my toes against the toe-rail lining the edge of the boat and knelt down, grasping her safety harness cable. I pulled it toward me hand over hand until she could get her elbows on the deck, then helped her slide onto the deck on her stomach. She let me help her up, and though her eyes were wide, she seemed to be all right, if soaked from splashing waves. She nodded at me quickly in reassurance and even attempted a smile, which rapidly changed to an expression of horror.

I wheeled to see a figure jump onto *Rosie*'s deck from the other yacht, and I didn't like the looks of what he had in his gloved hand. It was small and dark and bore an uncanny resemblance to a gun.

"Flares," I shouted at Sarah, who rapidly disappeared below, as I moved to intercept the intruder before he could gain a foothold. He had fallen after a chancy jump and was picking himself up off the tossing deck on the opposite side of the boat. I unfastened my safety harness and lunged for the man's arm. It was up to me to contain him while she created a helpful diversion, which we had planned carefully earlier in the day.

I gripped the wrist that held the gun for dear life, fighting to point it out to sea while he struggled to turn it toward me. I used the advantage I had over him, which was that I was farther from the edge of the boat than he, and edged closer and closer to him, pressing my hip against his, forcing him to lean backward over the guardrail.

But he wasn't about to lose the fight so easily. He stopped trying to loosen my grip with his left hand and planted it in a stranglehold on my neck. "You haven't got a chance in hell." He forced the words out between his teeth, grunting and straining as he fought to maintain his footing. "The old man doesn't either."

Old man? Did he mean Ian?

He pushed steadily against my windpipe as I tried to push him overboard, and I cursed the guardrail for impeding his progress. I pushed harder against him with my side, willing him to lose his footing, but somehow he held on. After a moment I was seeing stars, but I knew if I let him point his gun at me it would all be over. So I clung to his wrist like a dog to a bone, stupidly refusing to give in.

When I saw the explosion I wasn't sure if he had finally succeeded in pointing the gun at me, or if Sarah had got the diversion underway. But then in quick succession I saw a second burst of light and knew it had to be the flares we had planned. My opponent's eyes couldn't resist following the glowing orange missiles for just an instant, and his hand momentarily loosened from around my neck. I let him have a stunning punch that sent him reeling backward over the top wire of the guardrail. His hand hit the metal stanchion that held the wire, and the gun sailed out of his hand and into the water. Before he could recover I mustered all the strength I had and hit him solidly in the stomach, at which point he finally lost his balance completely and fell, as if in slow motion, into the icy waves. I glanced at the other yacht, which was drifting away, and moved to *Rosie*'s stern. Then I jumped over the edge into the black water.

The iciness of it made me suck in my breath, and my head hurt intensely. I would have to act quickly, I knew, or the sea would claim me as it had countless others. Unfortunately, there hadn't been time to put one of Frank's wetsuits on first, though I'd had the foresight to put on the elastic strap that secured my glasses when we'd reefed.

I had seen four people on the deck fighting the fire, all of them young and strapping. No Romney. It was possible that there was another boat somewhere, one that had either sent them to board us or had them patrolling the area for strangers.

I swam as fast as I could in the rough water across the ten yards or so that now separated the boats. The other yacht had also left its running lights off, but Sarah had serendipitously started a fair-sized blaze in their cabin by shooting the flares directly into it. The flame was licking at their sail helpfully now, and I had no trouble spotting them. I'd have to be careful not to get too close, I thought; just close enough to get my safety harness and cable nicely entangled in the blades of their propeller.

I was close now, just two feet from the blades. The crew was running about on deck, shouting and fighting their fires in a panic-stricken, ineffectual way. I got my Swiss Army knife out of my sock and quietly but thoroughly slashed their rubber tender. After folding and replacing the knife, I unfastened my harness and slid it off, feeding the cable end down toward the propellers. The cable was sucked into the motor's eddy almost immediately, pulling the harness fast with it, down and around the blades of the motor in a hopeless snarl. The motor whined against its restraints, then began to smoke in the cold air, and finally went silent. There was little chance that they would be motoring after us—or anywhere else, for that matter—without extensive repairs.

I swam underwater as much as possible to the far side of *Rosie,* where Sarah waited. She helped me into the cockpit and threw an old blanket, evidently one of Frank's provisions with the boat, around me. Her face was full of concern.

"Your lips are blue," she said, frowning.

I nodded. "We need to put on the wetsuits. If you can get her underway, I'll put mine on now. Any minute they'll discover that their motor has burned itself out, though, so we've got to keep moving." She nodded and as I struggled, shivering, into the rubber suit below I felt *Rosie* move forward with a tug.

We traded places while Sarah put on her suit, and I stared in awe at the other yacht as we sailed toward the inlet and, I hoped, Ian. Sarah had done a beautiful job of turning their boat into a disaster area. Flames leapt from the cockpit and I was buoyed by the knowledge that we were on the right track. Romney wouldn't have sent his goons after us if we weren't very close to Ian.

It was worrisome that Romney's boat, assuming it was somewhere near, would be staring at the same sight and becoming suspicious, but there was nothing to be done about that. I couldn't see anything in any direction aside from the flames from the yacht and lights from the island, but I knew that Romney could be anywhere. We hoped to approach quietly, but I knew that we might come upon him as suddenly as we had the others. Thank God for the wind, I thought, so we don't have to use our motor.

The coordinates said we weren't far now—about fifty yards, I guessed. Since the inlet wouldn't be visible in any way, when we were really close we would have to watch the coordinates closely and turn into the deep pocket of water at precisely the moment we reached it.

When I told Sarah our position, she insisted that I go below and navigate. "One of us should be watching the depth chart as we approach the inlet, and it might as well be you. You're wet; you should be out of the wind," she said.

I seriously considered it for a moment, because I knew how quickly hypothermia could sneak up on a person, first dulling the wits and then incapacitating the body.

But if we were soon to come upon Romney, I didn't want her out there alone, even for a moment. He was ruthless, and if he saw us he wouldn't be pleased. I much preferred the thought of Sarah safely below, studying the chart.

"No," I said. "I promised Frank I'd be the one sailing the boat."

She gave me an exasperated look and said, "Coming about."

I ducked into the cockpit to avoid the boom knocking my block off, and thought that this might be our last tack before turning into the inlet. Sarah cranked on the winch and had the main sheet securely anchored before the wind caught the sail and pulled us forward with a violent tug.

"All right," I said. "I think it's time for you to go below. We must be nearly there. Just shout any course adjustments up to me, okay?"

Sarah looked at me defiantly. "Aren't you forgetting something? I don't mean to rub it in, but your eyesight is terrible. How do you think you're going to see them if they're out there?" She went on in a gentler tone. "Come on, Alex. Let me help you for a change. Frank would rather get his boat back intact than have you keep your promise about being at the helm."

There was no arguing with her logic; it didn't make sense for a half-blind person to keep a lookout for a dark yacht on a cloudy night. I hated the thought of putting her at risk, but I supposed I was doing that already.

"You'd better hurry, Alex; we don't want to miss it."

"All right. I'm going. But let me know the moment you spot anything."

She nodded and put her mind immediately to the task. Even after I turned to go below, I could see her in my mind's eye standing at the tiller, tall, confident, and capable, with dark wisps of wind-tangled hair blowing in her face. I loved her more than ever for putting herself in this crazy situation for my sake, and prayed that she would be all right.

The little blue numbers, when I saw them, prompted me to call through the hatchway to Sarah immediately, though of course she had a display in the cockpit, too. "Get ready to turn," I bellowed into the wind. I waited for our position numbers to match the destination numbers, and leaned out the hatchway. "Now!"

I watched, first confused and then worried as Sarah let the yacht turn itself into the wind and stall. I strained to see her and thought I saw her doing something with her left hand in front of her face as she completely released the main sheet. As I started up the stairs she hurried toward me. "Alex, she's here." An undercurrent of excitement rippled through her voice. "*Carpe Diem.* I'd know her anywhere."

She moved back for me to climb out and I looked, nearly tripping over Frank's blanket, which now smelled of wet wool. I couldn't see a thing.

"Are you sure?"

She nodded violently. "For just an instant there was a light—a cigarette, maybe—and then I could make out the outline."

If she said it was there, I would stake my life on it. I wondered what sort of trouble I'd have got myself in without her.

"Okay. How close are they? Should we go from here?"

"I think so. They're maybe fifty yards away. They might spot us if we took her any closer."

Sarah and I dropped *Rosie*'s anchor as quickly and quietly as we could. While Sarah grabbed the oars for the rubber tender from the cockpit locker, I pulled on the rope that kept it in tow. I untied the knot and held the tender as still as I could for Sarah to climb in, then handed her the oars. She threaded them through the little plastic circles on either side of the big innertube while I climbed in. It wasn't easy, considering that it was bobbing with all the stability of a Styrofoam cup on the waves.

"I'll row the first bit, then you can have a go." We balanced ourselves in the flimsy little craft, she in the front and I in the back, and I began to row. It wasn't exactly like rowing in an eight, but at least some of the right muscles were in shape. I kept looking where Sarah looked but couldn't see even a vague mass where the *Carpe Diem* was supposed to be.

We were soaked anew within moments, as the wind blew spray off of the waves. I was grateful that Sarah was experienced on the water; many people would be intimidated by such a rough sea in a questionable craft like the tender, not to mention the danger we were heading into. At times, in the trough of a wave, we were five feet below the crest. Rowing was extremely difficult, and the wind blew us sideways, so that I expended half my energy counteracting it and the other half ever so slowly moving toward *Carpe Diem.*

All told, probably ten minutes had passed since we left the burning yacht behind, but my internal timeclock told me it had been an eternity. Please don't let it be too late, I prayed. Please let us get there in time. I struck up a sort of litany of that phrase with every stroke, and was startled when Sarah reached out and stopped my hands, motioning that it was her turn.

I let go of the oars with difficulty, my hands having frozen into a grip. I was out of breath from the exertion, but warm at last, aside from my exposed hands. We didn't have to switch places since the oarlocks rotated freely, and Sarah took over, turning the handles toward her and straining a little against the waves. She was one in eighteen million, I thought, and turned my attention to the plan for boarding *Carpe Diem.*

Sarah had probably been doing the same thing while I rowed, I thought. Earlier in the afternoon we had gone over our plan to row silently to the yacht and create another diversion to draw the hired help away from Romney. I knew it was chancy, but I had to try to get them out of the way so I could tackle Romney one on one. Then it was another leap of faith to believe that I could outmaneuver him if he had a gun, tie him up, and find Ian—alive, God willing.

I couldn't help but believe that he was alive if *Carpe Diem* was still out at sea. If they had killed him, surely they would have scattered as quickly as possible from their meeting place. Besides, the goon that had fought me on *Rosie* had said, "The old man is as good as dead"—which meant that he wasn't. Not yet, anyway. Now that we were so close, I had to suppress an unreasonable fear that we would hear a shot any moment, right here next to the yacht, and fight our way aboard only to find it was too late.

When we were twenty feet away, I leaned forward and shouted into Sarah's ear, "Can you see anyone on board?" Though we were close to the yacht now, the sound of the wind and the waves was so loud that I knew it would far overwhelm my voice. The wind was also blowing away from the yacht and toward us, ensuring that we would hear their noises long before they heard ours.

She stopped rowing and looked, panting from the effort of rowing, then nodded. Evidently it seemed too much of a struggle to her to shout against the wind; she disengaged from the starboard oar and held up two fingers. Then she pointed to the stern end of the yacht. I looked where she pointed but couldn't see anything on the deck. She tapped my knee and made little circles around her eyes with her fingers, then pointed in the direction of the flaming yacht.

I nodded briskly to show that I understood her sign language. Evidently the men were watching the remaining flames from their companion yacht. It would have been impossible for the other boat to use its radio during and after the fire, so they were probably trying to determine if their friends were all right. I took the oars, gave a quick thumbs up signal, and started rowing again.

I could see her nod, looking very serious. We were almost there. It wasn't surprising that we were invisible to the men aboard as we approached; everything was working to our advantage. Besides the fact that it was a moonless night, *Carpe Diem* was a large yacht. We were at least six feet below them. And the sea was so restless that it would have been virtually impossible for them to notice a disturbance in the water, let alone an occasional slap of water against one of our oars.

Sarah unzipped her wetsuit to a tantalizing point just between her breasts, reached down and pulled what was by now our old standby diversion of the flare gun from the inside of her down jacket. Fortunately, there had been several in *Rosie*'s emergency kit. She stuck it firmly between the innertube and the bottom of the tender so it pointed upward, then looked at me. Abandoning our tender, we gently let ourselves down into the icy water, and even across the tender I thought I could hear Sarah suck in her breath. Then she looked at me again, and I nodded. She pulled the trigger and we dived as deeply as we could into the churning water on either side of the yacht. With luck, the flare would shoot up into the sky above the bow and attract Romney's goons to that end of the boat, where we wanted them.

I kept tight against the side of the yacht whenever I came up for breath, which I did only three times on my way to meet Sarah at the stern. Even if they looked over the edge, they wouldn't see me that way. Besides, the water was violent enough that it was comforting to have a solid surface to hand. I worried about Sarah, and in the brief instants that I gulped air I listened for indications that they had fallen for the ruse. I heard raised voices the first time I came up, but nothing the second or third times, which I optimistically interpreted as a signal that our scheme to attract them to the bow had succeeded. When I finally came up five feet short of the stern, I was relieved to hear nothing at that end of the boat.

I rounded the corner cautiously and with considerable relief saw Sarah, very much alive and looking as miserable as I felt in the water. We met by the rudder, and I pointed up onto the yacht. She grabbed hold of the painter that stretched from the yacht back to the motorized tender in tow, and started to haul herself up. I helped by pushing her up onto the deck as best I could from below. She stayed still for a moment, dripping, shivering, and watching, then turned to offer me a hand.

According to plan, she went round the starboard side and I went to port, each of us threading our way through cables and ropes as quietly as we could on the lurching deck. As we passed the bulge of the cabin I heard raised voices again, but this time it wasn't the hired help; it was Romney and a familiar voice I couldn't quite place.

Looking back on it, I know now that it was a voice I could have placed but didn't want to.

I couldn't have hoped for better circumstances, logistically. Romney's two goons were looking over the bow and never saw us coming. One of them was holding the binoculars and saying something as he focused on the tender, while the other held both of their snub-nosed little machine guns and stared down into the water.

Sarah was looking at me, and I indicated that she should take the one with the binoculars. Both of us had pulled our "weapons," winch handles from *Rosie*, from our jackets after boarding, and now raised them as we tiptoed toward our targets. I desperately hoped to avoid a scuffle by knocking them out with a good hard first blow, and had told Sarah so. It might be cruel and dangerous, but let's face it, they wouldn't go easy on us. Besides, if we got into a loud fight, those below would hear and it would ruin our surprise.

227

We were within a foot of them when we struck. Remarkably, unbelievably, they slumped over the guardrail. One of the guns bounced off the deck as the weapons fell into the waves, but it hit one of the men's shoes instead of the teak deck. If it had landed directly on the wood, it would have made enough of a clatter to bring reinforcements running.

We gently lowered the men to the deck, and I noticed that a trickle of blood came from the back of the head of the man who had held the guns. I grabbed ropes from the deck to tie them and I felt a wave of panic at the thought that I might have killed him. I knelt and felt for a pulse on his neck; it was there. Hurting people was a miserable business, and this was the second time this week I'd had to do it. But as I wound the ropes carefully around their hands and feet and then tied them to the rail, I told myself that the man I'd clobbered might have shot Ian—assuming he hadn't already done the job.

We made our way back to the cabin together, and I felt supremely confident in the afterglow of our success. Now it was down to those in the cabin and us. I signaled to Sarah that I was going to listen for a moment, and we put our ears close to the narrow horizontal Plexiglas windows that let light into the cabin during the day. Romney and his companion were shouting down there in the dark, and even with the wind and the waves I could hear them easily.

"Use reason, man!" It was Romney. "If you kill me, you'll be worse off than you are now. They just might pardon you for what you've done, possibly even for embezzling from the charity, given your years of service. But if you kill me, or Arthur, you'll never get out of jail."

I was confused. Romney wasn't the aggressor; he was the victim.

But then who . . . ?

The voice that answered was, suddenly, all too familiar.

"I'm tired of your arguments. Don't think I don't know you've been resourceful in delaying me this long." There was a pause.

"Simon Bow," I stage-whispered into Sarah's ear. Her eyes widened to match my own. So the man to whom I had been prepared to sign away part of Plumtree Press was my father's deadliest enemy. Unfortunately, my father hadn't lived to work out the final detail of his identity. That, and the writing of the books, had been left to Ian. Bow was the kidnapper of the children, the would-be murderer of Arthur.

I wasn't sure which was the greater shock; that Bow was the criminal or that Romney wasn't.

He continued. "I'm not stupid, Marsh. If I kill you and 'Arthur,' as you insist upon calling him, the only people who know about the kidnappings will be unable to inconvenience me again."

"Damn it all, Simon, I've told you. There's no way out of this. My people know to call in the Coast Guard if they haven't heard from me by now. They're already on their way."

A short, derisive laugh exploded from Bow. "My God, but that's pitiful. Someone with your years in MI6 should know better. We both know there's no Coast Guard on the way. Get up. We're going up on deck."

There were sounds of movement. I put my mouth to Sarah's ear and said, "This is it. Both of us on Simon, as soon as he's out the hatchway." She nodded ferociously and moved closer.

The hatch opened, and the top of Romney's head appeared as he climbed the stairs. Halfway up, he turned and spoke, evidently figuring he had nothing to lose.

"Why, Simon? You've always had so much going for you. Why did you kidnap the children?"

Sarah and I crept closer, hiding behind the open sliding door of the hatch.

"Don't suppose there's much harm in telling you, if you're so curious." Bow's voice was bitter, cold. He dropped the volume, and I strained to hear. "Children are everything that is wrong with my world. I loathe them. The only thing that would have made me acceptable in my father's eyes was for me to have a boy, an heir. He talked about nothing else . . . that nonexistent child was more important to him than I ever was. I married young to satisfy him, and we set about producing the boy right away." He paused. "But Mary had a difficult delivery, and to save her, they had to take—it. She couldn't have more." There was another pause. "My father couldn't hide his disappointment; he never looked upon me in the same way again. I, his only child, was the last of the Bows. That's when I realized that he had never really cared for me; I was just a way for him to carry on living. So when Mary's father got me a commission in London to be near her, perhaps out of spite to manage the evacuation of the children, there were all those children in one place. I realized I had the power to do with them as I pleased.

"I made sure that I was in charge of the three ships that evacuated the HELP-sponsored children to the States, and I even knew of a desolate place to take them. I'd been on Nantucket on leave while I was part of the Anglo-American Liaison with Wexford, Plumtree, and Higginbotham the year before, before being sent back home. They were fortunate to have lived, those children—always complaining, always crying. They weren't desirable children, either, you know—urchins from the East End, most of them. A thousand times on the Atlantic crossing I wanted to throw them overboard."

His voice became less angry, almost dreamy. "But then I thought of something better. Something far less messy, equally painful for them, and profitable for me as well. God knows, Bow and Bow has rarely been in the black. A quarter of a million dollars came in very handy."

I realized that I was listening to a very sick man. A conniving, deceitful, criminal mind, and a very warped one as well. The extent of his perversity made me feel sick to my stomach.

"Hang on—" Bow's voice was brusque, businesslike. "Where're my lads?" Romney was propelled up the stairs as Bow shouted, "Sanchez! Higgins!"

It was now or never. I dived at Bow before he got up the stairs, my hands fastening around his gun. The look on his face was worth five best-sellers. The only problem was that by landing on top of him, I had ensured that his gun was pointing directly into my belly. We tumbled backward down the stairs as I fought to turn it away, knowing that any moment it might explode, and me with it. I rolled sideways when we hit the floor, but didn't release my grip. As I rolled I heard and felt a white-hot explosion, and vaguely wondered if I'd been hit. There was too much adrenaline flowing; I couldn't feel pain, but there was an odd sensation in my right side.

The adrenaline got me on my knees, and I dived for Simon's shoulders, pinning him securely to the floor with the sheer ferocity of my anger more than bodily strength. Now that his arm was immobilized, Romney pitched in and tried to pry the gun from his fingers. Simon writhed like a snake and fought both of us for all he was worth, but it got him nowhere. In the end Romney got the gun out of his hand by stepping firmly just above it. Simon was furious, sputtering and swearing vociferously.

"No one's going to believe you, either of you," he spat. "Everybody's written you off," he said with an ugly smile, looking at me, "and Marsh, you're a ridiculous old fart. People will assume you've gone round the bend."

I didn't bother to answer him, to mention that we had mountains of proof in the form of my father's diaries, as well as a photo from an old woman on Nantucket who had fallen in love with him long ago, which Lisette would have for me when I got home. I was certain it would show a young Simon Bow with captivating eyes.

Romney, looking down at Simon over my shoulder, said, "I'll never understand how you got here, Alex, but by George I'm glad you did."

I couldn't seem to find the words to answer him, either, so I said nothing. Sarah came down the stairs with another set of ropes to secure Simon, flicking on the cabin light as she came. If anything, the scene seemed even more unreal with the lights on. She trussed up his hands and feet while I stayed on top of him, and for good measure also tied his hands to the leg of the built-in navigator's desk near the floor.

My mind was on Ian in the next cabin—if he were really there—and I fished in Simon's pockets, with considerable resistance from him, for the keys. I was certain he would have locked him in. I found a key ring and finally pulled it out. As I stood, I said, "You'll keep an eye on him?"

Romney and Sarah stared at me and didn't answer. "Well?" Sarah gulped. "Alex, you're bleeding."

I looked down at my side where they were looking, and saw that I was indeed making quite a mess. The outside of the wetsuit on my right leg was covered with blood. The odd thing was, I couldn't feel a thing.

She came toward me and began to steer me toward the built-in bench that surrounded the cabin dining table. Romney came forward to help. "Here, give me the keys. You sit down—"

"I'm fine. Honestly. Besides, Ian's in there, locked up." I moved away and toward the door, and as I started trying keys in the lock I heard a wail not unlike an American police siren. The Coast Guard. Romney hadn't been bluffing.

"I knew they'd come through," Romney said, and looked as if he'd rather go meet them than find out what lay on the other side of the cabin door. None of us had said it, but it had been very quiet on the other side of the door and I think all of us expected the worst.

They were both standing close behind me as the fifth key I tried turned in the lock. I swung open the cabin door and reached for the light switch. As I groped for it on the dark wall, I sensed rather than saw someone behind the door. I turned quickly; evidently the wrong thing to do. Something hard smashed down on my head, and a thousand flashbulbs exploded somewhere behind my eyes.

I blinked, and everything went black.

10

I woke up in a wretched mood, with a splitting headache and a bad case of cottonmouth. From the grayish light I guessed it was just before dawn; not dark, but not exactly light, either. I wondered peevishly why I had awakened so early, and let my eyelids slam shut, only to open them wide a second later.

Ian. What on earth had ever happened to Ian?

I sat up and barely managed to stifle a roar. Someone seemed to have stuck a white-hot poker into my side. Gingerly, I lifted the top of the pair of plaid flannel pajamas I was wearing and saw a white gauze bandage taped into place just above my waist, on the right side. Simon would be pleased that his bullet hadn't been spent in vain.

Leaning back against the headboard of the bed, I reached out to what appeared to be the bedside table, feeling for glasses. Half my life was spent searching for glasses, I thought irritably. They were there, on top of a white rectangle. I put them on and turned on the bedside lamp, wincing at the sudden brightness. The rectangle turned out to be a plain white envelope printed with my first name in the Zapf Calligraphic typeface.

My heart leapt as I thought of the one person I knew who always used that typeface and never put return addresses on his envelopes.

I ripped it open and reached inside. There was one sheet of paper, laser printed as usual on fine white bond.

Dear Alex,

Please accept my sincere apologies for my treatment of you aboard <u>Carpe Diem.</u> I hope that any anger you may feel will be mitigated by the understanding that it is best for all of us if I remain anonymous.

I will be forever in your debt for saving my life, and will endeavor to repay you—somehow—for the hardships you have suffered for my sake.

With sincere gratitude,
Arthur

P.S. Never fear; the remaining five chapters of *Those Who Trespass Against Us* are forthcoming.

I sat and stared at it, wondering. We really had saved Arthur, then. But we still didn't know for certain if he was Ian.

The sound of waves breaking finally penetrated my thoughts, and I gazed out of the window into the gray light and pounding surf past an autumnal bouquet that looked vaguely familiar. A house on the beach. Sarah's? I turned back to the room and took it in in a glance. It was simple and tasteful, with yards of white eyelet at the windows, two four-poster beds, flowered wallpaper, and a braided rug on the wooden floor. A clock on the table said five-thirty.

Bits and pieces of the struggle aboard *Carpe Diem* came back to me like the fragments of a dream. The fight for Simon's gun, the hot sensation in my side, opening the door to what I thought was Ian's cabin, the noise behind the door. My fingers reached up and gently investigated an unnatural bulge about two inches in diameter, halfway down the back of my head.

I swore blackly.

There was really no reason to feel so miserable, I told myself. Things seemed to have turned out all right. The manuscript was coming, after all. I supposed it was just that the task still seemed unfinished; I wanted to know for certain who Arthur really was.

I heard a quiet knock, and the door to the room opened a crack. Sarah popped her head in cautiously, then beamed and swung the door open all the way.

"You're awake!" Sarah bounced into the room looking surprised and genuinely pleased. I grunted a response and watched as she sat down on the edge of the bed opposite mine. It was like being in the same room with the sun; I couldn't help but feel better with her there.

My eyes drank in everything about her. Her dark hair was pulled back with a large tortoiseshell clip, accentuating her high cheekbones and almond-shaped, upwardly tilted eyes. She appeared not to be wearing makeup, and her face looked squeaky clean and shiny, very fair except for the usual bright red splotches in her cheeks. Her long legs were clad in jeans, and she wore a warm fisherman's knit sweater over a striped turtleneck. So many layers . . .

She spoke again, interrupting my wayward thoughts. "How are you feeling?"

I lifted a hand and wiggled my fingers in a so-so gesture.

She smiled ruefully. "Thank God you didn't say 'fine.' You wouldn't be human if you didn't feel wretched. The doctors said there were only four things wrong with you this time: concussion, bullet wound and corresponding loss of blood, hypothermia, and exhaustion." She sighed. "You do go to extremes, Alex."

"Well, I apologize," I said sarcastically. "Now will you please tell me what happened?"

She looked down at the pattern in the duvet cover. "I was afraid you were going to ask that."

"Uh-oh." I had an ominous feeling that she was going to tell me that all our efforts were for naught, that Ian had never been found.

"It's not exactly bad. It's just a bit—well, strange." She frowned and sat forward on the edge of the bed, her head to one side. "I was just behind you when you went into the cabin, then I heard a thud and you fell against me. But it was dark in there, and I couldn't see very well, so I felt for the light switch and turned it on. I saw someone's shoes just disappearing up the hatch, and heard him run across the deck just above us. I stayed with you while

Romney went up to investigate—we thought maybe one of Simon's men had gotten free—but by the time he got up there he couldn't see or hear anyone. And Simon's men were still tied up where we'd left them. The Coast Guard reached the boat just after that. They took you to the hospital, carted Simon off, and took our statements."

"But what happened to Ian? Where is he?"

She shrugged apologetically. "That's just it, Alex. We've all gone over it time and again, but we just don't know."

"What do you mean, you 'don't know'?"

"We don't know if he was ever on the yacht, or if he—um—disappeared before we got there, or if he just got off."

"Got off?"

She shrugged. "Well, we don't know who that man was climbing out of the cabin, and the Coast Guard said that the motorized tender had been cut free from the yacht. It was found at six this morning. So *someone* left after we came on board. It could have been Ian."

"It *had* to have been Ian," I said, almost to myself. "It had to be." A smile spread across my face as I realized that I almost had proof that Arthur was Ian after all.

Sarah looked at me questioningly, and I handed her the note from Arthur.

Her mouth dropped open. "So it's true," she said in awe. "I don't believe it! It's a good thing I didn't mention Ian's name to the Coast Guard, though at the time I wondered if it was the right thing to do." She was smiling now, too.

Then something she had said a moment ago clicked. I frowned. "Wait a minute. How could they have found the tender at six this morning?" I glanced at the clock. "It's only five-thirty."

She laughed. I wondered again what instrument it was that her voice reminded me of. It was mellow, rich, lower than an ordinary voice.

"How long do you think you've been sleeping?"

"I'm afraid to ask."

"Eighteen hours."

I groaned and ran a hand over two days' stubble. I could only imagine what her parents thought of me, not to mention Sarah herself.

"Oh, come on. Don't look so worried. The doctor said you'd need sleep; he said he didn't think the concussion was too bad, but he said that you had lost some blood, and the bullet wound would be painful. He looked in your eyes, had you count to ten backwards and forwards, then bandaged you up and sent you home with us. This is my parents' house, by the way. We finally got to bed at about three in the morning. I don't suppose you remember any of it."

I shook my head and immediately regretted it: it felt as if my brain was bouncing around in my skull like a handball. As the hammering receded I said, "No doubt your parents were thrilled that I got you involved in this."

She raised her eyebrows and shrugged. "Nothing happened to me that a hot toddy couldn't cure. Besides, they're grateful to you for getting *Carpe Diem* back." She smiled encouragingly. "By the way, I asked them why Simon had it, and they said they couldn't imagine. Evidently a friend of theirs had it on holiday—I guess he often takes it at this time of year—and when they didn't hear from him they just figured he was enjoying himself and hadn't bothered to get in touch. But it turns out he got sick somewhere along the way, and the yacht was stolen while he was on shore recuperating. They're eager to meet you, by the way, to thank you in person." Her words brought a vague thought to mind, but it faded as she stood to leave. I felt as if my mind was operating in slow motion. "How about something to drink? Orange juice, maybe?"

"That would be great, thanks."

"I'll be right back with it. By the way, you're welcome to come downstairs or stay up here and recuperate, whichever you please. No one expects anything either way. I put some of Rob's clothes in the closet, just in case."

She was gone before I could answer. I liked the way she did things without a lot of fuss. I sighed and thought again that she must have some faults, somewhere. I hoped I would have the chance to find out what they were.

I sat gathering steam to roust myself out of bed and stared out the window. It was strange to be an utter outcast one day and accepted back into the fold the next. Once people heard the truth about Simon, and he was extradited to England to serve what would undoubtedly be a lengthy prison sentence, my family's name would be cleared.

Now, I thought, if only Sarah loved me, and I had the last five chapters of the book in hand, and I knew where Ian was, things would be perfect. But as I knew full well, things were never perfect in the real world.

Something caught my eye on the beach below, and I was surprised to see a flashlight, held by a uniformed man who was stamping his feet in the sand to keep warm. Sarah came back and I asked her who he was.

She set a tray with a newspaper, a pitcher of orange juice, a glass and two pieces of toast on the bedside table. "We had to hire him to keep the press away. When they couldn't get in the front door, they started coming onto the beach in boats." She rolled her eyes and stood back, arms akimbo. "News about Arthur seems to travel fast, and I'm afraid the story about Simon is out. You are the man of the moment. Oh, I forgot to tell you earlier—Lisette and George tracked you down here and said to tell you that they neutralized Charlie, whatever that means, but when you feel up to it you might want to give him a call."

I felt a mental grimace. I had stood Charlie up. My eyes went to the flowers; of course, they were from Charlie, like the flowers at Great Portland Street Hospital. No wonder they had looked familiar. At least he wasn't angry.

"Lisette also said to tell you," Sarah adopted a thick French accent and the accompanying pout, "to 'stop being such a bloody hero and get the hell back to work.' "

I smiled at the backhanded way Lisette went about making people feel good and looked at the newspaper on the tray. It wasn't the *Nantucket Inquirer and Mirror,* as I had assumed. It was the *Tempus* of London. I gaped as I picked it up, and Sarah stayed while I drank juice, ate toast, asked questions, and absorbed the front-page article.

CRIMINAL OF "ARTHUR" NOVELS FOUND; COMPETING PUBLISHER SUSPECTED OF MURDER, KIDNAPPING

Nantucket, Mass. — London publisher Simon Bow today confessed to murder and numerous kidnappings after

238

Alexander Plumtree, a rival publisher, and a friend found him on a stolen yacht near this remote island. Bow was using the craft to hold hostage the renowned anonymous novelist "Arthur" in an attempt to prevent the publication of his next novel, which apparently implicates Bow in other serious crimes. Also captive on the yacht was an undercover investigator for the Charities Commission.

Bow confessed to hiring a man to kill Barnes Appleton, a literary critic for the *Sunday Tempus* who was found dead last Friday. He also admitted abducting the novelist Arthur to obtain the final portion of a manuscript to be published by Plumtree Press. As the result of a review published by Barnes Appleton, Bow feared that the manuscript would reveal him to be the perpetrator of a third crime: the kidnapping and selling of thousands of evacuated British children to Americans during World War II.

Although Arthur was apparently aboard the yacht at the time it was boarded and captured by Plumtree, he had disappeared by the time authorities arrived. His whereabouts and identity remain unknown. The Charities Commission investigator, who by government request shall not be named, was unharmed when the Coast Guard arrived at the vessel at eleven o'clock last night.

Alexander Plumtree sustained a gunshot wound in a struggle with Bow, but has been released from hospital.

So Romney Marsh had been conducting a secret investigation for the government of Publishers for Literacy and Simon's role therein. Perhaps they had already suspected his kidnappings of years ago.

Simon's lawyer had evidently advised him to make a full confession. Further down in the article, he'd also admitted to embezzling from Publishers for Literacy through the years to fund his publishing enterprise. I smiled at the irony of Simon having been found out by Nick, who wouldn't have been able to conduct his sophisticated analysis of the charity's accounts without his education from Publishers for Literacy.

But interestingly enough, Simon couldn't or wouldn't provide Arthur's true identity, according to the paper. That puzzled me, especially because he knew Ian Higginbotham quite well. It made me wonder again if Arthur were Ian. If he were, why wouldn't Simon have revealed the secret that Arthur so desperately wanted to hide?

To my relief, Sarah said that the Coast Guard had had no trouble finding *Rosie,* and she had already been returned to Frank. *Carpe Diem* was undamaged, aside from the sloppy new paint job and one bullet hole.

"I'll leave you alone for a while," she said. "Ring that bell on the nightstand if you want anything, okay?"

"Thanks, Sarah. Again."

She smiled and was gone. I wondered how I had ever doubted her.

I was surprised at the effort it took to get to the shower, let alone to take one, shave, and brush my teeth. Even after making repairs, I didn't look particularly well. My grayish, pinched face was a remarkably accurate reflection of how I felt. I sat a couple of times in order not to fall down, and did everything in slow motion so as not to jar my side. After an eternity I got Rob's clothes on—he was the same height, only a bit bulkier—and made it to the door. So far, so good, I thought.

I nearly bumped into Rob charging down the hall as I opened my door.

"Hey! Good to see you up and around. How're you feeling?" His genuine sincerity and boyish enthusiasm made him immediately likeable.

I told him honestly and succinctly how I felt, and he laughed at my choice of words. As we started down a wide circular staircase to the living room, it occurred to me that the Townsends didn't exactly live in a beach cottage. It was a stately home furnished in Nantucket colonial style. The ceilings were high, the banister well worn and highly polished, the walls painted cream and then covered with original paintings. In the upstairs hall, the paintings were of Nantucket scenes, lots of lighthouses, dunes, and harbor studies.

Rob considerately slowed to my pace and began to dish out some good-natured abuse, as if I were one of the family. He looked down his nose at me sideways. "Yeah, well, considering you looked like a zombie when we dragged you in, there has been some improvement."

"Thanks a lot." The better I knew him, the more I liked him. I chuckled at the memory of my antipathy for Mr. America.

"What's so funny?"

"When I saw you in London, I thought you were Sarah's boyfriend. I could have throttled you."

"No kidding?!" He looked surprised and a bit pleased. He glanced around surreptitiously and whispered in my ear, "If there'll ever be anyone again after Peter, it's you. I have it on good authority."

I stopped and turned to look at him, staring. The blood pounded in my head and the space before my eyes went dark, and for one horrible instant I thought I was actually going to fall down the stairs.

"Alex—are you all right?"

I felt a smile creep across my face and nodded dumbly to reassure him that I was very much all right. He clapped me lightly on the back, like the brother I'd always wished Max could have been, and we went down the stairs grinning like a couple of Cheshire cats. I was still somewhere in the clouds over his announcement when a man and woman came to the foot of the stairs to meet us and threw me off balance a second time.

I couldn't help it; I stared. It was the couple I'd seen with Ian in the photograph aboard *Carpe Diem*.

I did my best to hide my astonishment, chiding myself for not figuring it out sooner. Mrs. Townsend's resemblance to Sarah was astonishing. No wonder she had looked familiar in the photo. And her resemblance to someone else was even more astonishing. Less obvious, perhaps, but definitely more astonishing.

"Alex, dear," she was saying, her eyes worried. "What is it?" They all looked at me with concern and I realized I hadn't hidden my thoughts as well as I'd thought. I tried to restore my smile. "It's just—well, there's a remarkable resemblance between you and your daughter, Mrs. Townsend." It was a bit lame, but the best I could do.

They looked as if perhaps they didn't believe me, but Sarah's father relieved the awkwardness. "Remarkable, isn't it, Alex. Good thing Sarah didn't turn out looking like me, eh?" Everyone laughed and the moment had passed. He was a big man, tall and sturdy but not exactly fat, with bulldoglike features. Like his son, he was instantly likeable.

Sarah's mother said, "You must call us Liz and Fred." She smiled warmly, her gray hair curving under in a chic, natural-looking pageboy. She too was tall and had a poise and presence that made me wonder if she had once been a dancer or a performer of some sort. "We feel we know you already—a college friend of Sarah and Peter's, and you saved the yacht besides. We can't thank you enough."

I was glad to see that Peter's name was not taboo in the household; that was healthy, I thought.

"Please—don't thank me. It wasn't exactly unselfish. I suppose Sarah has told you that we were looking for one of Plumtree Press's authors." They nodded but didn't pursue the subject. Sarah had probably given them the full story, with the exception of Ian's name, as promised.

Fred looked at his watch apologetically and invited me to sit down. "I'm sorry to say that the Coast Guard called again a few minutes ago, inquiring about when they could get your statement. When they heard you were awake, we couldn't stall them beyond seven. They'll be here any minute, but after that we can all relax."

He indicated a chair and I sat gratefully. I was considerably weaker than I'd thought, and hoped that it wasn't obvious. Sarah came to sit next to me, and I searched in her eyes for assurance that Rob had been right. She returned my gaze and I saw it, a clear "I feel it too."

I reveled in my newfound status and thought I had never been happier. I also warned myself not to blow it now, having come this far.

Liz brought soft drinks while Fred and Rob told me about their day looking over *Carpe Diem*. The tender was missing, but insurance, they said, would take care of that.

The doorbell rang, and after ushering in a spectacularly uniformed officer from the Coast Guard, Fred and the others offered to leave Sarah and me alone with him. He'd taken their statements as owners of the yacht night before last.

I said, "Please stay, if you like." The officer nodded his approval, and they sat down with him, looking pleased.

Sarah and I spent the next hour and a half enlightening the officer. As it happened, he was an Arthur fan. Though he already knew some of the details from Sarah's statement, his eyes went wide when I explained that I had "overheard" a telephone conversation that implied Arthur was in grave danger.

Again, Sarah and I left Ian's name out of it by unspoken agreement. If he were indeed Arthur, we would leave it to him to reveal his identity when and if he chose. Moreover, I had decided not to let Ian know that I knew. After all, if he'd wanted me to know, he would have told me by now.

The Coast Guard officer was careful to inquire about details. Who exactly was Romney Marsh? What was my relationship to him? He asked the same about Simon Bow, who, he said, would remain incarcerated here on the island until his extradition to face charges in England. Then, looking serious, he asked if I had any idea who Arthur really was. He flushed slightly and added, "You understand that I need to ask as a matter of course in the investigation."

"Of course." I told him ruefully that I only wished I knew. He accepted it with a smile, obviously enjoying the intrigue of it all.

At eight-thirty he closed his notebook and stood almost regretfully. We all followed suit. "I think that's all I need," he said. "Can I reach you here if anything comes up?"

Sarah spoke up immediately. "Yes. He'll be here for the next few days at least." I was painfully aware of the fact that I had never been invited for this little visit, and that it was to have been a family holiday for Sarah. But all the signals I was receiving said that I was very welcome, so I let her statement stand and murmured a thank you.

Fred closed the door behind the officer and rubbed his hands together. "Now," he said. "How about a tincture of Scotch?"

I said that sounded like just the thing, except that he'd better make it a weakish tincture. Half an hour and a plate of crackers and brie later we were still in deep discussion about the last seven days. Sarah had already told them some of what had happened: the newsprint near-miss, Barnes's death, the fire in my flat, the missing five chapters, Max's article, the threats, the office break-in. They were full of questions, eager for details.

"But if these people were looking for you to get the manuscript, and they burned down your house, where did you hide from them?" Fred was intrigued.

"In my car."

"No, I mean, where did you stay at night?"

"In my car." I smiled at their shocked expressions.

"But surely you could have stayed with some friends . . ." Liz was horrified.

I shook my head. "No. Anywhere I went, I endangered the people around me. After Barnes and Riccardo died, I didn't take any more chances."

There was a stunned little silence, as if perhaps they hadn't quite realized that people had died over this.

"It's true," Sarah said slowly. "I never saw you after that night we found out about Barnes."

I nodded. "But I saw you."

"What do you mean?"

"I was afraid that they'd try to get to me through you—they seemed to know all about where I went and with whom. And Max knew that you and I were friends. Max is my brother," I explained to the others. "So I kept an eye on you from time to time."

Good old Max, I thought. I wondered what he was up to now.

I didn't think her parents would thank me if I told them about Acme and Red going up after her in the elevator. An involuntary shiver gripped me when I thought of how close they had come. Fred must have noticed; he quietly stood and turned up the thermostat. If only he knew, I thought.

Sarah looked at me, her head on one side, and evidently decided to change the subject. "Don't you think you should make an announcement about Plumtree's forthcoming novel?"

I looked at her parents and Rob, who looked back and forth at us as if they were watching a Ping-Pong match. "Didn't I tell you?" I laughed and shook my head, incredulous. My brain must have taken a worse beating than I'd thought. "The envelope that came for me"—Sarah nodded—"well, it was from Arthur. He promises that the chapters are on the way. It looks like we'll be publishing *Those Who Trespass Against Us* after all."

"Wow!" Rob exclaimed.

"That's great!"

"Can you believe it?"

Sarah beamed.

"There's one thing I've been meaning to ask you," Rob said. "How did you know that Arthur was even aboard *Carpe Diem?* And how on earth did you know where *Carpe Diem* would be?"

To my surprise, Liz broke in with a nervous laugh. "Um, Rob, dear, I think we've asked Alex enough questions." She looked at her watch. "Good heavens—it's after nine. Let's go in to dinner before Alex starves to death."

Rob looked at her curiously but accepted it willingly enough. We moved into the dining room, which was dominated by gleaming cherry wood and a deep red Oriental rug. To my surprise, the table was set with the same pattern of china my mother had used, an off-white basketweave. I commented on it, saying it felt like being at home again, and Liz beamed as she lit the candles.

We talked of other things besides Arthur and Simon over dinner: Nantucket, the whaling captain who had built their home in 1769, London, sailing in general, my job as flotilla babysitter. Eventually we had polished off lamb, potatoes, and tarragon carrots, followed by blueberry crisp and ice cream. I hoped I hadn't shocked them with my ravenous appetite, but was reassured by the fact that Rob consumed an equally outrageous quantity of food.

Rob and Sarah stood to clear the plates without fuss, and it was obvious that this was the normal routine. I pushed back my chair to help, but Sarah insisted that I push it right back in again. I didn't argue. I knew she wouldn't give in, and besides, I had something to discuss with the Townsends.

I would have to make good use of my moments alone with them.

"Mrs. Townsend," I began. "Liz, I mean." She smiled. "I'm assuming you don't want Sarah to know who Arthur really is, for her own good, so I'm going to say this quickly, while she's out of the room."

They were taken aback. Liz looked at Fred, and her mouth moved but no words came.

"Ian is your father—Sarah's grandfather—isn't he?" I willed her to say yes. "The blue eyes, the face—I saw the photo that he kept in his favorite book. It's impossible to miss." I spoke gently, knowing that my discovery could be a shock to her.

She looked totally nonplussed. Liz and Fred exchanged glances and returned their gaze to me.

Liz spoke, sounding concerned. "I'm sorry, but I really don't understand . . ."

Then Fred, frowning in confusion. "Yes, I'm afraid you've lost us. Who is this Ian?"

For a moment I had the old sensation of being on another planet, completely disoriented, without my bearings. They looked honestly confused, as if they had never seen or heard of Ian. I couldn't have been that far wrong.

Could I?

I tried again, working on the premise that they were bluffing. I desperately wanted to learn the truth about Ian while reassuring them that if they told me, I would never use the information to harm them.

"Please don't worry—I assure you, I wouldn't tell a soul. And I'm as eager to protect Sarah as you are, surely you can see that." I looked into their eyes. It was as good a time as any to tell them how I felt about their daughter. "This might sound crazy, but I've always known that Peter would be happy to have me look after her. I care for her a great deal."

They were still silent, but now there was warmth and understanding in their expressions. Something had glimmered for an instant in Liz's eyes, and I wondered if perhaps she had been ready to admit her relationship to Ian.

Against my better judgment, I continued. I simply refused to believe that I was on the wrong track.

"This is where he's been coming on his holidays all these years. To see the little girl he loved enough to seek out her foster parents in Boston after Simon Bow illegally sold her. And he wouldn't disrupt her or her children's lives by letting anyone else know. Sarah doesn't know about him, does she?"

Tears welled up in Liz's eyes and threatened to overflow.

I wanted them to know how much I cared about Ian. "I don't know if he's told you, but he's almost been a part of our family—as long as I can remember."

That last statement hung on the air for a moment, then Fred spoke calmly, almost gently, as if correcting a child. "Alex, I can see that you believe what you're saying, but Liz grew up with both a father and a mother." He glanced at Liz, who daubed at her eyes with her napkin. "She lost her father several months ago, as a matter of fact. I know that you mean no harm, but I'm sorry—you seem to think Liz is someone she isn't."

I wanted to ask a thousand questions. Why were they in the photograph with Ian? Why had Liz stopped me from answering Rob's question about looking for Ian on *Carpe Diem?* Who was the mysterious friend to whom they had lent the yacht for a vacation? Was Liz crying because her father had died recently or because I was right?

Why were they lying?

Were they lying?

They interpreted my silence as acquiescence. Fred said, "You've been through a great deal in the last few days, Alex. It's a lot to cope with, for anyone. That bump on the head probably didn't help, either. We should call the doctor back for a quick check tomorrow."

I mentally shook myself. This was more embarrassing than anything I could have envisioned. I knew I was right, but they were doing a very convincing job of persuading me that I had a screw loose.

"I don't know what to say," I said, looking from one to the other, feeling sick at having made such an irretrievable mistake. "I'm terribly, terribly sorry. I don't know if you can ever forgive me for barging into your private affairs like this."

They protested, truly unoffended, if still confused. They looked at me and smiled comfortingly, indulgently, for all the world as if they thought I really had been hit a bit too hard on the head.

Sarah burst in through the swinging door with a tray of coffee cups, and the smile died on her face. She stopped cold. "What is it?" she asked immediately. "What's wrong?"

I looked down at my napkin as Fred cleared his throat. "Oh—nothing, darling. I'm afraid we ventured onto the topic of the kidnapped children, the way they were separated from their parents." I looked at him as he shook his head sadly. "Such a tragedy for those families."

Liz picked up the story and ran with it. "Yes, I'm sorry I brought it up—not very happy dinner conversation. Let's talk about something else."

Sarah tried to reconcile this with what she saw on our faces and looked doubtful, but decided not to force the issue and began delivering coffee. To give them credit, Fred and Liz made a remarkable recovery, launching into an enthusiastic discussion of an islander who had designed a new kind of hull for yacht racing. I'm not sure I did as well.

We went to bed shortly after dinner. I probably looked as tired as I felt, not least because everything had been turned upside down again.

But, to my surprise, there was compensation. When Sarah and I drew even with the door to my room, she came near and kissed me. It was quick, and it was on the cheek, but it was definitely more than a sisterly peck. The tantalizing lips had graced my very own face. It happened so quickly, and I was so surprised, that I didn't have a chance to respond in kind. Before I knew it, she'd said "Good night" and was opening her own door down the hall. She turned and gave me a little wave as she went in.

I walked through my own open door and flipped on the lights, still tingling from her kiss. Now that she finally seemed to care for me, I couldn't quite take it in. I wondered if I had a built-in safety mechanism to keep my hopes from rising too fast.

I sank down on the bed to take off Rob's sweater, and the next thing I knew the sun was pouring through the windows. I was fully dressed. Disoriented, I looked at my watch and saw that I had done it again. Eleven o'clock.

It was much easier to get in and out of clothes and move about than it had been the day before, and I got myself decent as quickly as I could and started down the stairs. There was a lot of racket in the kitchen, and I found everyone assembled there with huge Portmeirion mugs of coffee.

There were cheery greetings all around, and the entire family seemed to be in a state of excitement and anticipation. Liz fired up the toaster while Sarah poured me coffee and juice. I was being hopelessly spoiled.

"Perfect timing, Alex—we were just debating whether to wake you," Sarah said. "Mom has made one of her famous picnics, and we're taking out *Carpe Diem*. It doesn't seem as rough today; we thought you might enjoy coming along."

I said it sounded like a great idea, thank you very much—a great way to spend my last day on Nantucket.

"Your last day!" They said it in chorus, staring at me in apparent disbelief.

"Well, yes," I said, slightly taken aback by the strength of their reaction. "I've got to meet with someone in Boston about copublishing, then get back to the mines. I'd love to stay longer—you've made me feel very welcome—but Plumtree Press isn't exactly Megabooks. It won't run itself."

They looked so disappointed I was almost sorry I'd mentioned it.

"But we're having so much fun . . ."

"You deserve a vacation . . ."

"If they've gotten along without you this long, can't they manage for a few more days?"

Sarah said, "You haven't forgotten that tomorrow's a bank holiday in England, have you? The new Commonwealth Day? So that's one less day you'd be missing at Plumtree Press." She wrinkled her nose, then smiled conspiratorially. "Come on. One more day."

I had forgotten. I laughed and said I'd love to stay, if they could put up with me for another day. They cheered and I bit into my toast with happy resignation.

Without saying it, Sarah and I had arrived at an understanding that things had changed between us, and I thought I saw my hopes for the future reflected in her eyes. I didn't jump to the conclusion that she would be ready to make commitments anytime soon, but it was enough to know that the possibility existed somewhere down the road.

As her family talked about all the things they'd like to do while

249

I was there, it struck me that I had been perfectly comfortable spending time with the whole family instead of Sarah alone, even given the change in her attitude toward me. Her family was a bonus I hadn't expected; mine had pretty well evaporated, and everyone needs a family of some kind.

That day and the next passed in a whirl of activity. I called Charlie, and then we looked at the stars from the Maria Mitchell Observatory, went to see the Wauwinet Home, visited the woman who'd mailed me the photo, walked along the beach, talked in front of the fire, and enjoyed Liz's culinary expertise. By the time I stood with them at the airport I was sorry to see it end. Fred and Liz had never brought up the subject of Ian again, nor had I, and nothing had changed in their manner toward me. There were hugs all around, and I suggested that they come for Christmas in England. They lit up at the idea and said they would be in touch.

When it was Sarah's turn for a hug, she said, "See you next Saturday." We both knew I'd be at Heathrow to meet her.

In Boston I walked out of the jetway to find Charlie Goodspeed standing proudly in the middle of a crowd of camera-toting journalists, resplendent in his well-cut navy blue suit and foulard tie. Disbelieving, I headed straight for him, temporarily ignoring the reporters' overtures. "What's all this about, Charlie?"

"Al, you look great, buddy." Lucky for me, I thought, he didn't mind doing business with people who weren't in full business dress. I was wearing some of Rob's clothes, as the other garb I had taken with me had been thrown away as too bloodstained to be of use; it was under the wetsuit when I tackled Simon. The only fortunate survivor was my leather jacket, which was still safely aboard *Rosie* when they found her. "What's what all about?" Charlie said, looking around. "Oh, you mean these guys? I couldn't think of a better way to announce our little agreement. I called 'em, told 'em to come on out to meet you." He smiled proudly.

I shook my head but had to smile as I fielded the first of the questions. Not only did his action confirm that he was ready to do business this time, but it showed me how he had managed to make a $10 million company out of nothing in just ten years. Marketing was no chore for him; it was a way of life.

To my surprise, Charlie was understanding and gracious about getting me back to Logan for the flight home in just three hours. I was fascinated to note that he could be as efficient as he was kind, and vowed not to underestimate him again. He monitored every moment closely without ever seeming to look at his watch. We spent fifteen minutes with the press, fifteen getting to his office in a black stretch limo, an hour going over the changes in the contracts and signing them, thirty seconds transferring the check (short but very sweet), half an hour discussing plans for the immediate future (over a celebratory champagne toast to the venture), and fifteen minutes getting back to the airport in the limo. We had fifteen to spare as we stood together at the airport curb.

"Al, it's a pleasure doing business with you. Your anthologies, our distribution and marketing—our future's so bright we gotta wear shades." We laughed. I was feeling pretty good with the champagne in my bloodstream and the check in my pocket. "Hey, next time, though, tell me in advance if you're gonna pull a publicity stunt, okay? No sense in wasting it." He winked and reached out to shake my hand, which he did like an Olympian discus thrower, then ducked back into the limo. I saw him pull out the car phone as he was whisked quietly back into the marketplace.

I sighed with satisfaction and walked to the ticket counter, where I upgraded my ticket to business class. I told myself that I had, after all, managed to save Plumtree Press from ruin, and the business would be able to afford the additional expense. Not only would Ian's—Arthur's—book be out soon, but I had a comfortable sum in my wallet. After takeoff I stretched out in my reasonably sized seat and let my mind wander. Although I hadn't thought I was dwelling on my old troubles while I was at the Townsends', my mind had pretty well put things in order.

For instance, I had once again arrived at the conclusion that Ian almost had to be Arthur, despite the Townsends' remarkable performance and the knock on the head. There were too many coincidences for this not to be true, but several stood out in my mind. First, there was Ian's picture with them aboard *Carpe Diem*. Second, there was Ian's abrupt discontinuation of communication with his answering service, which the operators themselves admitted was unusual. Finally, there was the note I'd received from Arthur.

Consequently, I fully expected Ian to be back in his swivel

chair on Monday morning as if nothing had happened, nonchalant
and reluctant to discuss his holiday as usual. I also expected the final
five chapters to appear sometime in the next few weeks. Arthur's
original deadline for the chapters had fallen one month into Ian's
holiday, which was to have been a total of six weeks long, so I
speculated that the bulk of the work had already been done when he
was kidnapped.

I was still curious about how he had kept the manuscript away
from them, considering that they would have found his computer
when they found him. I would have to casually raise the matter with
Ian back at the office, and see what he said.

As for Rupert, I had a feeling that Simon had worked him into
a jealous frenzy and given him a way to get back at my father
through me and Plumtree Press. Rupert, like Max, had merely been
used by Simon to make my life miserable so that when Simon
squeezed, I would give. Rupert, I thought, was basically harmless
and might even choke out an apology at some point. I didn't think
I could prosecute him or his cronies for industrial conspiracy, or
whatever one called this sort of thing, even if I'd wanted to. But I
was curious about what Nigel Wexford, the editor of the *Tempus
Book Review*, would say to me at the next press party.

I walked up to the office door seven hours later, straight off the tube
from Heathrow. It struck me immediately that something was
wrong. It was eight o'clock in the morning and the lights were still
off in the building. Granted, eight o'clock was an hour before starting time. But Lisette and Nick were early risers, not to mention Ian.
All of us were usually there by eight. Dreading another disaster,
such as our creditors having claimed our real estate, I unlocked the
door and pushed it open.

A deafening roar nearly knocked me off my feet.

"Surprise!"

Everyone in the company, from the basement mail room to the
editors on the top floor was there, obviously delighted at having
surprised the socks off of me. There was a poster at the rear of
reception that read, "Welcome back Alex!"

Lisette, Nick, and Ian were at the front of the crowd, and

Lisette ran forward to deliver a hug. The employees came forward one by one as if in a receiving line. Startled, I responded to all of them as best I could, thanking them for their faithfulness. My gaze kept returning to Ian, who smiled benignly on the proceedings, looking incredibly tan and fit and very unlike a hostage.

"Great to have you back!"

"We read about you in the paper . . ."

"Simon bloody Bow, of all people . . ."

"You did it!"

"Any word on who Arthur is, then?"

After most of them had had a go, Ian stepped forward and took my hand in both of his with a strong, almost rough grip. Aside from the tan, he looked exactly the same as he had six weeks ago. If the last couple of weeks had been hard on him, his appearance didn't give it away.

"Your father would be so proud," he said, his lip trembling. "I'm sorry, Alex. If only I'd known . . . I could have helped. It's irresponsible of me to take these solitary holidays, and I shall have to stop it." He shook his head regretfully.

"No, I don't think you should stop," I said, unable to resist a smile. Who would continue to write our best-selling books, I thought? If he caught the double entendre, he didn't show it.

He looked me up and down, frowning slightly. "Are you sure you should be back at work so soon?"

"Absolutely. We've a lot to catch up on, lots to do. In fact . . ." I looked around the room, and the party was still in full swing. It was only half nine, still plenty of time for them to have fun before the work week officially began. Ian caught my drift, and we sneaked out as unobtrusively as we could and climbed the stairs to our offices.

"How extraordinary that you actually had contact with Arthur, even if you didn't see who he was." He led the way into the conference room and fixed coffee for me, hot water with lemon for himself. He wanted every last detail of the story again, in my own words. No doubt he wanted to see how I had rationalized it for myself.

I was happy to oblige, except that I omitted any mention of searching his house, and the photo I found there, and the break-in. I was continually aware that if I was in fact speaking to Arthur, he must be enjoying my masquerade as much as his own. We pretended that nothing had changed but were very much aware of one another's small deceits for the sake of Arthur's anonymity.

"Remarkable. Absolutely remarkable," he said, shaking his head. Two hours had passed, and we had come to the end of it. "But it sounds to me as if Arthur hit you over the head rather more soundly than he intended," said Ian, poker-faced.

"He was more enthusiastic than I would have liked. But then, I don't suppose he's accustomed to violence. It must have been quite difficult for him, now that I think about it."

"Mmm. Perhaps you're right. And he had to ensure that you never found out his identity."

"Yes, I suppose he did."

We looked at each other, and Ian smiled.

Epilogue

"Done!"

I turned to see Sarah high on her ladder, holding out a paint roller in triumph. She rubbed her shoulder with her free hand, and there was a dollop of cream-colored paint on her nose.

"It looks beautiful," I said, and meant it. She had painted her third ceiling of the day, and she did good work. "Have you considered doing this professionally?"

"Thanks," she said, tongue in cheek. "But I'm very happy in my job. Why—how many more rooms do you want to do tomorrow?"

I had decided to live at The Orchard and was systematically fixing up the few remaining dark and dingy corners that my mother's redecoration had missed. The insurance money from the Bedford Square house, which I had put up for sale, was paying for major roof repairs. In the spring I would try to come to grips with the garden.

"Um, I haven't decided yet. But if it means you'll stay till tomorrow, I think we'd better paint several more."

She smiled, her rosy cheeks making her look like a model for a portrait, and climbed down off the ladder. "I'd better check the roast and get cleaned up," she said. "It's six o'clock already. They're coming at seven-thirty, right?"

I nodded and finished up the last several feet of the wall. Ian and Romney were coming to dinner tonight for a sort of celebration, and to rehash the events of the last few weeks. The dust had settled somewhat, as we'd all been back for a couple of weeks, and it seemed to me the time was right for a reunion.

It was altogether satisfying that Ian and I had fallen easily into our old routine, neither of us dwelling too much on the extraordinary events of the last few weeks. Arthur's last five chapters had appeared unceremoniously in reception, presumably via the poor Deadline Deliveries courier, and had been rushed through editing and production. They'd gone to the printer, along with the rest of the book, several days ago, and we would be seeing the first bound book from Singapore in just a week.

Things had changed considerably from when Ian and my father had started in this business, I thought; then it had taken at least a year for a manuscript to become a book, and in those days they weren't even printed halfway across the world.

I followed Sarah upstairs. I'd assigned her the guest suite, of which I was secretly proud. My mother had known how to make a guest feel like royalty, even if the rest of us lived in comfortably Spartan sleeping quarters.

It was a pleasure just to take a bath in my old cracked porcelain tub and know that Sarah was in the same house. As I soaked I thought of our conversation that afternoon, which had been conducted largely atop paint ladders. I'd tried to sound nonchalant, keeping my eyes on my paint roller as I asked the question that had tormented me for several weeks now.

"Do you remember saying at some point, 'The really funny thing is that he'll never even know how it happened'?"

I allowed myself a peek at her face out of the corner of my eye. She snorted and kept working.

"I sure do. Do you remember the night we had Indian food at your office, and I told you about that crotchety old investor who was driving me batty?"

"Mmm," I said.

"Well, he got into a dispute with his partner, who . . ."

I felt her eyes on me suddenly. "I don't remember discussing it with you after that night at your office."

She was sharp, all right.

"No, that's right. We didn't discuss it after that." I met her eyes straight on. "I couldn't help but overhear you while I was following you one night."

I saw the thoughts passing through her head; how much had I seen and heard while following her? Why had I asked the question? Then her eyes released mine and she went back to rolling.

"The man's partner managed to buy him out of his largest holding secretly. The old man didn't find out until he saw it in the paper the next day." She paused. "It might sound terrible, but it almost seemed a just punishment for having been so miserable to everyone all his life."

Her response had been a relief then, and still was, hours later. I shook my head in disbelief that I had ever suspected her.

When I emerged from my quarters ready for guests, I was surprised that she was already downstairs making noises in the kitchen. I hurried down and opened the kitchen door.

I stopped, transfixed, and watched her bend down to insert a tray of hors d'oeuvres in the oven. Her back was almost completely exposed, framed by lines of black velvet, and her hair was a mass of dark braid wound into a coil on the back of her head.

She closed the oven door and stood, noticing me as she turned. In the front the dress came high enough to cover the necessary parts but plunged into a V that invited speculation.

She must have seen my appreciation. A confident smile crept across her bright pink-lipsticked mouth.

"Your back," I said. "It's beautiful." My lips felt numb, and I was glad to get the words out without stumbling over them. Seeing her back in its entirety had made me weak in the knees; it was the most appealing sight I'd ever seen. The muscles were well defined, but the expanse of creamy skin was spectacularly feminine.

"I've never done this before, you know," she said.

I almost stopped breathing. "What?"

"Camembert *en croûte*," she said, turning away to peek through the oven window. "I hope it turns out all right."

I breathed again. "Don't worry. It'll be wonderful. I'm sorry you beat me to it, though. I didn't mean for you to do this."

I didn't want her to think that I was some sort of old-fashioned European male who expected women to do all the cooking. My father had been the first Plumtree to do away with that tradition; he'd been a magnificent pastry chef. Earlier in the afternoon I had set the table, chilled the wine, prepared and started the roast, cleaned and trimmed the brussels sprouts for steaming, whipped the cream for the gooseberry fool, and laid out the smoked salmon, capers, and lemon for the starter. Like running a publishing house, I had seen my father do it all so many times that it came to me as if by osmosis.

We had barely started a fire in the library, put ice in the bucket, and turned on the lamps when the doorbell rang.

"Alex. Sarah." Romney took each of our hands and squeezed them, and we ushered him in out of the cold. "I'm so pleased that it's turned out this way—for all of us." I had recently hired Romney onto our staff at Plumtree. He had decided that special government assignments were more than he cared to take on at this point, and was in charge of Plumtree Press's effort to help reunite families brought together by Barnes Appleton's research.

He'd called the day I returned to apologize for the Ministry of Defence story, and for suggesting that Arthur had been a criminal, and Barnes an inaccurate journalist. But, he said, he knew I'd never reveal Arthur's whereabouts—assuming I knew them—unless he persuaded me that Arthur was a contemptible beast. He hadn't bargained on intuition, which had turned out to be worth something after all.

Romney had cleared the air on another subject that day: why my father had come to dislike him so intensely. "It was another special assignment," he'd said sadly, shaking his head. "I had to pretend for several months to be an agent for a foreign government. Naturally I kept my undercover activities in London separate from my normal life in Hertfordshire, but your father had his finger on everything; no doubt you know by now that he was active in intelligence in the war years."

In fact, I hadn't known, but I'd speculated that the Anglo-American Liaison had been involved in a lot more than arranging diplomatic cocktail parties.

Romney continued, "He heard that I was involved somehow. I never could tell him the truth, of course, because we weren't allowed to talk about our work while there was still a Soviet Union."

Moments after Romney arrived, Ian appeared on the doorstep.

"This is a great pleasure," he said formally, and thrust a huge bunch of flowers into Sarah's arms. "I count myself very fortunate indeed to have you as friends."

We smiled and pulled him inside. Sarah thanked him for the flowers and went to put them in a vase while I hung his coat in the hall closet. As I steered him toward the library, I thought about how often Ian had made similarly ambiguous comments over the last two weeks. He danced close to the flame, in my opinion, almost letting out the secret, but never quite revealing enough for me to be absolutely sure.

Sarah joined us at the door to the library, and I ushered him to a seat next to her on the sofa, opposite Romney. I went to the ice bucket, demurely covered with a towel, and produced the stuff of which a toast was made, a toast to all that had gone well with Plumtree Press, Arthur, and the four of us.

"Good heavens, Alex. You don't pull out the Dom Perignon for just any occasion, do you?" Romney looked shocked.

Ian merely smiled.

"This," I said, "is not just any occasion." I poured four champagne flutes of the toasty liquid with its tiny bubbles and distributed them. "To Arthur." I held my glass high and drank.

"Hear, hear."

"To Plumtree Press," said Ian.

"Hear, hear."

"To families," said Romney.

"Hear, hear."

"To all of us," said Sarah.

"Hear, hear!"

After the third and fourth coffees had been poured and our guests had made their way home, I sat with Sarah before a newly replenished fire in the library. She nestled happily in the crook of my arm as we stared at it, totally satisfied.

Or so I thought until she spoke.

"It's odd," she said, frowning slightly. "I almost feel that I know Ian somehow. It's almost as if . . ." She shook her head, looking mildly amused. "No. Never mind."

"Tell me," I said neutrally.

She looked up into my eyes, melting me again. "You'll think I've gone round the bend."

"Never."

She sat up, pulling away slightly, and looked at me.

"All right. I'll tell you." She smiled intriguingly. "It's as if he knows me."

"Well, you've met often enough."

"No, I don't mean that. I mean—this sounds crazy, but—it's as if he's a grandfather to me."

She had caught me totally off guard.

"A grandfather?" I worked hard to keep my muscles relaxed.

"Mmm." She nestled back in. "It's hard to put a finger on it, but . . ." She moved her shoulders around in what might have been a shrug, and I liked feeling her against my chest. "There's something else, but I just can't seem to put a name to it."

I sat wondering if she was trying to tell me that she knew. I knew far better than to underestimate her, and more than once I had thought it was unfair to keep her relationship to Ian, and or Arthur, from her. But after all, I couldn't be certain. Not after her parents' reaction around the dining room table in Nantucket.

I wondered if a casual change of topic would work. "Maybe someday a name will come to you. Until then, what do you say we start planning this Christmas at The Orchard? It'll never be the Ritz, but it can be quite warm and cheery—especially at Christmas."

She turned and smiled at me again. "You don't have to worry," she said. "I'm not going to tell anyone."

As if my heart wasn't beating wildly enough at the realization that she might have known for some time, her mouth came closer and closer to mine and finally put a stop to the words of protest rising in my throat.

Her scent drifted up and all thoughts of anyone or anything else evaporated.

We were home.

Concluding Note

In the autumn of 1940, thousands of British children were successfully evacuated to the United States and placed with families eager to help. This tremendous feat of organization and sheer goodwill was accomplished through the dedication of many talented volunteers and child care specialists, among them the Children's Overseas Reception Board, Marshall Field and the London-based U.S. Committee for the Care of European Children, and the U.S. Children's Bureau.

It is to their great credit that what you have read never actually took place in 1940, though, sadly, it has happened since with children from other countries.